New York Times bestselling author
KRESLEY COLE
Winner of the 2007 RITA Award
for Best Paranormal Romance

The critics love her "devilishly passionate"
(*Romantic Times*)
series The Immortals After Dark

NO REST FOR THE WICKED

"Sizzling sex and high-stakes adventure are what's on tap in mega-talented Cole's sensational new paranormal release. . . . One nonstop thrill ride. Brava!"

—*Romantic Times* Magazine (Top Pick)

"What a fabulous story! I can hardly wait to get my hands on the next one in the series."

—Bella Online

"Oh, wow! Kresley Cole writes another spine-tingling, adventurous, and passionate romance. . . . I recommend readers grab a copy of Kresley Cole's *No Rest for the Wicked* today. It's a definite keeper."

—*Romance Reviews Today*

Dark Needs at Night's Edge
is also available as an eBook

A HUNGER LIKE NO OTHER
2007 RITA Award Winner

And her gripping historical romances
featuring the MacCarrick brothers

IF YOU DECEIVE

Books by Kresley Cole

The Sutherland Series
The Captain of All Pleasures
The Price of Pleasure

The MacCarrick Brothers Series
If You Dare
If You Desire
If You Deceive

The Immortals After Dark Series
A Hunger Like No Other
No Rest for the Wicked
Wicked Deeds on a Winter's Night

KRESLEY COLE

DARK
NEEDS AT
NIGHT'S
EDGE

POCKET BOOKS
New York London Toronto Sydney

Pocket Books
A Division of Simon & Schuster, Inc.
1230 Avenue of the Americas
New York, NY 10020

This book is a work of fiction. Names, characters, places, and incidents either are products of the author's imagination or are used fictitiously. Any resemblance to actual events or locales or persons, living or dead, is entirely coincidental.

First Pocket Books paperback edition May 2008

POCKET and colophon are registered trademarks of Simon & Schuster, Inc.

For information about special discounts for bulk purchases, please contact Simon & Schuster Special Sales at 1-800-456-6798 or business@simonandschuster.com

Art by Jon Paul

Manufactured in the United States of America

10 9 8 7 6 5 4 3 2 1

ISBN-13: 978-1-4165-4707-5
ISBN-10:   1-4165-4707-X

For Lauren,
my phenomenal editor and a dedicated champion
of the books. This is our tenth project together,
and it's still as crazy and exciting as the first.

Acknowledgments

Many, many thanks to my fantastic agent Robin Rue. So happy to be working with you. To Caroline Phipps, my steadfast friend who's always willing to do a midnight line-edit. To Gena Showalter, because my life's a more meaningful (and riotous) trip with you in it.

And to Roxanne St. Claire, a.k.a. G.U.F. Did I happen to mention you're my rock?

Glossary of Terms from the
Living Book of Lore

The Lore

". . . *and those sentient creatures that are not human shall be united in one stratum, coexisting with, yet secret from, man's.*"

The Lykae Clan

"*A proud, strapping warrior of the Keltoi People (or Hidden People, later known as Celts) was taken in his prime by a maddened wolf. The warrior rose from the dead, now an immortal, with the spirit of the beast latent within him. He displayed the wolf's traits: the need for touch, an intense loyalty to its kind, an animal craving for the delights of the flesh. Sometimes the beast rises. . . .*"

- Also called werewolves, war-wolds.
- Enemies of the Vampire Horde.

The Vampires

Two warring factions, the Horde and the Forbearer Army.

- Each vampire seeks his *Bride*, his eternal wife, and walks as the living dead until he finds her.
- A Bride will render his body fully alive, giving

him breath and making his heart beat, a process known as *blooding*.

- *Tracing* is teleporting, the vampires' means of travel. A vampire can only trace to destinations he's previously been or to those he can see.
- *The Fallen* are vampires who have killed by drinking a victim to death. Distinguished by their red eyes.

The Horde

"In the first chaos of the Lore, a brotherhood of vampires dominated, by relying on their cold nature, worship of logic, and absence of mercy. They sprang from the harsh steppes of Dacia and migrated to Russia, though some say a secret enclave, the Daci, live in Dacia still."

- Their ranks are comprised of the Fallen.
- Enemies of most factions in the Lore.

The Forbearers

". . . his crown stolen, Kristoff, the rightful Horde king, stalked the battlefields of antiquity seeking the strongest, most valiant human warriors as they died, earning him the name of Gravewalker. He offered eternal life in exchange for eternal fealty to him and his growing army."

- An army of vampires consisting of turned humans, who do not drink blood directly from the flesh, unless from an immortal Bride.
- Kristoff was raised as a human and then lived among them. He and his army know little of the Lore.
- Enemies of the Horde.

The Demonarchies
"The demons are as varied as the bands of man. . . ."

- A collection of demon dynasties. Some kingdoms ally with the Horde.
- Most demon breeds can *trace* like vampires. Some breeds are bound to obey summonses.
- A demon must have intercourse with a potential mate to ascertain if she's truly his—a process known as *attempting*.

The House of Witches
". . . immortal possessors of magickal talents, practitioners of good and evil."

- Mystickal mercenaries who sell their spells.
- Strictly forbidden to create personal wealth or grant immortality.
- Separated into five castes: warrior, healer, enchantress, conjurer, and seeress.
- The only witch known to possess the powers of all five castes is Mariketa the Awaited.

The Valkyrie
"When a maiden warrior screams for courage as she dies in battle, Wóden and Freya heed her call. The two gods give up lightning to strike her, rescuing her to their hall, and preserving her courage forever in the form of the maiden's immortal Valkyrie daughter."

- Take sustenance from the electrical energy of the earth, sharing it in one collective power, and give it back with their emotions in the form of lightning.

- Possess preternatural strength and speed.
- Without training, they can be mesmerized by shining objects and jewels.
- Enemies of the Vampire Horde.

The Talisman's Hie
"A treacherous and grueling scavenger hunt for magickal talismans, amulets, and other mystical riches over the entire world."

- The rules forbid killing—until the final round. Any other trickery or violence is encouraged.
- Held every two hundred fifty years.
- Hosted by Riora, the goddess of impossibility.

The Turning
"Only through death can one become an 'other.'"

- Some beings, like the Lykae, vampires, and demons, can turn a human or even other Lore creatures into their kind through differing means, but the catalyst for change is always death, and success is not guaranteed.

The Accession
"And a time shall pass that all immortal beings in the Lore, from the Valkyrie, vampire, Lykae, and demon factions, to the phantoms, shifters, fey, and sirens . . . must fight and destroy each other."

- A kind of mystickal checks-and-balances system for an ever-growing population of immortals.
- Occurs every five hundred years. Or right now . . .

DARK
NEEDS AT
NIGHT'S
EDGE

A femme fatale? With a history of burlesque dancing? You must have the wrong girl. I'm naught but a humble ballet dancer, a mere delicate sparrow.
—Néomi Laress,
prima ballerina, former femme fatale and burlesque dancer
(b. approx. 1901—d. August 24, 1927)

I hereby vow to devote my life to annihilating the vampiir. None shall know my presence and live.
—Conrad Wroth, age thirteen,
upon being inducted into the Order of Kapsliga Uur
in the year 1609

Prologue

I'll kill you for spurning me. . . .

Struggling to block out memories of Louis Robicheaux's latest threat, Néomi Laress stood at the top of her grand staircase and gazed out over the packed ballroom.

As she might cradle a babe, she held bouquets of roses swathed in silk. They were gifts from some of the men in the crowd of partygoers below, a motley mix of her rollicking set, rich patrons, and newspaper reporters. A sultry bayou breeze slid throughout the space, carrying strains of music from the twelve-piece orchestra outside.

. . . you'll beg for my mercy.

She stifled a shiver. Her ex-fiancé's behavior had become more chilling of late, his atonement gifts more extravagant. Néomi's long-standing refusal to sleep with Louis had frustrated and angered him, but breaking off their relationship had *enraged* him.

The look in his pale eyes earlier tonight . . . She

gave herself an inward shake. She'd hired guards for this event—Louis couldn't get to her.

One admirer, a handsome banker from Boston, noticed her aloft and began to clap. The throng joined in, and in her mind she envisioned a curtain going up. With a slow, gracious smile, she said, "*Bienvenue* to you all," then began descending her stairs.

No one would ever sense her anxiety. She was a trained ballerina, but above all things, she was an entertainer. She would work this room, dispensing teasing nibbles of sarcasm and softly spoken *bons mots*, charming any critics and coaxing laughter from even the most staid.

Though her arms already ached from cradling so many bouquets, and flashbulbs went off in glaring succession, her smile remained fixed. Another gliding step down.

She'd be damned before she'd let Louis ruin her night of triumph. Three hours ago, she'd given the performance of a lifetime to a sold-out house. For tonight's soirée celebrating her newly renovated estate, Elancourt, the Gothic manor house was resplendent with the glow of a thousand candles. Through her dancing, she'd paid for the painstaking restoration of her new home and all the sumptuous furnishings inside it.

Every detail for the party was perfect, and outside, a sliver moon clung to the sky. *A lucky moon.*

Her dress for this evening was a more risqué version of the costume she'd worn earlier, the satin as black as her jet hair. It had a tight bodice that she laced up the front like a bygone corset and a slit in the skirt that almost reached up to where her garter belt snapped to her stockings. Her makeup was styled after the Hollywood vamps—she'd kohled her eyes with a smoky hue, donned lipstick of oxblood red, and painted her short nails a dark crimson.

With her jeweled choker and dangling earrings, the ensemble had cost a small fortune, but tonight was worth it—tonight all her dreams had finally come true.

Only Louis could ruin it. She willed herself to ignore her apprehension, inwardly cursing him in English and in French, which helped ease her tension.

Until she nearly stumbled on the stairs. He was there, standing at the periphery, staring up at her.

Usually so perfect and kempt, he had his tie loosened, his blond hair disheveled.

How had he gotten past the guards? Louis was filthy rich—had the bastard bribed them?

His bloodshot eyes were burning with a maniacal light, but she assured herself that he wouldn't dare harm her in front of so many. After all, there were hundreds of people in her home, including reporters and photographers.

Yet she wouldn't put it past him to make a scene or expose her scandalous history to everyone. Her uptown patrons winked at her and her friends' colorful antics, but they had no idea what she was—much less of her past occupation.

Chin raised and shoulders back, she continued down, but her hands were clenching the roses. Resentment warred with her fear. So help her, God, she'd scratch his eyes out if he ruined this for her.

Just before she reached the bottom step, he began elbowing his way toward her. She tried to signal the burly guard at the opened patio door, but the crowd enveloped her, effectively trapping her. She attempted to make her way to the man, yet everyone wanted "to be the first to congratulate her."

When she heard Louis pushing people behind her, Néomi's soft-spoken apologies—"*Pardonnez-moi*, I'll just be a moment"—turned to "Let me pass!"

He neared. Out of the corner of her eye she spied his hand fiddling with something in his jacket pocket. Not another gift? *This will be so embarrassing.*

When that hand shot out, she whirled around, dropping her bouquets. Metal glinted in the light of the candles. Eyes wide, she screamed—

Just before he plunged a knife into her chest.

Pain . . . unimaginable pain. She could hear the blade grating past her bones, felt a force so jarring the tip pierced through her very back. As she clawed at his arms, ugly sounds erupted from her throat; those nearest her backed away in horror.

This can't be happening. . . .

Only when he released the knife with splayed fingers did her body collapse to the floor. Rosebuds scattered around her, their petals wafting around the jutting hilt. She stared dumbly at the ceiling as warm blood seeped from her back, pooling all around her. She perceived the silence of the room over Louis's harried breaths as he knelt beside her, beginning to weep.

This isn't happening. . . .

The first hysterical scream rent the quiet. People fled the scene, shoving and tangling all around them. She heard the guards finally yelling and fighting past the crowd.

And Néomi lived still. She was dogged, a survivor—she would not die in her dream home on her dream night. *Fight*—

Louis fisted the hilt once again, jarring the knife inside her. *Agony . . . too much . . . can't bear this . . .* But she had no breath to scream, no strength to raise her limp arms to defend herself.

With a choking bellow he twisted the blade in the pocket of her wound. "Feel it for me, Néomi," he gasped at her ear. Pain exploded, radiating out from her heart to every inch of her body. "Feel what I have suffered!"

Too much! The temptation to close her eyes nearly overwhelmed her. Yet she kept them open, *kept living*.

"See how much I love you? We'll be together now." The knife made a sucking sound when he yanked it from her. Just before he was finally tackled to the ground, he sliced his own throat ear to ear.

Her blood had begun to cool by the time a doctor crouched to grasp her wrist. "There's no pulse," he said to someone unseen, his voice raised over the commotion. "She's gone."

But she wasn't! Not yet!

Néomi was young, and there were so many things she had left to experience. She *deserved* to live. *I'm not dying.* Her hands somehow clenched. *I refuse to!*

Yet as the breeze picked up once more, Néomi's vision guttered out like a candle. *No, no . . . still living . . . can't see, can't see . . . so scared.*

Rose petals caught on the wind and tumbled over her face. She could feel each cool kiss of them.

Then . . . nothingness.

1

Outside Orleans Parish
Present day

*S*tay sane, act normal, he chants to himself as he
strides down the rickety pier. On either side of him,
water black like tar. Ahead of him, muted light from
the bayou tavern. A Lore bar. A lone neon sign flickers
over flat skiffs below. Music and laughter carry.

Stay sane . . . need to dull the rage. Until the endtime.

Inside. "Whiskey." His voice is low, rough from
disuse.

The bartender's face falls. Like last night. Others grow skittish. *Can they sense that I ache to kill?* The
whispers around him are like metal on slate to his
ragged nerves.

—"Conrad Wroth, once a warlord . . . madder
than any vampire I've seen in all my centuries."

—"A killer for hire. If he shows up in your town,
then folks from the Lore there'll go missing."

Missing? Unless I want them found.

—"Heard he drains 'em so savagely . . . nothing's
left of their throats."

So I'm not fastidious.

—"I heard he eats them."

Distorted rumors. *Or is that one true?*

Tales of his insanity spreading once more. *I've never missed a target—how insane can I be?* He answers himself: *Very fucking much so.*

Memories clot his mind. His victims' memories taken from their blood toll inside him, their number always growing. *Don't know what's real; can't determine what's illusion.* Most of the time, he can scarcely understand his own thoughts. He doesn't go a day without seeing some type of hallucination, striking out at shadows around him.

A grenade with the pin pulled, they say. Only a matter of time.

They're right.

Stay sane . . . act normal. Glass in hand, he chuckles softly on his way to a dimly lit table in the back. *Normal?* He's a goddamned vampire in a bar filled with shifters, demons, and the sharp-eared fey. Christmas lights are strung up in the back—through the eye sockets of human skulls that frame a mirror. In the corner, a demoness lazily strokes her lover's horns, visibly arousing the male. At the bar, an immense werewolf bares his fangs, bowing protectively as he tosses a small redhead behind him.

Can't decide if you should attack, Lykae? That's right. I don't smell of blood. A trick I learned.

The couple leaves, the redhead all but carried out by the Lykae. As they exit, she peers over her shoulder, her eyes like mirrors. Then gone. Out into the night where they belong.

Sit. Back against the wall. He adjusts the sunglasses that shade his red eyes, dirty red eyes. As he scans the room, he resists the urge to rub his palm over the back of his neck. *Watched by someone unseen?*

But then, I always feel like that.

He swoops up the drink, narrowing his eyes at his steady hand. *My mind's decayed, but my sword hand's still true.* A ruinous combination.

He takes a liberal swallow. *The drink.* The whiskey dulls the need to lash out. Not that it has disappeared.

Small things enrage him. An off look. Someone approaching too quickly. Failing to give him a wide enough berth. His fangs sharpen at the slightest provocation. *As though a living thing hungers inside me.* Ravenous for blood and a throat to tear. Each time he acts on the rage, others' memories blight more of his own.

He still has enough sanity to stalk his targets—his brothers. He will mete out retribution to Nikolai and Murdoch Wroth for doing the unspeakable to him. Sebastian, the third brother, was a victim like him, but must be slain—simply because of what he is.

And my time grows nigh. Like an animal, he recognizes this. He's found them in this mysterious place of swamps and haze and music. He's seen Nikolai and Sebastian with their wives. He might have felt envy that his brothers laugh with them. That they touch them possessively, with wonder in their clear eyes. But hatred drowns out any confusing jealousy.

Offspring will follow. He'll kill their females as well. *Destroy them. Destroy myself. Before my enemies catch up with me.*

He adjusts the bandage under his shirt on his left

arm. The slashed skin beneath it will not heal. Five days ago, he was marked by a dream demon, one who tracks him by this very injury. One who promised that *most coveted dream and most dreaded nightmare* would follow the mark.

His brows draw together. The hunter will soon become the hunted—his life is nearing its end.

A whisper of regret. The thing he regrets most. He tries to remember what he covets so dearly. Another's memories bombard him, exploding in his mind. His hand shoots up to clasp his forehead—

Nikolai enters the bar, Murdoch behind him. Their expressions are grave.

They've come to kill me. As he expected. He thought he could draw them out by returning here again and again. He lowers his hand, and his lips ease back from his fangs. The bar empties in a rush.

Then . . . stillness. His brothers stare at him as if seeing a ghost. Insects clamor outside. Rain draws near and steeps the air. Just as lightning strikes in the distance, Sebastian enters, crossing to stand beside the other two. He's allied with them? This he hadn't expected.

He removes his sunglasses, revealing his red eyes. The eldest, Nikolai, stifles a wince at the sight, but shakes it off and advances. The three seem surprised that he'll stay to engage them, that he hasn't traced away. They are strong and skilled, yet they don't recognize the power he wields, the thing he's become.

He can slaughter them all without blinking, and he'll savor it. They haven't drawn their swords? Then they walk to their doom. *Can't keep them waiting.*

He lunges from his seat and hurdles the table, knocking Sebastian unconscious with a blow that cracks his skull and sends him flying into the back wall. Before the other two can raise a hand in defense, he snatches them by their throats. One in each tightening hand as they grapple to free themselves. "Three hundred years of this," he hisses. Their struggles do nothing; their shocked expressions satisfy. Squeezing—

Wood creaks behind him. He shoves back and heaves his brothers at a new enemy. Too late; that Lykae's returned and slashes out with flared claws, ripping through his torso. Blood gushes.

He roars with fury and charges the werewolf, dodging claws and teeth with uncanny speed to barrel him to the ground. Just as his hands are about to meet around the Lykae's corded neck, the beast claps something to his right wrist.

A *manacle*? Clenching harder, he grates out a rasping laugh. "You don't think that will hold me?" Bones begin to pop beneath his palms. The kill is near, and he wants to yell with pleasure.

The werewolf cuffs his left wrist.

What is this? The metal won't bend. Won't break. *They goddamned mean to take me alive?* He leaps to his feet, tensing to trace. Nothing. Sebastian on the floor, pouring blood from his temple, has him by the ankles.

He kicks Sebastian, connecting squarely with his brother's chest. Ribs crack. He whirls around—in time to catch the bar rail the Lykae swings at his face.

He staggers but remains on his feet.

"What the fuck *is* he?" the Lykae bellows, swinging the rail again with all his might.

The brutal hit takes him across his neck. A split second of faltering. Enough for his brothers to tackle him.

He thrashes and bites, snapping his fangs. *Can't break free . . . can't . . .* They attach the manacles at his wrists to another chain. He kicks viciously, stunned when they trap his legs as well.

Choking with rage, he strains against his bonds with all his strength. The metal cleaves his skin to the bone. Nothing.

Caught. He roars, spitting blood at them, dimly hearing them speak.

"I hope you came up with a good place to put him," Sebastian says between ragged breaths.

"I bought a long-abandoned manor," Nikolai grates, "place called Elancourt."

Chills course through him even through his fury; pain erupts from the injury on his arm. *A dream. His doom.* He can never go to this Elancourt—knows this with a savage certainty. He's too strong for them to trace him—there's still time to escape.

If they take him there, they won't take him alive. . . .

Under a clouded nighttime sky, the spirit of Néomi Laress knelt in the drive at the very edge of her property line, gazing hungrily at the newspaper, lying wrapped in wet plastic.

Today the deliveryman—that capricious fiend— had missed the drive again, this time tossing the bundle squarely onto the desolate county road.

Néomi was starving for that paper, desperate for

the news, reviews, and commentary that would break up the monotony of her life—or her eighty-year-long *afterlife*.

But she couldn't leave the estate to seize it. As a ghost, Néomi could manipulate matter telekinetically, and her power was nearly absolute at Elancourt—she could rattle all the windows or tear off the roof if she wanted to, and the weather often changed with her emotions—but not outside the property.

Her beloved home had become her prison, her eternal cell of fifteen acres and a slowly dying manor. Among fate's other curses, each seemingly designed to torture her in personal and specific ways, Néomi could never leave this place.

She didn't know why this was so—only that it was, and had been since she'd awakened the morning after her murder. She recalled seeing her haunting reflection for the first time. Néomi remembered that exact moment when she'd realized that she'd died—when she'd first comprehended what she'd become.

A ghost. She'd become something that frightened even her. Something unnatural. Never again to be a lover or friend. Never to be a mother, like she'd always planned after her dancing career. As a storm had boiled outside, she'd silently screamed for hours.

The only thing she could be thankful for was that Louis hadn't been trapped here with her.

She stretched harder. *Must . . . have that . . . paper!*

Néomi wasn't certain why it continued to arrive. A past article had recounted the problems inherent with "recurrent billing of credit cards," and she supposed she was the benefactress of her last tenant's credit card negligence. The delivery could end at any time. Every one was precious.

Eventually she gave up, defeated, sitting back in the weed-ridden drive. Out of habit, she made movements as if she was rubbing her thighs, yet felt nothing.

Néomi could *never* feel. Never again. She was incorporeal, as substantial as the mist rolling in from the bayou.

Thanks, Louis. Oh, and may you rot in hell—because surely that's where you went. . . .

Usually, at this point in the newspaper struggle, she'd be battling the urge to tear her hair out, wondering how much longer she could endure this existence, speculating what she'd done to deserve it.

Yes, on the night of her death, she'd refused to die, but this was ridiculous.

But even as desperate as she was for the words, she wasn't as badly off as usual.

Because last night a man had come into her home. A towering, handsome man with grave eyes. He might return this night. He might even *move in.*

She shouldn't get too excited about the stranger, to have her hopes crushed yet again—

Lights blinded her; the shriek of squealing tires ripped through the quiet of the night.

As a car shot forward onto the gravel, she futilely raised her arms to protect her face and gave a silent cry. It drove straight through her, the engine reverberating like an earthquake when it passed through her head.

The vehicle never slowed as it prowled down the oak-lined drive to Elancourt.

2

Néomi blinked, her strong night vision returning slowly. Even after all these years, she was still surprised that she was unharmed.

She recognized the sharp, low car from last night, so markedly different from the trucks that usually chugged by on the old county road. Which meant . . . which meant . . .

He's returned! The grave-eyed man who came here last night!

The paper forgotten, she materialized to Elancourt's landing, overlooking the front entrance. She moved as if to clutch the sides of the window there, her arms floating outspread.

And there sat his car in the drive.

Won't you move in? she'd wanted to beg last night as the man had examined the manor. He'd tested the columns, drawn sheets off some of the remaining furniture, and even yanked on the radiant heater in the main salon. Appearing satisfied that it was solid, he'd followed the contraption's underfloor pipes by stomping on the marble tiles.

The heater will work, she'd inwardly cried. Ten

years ago, the manor had been modernized by a young couple who'd stayed for a time.

Yet she couldn't relate the merits of Elancourt to this mysterious stranger. Because she was a ghost. The act of speaking, or at least talking in a way that others could hear, had proved impossible for her, as had making herself visible to others.

Which was probably for the best. Her reflection was haunting even to her. Though Néomi's appearance was a close facsimile of how she'd looked the night she died—with the same dress and jewelry—now her skin and lips were as pale as rice paper. Her hair flowed wildly with rose petals tangled in it, and the skin under her eyes was darkened, making her irises seem freakishly blue in contrast.

She focused on the car again. Deep masculine voices sounded from within it. Was there more than one man?

Maybe there'd be two more "confirmed bachelors" like the handsome couple who had lived here during the fifties!

Whoever was within the car needed to hurry inside. Autumn rains had been tentatively falling all night and lightning had begun flaring in a building rhythm. She hoped the men didn't catch the front façade lit by the glow of lightning. With its arches and overhangs and stained glass, the manor could appear . . . forbidding.

The very Gothic traits she'd admired seemed to drive others away.

The vehicle began to rock from side to side on its wide wheels, and the voices grew louder. Then came a man's bellow. Her lips parted when two large boots kicked through the back window, shattering it, glass spraying out into the gravel.

Someone unseen hauled the booted man back inside, but then a rear door began to bulge outward. Were cars so weak in this age that a man could kick it out of shape? No, no, she'd dutifully read the crash test reports, and they said—

The door shot off its hinges, all the way to the front porch. She gasped as a wild-eyed, crazed man lunged out of the vehicle. He was manacled at his wrists and ankles and covered in blood. He immediately fell into a deep slick of mud, only to be tackled by three men.

One of them was her prospective tenant from last night.

She saw then that they all were covered in blood—because the chained one was spitting it at them as he thrashed.

"*No . . . no!*" he yelled, struggling not to enter the house. Could he possibly sense there was more here than could be seen? No one had before.

"Conrad, stop fighting us!" the tenant said through gritted teeth. His accent sounded Russian. "We don't want to hurt you."

But the madman named Conrad didn't let up one bit. "God damn you, Nikolai! What do you want with me?"

"We're going to rid you of this madness, defeat your bloodlust."

"You *fools!*" He laughed manically. "No one comes back!"

"Sebastian, grab his arms!" this Nikolai barked to one of the others. "Murdoch, get his damned legs!" As Murdoch and Sebastian rushed to action, she realized that they both resembled Nikolai. All three had the same grim expression, the same tall, powerful bodies.

Brothers. Their captive must be one as well.

They carried the bloody and flailing Conrad toward the front double doors. Blood in her home. She shuddered. She detested blood, hated the sight of it, the scent of it. She'd never forget how it'd felt to be bathed in her own, to have it thicken and cool around her dying body.

Hadn't Elancourt seen enough of it?

In a panic, she raced downstairs and shot her hands up, exerting an invisible force against the doors. She used all her strength to keep them sealed tight. No one could bust through this hold—

The doors flew open. The men barreled through her, making her shiver as though she'd walked through a cobweb. A gust of wind rushed inside, following them in to stir the leaves and grit coating the floor.

Just how strong were they? Yes, they were huge, but she'd held the doors with what had to be the strength of twenty men.

Once inside the darkened room, Nikolai cast a chain across the floor with no care for her Italian marble.

The lunatic broke free once more, making it to his feet. He was towering! He lumbered toward the door, but his bound ankles ensured that he careened into an antique armoire covered with a sheet. It collapsed under the impact. *Crushed.*

She'd had to dance two performances to afford that

piece, and remembered lovingly polishing it herself. It was one of the few original furnishings that remained.

After Murdoch and Sebastian hoisted him out of the wreckage, Murdoch wrapped his thick arm around Conrad's neck, cupping the back of Conrad's head with his free hand. She could see that Murdoch was tightening this hold with all his might, his face drawn with the effort, the muscles in his neck standing out with strain.

Somehow Conrad was unaffected for long moments. Eventually, his thrashing eased and he went limp. While Murdoch laid him on the ground, Nikolai hastily affixed the chain to the same radiator he'd tested last night, then attached the other end to Conrad's handcuffs.

That's why Nikolai had been inspecting it? Because he intended to jail this lunatic here?

Why here?

"Could you have found an eerier place to keep him?" Sebastian said between breaths as they all stood. At that instant, lightning crackled just outside. The high stained-glass windows were broken in places and cast tinted light, distorting the shadows within. "Why not use the old mill?"

"Someone might come across him there," Murdoch answered. "And Kristoff knows about the mill. If he or his men discover what we're planning . . ."

Who's Kristoff? What are they planning?

Nikolai added, "Besides, Elancourt was recommended to me."

"Who would ever recommend this?" Sebastian waved a hand around. "It looks straight from a horror movie." She wished he was wrong, but a bolt flashed then; hued shadows appeared to slither and pounce. Sebastian raised his brows as if his point had been made.

Nikolai's gaze focused on his brothers' faces, studying their reactions as he answered, "Nïx did." He hesitated, seeming not to know if they'd laugh, rail, or nod.

Murdoch shrugged and Sebastian nodded grimly.

Who's Nïx?

Sebastian glanced around. "Raises my hackles, though"—another flash of lightning—"almost like it's . . . *haunted*."

Sebastian gets a cookie.

"And you know that's something for me to say. It's spooked Conrad as well."

Yes, because otherwise he clearly would be fine.

"The weather makes it seem worse." Nikolai ran his hand through his wet hair, then wiped his face with his shirttail. "And if there are spirits lingering about? You forget what we are—any ghosts would do well to fear us."

Fear them? No living thing could touch her.

"It's actually ideal because the place scares people away," Nikolai continued over another bout of thunder. "And the Valkyrie compound isn't far from here—not many from the Lore will venture anywhere near their home."

Valkyrie? Lore? She remembered a newspaper article a few years back on "Gang Speak." These men were speaking Gang. They had to be.

Murdoch said, "Perhaps the Valkyrie won't appreciate vampires so close to Val Hall."

Vampires? Not Gang? They're all mad. Mon Dieu, I need a bourbon.

"Is it even *habitable?*" Sebastian asked in a scoffing voice.

Nikolai nodded. "The structure and the roof are solid—"

As rock.

"—and once we do some modifications, it'll be suitable for our purposes. We'll fix just what we need: a couple of bedrooms, a shower, the kitchen. I already had the witches come around today to do an enclosure spell along the perimeter of the estate. As long as Conrad's wearing those chains, he can't escape the boundary."

Witches? Oh, come now! Néomi moved to rub her temple, felt nothing, but was somewhat soothed by the familiar act.

In the lull, Murdoch cased the main salon, plucking at cobwebs. "Conrad knew we were going to be at the tavern."

"No doubt of it," Nikolai answered, crossing to a dirt-caked window to glance outside. "He was awaiting us. To kill us."

"Obviously he's gotten good at it." Sebastian patted his ribs in an assessing manner and winced. Looking more closely, she could see that they all seemed injured in some way. Even Conrad appeared to have been clawed across the chest by some beast. "He likes it."

Likes to kill? A murderer in my home. Again. Was he the same kind of man as Louis—one who would stab a defenseless woman through the heart? *Tamp it down, Néomi. . . .* The wind picked up. *Control the emotion.*

Murdoch said, "I suppose he'd have to, if the word about his occupation is true."

A professional killer?

"Finding him now . . . it couldn't come at a worse time," Sebastian said. "How are we going to manage this?"

"We fight a war, deceive our king, try not to worry about our Kaderin and Myst, all the while attempting to salvage Con's sanity," Nikolai replied evenly.

Murdoch lifted a brow. "And here I thought we would be busy."

The brothers began exploring nearby rooms, testing wood for rot and pulling sheets from furniture, examining their surroundings.

In the past, she'd been fortunate with those who'd occupied Elancourt. Nice families had come and gone, a few harmless vagrants. Nothing about these men said *We're nice and harmless!*

Especially not the chained murderer. He lay on the floor, blood collecting at the corner of his parted lips to drip down.

Drip . . . drip . . . A crimson pool was stark against her marble. Just as before. *Tamp it down. Control it.*

The madman's eyes flashed open. She couldn't warn the others! In the space of a bolt of lightning, he somehow shot to his chained feet, hobbling forward with unnatural speed. Before she could even raise her arms to exert pressure against him, he'd stretched the chain taut . . . the radiator was bending under the pressure.

He couldn't break it. Imposs—

Like a whip, it snapped free as he charged across the room for the door—the door where she stood. As she stared in disbelief, the radiator trailed in his wake, destroying everything in its wildly sweeping path.

Suddenly, the underfloor web of attached heating pipes burst up through the floor, foot after foot of groaning metal and exploding marble and splinters.

The three men dove for him once more, the pile of them skidding to a stop right at her slippers.

She gaped. Her home, her beloved home. In fifteen minutes, the madman had wrought more destruction to Elancourt than it had sustained in the last eighty years.

Her hands fisted. *Control it.* But her hair had already begun to swirl about her face, rose petals floating in a tempest around her body. Outside, the wind kicked up, streaming through the holes in the high windows, sweeping the grit and dust until she was able to see all the destruction.

The marble! When her eyes watered with frustration, rain poured outside.

Tamp it down.

Too late. Lightning bombarded the house, illuminating the night like successive bomb blasts. From under the pile of men, Conrad yanked his head up at her.

In a flash, Néomi twisted round, sweeping her hair over her face as she dissipated. Reemerging on the landing, she gazed down at him.

Conrad continued to stare at the spot where she'd stood, blinking and easing his struggles as if dumbfounded.

Had he . . . had he possibly seen *her?*

No one ever had before. Ever. She'd been so uniformly ignored for so long that she'd begun to wonder if she truly existed.

Up close, she'd been able to see that the whites of his eyes were . . . red. She'd thought he'd been injured, with burst blood vessels shooting across, but in fact, they were wholly glazed with red.

What were these beings? Could they truly be . . . *vampires*? Even in light of what she'd become, she still struggled to believe in anything supernatural.

With a shake of his head, Conrad frenziedly renewed his flight for the door, gaining inches, even as the three wrestled with him.

"I didn't want to have to do this, Conrad!" Nikolai said, digging into his jacket pocket. As the others pinned Conrad, he bit the end off what appeared to be a syringe and injected its contents into Conrad's arm.

Whatever it was slowed him, making him blink his red eyes again and again.

"What did you give him?" Sebastian asked.

"It's a concoction from the witches—part medical, part mystickal. It should knock him out."

For *how long* would it knock Conrad out? How long were they expecting him to stay here? To spit across her floor and roar within her halls? She'd be damned if she allowed another of Louis's ilk to taint her home once more! This Conrad was an animal. He should be put down. Or at the very least, *put out.*

She'd show these trespassers power like they'd never seen, sweeping them into the yard like trash! She'd toss them by their feet all the way to the bayou! Néomi would demonstrate what happened when a ghost went poltergeist—

"*Where . . . is she?*" Conrad grated between heaving breaths.

Néomi froze. He couldn't be talking about her, couldn't have seen her.

"Who, Conrad?" Nikolai demanded.

Just before the shot knocked him unconscious, he rasped, "Female . . . *beautiful*."

3

Dawn had come and gone, and still Néomi was reeling. Because apparently Elancourt was filled to the rafters with real vampires.

Any lingering doubt had evaporated when she'd seen the brothers vanish and reappear as they'd gone about repairing parts of the house.

And this wasn't even the most astonishing development of the night. When Conrad had said, *"Female . . . beautiful,"* had he possibly been talking about her?

Now she could only wait impatiently for him to regain consciousness so she could find out.

He remained as the brothers had left him last night—lying on the new mattress they'd brought in for him, with his wrists chained together behind him, his muddy boots and the ankle restraints removed. His ripped clothing had dried, the material stiff with dirt. The angry red gashes on his chest had healed within mere hours.

She floated in a sitting position above the foot of the bed wondering how much longer he would be out. She'd thought all vampires would be comatose during the day, but his brothers were in and out downstairs, busily teleporting goods into the manor.

This waiting was unbearable. *Because he possibly . . . saw me.* Yes, no one ever had before, and, yes, this development was based solely on the idea that he'd deemed her beautiful. Maybe if he wasn't one to quibble about pink cheeks and the appearance of blooming health . . . ?

Néomi didn't necessarily seek an acknowledgment of her presence. She could float a sheet spray-painted with "*Bonjour! from le spectre!*" if she wanted bad attention, or a possible exorcism. No, she wanted to be *seen*. She yearned to converse.

The possibility of this meant that all her grand plans to evict them had evaporated, her rancor over the damage to Elancourt temporarily soothed. Now she wanted to keep them close—especially Conrad.

Curiosity ruled her. Why after eighty years of sporadic tenants had the blood-spitting vampire been able to see her? Why not his brothers? When they'd been chaining up Conrad for the day, she'd waved her hands, yelling as loud as she could. She'd even thrown herself through their torsos, to no effect.

Was Conrad able to see her because he alone had red eyes?

She stood to float from one peeling blue wall to the other. The brothers had unerringly chosen for Conrad the Blue Room, the most masculine of all the guest rooms. The heavy curtains were a deep navy, and the spare pieces of furniture—the bedstead, the nightstand, and a high-backed chair by the fireplace—were dark and stout.

Though she'd expected them to sleep in coffins, they'd put Conrad in the made-up bed. She'd also believed that even indirect sun would burn them, but the room was aglow with enough pallid sunlight to illuminate the dust motes. And when the curtains wavered from a draft in the house, light would encroach all the way up to his feet.

He turned over on his back then, reminding her how massive he was, his broad shoulders seeming to span the bed, his feet hanging over the end. He must be over six and a half feet tall.

She floated above him, tilting her head as she peered down. He looked to be in his early thirties, but it was difficult to tell with the mud and blood covering his face. With a nervous swallow, she concentrated and used telekinesis to draw back his upper lip, jabbing his nose before she got it right.

She saw a slash of white teeth gleaming against his dirty face and . . . unmistakable fangs. Just like in the novels she'd read long ago. Just like in the vampire movies the last young couple had loved to watch.

How had these men become vampires? Were they turned? Or born that way?

At that moment a loud bang sounded from downstairs. Though she dearly wanted to investigate what they were doing to her house, she feared Conrad would wake in her absence.

The brothers had already boarded many of the windows that didn't have heavy curtains, and had brought in folding chairs, mattresses, and sheets—even a modern refrigerator. The plumbing had been repaired in the master bathroom. Earlier, electricity had surged to life so abruptly that the lightbulb and fixture overhead had popped and shattered, raining glass.

She'd floated the shards off the prisoner, a good

move because he now began to twist in the tangled sheets.

When his ripped shirt rode up a few inches, she noticed a thin scar beginning just above the waistline of his loose pants. How long was it? She waved her hand to tug the shirt farther up his torso. The scar continued. Nibbling her lip, she painstakingly manipulated the buttons until she could unfasten them all and spread the sides wide.

The scar nearly reached up to his heart. It appeared as if a razor-sharp blade had entered at his stomach and slashed upward.

When she could drag her gaze from the mark, she surveyed his bared chest. It was broad and generously packed with muscle. With his hands behind his back, those rippling muscles seemed to flex even at rest. His entire torso looked hard as rock, with not a spare ounce on him.

She wondered what his skin would feel like. She would never know. . . .

His pants waist sat so low that she could see the line of crisp, black hair descending from his navel. That dusky trail taunted her to ease his pants lower, but she resisted—barely.

The men Néomi had been attracted to in the past had been older and handsome in a soft, cultured way. In contrast, this male was all hardness and sharp edges.

So why did she find his battle-scarred body so attractive?

"*Oh, wake up, Conrad,*" she said with difficulty. Speaking was an arduous undertaking for her—she often felt like she was trying to shove elephant-sized sounds through a pinhole. To her, the words came out echoing and extended. "*Just . . . wake up.*" She wanted to jump on the bed or scream in his ear. If she'd had a bucket of water—

Conrad's eyes shot wide open.

He comes to. The light is murder on his sensitive eyes. Pain shoots through him. He grits his teeth against waves of it.

Get free. He fights his bonds. Limbs feel leaden. *Drugged.* Rage stabs him, the need to kill strangles him like clenched hands around his own throat.

How long have I been out? He remembers where he is. The manor—as forbidding as he'd sensed it would be. When he'd been in the car, the sight of it had made him sweat and thrash.

The feeling of being watched is multiplied here, the tingle on the back of his neck unrelenting.

He tenses. He'd seen . . . *had* he seen a spill of shining black hair as some female twirled round? *Can't determine what's real and what's illusion.* Before she vanished, he'd thought he'd glimpsed blue eyes going wide with surprise. He'd smelled roses and had seen a bared shoulder—slim and impossibly pale. Yet no one else had reacted to her.

Which means she can't be real.

Anything he sees that others don't is suspect. She's likely a figment in his mind from another's memory. Someone that he's drunk had known her as a wife, a mistress . . . or one of their own victims.

He strains harder against the chains. Nothing.

Metal like this shouldn't be able to hold him. Unless . . . *Mystickally reinforced.*

Damn his brothers to hell! Why in the fuck would they bring him here? This place feels wrong, menacing. He doesn't know how or why. Doesn't care. *Just know I have to get free.*

Suddenly the smell of roses surrounds him. *I'm not alone in this room.* Though he sees nothing, there's another presence here. Is it the female from before? *Was* there a female before? He begins to sweat.

Something is inches from him, creeping closer . . . he could swear he feels warm breaths against his ear. He writhes, baring his fangs in warning. The need to kill seethes inside him.

Closer . . . closer . . .

From directly beside his ear he scarcely hears a voice. He can't make out the faltering words.

But he senses *expectancy*—a yearning that hits him in roiling waves. His head feels like it's about to explode. He's supposed to do something. "What? What?" He doesn't know . . . doesn't know what he's supposed to do . . .

He hates this need he senses.

"*Seeeeee meeeeee?*" the faint voice says. He jerks his head back and forth. Sees *nothing*.

He lunges upright, feeling a shock of something, like static electricity.

Conrad's body drifted through hers, making her gasp and him shudder.

He stumbled to his feet. Confusion appeared to

mount within him. "Someone's here. Real?" His voice sounded even raspier than last night.

"*Conrad, be calm,*" she said slowly.

His eyes glowed a deeper red. "Show—yourself!" Could he possibly be responding to her words? Or did he merely have some kind of vampire's sense that he wasn't alone?

With a low growl, he backed against the wall as he worked on the manacles. Finally he looped his bound hands under his feet to bring them forward. Seeming to relish the chance to fight, he intently scanned the room for an enemy, for a kill.

As Néomi hovered about him, waving her hand in front of his face, his eyes darted wildly, his head jerking right, then left. Frowning, she brandished her forefinger, stabbing his eye, passing straight through it.

He didn't blink.

She floated backward as if pushed. *He* can't *see me.* Heavy disappointment settled over her.

Beautiful female? Just the ramblings of a madman. She'd seized on the words no matter how unlikely they were because she'd been desperate.

The elation of the night had set her up for the bitterest disappointment. She gave one last frantic wave at his eyes—

He snapped his teeth, the sound like a bear trap; she reacted with a startled cry and raised her hands, shoving him away, sending him like a cannonball into the high-backed chair. When the chair slammed into the opposite wall, it collapsed from the impact, exploding into a cloud of splinters, tufts of upholstery filler, and plaster.

Battling to be freed from the shambles, he yelled in a foreign language, what had to be oaths. Yet he appeared to *like* the violence—or at least to be accustomed to it.

"Conrad . . . *wait!*" she managed to bite out. *Where are the brothers? With their syringes?* Yes, the three men were in and out, but they were never gone long.

Once he made it to his feet, he began tearing through the room, banging on the walls with his chained hands, knocking holes in the brittle plaster.

"Stop hurting . . . my house!"

He didn't. Instead, he snatched up the fireplace tools and swung them round, chucking them with so much force that the poker embedded itself into the brick of the fireplace, bobbing there. When his frenzied gaze landed on the defenseless nightstand, she said, "No closer."

Conrad charged for it. Without thinking, she swept him up to the ceiling. He closed his eyes tight, then opened them, seeming astounded to be still regarding the floor.

He thrashed and fought her hold. He was strong, and soon she was forced to drop him, more hastily than she'd intended—he landed flat on his face. When he rose, she saw that his forehead was gushing blood into his eyes and alongside his nose.

She hadn't meant to hurt him! *"Dieu, je regrette!"*

"Conrad!" Nikolai yelled from downstairs, appearing in the doorway a split second later. He swept a baffled glance over the chaotic scene. "What the hell are you—"

Nikolai never finished his question because Conrad swung his bound arms at him. As though hit by a battering ram, Nikolai flew out of the room and over the landing to the first floor.

Conrad charged out the door with a wide-eyed Néomi right behind him. Though his speed was still superhuman, he was slower than he'd been last night—even with his ankles free. They'd already weakened him drastically.

As Nikolai lumbered to his feet, Sebastian stood on the stairs, arms outstretched. But Conrad planted his chained hands on the railing and leapt down, evading any contact. When he turned toward the front entry, he found Murdoch barring his way.

Nikolai yelled, "Conrad, it's impossible for you to leave! Damn it, the sun!"

What would happen to Conrad in the direct light of day? She gasped when he charged Murdoch, tackling him into the mahogany front doors. They wrenched one completely free of its hinges, flattening it onto the front porch.

Just before they surged into the morning sun, Murdoch traced back to the protective cover of the porch; Conrad continued. Should she try to stop him?

Nikolai started to follow, but Sebastian snatched his shirt and lugged him back to the shade. "He won't get far, Nikolai."

Néomi stood beside the brothers. Out of habit, she shaded her eyes as the four of them watched Conrad racing down the drive. *I didn't mean to drop him like that. He must be so bewildered.*

"He's going to burn," Nikolai said, sounding in pain.

Just as Néomi had, Murdoch put his hand to his forehead. "And then he's going to learn."

The sun sears his eyes as if they've been doused with acid. *Fight on.* The bayou is just down the drive, then across the road. He can scent the dark water.

His skin begins to burn. He grits his teeth against the pain.

Bayou just across the road. He can make it, could survive in the shade there. *Flames growing.*

He nears the property line. Gaining distance away from whatever entity seems bent on tormenting him. A being he can't see to fight, with no throat to savage. A disembodied voice had echoed all around him.

Almost there . . . *Burning . . . burning . . .*

Suddenly his sight goes black; a force shoves him back on his ass. Once his vision clears, his eyes widen. Crumbling blue walls surround him. He yells in disbelief. Confusion wells.

The same bedroom! He's in . . . *the same goddamned room.*

Crouched on the floor, he knocks his head against the wall again and again until the needle pierces his arm.

4

Something is happening to the patient.

Over the last week, Néomi had begun noticing an eerie awareness in those red eyes that wasn't there before, the blankness in his gaze receding with each day.

And she would know. She'd done little else but study him since his bizarre return, seldom retiring to her own room—her secret studio, hidden downstairs. Even now as Conrad lay in the bed once more, sleeping, she floated above the end of his mattress, continuing her vigil.

When he'd returned that first morning, he'd been raging, banging his head against the wall as if to blunt whatever was inside his mind. Plaster had snowed down on him and stuck to his bloody cheeks. Once the brothers had rechained him—tethering him to the bed this time—Conrad had been unreachable, drugged and muttering foreign words in his low, harsh voice.

To be fair, she would've been addled, too. One moment she'd been watching him running, the next she'd heard his unholy roar just upstairs.

No longer was Néomi the only one trapped here. Apparently, witches truly had put a boundary spell on

Elancourt. As long as Conrad wore those chains, he couldn't cross the property line. The chains also rendered it impossible for him to teleport—or *trace*, as they called it.

Néomi couldn't put her finger on exactly when she'd first sensed a change in him. Whenever his brothers had spoken to him, Conrad had muttered incoherently, and yet she'd begun to get the feeling that he was . . . coherent. At least intermittently.

Sometimes it seemed as if he was trying to filter a million thoughts in order to speak only one, and that was why he had difficulty talking normally. On occasion, even his accent changed. . . .

He began twisting then, his head thrashing, no doubt caught in the grip of a horrific nightmare. Conrad routinely suffered them. With his fangs seeming to sharpen at intervals, he writhed, muscles straining, the chains cutting into his skin. She frowned. She didn't like to see that.

Even though everything about him should repel her, she found herself striving to be impassive. He'd destroyed parts of her house. He was a killer. He continued to have flashes of violent aggression. And he was filthy. His face was still coated with mud, blood, and caked-on plaster, his hair tangled in thick knots. Burn marks radiated over his skin and blackened his ratty clothes. When Sebastian had tried to wipe clean his charred face, Conrad had snapped his teeth at him so fast, Sebastian had almost lost his fingers.

Néomi should hate Conrad. So why did she find herself so drawn to this big male, with his terrifying dreams?

Because, like her, he knew the horror of being murdered? He might be reliving it even now.

Was Conrad merely a lost soul to be pitied? Or a man worthy of rescue? Néomi had never been very interested in Men Who Needed Saving. There were women enough out there for them—

At that moment, he jerked awake, his eyes darting yet blank. Arching his body around, he opened his mouth and sank his fangs into his own arm. With his brows drawn, he sucked slowly as if for comfort.

And her heart melted. "*Merde,*" she whispered.

When he gave a short, ireful growl against his arm, she eased beside him on the bed. "*Hush, vampire,*" she sighed, brushing his hair from his forehead with a telekinetic stroke. "*Hush, now.*" He stilled, gradually releasing his bite to lie back and slumber on, as if he'd been soothed by her. . . .

Each night until sunrise, as the brothers attempted to reach him, Néomi floated about the ceiling, listening. Though she simply enjoyed hearing the rhythms of the men's conversations, she had also been learning much about these people.

They were from Estonia, a Baltic country bordering Russia, which explained their accents. *Men from the Northlands.* They'd been turned into vampires— three hundred years ago. Before then, they'd fought in the Great Northern War against Russia as noblemen officers, though eventually they'd wrested control of Estonia's floundering army. Each brother had become a warlord, leading the defense of a section of their country, under the ultimate command of Nikolai, the eldest.

At first, she'd remained in Conrad's room because she'd been hopeful about him seeing her. Now she stayed because she was intrigued by the crazed vampire.

His history was like an incomplete puzzle, and with each piece of it she received, the whole grew more riveting. He'd been highborn, but ultimately had used his military experience and his vampiric strength to become an assassin. He'd planned to kill his own brothers in retaliation for some deed she hadn't yet learned.

He'd been alone and friendless for centuries.

His past was so different from hers—with all the dancing and laughter and letting the good times roll—they were poles apart.

Yet with each revelation came more questions. He was obviously a powerful man, so what could have broken his mind like this? And how could he remain in bed day after day? Did vampires have no bodily functions?

Each night they'd brought a thermos from the new refrigerator to Conrad, and Néomi was fairly certain she knew what was in it. But exactly where did they get it? And since Conrad was refusing to drink the contents, how long would it be before he starved?

She'd watched him sleeping for more hours than she could count—why had he never once grown hard as men unwittingly did in sleep?

When dusk approached, and the brothers returned downstairs, Conrad's eyes flashed open instantly.

She crossed to the door, floating in it, so that half of her remained outside the room, and half was inside. Still she could barely hear them downstairs. But she could see Conrad's reaction and realized that he could hear them, even with the heavy door closed.

"After seeing him in this condition," Sebastian said, "I'm beginning to understand why none of the Fallen have ever come back from bloodlust."

"No one before has had the tools we do," Nikolai answered. "We've agreed to spend a month trying to rehabilitate him. If he shows no signs of improvement, then we'll do what must be done."

Conrad's listening to them. Intently. She wondered what he must be thinking.

"That was before I saw him, Nikolai. Maybe we need to . . . to put him out of his misery." *Is he in misery?*

Conrad's jaw clenched, and his expression grew deadly. Yet then his brows drew together as if he was considering the possibility right at that moment. When he frowned and closed his eyes, she felt a twist in her chest.

The vampire is in misery. And he's sane enough to know it.

Misery? What the fuck do they know of it? He shakes his head as if to jar loose the thought.

He easily hears them downstairs as Murdoch explains what he's learned about the Fallen, vampires who kill by drinking blood. "Loud sounds other than their own yells enrage them. Quick movements do as well—they react to them as if they're threats, no matter how benign. Being taken unaware would send one into a fury. Any sense of their own physical vulnerability triggers rage."

"Why don't you just explain what *doesn't* enrage them?" Sebastian asks.

There is little that doesn't, he thinks, just as Murdoch says, "That would be a short explanation."

He blocks them out, his musings turning to the mysterious entity again.

The being can be one of three things. He thinks. An echo from a fractured memory, a hallucination, or a ghost. He has nearly three hundred years of experience with the first two possibilities—and none with the latter. The first pair are figments of his twisted mind. The ghost would be unimagined.

Can't determine what's real or what's illusion. For the last week the being has returned to his room. He's begun seeing her again, though not as much as that first night. Only a faint, glowing outline now. But he can scent her presence. Even now, he's awash in the smell of roses.

Whenever she comes to him, so do flashes of his lucidity. He doesn't understand the connection, just knows he's beginning to crave the focus of his thoughts.

A mystery. How could a figment of his mind *clear* his mind? Even as he's debating her existence—he's realizing that something is actually making him coherent enough to fucking debate her existence.

Maybe the shots they keep forcing on him are helping.

He can't recall much of what happened the morning he'd tried to escape. But he thinks that she'd been trying to undress him and possibly had attempted to kiss him—before casting him about the room.

Yet the being never attacked him again. Usually she stays near the window seat. Though he has sensed her at the foot of his bed on more than one unnerving occasion.

For years, he's constantly felt as if he was being watched by something unseen—now he actually could be.

No. He sees shadowy figures every day. Why should he think she's different? Because she has a scent? Because, for the first time, he wants a hallucination to be real?

He knows there's a line between suffering from hallucinations and interacting with them. You can live with the former; the latter means you're lost.

Over the last century, he's held on to the last of his sanity by his fingertips. Acknowledging her might just be the weight around his ankles needed to drag him down.

Even as he knows this, he speculates about her constantly. If she exists, then she's a ghost. Weren't ghosts born of violent deaths or murder? *So how did she die? And when? Is she even sentient?* He's seen her eyes and her long hair. *What does the rest of her look like?*

Why are my goddamned thoughts so lucid around her?

His brothers sound as if they're about to come to the room. He doesn't want this. Each day the entity grows clearer as the sun sets and the room dims. But when his brothers arrive, she fades. He's realized that the uncovered new bulb above is too bright—the unnatural light obscures her. Darkness would reveal her to him.

It wasn't in the lightning bolts that he saw her that

first night. It was in the dead black lulls between them.

Twilight's coming. Which means if his brothers will stay away, he would be closer with each minute to discovering what she looks like. He's hungry for the sight of her, hands clenching and unclenching behind his back in anticipation.

$$5$$

"Am I reaching or does he seem much better?" Nikolai asked when the three traced into the room.

"He doesn't appear as . . . disordered," Sebastian said.

As if to prove them wrong, Conrad began to mutter unintelligibly in a language Néomi had never heard, his gaze darting to the window.

"Why don't you try to talk to him alone?" Murdoch said. When Nikolai nodded, Murdoch and Sebastian left.

Nikolai set the thermos on the nightstand, then pulled up a folding chair, turning it around to sit astraddle. Néomi loved it when men sat that way. His voice low, he said, "Where have you been, brother?"

Brother. She was still startled at the idea that Conrad was part of their family. Sebastian seemed determined and studious, Murdoch was quiet and mysterious, and Nikolai was authoritative like the general he was. In contrast, the madman was aggressive and struck her as dishonorable, as if in a stand-up fight between gentlemen, he'd fling dirt in his opponent's eyes.

"What do you want with me?" Conrad abruptly grated. "Why haven't you killed me?"

Seeming surprised by the interaction, Nikolai said, "That's not our intention."

"What is—to drug and starve me?"

Nikolai shot to his feet for the thermos. "I've some blood here. Will you drink?" He quickly opened the top and poured into the attached cup.

Néomi saw that the liquid was thick and dark. When it made a *glug-glug* sound, she wondered if it was possible for her to vomit.

"You feeding me blood." Conrad's tone was scathing. "How *familiar*."

Nikolai seemed to stifle a wince at that, but then he brought the cup to Conrad's lips.

Drinking. Blood. Conrad accepted obediently, drawing deep.

I want to vomit—

He spit a mouthful at Nikolai, hitting him in the face. Then he laughed, a rough, sinister sound. His red eyes brimmed with a hatred so virulent, Néomi believed that only death would cure it.

Nikolai wiped his face with his shirttail. When he seemed to draw on an unearthly supply of patience, Néomi felt sympathy for him. How much he must care for his brother to tolerate this. Nikolai didn't strike her as a normally forgiving male.

Of course, Néomi didn't bother hiding her disgusted expression. Strangely, when Conrad's eyes darted in her direction, she could swear he became more restless. Then his gaze slid to the window once more.

"Bagged blood is all you're going to get," Nikolai said. "If you don't drink it, then you go without."

"I hunt. I feed from the vein. Unlike you unmanned traitors," Conrad bit out, facing him again. "I know you hide me from your king. Your *Russian* king. He'll execute you for this—favored general or not."

"Possibly. So you know the risk we take."

"Why?"

"We want to help you—"

"Like you did last time!" Conrad bellowed, wrestling against the chain that trapped him to the bed, those tremendous muscles straining.

Undaunted, Nikolai continued, "We're going to help you combat your bloodlust."

"Never." Conrad's bloody fangs seemed to sharpen. "No one comes back. The red on my eyes will never go away."

"It would if I bled you out, drained you completely dry. But you'd only want to return to that state, killing even more than before. And you'd lose all the power you'd amassed."

"I know this!"

"Then did you know you can learn to control the memories if you're not constantly adding new ones?" At Conrad's mildly surprised look, Nikolai said, "We're aware of the memories. They're a sickness. You can't differentiate between those of your victims and your own. They make you hallucinate constantly, and your head feels like it will explode from them."

What did they mean? Conrad was *sick*? Was there an actual medical reason behind his madness?

"Yet what if you could turn them on and off, accessing them at will?" Nikolai asked. "How much better do you think your life would be without them tormenting you? If we can get you stable, you can learn to hold them at bay."

Conrad shook his head sharply. "I want blood from the vein. Only from the vein—"

"That's why we're going to help you find your Bride. Because there is one drive that's strong enough to compete with bloodlust."

His Bride? Did Nikolai mean the need for sex?

"And the need to kill?" Conrad bit out. "I savor it . . . ache to end you right now."

"Just as there's one drive that can overcome bloodlust, there's one need that's stronger than the need to kill."

"And what's that?" Conrad sneered.

Nikolai said only, "You'll know when it hits you."

Conrad glanced at the window yet again. "What are you injecting me with?" Sometimes when he spoke, he would hesitate as if even he couldn't believe he'd just sounded sane. He must have been mad for a very long time.

"A soothsayer got it from the witches for us. It's a sedative of sorts. It'll continue to weaken you physically, but after a few days, it shouldn't put you in a stupor."

Attention back to his brother, Conrad snapped, "You've no right to drug me!"

"We'll do whatever it takes," Nikolai said, with steel in his tone. "You were a good man and can be again."

"Not *a man*! No longer!" He ground his teeth. "I'm a killer, that's all."

"Most in the Lore believe you're lost. That the red automatically means we have no choice but to destroy you. I do not agree. Mark me, Conrad. One way or another, you will be cured of this," Nikolai vowed, his voice fierce, his gray eyes turning *black*, as if with emotion. No matter what had occurred, she knew that Nikolai indeed loved his younger brother. "We have resources at our disposal that you can't begin to comprehend."

Nikolai's answer seemed to be just cryptic and confident enough to intrigue Conrad. "And exactly how long am I to be jailed and drugged?"

"A month. We're going to keep you from killing for a month. If there's no change by then, we will . . . reevaluate."

Any interest in Conrad's expression dimmed. "I don't have that long."

"Why? What do you mean?"

Conrad didn't answer, seeming to go adrift in his own thoughts, his red eyes skittering in *her* direction again. She could have sworn he began following her movements, so she floated to the window seat. But he continued staring at the spot where she'd just been.

She saw the exact moment Nikolai knew he'd get no further, because he looked whipped with disappointment. With a grave nod to Conrad, he traced out, and seconds later, Murdoch appeared.

He turned the folding chair around and sat, leaning forward, elbows to his knees. "We've missed you, Con," he said quietly. This brother seemed weary to

Néomi, like a man undertaking an arduous journey. And his expression constantly looked as if he'd just, at that very instant, determined he wasn't even halfway there.

"I know you hate Nikolai and me for what we did to you," he began. "But we can't take it back."

What did Nikolai and Murdoch do? These undercurrents, the tensions, the unspoken words—she had to admit all of this was fascinating to her.

"No matter how you treat us, Nikolai won't give up on this. Not until he's convinced you're beyond salvation."

Conrad smiled, his teeth still bloodied, fangs prominent—the most menacing smile Néomi had ever seen. As she shivered, he said, "Convince him then, brother. There's no delivering me from being evil."

6

When does the goddamned sun set in this place? He checks the sun's progress—no different from twenty seconds ago—then studies his brother's tired visage.

"Con, I can't convince Nikolai to give up on you, not when I won't," Murdoch says. "Just cooperate with us. Life can be good again."

Murdoch is much altered from how he'd been as a human. Back then, he'd been lighthearted. Women had found him charming, and he'd had few cares past servicing every pretty maid within a hundred-mile radius.

All I had was cares, no time for women, and a distinct lack of charm.

"Tell me what you've been doing these three hundred years. I haven't seen a glimpse of you since the night right after you died and rose."

He hates to be reminded of that. Swords in hand, he and Sebastian had been defending their four gravely ill sisters and father from marauding Russian soldiers. Two against battalions; they'd had no chance. Nikolai and Murdoch had returned home to find five dead from plague and two brothers mortally wounded, barely clinging to life.

Unconscious, he hadn't been able to fight off Nikolai when he'd dripped his vampiric blood down his throat. He'd woken a monster.

Neither Sebastian nor he had wanted to be turned, but then he'd had quite a bit more reason to resent the betrayal. *Changed to the very thing I'd been conditioned to hate and trained to destroy . . .*

"Don't want to tell me?" Murdoch says. "Then I'll leave tonight to dig on my own, now that I know what you were—"

"What I *am*. I'm still a killer for hire."

"Look at yourself." Murdoch seems to stifle his exasperation. "Who'd hire you?"

His face heats. "Fuck off, Murdoch." His brother makes him sound like a washed-up failure. Which he doesn't give a damn about—except that he doesn't want the female to believe this. *The one who isn't real. The one I'm about to see.*

Almost sunset . . . any second now. At the window she flickers in the last of the muted light. He begins to make out a more distinct shape.

"Very well," Murdoch says as he stands. "Con, you can resist us because you hate what we are or because you resent our actions. But don't fight just because you're prideful and stubborn." He gives a grin, a hint of the old Murdoch. "What am I saying? If you weren't prideful and stubborn, you wouldn't be Conrad Wroth." He traces out.

Shortly after, Sebastian enters and turns on the overhead light. The glare blazes, and she disappears.

"Turn it off!"

"What? Why?"

"My eyes pain me. Do it."

With a shrug, Sebastian flips off the switch, then sits with his long legs stretched out in front of him. "I understand the anger you feel for Nikolai and Murdoch," Sebastian begins in a measured tone. "I hated them too, you know. For so long, I yearned for revenge. But life can be good again. Better than ever before."

"According to you? There's nothing wrong with my life." *Everything's wrong with my life. . . . How much longer till I can see her?*

"Then you'll like it even better sharing it with your fated Bride," Sebastian continues. "She'll calm you, and will help you find clarity. I was on the edge myself before I met mine. One day I had nothing, no real home, no friends, no family. Then as soon as I recognized her as mine, suddenly there was *possibility*."

Sebastian's obviously musing about her right at this moment, his expression so satisfied. *Sickening.* "I want you to meet Kaderin soon. Once you're recovered."

They're acting like it's a given that I'll heal.

Impossible. He would know if there was a way to come back from bloodlust. There is no return. No instance of it.

But his brothers' confidence forces him to wonder.

"Kaderin's had . . . well, her history with fallen vampires is extensive, even for a Valkyrie."

"Kaderin the Coldhearted?" he asks with a slow nod. "An assassin like me. Rumored she snaps vampires' fangs from their decapitated heads, strings them together for her collection. Sounds really fucking calming, Bastian."

Darker outside . . . The female appears backlit by

an iridescent source. He can't discern her features yet. But he can see the outline of her figure. His lips part. *Of her breasts*.

Sebastian shrugs. "Like I said, Kaderin has a long history with them. Which means we're fighting on the same side. Who knows, you might even have a Valkyrie for a Bride."

Darker. Valkyrie were strange, fey-looking women, with far too much strength for their small bodies—and no hesitation to wade into battles or start wars. If one was his Bride, he'd greet dawn.

Dark.

And there the female is.

Though her image is flickering and colorless like an old TV show, he can make out her dress and her bared arms and shoulders. She's turned away as though perched on the window seat, with her head leaning against the window. He begins to see that she's not entirely colorless. Her nails, her choker, and the ties at her bodice are all a deep crimson.

Are those red petals sprinkled in her wild hair?

The more he can discern of her hazy form, the more he . . . *likes*.

She's small in stature, but she has generous breasts. His hands fist behind him again, his fangs subtly aching for that plump flesh. He's never drunk from a woman—and why in the hell has he never drunk from a woman?

He can make out the shine of her nails and the sheen of the slipper ribbons laced up her calves. A slit in her dress climbs up her thigh to reveal a garter.

For some reason, he raises his brows at this. As a vampire who hasn't encountered his Bride, he has no sexual ability or need; her breasts and garters shouldn't interest him whatsoever, not any more than food would.

But they do.

Then . . . for the first time, he sees her face. And just stifles a curse. He hadn't been deluded that first night.

Figures she'd be fucking beautiful. He grates a short laugh. He would imagine nothing but the best.

Those big blue eyes are another shot of color in her black-and-white image. She has a pert, slim nose and smooth, translucent skin. Her lips are pale, but they're full, especially the bottom one.

As if she feels his scrutiny, she turns to him, easing to her feet. *Eerie grace.* He makes his expression blank while keeping her in his field of vision.

She tilts her head. *Is she studying me? Can she see without the light?*

No, she's not real. There's a line between having hallucinations and interacting with them . . . *Can't cross the line.*

She appears to walk, though she is floating off the ground. And she's coming directly toward the bed. What does she want from him? Closer . . . closer . . .

He dimly hears Sebastian ask, "Do you know what will happen to you when your Bride *bloods* you? Your heart will start to beat again, and you'll begin to breathe once more. The air is cold and heavy in your lungs, but the pressure feels good if you don't resist it. And then, with some encouragement from her . . . *all* of you will come back to life, like a fire's been lit."

A *fire lit*. In other words, he'll be able to get hard again.

But unlike every other vampire he's known, he doesn't want to be blooded. He likes the stillness within him, will hold on to it with everything he is. Dying isn't so daunting a prospect when you're halfway there. . . .

Creeping closer to his side, the female lowers her tilted head. *Listening to my chest?* She's heard Sebastian explaining the lack of a heartbeat and decided to see for herself. Which means she's sentient.

He's held out hope that she is a mindless spirit, unaware of her actions. Or that she's been like him in bloodlust—unthinking, reacting on instinct. Instead, she is very aware. Suddenly, his position embarrasses him. Chained in bed, at the mercy of others. This is the weakest he's ever felt in his entire life.

No, there was another time. . . .

Up close, he can see flashes of her ghostly hair tumbling over her shoulder. He swallows, closing his eyes as he waits to feel her hair across his skin. He can't perceive more than electric pinpricks. They don't hurt him; they're not unpleasant.

When she flits away, he cracks open his lids. Her lips are parted in surprise. "*How strange, dément . . . your heart's truly still.*"

He just stops himself from jerking back from her, because the ghost is *addressing him directly*.

That's it. He's lost his fucking mind.

Her echoing words come slowly. As if they've traveled from miles away. He can scarcely hear them—which means no one else would be able to. His hearing is ten times more acute than even his brothers'. A hundred times more than a human's.

He knows she's not speaking to him in the hope of a response, seems to be just testing speech. She looks like she's tasting the words, determining how they feel rolling on her tongue.

Wait . . . *Did she call me dément?* It means *madman* in French. He feels heat on the back of his neck. Though most times he reacts just like an animal, sometimes, very rarely, he suffers the emotions he thought he'd lost—like shame.

There's a line . . . *But is that how she sees me?*

"You know all this, don't you?" Sebastian asks, exhaling. "Aren't you even curious about being blooded? We were forced to do without so much. There is a lot that your Bride could make up for."

This yanks his attention from the ghost. *Don't you dare, Sebastian! Don't bring this up. . . .*

7

Sebastian lowered his voice to say, "Wouldn't you want to bed a female once more? It isn't like you were a man of experience, glutted on women, Conrad. If you're anything like me, you can count the number of times on one hand."

Conrad didn't deny his brother's words, instead grinding his teeth, his jaws bulging. The number of *times* on one hand? *How awful*, Néomi thought, floating to the foot of his bed to hover there in a sitting position.

Though she herself hadn't taken as many lovers as she would have liked—the specter of pregnancy for a working ballerina was too daunting—the ones she'd had, she'd enjoyed to the fullest.

Even with the filth covering Conrad's face and the scars on his body, she could tell he had pleasing features. Women would find him attractive. At least enough that he could bed one when he wanted to. And Sebastian was handsome, yet he'd said they'd been forced to go without. She'd heard them talking about their small country having been decimated by plague, embattled for decades—were there no women to take succor from?

"Le dément . . . isn't a man of experience?" she murmured in her weird, ghostly voice. *"Intéressant."*

Though it was still difficult to speak, she marveled at how much more readily her words came with each try. The more she talked, the easier it was becoming, like training oneself to run through knee-high water. Too bad no one would answer, just when she was getting good at it.

Yet even if no one responded, talking made her feel more . . . real. Sometimes she felt like the proverbial falling tree in the forest. It could be argued that because no one had seen her or heard her since she'd died, she didn't exist.

She sighed and drew her legs to her chest. When the slit in her dress rode up, she had the strange impulse to cover her legs in front of the vampire. But why? She couldn't be seen, and she'd certainly never been modest when living. Indeed, she was just the opposite.

Any inhibitions had been drummed out of her when she'd been young. She'd been raised in tiny lodgings above a burlesque bar, with her dear *maman* eventually becoming one of its best draws.

From an early age, Néomi had flitted in and out of the performers' dressing rooms, fascinated with the silks, makeup, and exotic perfumes, enthralled by the sensual strains of music that compelled her to sway to them. . . .

Yet she could have sworn there had been a *lustful* aspect to the vampire's gaze.

No. It was time to face the facts. Either he found her spectral appearance *beautiful*, had mastered his

blink reflex, and simply refused to acknowledge her—
or he was just like every other person who'd set foot in
this house over the last eight decades.

She gave a humorless laugh. *"If I thought you could
see me,"* she began slowly, *"I'd show far more than a
garter."*

Besides, Conrad wouldn't be interested in her like
that. Never once in the past week had he grown erect.
Was it impossible for him? Was that the "fire" that
would be lit by his Bride?

Of all the subjects the men discussed, this Bride
concept intrigued her most.

Earlier, she'd heard Sebastian on the phone with
his, earnestly assuring her that she didn't need to
be here, that she should keep working with her sisters, and that he would be home soon. Even the mere
phone conversation with this Kaderin had seemed to
consume him.

Nikolai had also phoned his Bride, another Valkyrie named Myst, and was equally attentive. But with
her he'd sounded less confident about Conrad's recovery than he'd been with his brothers. In a low tone,
he'd said, "We might have to use Riora's gift."

Who is Riora? Another mystery.

The two men's devotion to their wives brought on
Néomi's own longings, because nothing was sexier to
her than a thoroughly smitten male.

She called her desire *longings* since it was different
from the physical symptoms of lust she'd felt while living. She suffered from what she remembered of desire,
still hungering to touch and be touched, but now the
need was more akin to an electrical stimulation, a

charge that built and built. It was like having pinpricks and itching all over her, but no way to scratch.

Néomi had eighty years of those pent-up longings. As it was impossible for her to alleviate them, sometimes she felt like a ticking bomb set to go off—an aching, hungry, Néomi-shaped bomb.

In the face of her never-ending frustration, she tended to behave . . . badly.

And when the brothers all returned to the room, the temptation was too much to resist.

When she rises from the bed, he waits a moment, then casts her another glance. And nearly coughs. Sebastian's money clip is floating from his coat pocket into her outstretched palm.

Then she deposits a . . . *pebble* in exchange? Sebastian doesn't notice, even when she transports the clip away.

Telekinesis? Yes, and well controlled.

After a cagey glance at him—he swiftly makes his gaze blank—the female prowls for her next mark. She maneuvers around them, yet even with her speed, sometimes they pass a hand or an elbow through her. Each time she grows still, then quivers as though shuddering.

Nikolai is next. With a wave of her hand, a cell phone floats out of his jacket. Again the entity drops a pebble before floating the phone over to the corner.

This cat-and-mouse game entertains him, and he wants her to fleece the bastards. She's far more interesting than Sebastian's patronizing speech about family and honor and forgiveness.

He wonders where the little being takes her spoils. *Why* does she take them? Is she *playing* now? Or is it a compulsion, like his need to kill?

For Murdoch's turn, she plucks a woman's jeweled hair comb right out of his pocket. Just who is Murdoch buying combs for?

She smiles delightedly at her prize. *That smile . . .* Her eyes glitter, her lips curving. She might as well have been carrying a weapon.

As she glides toward the corner, she raises her slender, bared arms above her and does a flawless pirouette. Then another. Her skirts flare out, and he hears them rustling. A single rose petal wafts from her wild hair to the bed, landing on the sheet beside him.

Her lithe body, the way she moves, those slippers—she must have been a dancer. A *tantsija*. Of course.

When she twirls around again, she suddenly laughs. The sound is haunting. But for some reason, his lips curl in response to it. The grin turns to a scowl when Sebastian regards him as if he's completely gone. *A vacant grin from a madman.*

Because he *is* mad—there is no raven-haired spirit who wants to show him more than her garters.

And still he can't take his eyes from her as Sebastian starts up again. He hears snippets of his brother's words. As he tends to do when he's weary and wanting to be left alone, he repeats them, muttering back in a different language. "It eats at Nikolai, the guilt . . . they've been fighting the Vampire Horde for three centuries. . . . We can join their army . . . kill them off. . . . Not all vampires are evil."

He blinks when Sebastian falls silent.

With a narrowed gaze, Sebastian says, "You haven't been talking to yourself. You're repeating all of our words. This time in Greek! You weren't hallucinating—you were *listening*." Sebastian nods, as if he's encouraged by this. "I wonder what else you can do that we don't know about?"

I can see ghosts. In Estonian, he asks Sebastian, "To your right, you see nothing strange? No female in the room?"

Sebastian glances around. In the same language, he answers slowly, "There are only the four of us in the room, Conrad." His tone is one he'd use to explain, "Actually, brother, the sky isn't green. It's *blue*."

The female seems to have concluded her stealing and appears slower, fainter. *Is she tired?*

"Conrad, do *you* see someone else?" Sebastian asks. "Your kind is supposed to suffer from severe delusions. . . ."

His "delusion" is now listening in on Murdoch and Nikolai's murmured conversation at the edge of the room. "He reeks of blood and mud," Nikolai says. "He might be improving, but to others he wouldn't look like it. If we ever had to defend our plan . . ."

Without warning, she's on the bed beside him. From too close by his ear, she asks, *"Is this true, vampire?"* Her words come much more quickly, almost normally. He's able to discern that she has a tinge of a French accent.

"Do you reek, dément? I can't smell. But it makes sense . . . considering how dirty you are."

He becomes acutely aware that his face is caked

with blood and mud, his hair stiff with it. *Dément.* Is that all she sees him as? A madman to be ignored? Or worse—pitied? That *is* how she sees him.

A filthy, sexually inexperienced lunatic.

She's seen him spit blood. Did she witness him mindlessly banging his head against the wall? Damn it, he's beginning to dislike this clarity! Again, he craves the oblivion of memories. It's easier to be awash in them, to hate, to hurt. . . .

Yet the female beside him moors his mind to the present like an anchor.

"*They should give you a bath,*" she says in her whispery voice, just as Sebastian intones, "Rest easy, Conrad. The hallucinations will disappear before you know—"

"Leave me!" he snaps. He almost said, "Leave *us.*"

The ghost drifts away, readying her loot to depart. *No, not you!* When she and the items vanish, all that's left of her is the petal on the sheet. He inches over, wanting to touch it. But it begins to fade. Then gone.

He shifts in the bed, restless and chafing in his bonds. *Want her here.*

Sebastian rises. "Very well, we'll go. Call out if you need anything—or if you feel like drinking."

They leave him in the darkened room. "Have you seen my cell phone?" Nikolai asks on the way out.

Before he has time to analyze why her absence could possibly disappoint him to this degree, others' memories bubble up in his mind as though from a wellspring.

Over the years, he hasn't killed honorable men, actually has taken out some who were even more monstrous than himself. And their memories, now *his* memories, chill him to his bones.

He sees scenes of torture he hasn't inflicted, harrowing murders of women and children he never committed. Glassy, sightless eyes stare up at him—but not *him*.

These memories demand to be acknowledged, to be experienced. Before they'll be allayed, each must be relived, eking away his sanity.

And he has none left to lose.

8

Néomi was fairly much an open book—open about her sexuality, her body, her opinions. But she had two dirty little secrets.

One of which was her penchant for relocating an odd item here and there that didn't belong to her.

Inside her hidden chamber, behind the concealed Gothic entrance, she placed her new acquisitions on the display table. Here lay all of her trinkets and treasures picked up from tenants over the years.

The table was nearly filled. Soon she'd have to employ the coffee table. Not a bad take, considering Elancourt had been occupied for only about a third of her afterlife.

So I tend to steal a lot.

She didn't necessarily appropriate things of value, more items that intrigued her. Among the contraband: a battery-operated TV with the batteries long dead, a fairly modern bra, a gramophone, and a box of condoms she would've paid thousands for in the twenties.

She had matchbooks and Mardi Gras doubloons, candy she'd never eat, and about a dozen spray-paint cans confiscated from myriad teenage vandals.

With slammed doors, flying sheets, and tempests

of leaves, she'd scared *les artistes graffiti* past the point of spontaneous urination, at which time they always dropped their paint and ran. This was Néomi's home, her entire world. She refused to read poorly crafted "art" for the rest of her days.

Like a bird feathering her nest, she'd collected things from outside and brought them within her hidden enclave. This room used to be her dance studio—with ballet barres, a wood parquet floor, and wall-to-wall mirrors. The studio itself was largely untouched, though newspapers were stacked everywhere, and the mirrors had been modified to fit her current appearance. In other words, she'd broken them.

In the days after her death, when movers had brought in boxes for all her belongings, she'd yearned so passionately to smuggle them back to this room, they'd actually *moved*. That was how she'd first recognized she had the ability to transport things with her mind.

In a mad dash, she'd levitated all the things she'd valued: her jewelry, clothes, scrapbooks, her prohibited stash of liquor, and even her weighty safe, conveying them to the hidden studio.

Yet now she could do nothing but watch her possessions age right before her. Just like her home. She couldn't feel any of them, couldn't run her greedy fingertips over a spill of cool silk or the tickling tip of a feather. . . .

"Now what?" she asked aloud.

The echoing silence seemed to mock her. *Alone . . . alone . . . alone . . .*

Néomi considered materializing to the vampire's room—or *tracing* there. She assured herself it was the pressing quiet that spurred her to debate returning, and not the madman himself. But he did seem to sense her the best of anyone who'd ever come to Elancourt.

Even if he was insane and unwashed, something about him drew her. She had the undeniable urge to talk to him more.

Yet in the end, she was too exhausted to return, her essence depleted from all the energy she used for her concentrated telekinesis. Needing to rest, she floated to her cot.

Long ago, she'd brought it into the studio. Though she couldn't feel it or the blankets she'd strewn over it, she slept there almost every night. As much as possible, she liked to behave as she had when alive—except for drifting through walls and tracing, of course.

She curled up an inch above it for her reverie. Néomi termed her ghostly sleep a *reverie* because it differed from what she'd known when living. She didn't have to have it every day. If she didn't use telekinesis for more than moving the newspaper, she could go days without it. Waking was instantaneous, with nothing altered except her energy level. She still wore the same clothes, her hair was unchanged, and she never needed to shave her legs and underarms. Normally, she only lost consciousness for about four hours.

That is, until the sliver moon came each month. On that one night, some force compelled her to dance. Like a ghostly marionette, she spun to the same gruesome end, left exhausted and shaken, wishing for a true death.

There were only three days left until her next performance. . . .

Her *maman* had always said the sliver moon was lucky for people like them—*people who hold on to the sky with all their might, and do it again and again. No matter how many times they lose it.* That was why Néomi had scheduled her party on that night.

Lucky wasn't the first term she'd use to describe that party—the one meant to celebrate the achievement of all her dreams. At twenty-six, Néomi had bought this place on her own, after working her way out of the Vieux Carré—all the while managing to keep her shady background a secret.

Her uptown patrons had never found out that Néomi was a French émigrée's bastard born in the seedy French Quarter. They hadn't connected Néomi Laress to Marguerite L'Are, the infamous burlesque dancer.

They hadn't discovered that, for a time, Néomi had been one, too.

After her *maman* had succumbed to influenza when Néomi had just turned sixteen, she'd begun doing shows. Néomi had been well developed then, and with the right makeup and costumes, she'd passed for twenty. Times had been tough, and the money was good.

She'd had no inhibitions, no moral convictions against it. Everyone got what they needed, and no one was hurt by it. Though she'd never been ashamed of what she'd done, she'd kept it secret because she'd understood that others wouldn't view it the same way she did.

After a year of saving up money, Néomi had quit. She'd always dreamed of being a ballerina and hadn't wanted to waste all those lessons her mother had scrimped to afford—and all the work Néomi had done to justify the incredible sacrifice. And somehow, she'd made it. . . .

Then I died.

She wished Conrad could have seen her as the ballerina she'd once been—onstage in a luxurious costume, flushed with pride, inundated with lusty applause. Would he have found her pretty?

She sighed glumly. She would never know. . . .

What would tomorrow bring with Conrad, the vampire assassin with his powerful body and ailing mind? As she drifted off to reverie, she wondered, *Can we save him when he doesn't want to be saved?*

We?

The ghost doesn't return the entire night.

And he resents her for it.

It takes till late the next afternoon before he smells the scent of roses. The room is lit with afternoon sun, but he can still see her floating directly through the closed door. He knows what to look for now, *how* to look for her, like a hidden message in a visual puzzle.

She acts as if she's never left, absently lying back across the mattress and stretching her slender arms above her head. Her long hair flows out over the sheet—shining black, stark against the white. Her pale breasts are barely contained by her dress.

She's forgiven.

If he isn't blooded, then why does this view captivate him? Why does it make his fangs ache?

He continues to debate the possibilities of fractured memory, hallucination, or ghost. As far as a fractured memory goes, she *fits* this place, this situation, too perfectly. And if she's a figment of his imagination, why would he imagine a woman the opposite of what he is normally attracted to?

He thought he liked tall, Nordic women with fair hair and their skin sun-pinkened from the outdoor life. But this female's tiny and pale, not much over five feet tall. Her hair is black as night.

During his harsh human life, he would've scarcely spared a pitying glance at her, predicting the delicate girl wouldn't last though the next winter in their war-torn country.

And she *hadn't* survived long. She appears to be no more than in her early twenties. If ghosts were born of violence, then how had she met her end so young?

She wouldn't have if she'd had a strong protector. *I was strong.* He stifles a low growl. *I'd have kept her safe if she'd been mine.*

Maybe he wouldn't have predicted her doom over the winter and turned away. Maybe he would've approached her. In his rough way, he could have attempted to garner the position as her protector. He was a skilled officer. He'd been born a nobleman—and at least before the Great War, that had meant something. Perhaps she would have accepted him.

My God, to have had such a woman in my keeping . . . to have taken her each night.

He can imagine what that would be like. During the day, his nightmares have been varied with strange new dreams of pinning her arms over her head and mounting her luscious little body.

There's a line . . . there's a line . . .

Could this woman possibly be real? This would mean that not only is the ghost not imagined—it would mean he's gone three days without a single hallucination. A hundred years have passed since that happened last.

Which would mean, he might be . . . *healing*.

Like a starburst between his eyes, he finally remembers what he'd regretted, what he'd coveted so badly—

Nikolai and Sebastian enter then, their expressions grim. *Why is Nikolai holding a syringe?* In a tone low with warning, he says, "What's the goddamned shot for? I haven't done anything."

"No, but we fear you will," Nikolai says. "We need to take you from the room—and this will keep you from getting hurt."

When Nikolai nears, he yells, "Get the fucking thing away from me, Nikolai!" He doesn't want to be mindless, can't have that happen again. *"No!"*

I don't want her to see me like that.

"Damn you, I said no!"

9

Néomi was stunned anew at how viciously Conrad fought the two men, pounding his forehead against Sebastian's and nearly taking off Nikolai's hand with his fangs.

In the end, his resisting gained him no ground. They injected him once again. Just before it took hold, Conrad stared in her direction with his brows drawn and teeth gritted, and she found that so much harder to see now.

When did my curiosity turn to caring?

His brothers had treated him like an animal—because that was how he'd acted mere days ago. She understood the need to keep him contained, because he was so incredibly powerful and could be dangerous if freed.

But he'd been doing so much better. And they hadn't even given him a chance. . . .

As Nikolai and Sebastian led him, docile and barefooted, into the oversize master bathroom, Conrad's eyes were heavy-lidded, and he'd begun speaking in that low, unnerving voice. His wrists remained chained behind his back. They must be intent on washing him. Curious, she followed them in.

Néomi's second dirty secret? As a ghost, she'd become quite the voyeur.

She'd watched men shower before, but she'd never been so intent to discover what a particular man's body would look like as she was now.

While Sebastian adjusted the water temperature and opened a bar of soap, Nikolai ripped away the remains of Conrad's tattered shirt.

From her spot halfway up the far wall, Néomi sighed, admiring Conrad's powerful physique. She hadn't appreciated exactly how tall he was because he'd been lying down for so long. He would tower over her if she stood near him.

He had a narrow waist and hips and broad shoulders that looked tailor-made for a woman to hold on to during sex. With his hands behind his back, the corded muscles of those shoulders and his chest were stretched taut, displayed so attractively.

He was all male hardness, with so many scars marring his flesh, like the narrow one slashing up his torso. But she'd begun to find the evidence of his formidable life attractive, had begun imagining a scenario for each battle wound.

She'd seen Conrad fight with a ferocity that astonished her. She could all too easily see him brandishing a sword three hundred years ago, a massive warlord fearlessly storming a battlefield. . . .

A ragged bandage on his arm caught her attention. Sebastian too frowned at the gauze, tearing it off to reveal a peculiar, blackened injury. "What the hell is this?" It appeared as if he'd been attacked by a beast, and then the skin around the mark had died.

Why would Conrad have healed from the gashes across his chest, but not from another wound?

Nikolai narrowed his eyes. "With his strength, he should have mended that easily by now. Maybe if he cleans it, it will improve."

"Christ, look at all the scars, Nikolai."

"I had no idea he'd sustained this many hits during the war," he answered, moving behind Conrad to inspect his back.

"Maybe he had them before the war." Sebastian yanked free Conrad's belt. "Think about it—he never worked without his shirt, and he continually went off by himself. He could have been a highwayman for all we know. . . ." He trailed off at Nikolai's expression. "What?"

"Come look at this," Nikolai said, so Néomi followed Sebastian around. All three of them frowned at an elaborate black tattoo covering his entire right shoulder blade. It was unusual, with its slashing lines, but compelling in a way. "Isn't that the mark of the Kapsliga Uur?"

What's the Kapsliga Uur? Why did their faces pale at the very idea?

"That can't be right," Sebastian said, an edge to his voice. "We'd have known. They recruit young. He couldn't have hidden his involvement for two decades."

Seeming lost in his own world, Conrad continued his rasping mutter, unaware of their discovery.

"He always did his own thing, always brushed off questions about where he'd been or with whom," Nikolai said. "My God. He'd been out hunting vampires with the Kapsliga. No wonder the turning maddened him."

Sebastian's face was grim. "He would have been trained to destroy vampires, his hatred of them stoked from the time he was a boy."

"And then I turned him into what he despised." Nikolai released a breath through his teeth as though he'd been kicked in the stomach. "It would have been unendurable."

"What about their vow?" *What vow?*

If possible, Nikolai paled even more. "For all his faults, Conrad never broke a vow in his life. Unless it happened before he'd turned thirteen . . ." *Unless what happened?*

The two were silent for long moments, Sebastian's expression grave while Nikolai's was filled with guilt. "His life had been given over to a cause greater than himself. I should have"—Nikolai ran his hand over his forehead—"I should have talked to him, given him, and you, the choice that night."

"I wouldn't have chosen the turning, and then I wouldn't be with Kaderin." He spoke as if he'd sidestepped the direst tragedy. Sebastian was lost for his Bride. "Besides, Conrad was too far gone. The soldiers gutted him before me, hours before you and Murdoch came. I don't believe he would ever have regained consciousness."

She floated in front of Conrad to face him. He'd been stabbed in the stomach, she in the heart. Then against their wills they'd both been changed into something else entirely. Neither of them had asked for their current existences.

He'd been a hero, his *life given over to a greater cause*. She sighed, waving her hand to send a gentle touch along his cheek. *What happened to you out there, vampire?*

Sebastian said, "But he'll never reconcile himself to our existence unless we can convince him that we aren't evil."

Shaking his head hard, Nikolai said, "We can't convince him of anything until his mind heals more. Let's get this over with."

They stripped off his pants, leaving him naked.

And she swayed weightlessly. *Le dément est exquis.*

Her gaze slid from his navel, following that trail of black hair. *Oh, my, my, my.* Even flaccid, his size was brow-raising.

"Conrad, look at me." Nikolai waved in front of his vacant stare.

Conrad blinked as if he had no idea where he was or how he'd gotten there.

"Do you want to wash yourself?" Nikolai asked. "If we chain your hands in front of you?"

Seeming to shake off some of his confusion, Conrad eased his muttering. A flicker arose in those red eyes.

He's calculating. At length, Conrad grated, "Alone."

The brothers shared a glance, no doubt reviewing all the ways Conrad *couldn't* escape. "Very well," Nikolai said.

Conrad held his wrists up behind him, and all the rippling muscles of his torso flexed into sharp rises and indentations that spoke of a terrible strength.

After removing the cuffs, Nikolai refastened them

in front, then pulled a pin to loosen the chain between the wrists so Conrad could have more freedom. When Conrad made no attempt to escape, they glanced at each other as if their brother was making outrageous progress. Which, she supposed, he was.

"I've left a towel and a change of clothes on the rack," Sebastian said. "They should fit. But if not, we've brought plenty more—"

"Alone!" Conrad snapped. When they finally left, he entered the spacious shower stall.

Still facing her direction, he stepped under the water and let it cascade over his back. He appeared exhausted from the medicine, as if his limbs felt heavy and ungainly, but he seemed to enjoy the simple pleasure of the water sluicing over his body.

I envy him every drop!

He picked up the bar of soap, smelled it. Finding it acceptable, he lathered his face, then leaned back against the tile so that the water ran over his front.

And all she could do was stare because, as the blood, plaster, and burn marks washed from his skin in thick, grimy rivulets, a handsome visage surfaced.

No, not merely handsome, more like *extraordinary*.

She'd known he had pleasing features but hadn't been able to look past the unnatural eyes and dirt to truly appreciate his firm lips and wide, masculine jaw, or how his nose was aristocratic and strong.

Punch-drunk. That's how she felt about seeing his clean face and unclothed body as a whole. She'd heard women talk about encountering a man so devastatingly gorgeous they'd felt breathless, dizzy. Now she understood.

It dawned on her that though she'd spied on men before, never had any male as sexually attractive as this graced her shower stall.

When he began to rub the soap over his chest and under his arms, the slick muscles in his torso bulged in a breathtaking display. It'd take her weeks to learn just those muscles alone—how they flexed, how his body could move. . . .

The soap went lower.

She swallowed.

Lower still . . .

She didn't think she breathed when he lathered between his legs with his big, scarred hands, washing his long shaft and the flesh hanging behind it without interest, while she was dumbstruck.

Am I shaking? For eight decades, she'd never yearned to touch anything as much as his body. Even though she knew she couldn't feel him, it was everything she could do not to reach forward.

His hands abruptly stilled at his privates, and his handsome face flushed. His gaze landed directly on her, before skittering away. He acted the way a reserved, inexperienced man would when he'd realized he was washing himself in front of an audience of one.

Her eyes went wide. *He damn well can see me.* She frowned. *Then that means I'm being . . . ignored.*

"Vampire, look at me. Please talk to me."

But he gave no reaction. The one man on earth she could communicate with *wouldn't* talk to her.

Which meant . . .

"Do you think I'm pretty, Conrad? Beautiful, even? After all, you can see me, can't you? And I know you can hear me, too. Now I'm going to prove it. You dare throw down that gauntlet to a woman who entertained for a living? You can't simply shut me out."

Few knew there was a second reason that Néomi had chosen her dream of ballet over following in her *maman*'s footsteps, tempting crowds of men as a femme fatale: Turning males into frothing, gawking, mindless beasts had been too . . . *easy.*

With merely a throaty laugh and a dab of her tongue at her bottom lip, Néomi could send a man diving for his hat—to cover his stirring lap.

Too easy. And Néomi had always craved a challenge.

With a wicked grin, she decided it was time to draw on her shady background, time to put away the popguns and engage the cannons. And Néomi had a hidden arsenal he couldn't even comprehend.

10

Perhaps I haven't been stimulating enough for you, vampire?" Néomi made her voice a breathy murmur. "And didn't I promise that I'd show you more than a garter if you could only see me?"

She tugged her skirt up slowly, making the fabric appear to bunch in her hands. "I have a bit of experience with what men like to . . . *be shown.*"

When she'd bared the tops of her thigh-high hose, she asked, "Still not stimulating enough? Maybe Conrad wants to see my panties instead?" Just before she revealed them, she floated into the corner, the one that was farthest from his vision. He'd have to turn fully to see her there.

"The line . . . the line . . ." he muttered urgently.

He must be talking about some line *with her* that shouldn't be crossed. "Yes, Conrad, the line! Let's cross it! Or am I going to have to up the ante? Very well," she sighed. "You drive a hard, hard bargain. But I feel overdressed anyway, and since you're so deliciously naked . . ." His body shot upright with tension, muscles bunching in his neck and shoulders. "Here I am, in the corner, unlacing my dress." She made her voice drip with sensuality and her dress rustle as she removed it. "I'm doing it slowly for my vampire. *Oh . . . so . . . slowly.*"

Did he just growl?

She moved forward to dangle her dress in his line of vision. Like a lure for an animal, she eased it back toward the corner.

He gave a groan as if defeated and turned. His jaw slackened.

She stood with her back to him, peering over her shoulder, wearing only her garter belt, hose, and her tight black panties. "I knew it, vampire," she said with delight.

His riveted gaze lingered over her face, descending to her back, her ass, and her legs, then slowly back up again. His voice broke when he rasped, "Turn around for me." Had his accent ever sounded so heavy?

He was talking to her, the first person to address her in eight decades. She was trembling with happiness and gratitude, elated by the interaction—and helpless not to be excited by his heated looks. She faced him with her arms crossed over her breasts, not shyly, but provocatively.

He ran a palm over his mouth. "Y-your arms now."

Standing against the wall, she removed one arm, then the other, raising them above her, appearing to rest them against the wall. With his gaze locked on her breasts, he clenched and unclenched his hands as if he was imagining squeezing them. She felt a thrill when he subtly rubbed his tongue over a fang, those red eyes smoldering like embers.

"Did you think I was bluffing?"

Never glancing up, he gave her a sharp nod, as if he didn't trust himself to speak.

"I never bluff. If it took baring my body to prove you can see me, then look your fill, Conrad." When he finally raised his eyes to meet hers, she tilted her head and cast him a flirtatious smile. "But why have you ignored me?"

He said, "Because you're not . . . you weren't real," then winced as if he found his comment idiotic.

He'd thought she was a hallucination! *Poor vampire!* He hadn't ignored her for any reason other than the need for self-preservation. "Do you want me to be real?" Drifting away from the wall, she sauntered toward him, her eyes holding his. He didn't seem to realize that he was easing toward her, leaving the spray of the water. "I'm Néomi," she purred.

"*Néomi,*" he repeated absently. "Does nothing abash you?"

She shook her head, and her hair bounced over her shoulders and lower. When the locks swayed across her nipples, his gaze dipped once more. "And it's difficult for me to regret undressing when my vampire's giving me a look that makes my toes curl."

He swallowed hard, his Adam's apple working. "I make your toes curl?"

She nodded. "Would you like me to come in with you?"

His brows drew together. "Why would you want to?"

She told him honestly, "Because right now you are my favorite man in the entire world."

* * *

A half-naked ghost with high, plump breasts wants to get into the shower with him.

And he has no idea how to go about processing this. He starts sweating, his teeth grinding. He has no experience like this to draw from.

He was born and raised in a conservative culture. As an adult, he's never been wholly unclothed in front of a woman, certainly has never washed himself in front of one.

Yet this female is standing before him, clad in only her hose, garters, and a pair of wicked panties. They're black and lined with a tight band of jet lace that cuts up across the generous curves of her ass. Her breasts are proudly bared.

She's acting as natural as if he and she were wed. *I don't even know her last name.*

Unable to help himself, he rakes another hungry gaze over her body. She's surprisingly defined, her legs taut and strong. The lines of her form are lithe—a dancer's body, with softly flaring hips and a tiny waist he can span with his hands.

And those breasts . . .

He shakes his head. She's *too* pretty. A half-naked beauty dropped into his shower? Into his life? This simply isn't in keeping with his fortunes over the centuries. "You're probably not real." When she grins, he curses his clumsiness with this. He wishes for Murdoch's ease with women—he never has before, even when he'd recognized at a young age that he lacked charm.

"Do you often see things that aren't real?"

"Daily." But if she *is* real . . . "Come in. If you wish to."

Her gaze holds his as she drifts toward him. She has sultry blue eyes, knowing eyes. *Hypnotic.* He finds his body arching toward her of its own will.

She floats into the stall with him. Inside, the water doesn't wet her, instead sparking off her like minuscule electrical flares, seeming like glitter.

A *dream—an erotic one.* Can he really be naked with an almost nude dancer? *Enjoy it.*

Bloody how? He can't feel lust. He isn't erect. And . . . *she's a ghost!*

That doesn't seem to be stopping her. He can sense her energy, as strong as it's ever felt to him. It radiates off her in waves, slingshotting from her to him and back again.

"*Le dément* has a magnificent body, *n'est-ce pas?* So strong, virile."

He feels that increasingly familiar heat on the back of his neck. "Do not call me that again."

"So you speak French among all your many languages?" When he replies with a curt nod, she says, "Well, what shall I call you, then? Conrad the Mad? Conrad the Crazed? Or I could call you *my vampire?*" Softening her tone, she says, "I think you like that."

How can she read him so well?

She murmurs, "If you can hear me, and you can see me, I wonder what else is possible. Perhaps I can . . . maybe I can try to feel you?" The yearning in her voice staggers him. "I feel nothing, you see. My hands pass through everything."

She can't touch, and he can't get erect. But at least

he still experiences pleasure—the tang of blood on his tongue, the exhilaration of a bracing wind.

"Maybe if I concentrate very hard, maybe with you . . . I could *feel*." Before him appears a fragile, pale hand with shining dark nails. A petal lies starkly on the back of her wrist, then tumbles away to vanish. "Can I try to touch you?"

At least she asks this time. His voice a rasp, he says, "Do as you will."

Her hand begins to tremble as she inches it closer to him. Electricity pricks his skin as she nears. *Can* she feel him? Does he truly want this? Yes, Christ, yes, he does. But it glides right through his chest. His skin tingles at the spot, making the muscles tense, but he has no perception of pressure.

She seems to sag with disappointment. Once more she attempts it, running her hand down his torso. He experiences the same electrical feel, which isn't *un*pleasurable.

"I suppose it's not meant to be." Her tone is wistful, and this bothers him—he feels as if he's disappointed her.

After coughing into his fist, he says, "I could try . . . to touch you."

In an instant, her expression brightens again. He's effected that. So easily?

"Where would you like to, Conrad?"

Before he can stop himself, he's peering hard at her breasts.

"Then touch them," she murmurs, each sultry word like a stroke.

Her energy begins to make him restless. Strange

urges rack him. He wants not only to touch her there, but also to kiss her flesh until she clings to him, to drag his tongue over her jutting nipples. Would she like that? Could he make her moan?

He needs to cage her in with his body, to keep her from getting away from him, and finds himself backing her against the shower wall. She could have floated through it, but she lets him surround her. He raises his knee beside her and his chained hands over her head.

Positioned like this, he gazes down into the loveliest eyes he's ever seen. As if a breeze has swept a path through the fog of memories and confusion, he feels clearer as he beholds her face. He feels centered.

Feels . . . feels . . . felt . . .

He felt clearer. Conrad felt centered. His very thoughts seemed to arise differently. They were more focused, each one distinct in his mind.

And Conrad wanted to understand *why*.

Was it her, or the drugs? What exactly was she to him? A suspicion prodded at his consciousness, but he pushed it away.

Her lids grew heavy, her breathing faster, as if she was losing herself in the moment. She was small and perfect. Yet even with his red eyes and scarred, hulking body, she looked at him . . . hungrily. Could ghosts feel desire?

Not only was she a ghost, a creature he had no experience with, she was a sensual female—again, a creature he had no experience with.

Conrad wanted to try to touch her—because she was both.

With an audible swallow, he eased his hands toward her mouthwatering breasts.

Had she arched to him? He covered their outline with his big palms, but he only experienced the same electricity.

He saw her lower her gaze, as though to see if he'd reacted. He dropped his hands, shamed that he wasn't hard. At that instant, he wished he could be. "You can't get me aroused." He backed away from her, standing under the water. "I haven't been in three hundred years."

"Do you not wish to be?"

"Do *you* want me to be?"

"Yes," she began with a smile in her voice. "I was thinking that might be nice to see."

He'd once been so proud. Now a creature who didn't even have a body made him feel shame. If he was blooded, his shaft thick with lust, what would she think then? "It takes a special female to tempt me back to life. I'm thinking one with flesh and blood. So you're not her."

"You're speaking of your Bride?"

"Be glad you're not," he said, but with this new clarity, he began to wonder.

Tonight Conrad had recalled what he'd once coveted, what he'd been filled with regret never to possess.

I'd wanted a woman of my own.

One to claim and protect. One to pleasure. As a mortal, he'd longed for this constantly. What if this female was *his*?

His arm injury ached under the spray of the water. If the curse of that mark was true . . .

Was this little ghost the one his life had been leading toward? He recalled the chills he'd felt when Nikolai had merely uttered the name of her home.

Conrad had been forced here, sensing it was the first step on a doomed path. *His dream . . . her doom.*

"You need to stay away from me." *I have to escape this place.* "For your own good."

Her brows drew together. "Vampire, I don't know if I can."

Nikolai walked in then, Sebastian behind him. "What's going on in here?"

Conrad lunged in front of her, snapping his teeth at his brothers. Fury churned at the idea of her undressed and in the same room with them. His fangs sharpened with his aggression. To her he gave a half-growl, half-hiss over his shoulder. "Leave. Now."

"But they can't—"

"I said *now!*" he bellowed, making her squeeze her eyes shut. She flickered before she vanished.

He'd frightened her. He *should* frighten her.

"What the hell's going on, Conrad?" Nikolai had another syringe at the ready.

Can't have another. He needed to process what had just happened with the female. Clutching his forehead, he struggled to beat back the rage. To stifle the memories that accompanied the fury. Nikolai hesitated with the shot—he was the one who'd said mastering the memories was possible. Conrad endeavored to do it now. . . .

Time ticked by . . . *Control it.* He must have been *succeeding* because Nikolai ultimately pocketed the syringe.

"You brought it back, Conrad," Sebastian said proudly. "That's the first step."

Nikolai was more cautious. "Who were you talking to?"

"Just leave me to dress." Conrad's tone was weary now, his body fatigued from the battle in his mind. "You wouldn't believe me if I told you."

Now that the female was gone and her scent had faded, Conrad had doubts about what had just happened as well. His brothers didn't pursue it—because they probably knew they wouldn't believe him. Hesitantly, they left to wait outside.

After turning off the water, he dried himself. For the first time in perhaps three hundred years, he decided to study his reflection. *Stubble, eyes blood red, hair too long and cut unevenly.*

His appearance was disturbing even to him. And this was an improvement over the last several days. He bit out a curse. When human, he'd never given his looks more than a rare and passing thought.

But then, he'd never wanted to impress anyone before.

As he changed into the jeans his brothers had left for him—the shirt would be impossible to put on with the cuffs—he considered taking down Nikolai and Sebastian, but he was weakened.

Besides, he had a better idea. . . .

When Conrad exited the room, Sebastian said, "What made you so riled back there?"

Need to make them think I'm recovering. "Nothing." *Am I recovering?* He'd go along with his brothers for now, until he could escape them.

When Sebastian held up a roll of bandage gauze with his brows raised, Conrad hesitated, then extended his injured arm.

As Sebastian rebandaged it, Nikolai asked, "How'd you get this?"

Conrad muttered. "Occupational hazard." Courtesy of Tarut, an ancient and powerful dream demon who worked with the Kapsliga.

He and the demon had been trying to kill each other for centuries, but neither could quite manage it. Yet just two weeks ago, Tarut had scored a crucial victory.

He'd marked Conrad with his claws. If the tales about dream demons were true, then whenever he and the demon slumbered at the same time, Tarut could retrieve clues to his whereabouts.

Conrad had believed the curse of the mark was just folklore, the demons using tales of it to their advantage. But the injury refused to mend.

And that was only the first part of the curse. Legend held that Conrad couldn't heal until either the demon had been slain—or Conrad had had both his most fervent dream and most feared nightmare come true.

"*You have to have a dream to lose it,*" Tarut had said at their last clash.

Conrad might actually be closing in on one. He stifled a shudder. *His dream . . . her doom.*

"You look a thousand times better after the shower," Sebastian said. "You're definitely getting more focused."

He shrugged. It wouldn't matter. Besides Tarut,

Conrad was being hunted by at least half a dozen contingents that wanted him either captured or executed.

The Kapsliga, his former order, sought his death because he was an abomination to them—a vampire who wore their symbol on his back. They'd made him their priority, dispatching Tarut and other assassins after Conrad.

Then there were countless offspring of Conrad's victims, all seeking to avenge their fathers, swords in hand.

And it was only a matter of time before he became the target of Rydstrom Woede, the fallen king of the fierce rage demons, and Cadeon, his heir.

Conrad had come by information that they would kill for.

Dozens of demonarchies held Conrad as enemy number one; he worried about none of them—except for the Woede, as the pair was called.

None of these adversaries would hesitate to destroy anyone who stood in their way. It was possible that Conrad and his brothers could be taken down without his lifting a finger.

"Are you ready to drink?" Nikolai asked.

"The only thing I drink that's not fresh from the vein is whiskey," he lied.

In the past, Conrad had drunk bagged blood, but he refused now. Though he was getting thirstier, he didn't need nourishment as often as other vampires, and he'd be damned if he bent to their will in this.

Murdoch had called him stubborn, and Conrad couldn't deny it. After being captured, chained, and drugged, Conrad wouldn't prove obliging to their futile plans—especially when he wouldn't be here much longer.

He'd noted that each brother had a key to his chains. When the ghost returned, he would get her to steal one. And then he'd be gone.

Nothing could be simpler.

11

Two goddamned days. The female hadn't come back to his room for two days. For that time, Conrad alternated between a burning desire to get free and a need to discover what she was to him.

During the nights, his brothers had returned and tried to reach him, but he had no time for them. Even if he was improving, the part of him that might have responded to his family was dead.

Besides, his mind was consumed with thoughts of Néomi.

Now he gritted his teeth, struggling to remain calm. He was trapped, unable to seek her out. If he went into another rage, his brothers might force him to leave this place, jailing him somewhere else.

And he wasn't through here, not yet, not until he figured out if she was affecting his mind. Though he was still having episodes of uncontrollable violence, his aggression and rage were becoming more manageable. Just the fact that he'd pulled back from the edge in the shower attested to that.

Maybe it's not her—maybe it's something about the house. After all, he was lucid now, and she wasn't here.

No, that didn't matter. He could still sense her

constantly. Yesterday, it had drizzled all day, and he could swear he'd felt that she was . . . sad. He routinely heard her late in the night, roaming the hallways of her home. He could make out the ghostly rustle of her skirts or even an occasional sigh. When she passed his room's door, he perceived the change in the air and had learned to search for that faint scent of roses.

He'd called for her, but it was always Nikolai who'd hastened into the room. "Who are you talking to?" he'd asked in an anxious tone.

Now Conrad felt like he suffered a different kind of madness. *Need to find her. Want her here.* Questions about her plagued him. She wore jewelry—earrings, a choker, a wide band on her forefinger—but she'd had no wedding ring. If this had been her property, then she'd been wealthy, but apparently she wasn't wed. And he didn't think she'd been born well-off—there was something about her demeanor that spoke of a past with nothing to lose.

Would a dancer have made enough to afford this place?

Hell, with her sensuality and complete lack of inhibitions, she could have been a courtesan.

She'd have made a fortune.

Whoever this Néomi had been in life, she was now dead. Was he sick to desire a woman's ghost so much? Over the past two days, he'd envisioned her nude form again and again. He might not have been hard for her before, but he'd *wanted* to be.

He *was* sick. Not only mad, but sick.

If Conrad was wise, he'd crush this growing obsession with the ghost and get on with his business, with his escape.

He was driven; he wouldn't be sidetracked because he couldn't stop recalling how she'd arched those pale breasts right to his hands.

At twilight, the last of the sun's rays painted the bayou in hazy hues. Along the cypress-cluttered banks, moss dripped from limbs. A rickety folly persisted near the water's edge.

Decades ago, this little inlet of Elancourt's had been navigable, but over the years, debris and grasses had choked the cove until the area looked more like a swamp.

Wildlife teemed. Snakes, alligators, and mink made their home here. Nutrias—large, aquatic rodents—frolicked among the lily pads, flashing their orange teeth.

This was one of Néomi's favorite spots on the property. She'd spent the entire day on the bank, crouched at the edge of the water, watching tadpoles growing limbs.

It was the best she could come up with to occupy her so she wouldn't return to the vampire's room.

"Stay away from me," he'd warned. *Bonne idée*, Néomi had decided.

Because she was attracted to him. Softened by the knowledge of his heroism in the past—and awed by the sight of his naked body—she'd begun feeling a strong pull toward him. Their interaction had been heady and addictive for Néomi. Even his fearsome bellowing hadn't dampened it.

And it would only get worse.

So what would happen when he left? Again, she'd be all alone in her empty house, enduring her empty life. With no mad but sexy vampire to distract her from her existence.

For someone as sociable as Néomi, getting used to the loneliness and the interminable days after her death had been grueling; it was even more devastating when the tenants left.

They always left.

Conrad Wroth will, too.

The idea so depressed her, she'd vowed to stay away from them all. *I'd best not get accustomed to them being around.*

Her battle to stay away this long had taken all her willpower, but she didn't foresee a victory this eve. Soon the sliver moon would rise like a pale rip in the fabric of the sky, and she was feeling vulnerable, as she always did.

Néomi had told Conrad that she felt nothing, which wasn't entirely true. When she danced at midnight, she would feel the pain of her death, that agony relived.

I don't want to be alone. Not tonight . . .

At twilight, she found herself making her way to him as if pulled by an invisible string. When she hesitated just outside his door, he said, "Ghost, come to me!"

Enjoy the interaction, she commanded herself. *Just don't get used to it!*

"I know you're there." His voice sounded weary. "Are you frightened of me now?"

She'd never forget the terrifying sound he'd made, the aggressive growl that threatened pain, a sharp reminder of what he was. But she wasn't afraid of him.

She bit her lip. *When I go inside, I won't find him as handsome as I've been thinking.* She floated through the closed door and immediately glared. No, he was *more* handsome. *Très beau.*

Why was he so appealing to her? She'd always favored older men, established in their lives, with some of their fire already subdued by life's trials.

Conrad was *all* fire. . . . A *beautiful madman.*

"Where the fuck have you been?" he immediately snapped. His red eyes flickered over her face, her breasts, down her body and up again with a greedy gaze, surveying her as men had before she'd died.

How was she going to go another eighty years without smoldering looks like that?

Unaffected by his tone, she said, "Did you miss me?" Her demeanor was breezy. He'd never know about her struggle to remain away. "Should I have been here instead?"

"You'd come every day before," he said gruffly.

"You warned me away, remember? And then you bellowed at me like some rabid bear."

"*Rabid bear?* I didn't want my brothers to see you unclothed."

"Conrad, they couldn't see me at all."

He scowled. "I didn't . . . recall that! Not at the time. Sometimes, it's difficult for me . . ." He trailed off, then added, "Damn it, I'd just had a shot."

Unwelcome sympathy for him bloomed inside her—again. She wondered what it would take for him to actually rattle her unwavering attraction. "Why would you care if they saw me naked?"

He looked away and muttered, "I wish I knew."

Néomi stifled a smile. He was becoming as attracted to her as she was to him.

"What were you doing outside the house earlier?" He sounded accusatory.

"How did you know I was outside?"

"Didn't hear you all day."

She frowned. "Do you ever sleep?"

"Not if I can help it."

Néomi had noticed that he only slept about three or four hours in a twenty-four hour period. "And you never sleep at regular intervals. I can't see a pattern."

"Then no one else can either," he said, but before she could question his words, he said, "Now, tell me what you were doing."

"If you must know—I was studying tadpoles. I've decided to determine how long it takes their legs to grow. To the minute."

"Tadpoles. Why would you do this?"

"Give me an alternative, Conrad. What should I do?"

He was clearly at a loss.

"The one newspaper I was able to snare on the drive has been read. The house is empty of insatiable newlyweds or teenage thrill seekers with spray-paint cans, so I've no one to ogle or to frighten away. But I'm here now, so what did you want?"

Seeming not to know what to say for several moments, he opened and closed his mouth twice.

"Nothing?" she asked airily, waving him away. "Very well, have a good—"

"Stay!" he bit out. "I want you to stay."

"Why? Because you find me more stimulating than watching the paint peeling above the bed?"

He shook his head. "Want to talk to you."

With her chin up, she nonchalantly crossed to the window seat and floated atop it. "Perhaps I'll stay if you agree to answer some of my questions."

"Like what?"

"I overhear your brothers talking, but a lot of times, I have no idea what they mean. You could explain some things."

As though put out, he gave a short nod.

"What do they mean about your memories?"

"If a vampire takes blood straight from the vein, it's *live*, laden with a lifetime of memories. The memories have accumulated, until I can't control them. I can't tell them from my own."

"Every night Murdoch returns with more information about you. He said you have all kinds of people who want you dead."

"True."

"He also said he suspects you played with your victims before you killed them."

"I did only what I was paid to do."

"Did you get paid to behead people while you drank them to death?"

He narrowed his eyes. "Drinking another gives you his memories. Drinking another as you kill him also gives you much of his strength, even some of his mystickal abilities. And beheading is one of the only ways to slay an immortal."

"Have you killed women and children before? Or humans?"

"Why would I bother to?" He seemed genuinely perplexed.

Somewhat reassured by his answer, she asked, "How did you become a vampire?"

His face was drawn with anger. "Nikolai decided to drip his tainted blood down my throat just before I died."

"He didn't have to bite you?"

"That's only in the movies," Conrad said. "Blood is the agent of the transformation, and death is the catalyst. It's this way for any species to be turned in the Lore."

"It's that easy to become a vampire?"

"Easy? It doesn't always work. And if it doesn't, you die."

"Who did it to them?"

"Kristoff, a natural-born vampire—and someone I have no intention of speaking about. Ask something else."

"Very well. Can you still eat food?"

"Yes, but I have as much interest in eating food as you would have in drinking blood." When her expression screwed up with distaste, he said, "Exactly. Though I do enjoy a good whiskey."

So had she. She had a stash of it in her studio. "What about your teleportation, your *tracing*? How far can you go?"

"We can cross the world—not just the living room of a haunted manor." She pursed her lips at that. "But we can only travel to places we've previously been or that we can see."

"And the Accession?"

"Phenomenon in the Lore, every five centuries or so. Families get seeded and immortals get sowed. Fights break out, and factions war. Lots of immortals get to die."

Néomi had heard these uncanny men speak of *the Lore,* as if it was a separate sphere of beings. She'd heard them talk about Valkyrie, witches, ghouls, and the "noble fey." There were werewolves and wraiths—and apparently all these beings . . . interacted.

"Are mermaids real?" she asked.

"Yes."

She gave a wide-eyed gasp, unable to hide her excitement. "Have you seen one? Do they have big tails? With scales? And what about Nessie? Is she real? Does she bite, and is she actually a Neddie—"

"How old were you when you died, ghost?" he interrupted with a patronizing mien. "Did you reach any level of maturity?"

She straightened her shoulders. "I was twenty-six."

Brows drawn, he murmured, "How did you die so young?"

How to answer? She couldn't very well admit that she'd been murdered without going into details. And the details made her sound weak. But then, being murdered was the ultimate weakness, wasn't it? Only someone who'd succumbed could understand.

This male would understand, her mind whispered. He would comprehend like no other the pain she'd endured. "I was murdered," she eventually answered.

"How?"

"What do you suppose?"

"A jealous wife shot her husband's pretty mistress."

"You think me pretty?" When he gave her an impatient look, as if they were retreading old ground, she felt a flush of pleasure. "I was never with a married man."

"A spurned lover pushed you down a flight of stairs."

"Why do you assume it was a crime of passion?" she asked.

"A feeling."

"Then your feeling's right. My ex-fiancé . . . stabbed me in the heart." Saying the words out loud sent chills racing through her. "He did it here. And I woke up trapped on the property, unable to leave, unable to feel."

The vampire's red eyes . . . softened. His voice a rasp, he asked, "Why would he do that to you?"

"He couldn't accept it when I broke it off with him." Louis had told her again and again that he would rather die than live without her, that nothing could make him let her go. "He turned the blade on himself right after me."

Conrad tensed, getting that violent expression again. "Is he *here*?"

"No. I don't know why I'm here and he's not, but it's the one thing I'm thankful for."

He relaxed marginally. "When did it happen?"

"The twenty-fourth of August, nineteen twenty-seven. On the night of my party celebrating my move into Elancourt. I'd just finished restoring it." The run-down estate had called to her very soul. She'd lovingly overseen every tiny detail of its restoration, slowly bringing the manor and gardens back to life.

She'd had no idea it would be her eternal home. . . .

"Enough about him," she said, shaking off the pall of Louis. Now that she was here with Conrad, she was determined to enjoy this conversation.

The second-ever conversation of her afterlife.

"Why do you think you became a ghost?" he asked.

"I was hoping one of you might know."

"I haven't heard the subject talked about much in the Lore—ghosts are a human phenomenon—but I understand your kind is very rare. In all my years, I've never seen one before you."

"Oh." She hadn't expected him to impart the secrets to all ghostly life, but a tad more trivia might have been nice.

"Are you . . . buried at Elancourt?"

"How strange that question sounds, *non*? Well, unless something went horribly wrong, I was buried in the city, in the old French Society's aboveground tomb." Néomi's . . . remains were in a coffin amidst that towering vault. There were at least thirty other bodies within. "But then, crypt robbers might have stolen my body for voodoo rituals."

He frowned at her. "Are you *jesting* about this?"

"Tell me, Conrad, what's the etiquette when speaking of one's own dead body? No jesting about one's bones? Am I gauche?"

He gave her a look that said he would never understand her, and might not bother trying to. "How did you come by this property?"

"I bought it. All by my female self."

"And how would you afford it?" His tone was tinged with disbelief.

Typical. "I worked," she said, unable to disguise her satisfaction. "I was a ballerina."

"A ballerina. And now a ghost."

"A warlord and now a vampire." She couldn't help but chuckle at the disparity. "What a pair we make."

He studied her. "Your laughter . . . seems out of place."

"Why?"

"Aren't ghosts supposed to be steeped in misery?"

"Right now, I'm enjoying talking to you—so I'm happy. I have plenty of time to be unhappy later."

"Are you usually unhappy?" he asked.

"It's not my nature to be, but my present circumstances are hardly ideal."

"Then we have that in common: Néomi, when my brothers return, I want you to steal a key to my chains."

She breathed, "Steal? *Moi?* Never."

"I saw you taking things from them already," he said. She gazed up at the ceiling, resisting the urge to whistle with guilt. "Why did you exchange pebbles for your thefts?"

"Well, it's one thing to take something from the living, another to give. I wanted to hear someone say, 'Now, where'd this pebble come from?' well after the fact—it would be like a record of my existence. I thought it would prove me real."

"And now, because I interact with you, you know you're real?" When she nodded, he said, "Then you'd think you'd be more appreciative, more inclined to help me. Néomi, I'm going mad just lying in this room hour after hour."

"You're already mad."

He cast her a glower. "Aren't your kind supposed to be territorial? Get me that key, and then you can be all by yourself again."

"I'm not always alone here," she said. "Families live here at times. And contrary to most ghost stories, I adore having people here. Even if they can't see or hear me, they at least entertain."

"When were the last ones here?"

"Ten years ago. A charming young couple moved in." The husband and wife had been dazzled by the incredible bargain they'd gotten on Elancourt—having no idea it was the scene of a "grisly murder-suicide," as the papers had called it.

The two had worked diligently to restore and modernize as much as they could themselves. When their first baby had come, Néomi had cosseted the little girl, rocking her cradle and putting on floating puppet shows, helping out the exhausted parents as much as possible. Yet when the toddler had begun to cry for an invisible puppeteer, the parents had gotten spooked and moved.

Néomi had been heartbroken—and alone for the next ten years . . . until Conrad and his brothers had come.

"You've never frightened anyone away?" he asked, as if that was precisely what he would've been doing in her position.

"In truth, I do get very territorial with vandals. I scare them off—and they *never* return," she said proudly.

"I've already done much more damage to your

home than some vandals. Yet you won't help me leave?"

If she gave him a key, he would be gone before the chains hit the ground. And she knew she would never see him again.

Merde, that pang hurt. She inwardly shook herself. "Even if I could get it, why would I give it to you? So you could make good on your threats against your brothers?"

"You would give it to me because, if you don't, then I'm as much your prisoner as theirs."

"Why are you so keen to get away from them, Conrad? They're only trying to do what's best for you."

"You know nothing."

"Then tell me why you hate them so much. Because they turned you?"

He gave a bitter laugh. "That's not enough?"

"It was a long time ago, and they're doing so much for you now. They aren't sleeping. They trace across the ocean, warring against evil vampires when it's night over there, and then they rush back here to try to help you."

His expression inscrutable, he asked, "Do you hate?"

"Pardon? As in hate a person?"

He nodded. "Picture who you hate most in the world."

"That's easy—Louis. The man who stabbed me."

"Imagine dying and then waking, only to be bound to that miserable fuck for eternity. Would you not resent whoever put you in that situation?"

Oh, Lord, he has a point.

"They took from me my mission, my comrades, my life as I knew and wanted it—"

"Would you rather be dead?"

"Without question."

She could see there was no convincing him of anything different in this matter.

"You've heard that I have all kinds of factions gunning for my head," he said. "It's only a matter of time before they find me here. I need that key, ghost."

"My name's not 'ghost.'"

"Mine's not *'dément.'*"

"Touché, *dément*," she said blandly.

"Damn it! I've told you not to call me that—"

Murdoch suddenly appeared in the room.

12

Call you what?" Murdoch asked, but Conrad only shrugged. "Even with your one-sided conversations, you still seem a hundred times better already." Murdoch wasn't nearly as surprised as he should be about his progress.

They had an ace in their pocket. Conrad narrowed his eyes. *They know something I don't about the bloodlust.* "If I'm so much better, then free me."

"Can't do that. You could relapse. It's not even an option until you're drinking bagged blood, and you go at least two weeks without a rage."

Barely reining in his temper, Conrad said, "Am I to stay here the entire time?"

"No. Of course not. At the end of the next week, we're tracing you to a meeting about the Accession. A huge crowd is expected, with Lorekind from all over the world attending. Thousands of females will be there—Valkyrie, sirens, nymphs. You might find your Bride among them. Especially now, on the cusp of the Accession. We're also going to search for Nïx, a Valkyrie soothsayer. She's been aiding us with you. When we can find her."

Conrad had heard of Nïx the Ever-Knowing. She

was powerful and supposedly as mad as he was. But whereas his mind was clotted with memories, hers was filled with visions of the future. "Why would she help you?" Just because Sebastian and Nikolai had married Valkyrie didn't mean the rest of their kind accepted vampires. "Leeches" were universally hated in the Lore, even the clear-eyed ones.

"We're not entirely sure," Murdoch admitted. "But she could help locate your Bride."

"And what about your Bride, Murdoch? Your heart beats. Sebastian and Nikolai know it. You can't hide it."

When Murdoch stood and crossed to the window, Néomi relocated from her window seat to the spot beside Conrad in the bed. *The first female ever to move away from Murdoch in favor of another Wroth.* He felt a surge of satisfaction.

"I've made a vow to my Bride that I would tell no one, and Wroths keep their word." Murdoch ran his hand over the back of his neck. "I ask you not to bring it up to them."

"It's none of my concern—just as my Bride isn't yours," Conrad said.

"But we believe finding your female could help you recover fully."

"Fully recovered still means I'm a vampire."

"That's true," Murdoch said. "Everything we're doing will be wasted if we can't convince you that some vampires aren't evil. Not all of our kind have to be destroyed."

"What did Nikolai mean about controlling the memories, pulling them up at will?"

"You can learn to do it—but you have to be stable first."

Stable? When was the last time he'd been stable? "What have you been injecting me with?"

"A sedative and muscle relaxant concocted by the witches. They also put some element in it that's supposed to make you more susceptible to your Bride's influence. If we can help you find her."

Son of a bitch. "You don't say." His gaze landed on Néomi. She tilted her head at him.

Was she . . . *his?* Was this why she affected him so strongly? Then why hadn't she blooded him? Especially if he was more susceptible to her from the shots?

He inwardly shook himself. No, it wasn't possible. She wasn't truly *alive.* "What witches?" Conrad asked. "Mariketa the Awaited?"

"How did you know about the Witch in the Glass?"

He didn't remember Mariketa from his own experience but from the memories of one of his victims. "Someone I drank must have."

Conrad's casual tone had Murdoch raising his brows. "We couldn't ask Mariketa for assistance with this. Her male is Bowen MacRieve, the Lykae who helped us capture you. It happens that he wants you put down. At the tavern, he told us he'd give us two weeks to get you straight or he'd come destroy you himself."

"Why would he wait? Why assist you?"

"Sebastian saved MacRieve's life recently. He also spared the Lykae from what he considers a fate a thousand times worse than death."

"Then why come after me at all?"

"You're a fallen vampire who showed up not only in his town, but in a place he and his mate patronize. A little too close for his comfort. So MacRieve is sympathetic, but only to a point."

And the Lykae's witch could easily scry and find Conrad. Yet another enemy bent on destroying him. *The line begins here, gentlemen.*

"Conrad, the three of us have vowed to bring you back from the brink, even with you spitting and bellowing if we have to. I'm asking you, as your brother, to just . . . try."

How far are they willing to go?

Conrad shook his head. *What am I thinking? Imagining a recovery from this?* He'd made his choices. He'd suffer the consequences.

Even if there was a way, he wouldn't have *time*. Pain shot through his arm as if to punctuate his thoughts.

If the curse of the mark was true, then the fact that Conrad had begun dreaming of Néomi could mean far more than he'd imagined.

He needed to get free and hunt that bastard. If he could defeat Tarut and take the demon's blood, Conrad would truly be the most powerful male in the Lore. He would be unstoppable.

Which would help him defeat his next set of opponents: the Woede.

Months ago, Conrad had unwittingly drained a warlock who'd known a critical secret: the only way to defeat Rydstrom's usurper.

Now Conrad was the last living being with that

information—not that he consciously knew what it was or even how to find it.

Rydstrom would kill for what was in Conrad's mind. So would his brother, Cadeon the Kingmaker; as a mercenary, that demon had seated five kings. But he couldn't quite reclaim his own brother's crown.

Conrad said, "You risk much, taking me to the gathering."

"It will be wild there, so we'll stay on the periphery of the crowd and see if any female catches your fancy."

Conrad was to skulk in the bushes at some field party, looking for a woman. *My degradation is complete.* He willed himself not to look at Néomi. "I have no interest in having to care for and protect a female that I don't get to choose for myself." Even as he said the words, he lost himself musing what it would mean if fate had chosen Néomi for him. . . . Could Conrad find a way to bridge their existences? To make it so he could claim her? He'd dreamed about taking her—if it was a fraction as good as his dreams . . .

"Conrad!" Murdoch snapped his fingers.

He blinked. "What?"

"I said that we know about your involvement in the Kapsliga, and we know the vows involved."

Conrad's eyes shot wide. "Don't—"

"We know you've never been with a woman."

13

Cadeon Woede of the rage demons would rather have had his black claws pulled from his fingers or his horns filed than come to this bar—a grungy biker dive, patronized almost entirely by male demons.

But if Cade hadn't accompanied his brother and crew here, he would've gone to stalk *her*—and Rydstrom was already getting suspicious about his late-night activities.

Besides, they had a business meeting with a soothsayer this eve. "And here's the dove of the hour," Cade muttered when Nïx and another Valkyrie entered the bar. They'd been searching for Nïx for days now, and a mutual friend had arranged the meeting.

Rydstrom twisted around in time to see the two small females accosted by a pathos demon. The pathos was a brawny biker, but he looked young, too young to tangle with the much older Valkyrie.

"Step aside," Nïx told him, already glancing past him.

When he didn't, her companion tensed. "Move." The female was wearing a low-hanging cowboy hat. Good money said that the hat was shading the glowing face of Regin the Radiant, a combat-loving Valkyrie. "Or *hurt*."

"My friend here has been spoiling for a brawl for weeks now," Nïx said. "At this point she'll smack down unwary kindergartners over sandbox toys. I suggest you get out of our way."

"None doing, lovelies," the pathos said in a nineteenth-century Cockney accent. "Pretty little things like ye come in a place like this, methinks yer keen for a demon twixt yer thighs."

Nïx rolled her eyes. "Only about, oh, *always*," she said in an exasperated tone. "As long as they don't resemble you in any way."

The pathos put his arm in front of Nïx, blocking her. "Now, that's not nice."

Cade shook his head. *The fuckwit has no idea what he's provoking.*

"No," Regin began, "making you wear your bulbous horns out of your ass wouldn't be nice."

Rydstrom asked, "Should we warn that demon?"

"Let them sort out the tosser," Cade answered. "The Valkyrie'll be in a good mood after violence." And the spectacle would be something to take Cade's mind off his obsession.

In a flash, Nïx snared the pathos's hand and smiled, baring her small fangs. His eyes widened with belated recognition, just as she squeezed his hand in her own, pulverizing the bones. He yelled, alerting a kinsman, who unwisely decided to join in.

Rydstrom's battle-scarred face creased into a grin. "It's never dull with Valkyrie around."

"Hey, Nïx," Regin said minutes later, "my demon

screams like a singing bitch—what does yours scream like?"

Nïx replied conversationally, "Also like a singing bitch. Hmm. Only without balls." As Nïx plugged his left horn into a wall socket, Regin got to enjoy a round of the cheap shots she was known for, until her hat got knocked off in the skirmish. Her glowing face made everyone back away.

Though Nïx was older and therefore stronger, Regin had a notorious vicious streak.

The crowd quieted as a whole, but more than one creature cursed under his breath, *"Not Regin."*

A drunk hunched over the bar muttered, "That glowing one made me eat a transistor radio once."

In the lull, the Valkyries' two battered opponents fled.

With a shrug, Regin collected and dusted off her hat, then cast Nïx a blazing smile. "Nïxie, you were on *fuego!*"

Nïx tucked her black hair behind her pointed Valkyrie ears. "And your *waif fu* is as diabolical as ever!"

As predicted, the chits are in a great mood now.

Seeing the show was over, Rydstrom rose to go collect the pair, which meant Cade rose as well. "Nïx?" As Rydstrom strode to her, even hardened denizens of the bar dived out of his way. Nïx and Regin had to crane their heads up to look into his face.

"King Rydstrom," she said with a smile, "and behind you as usual is your guard Cadeon the Kingmaker."

"Why don't you have a seat with us?" Rydstrom led Nïx to their back table, with Regin and Cade following.

"Excuse Cade's mercenaries." Not bothering to

hide his disapproval, Rydstrom indicated Cade's crew. "Some of them are in town. Indefinitely." Rydstrom could be just as ruthless as Cade and his men, but he never wavered from his personal code.

Cade wondered where Rydstrom had gotten that code, because his own was missing.

Nïx gave them an exaggerated howdy wave, yet they all scowled. She seemed to recognize two of the five: the smoke demon Rök, a fugitive in two dimensions living under a "terminate with extreme prejudice" order, and Grimslade, who sat in the chair closest to the darkened corner.

Grim, one among a warrior breed of demons raised underground in the most hellish conditions, looked to have a heart attack when Regin sat beside him. She was unaware that Grim had only two aversions—one to bright things and one to beautiful things. Regin was both.

As Nïx took a seat, she said to Rydstrom, "Mariketa the Awaited told me you wanted to speak to me."

"Aye, I need your advice."

"My advice." She pressed her fingers to her chest. "But didn't you recently say that I was a 'mad creature' who was 'soft in the head'? Sniff, sniff, Rydstrom. Sniff, sniff. I was so crushed that I ate a gallon of Ben & Jerry's, except I didn't because Valkyrie don't eat."

Rydstrom narrowed his eyes. "Bowen told you I said that?"

"Ever-knowing here."

With uncharacteristic smoothness, Rydstrom said, "Then you also know I said you were a beauty."

She was a comely bit, but then, was there ever a

Valkyrie who was hard to look at? Cade had seen his first one when he'd just turned nine. He'd been fascinated with them ever since.

Nïx fluffed her long hair. "Though you merely observe the obvious with your aggressive flirting, you're still forgiven." Exhaling as if in resignation, she said, "I suppose that now you'll want to sleep with me." Over Rydstrom's sputtering, she added, "Alas, big guy—I am taken."

"No, you're not," Regin said.

"Am too," Nïx said. "Mike Rowe, the *star* of *Dirty Jobs*, is soon to realize I'm his beloved." She sighed dreamily. "He even got his lawyers to contact me on the pretext of a"—she made air quotes— "'restraining order.'"

Returning her attention to a bemused Rydstrom, she said, "So about this advice . . . do you want to find your fated female or defeat your usurper, Omort the Deathless? Which would you prefer to have? Your queen or the crown that your brother lost for you?"

Cade slammed his drink to the sticky table. He'd fucked up. He knew it, was reminded of it hourly. He did his damnedest to rectify the situation—and always fell short. "Am I never livin' that down?" he snapped, his lower-class demon accent standing out sharply. He usually masked it better than this.

He wanted to be like his older brother—he truly did. He often imagined what it would be like to be respected and sought out for his wisdom and even-handedness. Instead, he was "violent, impulsive, and misguided," according to Rydstrom.

Cade's crew made money doing the things the bad

guys would wince at. He just didn't have those moral checks on his personality.

But it isn't like Rydstrom doesn't have his secrets. And Cade was inadvertently privy to several. There were certain things that made King Rydstrom lose his cool in a catastrophic way.

"No, I checked. You're not going to live it down," Nïx said, with all the authority of a soothsayer who'd never been proven wrong—not once in at least three thousand years.

The other demons smirked, except for Grim, who was casting tense looks at Regin and absently puncturing claw marks into the table.

Rydstrom freely blamed Cade for losing his crown, and Cade had never apologized. Cade figured most brothers would have had an exchange of "Sorry" followed by "We'll work it out." Not he and his brother— they were prone to break out in fistfights just walking together.

Yet they'd rarely separated for centuries.

"Why make me choose?" Rydstrom asked. "You could tell me how to obtain both."

She blinked at him. "Because that wouldn't be . . . *fun?*" After casting an inquisitive glance at Cade, she focused on Rydstrom, seeming to will him toward an answer.

"I want . . . my crown."

Nïx glared. "Well, there went that decision tree. Four words and *both* of your fates just altered utterly." She turned to Cade. "What about you? What would you do to restore your brother's kingdom?"

He grated, "Bloody—*anything*."

She sighed as if she disapproved of his answer but wasn't surprised by it. "Would you relinquish your life for it?"

"I would," Cade said easily. *Life's too long anyway.* He was millennial in age, had no family other than Rydstrom and their sisters.

At least with his death, Cade could atone. If anyone got to die to save their kingdom, it *better* be him.

"Would you give up your own fated female?" she asked. The demons at the table grew quiet.

Not so easy to relinquish. *Answer the bloody question.* Cade couldn't have her anyway. She was forever forbidden to him. *Rydstrom's scrutinizing me.* Did he know? *Answer it.* "Yes, I would."

"Very well." She faced Rydstrom. "Your crown . . . You and Cade's gang have been searching for months for a particularly nasty warlock who's the only one with the knowledge of how Omort the Deathless can be vanquished."

Rydstrom narrowed his gaze. "We've told no one that."

She waved away his words. "Don't worry, I've been telling *everybody*." When he scowled, Nïx said, "Problem, though."

"Which is?"

"The warlock's . . . been murdered." She cupped her ear. "Wow, I can *hear* your hopes plummeting."

Cade ran his hand down his face. "How?"

"Sucked dry by a red-eyed vampire." Both Cade and Rydstrom tensed.

"This leech . . . he lives still?" Cade inched forward in his seat, already envisioning how to torture the vampire to retrieve the warlock's stolen memories. The Woede had no love lost for vampires.

"He does!" Nïx said. "And I even know where he is."

With a kingly motion of his hand, Rydstrom waved her on. Nïx grew still. Cade drank deeply. *Rydstrom, you just fucked up.* . . .

"You dare wave me about?" Nïx's eyes flickered silver with anger. "Like I'm your court seer, or the seer's coffee-fetching intern?" She lowered her voice. "I'm more than twice your age, and two of my three parents are *gods*."

Rydstrom had to know he'd botched this, but he plowed on. "Nïx . . ." he said slowly, *warningly*.

"Oh, Rydstrom"—she scratched him under the chin and gave him an embarrassed smile—"this mad creature is so soft in the head, she forgot where she put the leech!" She stood to go. "Toodle-oo, the night grows short, and Regin and I have much mayhem to hatch."

"Stay, Nïx. I'll leave. You can continue talking to Cade." Rydstrom obviously thought he'd have more luck with Nïx.

In general, Cade was considerably smoother with women than his brother was. Though Rydstrom did love to remind Cade what a "blathering idiot" he'd been the sole time he'd spoken with his fated female.

Admittedly, he hadn't been at the top of his game, but blathering idiot? Not in a million years.

Rydstrom indicated for the rest of the crew to go to the bar. Except for Rök, who gave a vile curse. "Summoned yet again," he grated, then began tracing.

Ballocks, there goes my ride. Neither Cade nor Rydstrom could trace any longer. They'd had that ability bound—a punishment for a failed coup.

I'm going to get Rydstrom's bloody crown back for him if it bloody kills me. . . .

When it was only Cade and the Valkyrie, Nïx said, "You'll be at the gathering this weekend, yes?"

He nodded. "How's the alliance shaping up?" He'd heard Nïx had been actively steering this Accession. For her to take such an interest meant this one could be apocalyptic. Otherwise, Nïx the Ever-Knowing would likely be out shopping, as Valkyrie fancied doing.

She said, "So far on our team, we have the Lykae, the Forbearers, the Furiae, the Wraiths, the noble fey, myriad demonarchies, the House of Witches, possibly the CIA, and probably a Colombian drug lord. The nymphs are straddling the fence."

Regin opened her mouth, but Nïx cut her off. "That one's too easy, Reege."

The Valkyrie shrugged, her attention returning to an arm-wrestling match.

In a nonchalant tone, he asked Nïx, "So you want to tell me about the leech?"

"I don't know if you can defeat this one," Nïx said. "He's unspeakably powerful."

Cade gritted his teeth. "Then I only wish you'd seen what I did to my last enemy. And that was piss easy for me."

Nïx peered at the ceiling, then down again with an expression of surprise. "Very nice. But I can't see what you did with his spine."

She could view the *past* as well? *There'd been*

rumors. . . . "Made him try to crawl for it before I beheaded him." He immediately frowned. "What do you do when you pluck a spine?"

"The same. You can't improve on a classic. Oh, and speaking of getting a spine—how are things with your lady love, Cade?"

He drank, studying her over the rim of his mug. *Nïx can tell how I feel. She knows.* Cade was notoriously brutal, a feared mercenary. Yet at times he found himself gut-sick with wanting his female, one who was too young and too human—the sole species forbidden to him.

Because the mortal wouldn't survive the initial claiming when he went demonic.

Cade no longer tried to deny that she was his, no longer bothered with his halfhearted pursuits of other females. Every time he saw her from the shadows, the certainty grew.

He wondered if Nïx knew about the picture he kept beside his bed.

Nïx smiled at that very moment; Cade swore. "Ever-knowing, Cade," she said softly.

Cade hiked his shoulders, pretending nonchalance. "Tell me about the vampire, or not, dove. But none of us really wants to be here."

"I'll tell you," Nïx said, her gaze rapt on his horns. "But only if you let me lick your rock-hard horns—"

"Nïx!" Regin's attention snapped back to this conversation.

Eyes wide, Nïx cried, "Who *said* that?? I didn't say that! Oh, very well—the vampire's named Conrad Wroth. Best be careful with that one. He single-handedly took down Bothrops the Lich."

"That was Wroth?" He'd heard of the assassin before. Cade grudgingly admitted that the leech did nice work, dealing deaths with a unique, gruesome signature to them. Which was important in their line of business. "Where is he?"

"To find him, you need to trail the one who seeks him in sleep."

"Soothsayerese? I don't speak it," he said, but she didn't elaborate. "That's all you're going to divvy?"

"Wanna know more?" Nïx raised her brows. "Then you should have let me lick your horns."

14

When Conrad's eyes slid shut, the muscles in his jaw tightening, Néomi realized he wasn't going to deny his brother's words.

Her lips parted. *Never been with a woman?* If Conrad had been attractive to her before, he'd just become *irresistible*. This man, with his tremendous body made for pleasing and protecting a woman, was a virgin.

Oh, but this revelation was a problem. Conrad—so secretive and proud—was plainly burning with embarrassment, restless in his chains. His arms were bulging so much, it was clear he was clenching his fists behind him. Her knowing this would be humiliating for him.

And his pride had already been taking a beating. She knew men, and she knew that any show of vulnerability in front of a woman they found attractive was crushing to them.

Her heart was breaking for him.

Murdoch frowned at Conrad's reaction. "Just think, if you found your Bride at the gathering, within a single week, you could be bedding her. Aren't you even curious about what it's like?"

His tone incensed, Conrad said, *"Leave me."*

"Things are heating up overseas—none of us will

be back until late tomorrow. Do you want to drink before I go?"

Conrad began straining against his bonds, the muscles in his neck standing out with the effort. "Get out of my sight!" As he rocked to the side, she saw blood on the sheets from where the manacles were cutting into his wrists.

"Conrad, calm yourself." Murdoch stood. "I'm leaving."

When Murdoch disappeared, Néomi took a breath, then sidled closer to Conrad. Making her tone casual, she said, "You seem discomfited by this, but you shouldn't be. *Et alors. Ce n'est pas grand-chose.* It's not a big—"

"Get out."

"Conrad, your brother seems to believe you could soon find your Bride and bed her, but I think he's glossing over a major component—she needs to want you, too. I could teach you what women like. I could show you how to seduce her."

That just made him more furious.

She hurriedly said, "Listen, this is your room and I'll respect your privacy, but maybe tonight, I could just sit with you? I won't say a word. I just don't want to be alone—"

"And you know what *I* want." She'd noticed that his fangs seemed to sharpen with aggression—they did now. "So be a good girl, and promise me," he began in a low tone, before yelling, "*that you'll get me a goddamned key!*"

"You said you wanted to kill your brothers. You said you *ached* to."

"So?"

She made an impatient sound. "So, if I free you, you could just lie in wait and attack them here. I'd be an accessory to murder."

Looking as if he could happily throttle her, he said, "I wouldn't do it here."

She shook her head. "I won't even consider it until you vow not *ever* to harm them."

"Why would you want this?"

"I feel like I know them, and I think they're honorable men," she answered. "They don't deserve to die, especially not for trying to help you."

"If you don't get me the key, I swear, I'll torch this rotting heap!"

"Why do you say these things?" she cried.

"Because I mean what I say. Now, get out! And don't return without my key."

"This is my house—I don't have to leave!"

"Of course you wouldn't want to! I suppose that's your lot, to follow the living around like a pathetic lapdog."

"L-lapdog?" Had he truly just called her that?

"Exactly. Doing your tricks, begging for a *crumb* of attention. Stripping off your clothes."

She gasped, tempted to reacquaint him with the ceiling.

"Run along, ghostling. Unless I haven't tossed you enough scraps?"

With a last glare, she twisted and disappeared from the room. Damn him, she didn't want to be alone. *Not tonight.*

Why did men get so *angry* after showing a vulnerability? Why did it cost them so much to let down their armor? She couldn't care less that Conrad was a virgin. Well, that wasn't true, but she definitely wasn't reacting the way he would think.

What if I just return and tell him that I'm attracted to him—and that this information doesn't lessen the feeling?

So he could yell more at her? Insult her? Was she the type of woman who would rather get insulted than be alone?

Never.

Now what to do? Where to go? Conrad's comments resounded within her as she moped through the hallways of her home.

At the week's end, the brothers were all going out and she . . . wasn't. Néomi had loved going to gatherings, had adored getting dressed up. She'd loved *anything* with a social aspect.

She recalled all the fun things she'd done—beach bonfires at the gulf, houseboat parties on the Mississippi, celebrating Mardi Gras with other *bons vivants*, lively and hedonistic stage people.

One Fourth of July, she'd splashed in the fountain in Jackson Square. Under the heat of fireworks above and surrounded by the soft strains of jazz, she'd kissed a complete stranger—his lips had tasted of absinthe.

I used to be proud, too, the life of the party. No longer. Now she wasn't above begging like a pathetic dog for a crumb of attention.

Her mood picked up a fraction when she heard a voice downstairs. Murdoch hadn't left yet. She traced to him, finding him dialing on his cellular phone. She decided to see if his pockets held any more of those lovely hair combs.

"Pick up, Danii," he muttered. When Danii didn't, he slammed his fist into a wall. *If another Wroth punches my house one more time . . .*

He was so preoccupied that he never felt a thing when she rooted through his pocket—

And fished out a key.

For hours, Conrad had wanted to call her back.

Something about her expression had put him on edge. She'd had a look on her face as if she'd been sentenced to the gallows—part fear, part resignation. Her eyes had been so sad, so different from her earlier excited demeanor, such as when she'd been asking about mermaids, of all things.

It wasn't her fault she'd overheard Conrad's shaming secret, but he'd treated her as if it were—because he was sick of feeling powerless and impotent, sick of *being* both. He was just about to swallow his pride and call for her when he smelled lit candles and . . . starch?

His hackles rose. Something was happening, something she'd known was awaiting her. All she'd wanted to do was stay with him during the day, because she'd been afraid. *Of what?*

And he'd cruelly sent her away to be on her own. A bewildering type of panic welled inside him, so strong it left him shaken. He began sweating.

Néomi should *never* be afraid. Not while he had strength in his body.

His eyes widened when he heard music downstairs. *Not right. This isn't right.* He grew frenzied, rocking back and forth, yanking against his chains, leveraging all his strength against one arm. Again and again, he heaved . . . until he dislocated his shoulder with a pop.

This gave him just enough leeway to thread his hands under his feet and unlatch the tether from the bed. He stood, pounding his shoulder into the doorframe to force it back in place, then charged downstairs. Searching for the scent of roses, he came to the ballroom.

This area had been wrecked by age—and by Conrad. Yet now it appeared as it must have been eighty years ago. The marble floor was an unbroken gleam under the light of what seemed like a thousand candles. The interior was filled with fresh-cut roses, starched tablecloths, and obviously expensive furniture. That ghostly music sounded from no apparent source.

Surreal. This situation had all the makings of a hallucination. But he didn't believe it was. Then he saw her enter the room, looking as though she were in a trance. "Néomi?" She didn't answer, just began to dance.

She started slowly, somehow keeping her chest, head, and arms perfectly still, while her leg unfolded and she pivoted round. When the pace quickened, she began to sweep her arms, the movements precise yet fluid.

The way she moved was like silk, as though her arms were boneless. Stunned, he muttered, "*Tantsija.*"

Even he recognized certain steps from classical ballet, but she infused them with sensuality. There was something . . . suggestive about the way she danced, as if she did it to attract a man.

It was working. When she moved, he *felt*.

Néomi appeared spectral at certain angles. But he'd still never seen anything so beautiful. Her skin was glowing, her pale lips like a bow. The smoky outlines around her eyes just made the blue irises stand out. Her cheeks only seemed sharper because of the shadows under them.

Her face was suffused with contentment, what looked like a nearly mindless joy. He was calmed watching her, his earlier frustrations soothed. Others' memories couldn't overcome his captivation with what he was seeing. They grew quieter with each second, and then, for the first time in centuries, they receded altogether.

A dead dancer with joy on her face made him feel . . . *expectation*. He had a sense of looking forward to something more with her—to watching her dance again, to talking with her.

Before, he'd been accepting of the fact that he would die soon, had believed he deserved it. He was a vampire, a being he'd been taught to hate all his life.

Now . . . he wasn't at all ready for the end. As he watched her, he thought, *I might not be able to miss out on her.*

He narrowed his eyes. *I want . . . the dancer.*

In the shower with her, he'd recognized she was special to him in some way. This evening the suspicion that she was his Bride had grown. Now he no longer denied it. She must not have blooded him because she wasn't technically alive.

Néomi's mine.

To have such a woman in his keeping . . .

For a chance with her, could he put away his plans for revenge—and his certainty that he would soon die?

She effortlessly twirled up on her toes, her black skirts and her long hair whipping around. So lovely his chest ached.

Yes, he could. *She's mine. And I'll have her.* There were obstacles, but he excelled at eliminating anything that stood in the way of what he wanted.

Soon her pace increased. She spun faster and faster. *Not right.* Outside, yellow lightning began to flash in front of the crescent moon, and the wind soon roared through the trees, raining leaves. The room slowly aged, decaying right before him. The music abruptly ended.

Rose petals littered the floor.

Conrad charged for her, unable to trace because of the chains. Before he could reach her, the pace quickened even more. "Néomi?"

The air grew heavier. Her expression changed, going from dreamy and seductive to terrified.

Once he reached her, he yelled, "Néomi, stop this!"

She didn't glance up, didn't seem able to. Her eyes were stark, her breaths ragged. When he tried to stay her, she passed right through him, making him shudder from a surge of electricity.

Every protective instinct in him screamed to life. *Keep her safe . . . keep her close.*

He *couldn't.* He roared with frustration when she moved through him again.

How long could she sustain this pace? Faster, twirling away from him, until . . . she vanished.

Turning in a slow circle, he bellowed, "Néomi!" But the sounds continued, sounds that he didn't want to identify: the wet scraping of bone; her scream—interrupted. Suddenly blood pooled out over the floor, soaking the petals.

Until they, too, disappeared.

15

He'd seen it. Somehow the vampire had gotten free.

When Conrad had begun yelling for her from all over the house, she'd evacuated from her studio to the bayou folly.

She planned to sleep out here, away from all the commotion. The crickets and owls were lulling, and a breeze blew. She couldn't feel it, but the cypress needles above her combed the wind, the sound sublime. She was just about to fall into reverie when he came upon her.

He stopped in his tracks, and his eyes briefly slid shut.

"What do you want?" Néomi murmured.

He wound around jutting cypress knees to reach her. "Are you injured?" he asked, crouching beside her, surveying her.

As much as she hated to admit it, his presence was comforting. "Don't be ridiculous, vampire. I can't be injured." Yet her essence was depleted—it always was. And she was shaken from the relived pain. Being stabbed in the heart tended to do that to a person.

Much less when the knife twists . . . She shuddered. *How much longer can I continue to endure this?*

"What the hell was that back there?" When she shurgged, he said, "You're even paler than before, fainter."

"Am I to expect more insults, Conrad? You should know that I'm *not* one of those women who will take disdain over nothing." Had she sounded as if she was trying to convince herself? "I'd rather not converse with you."

"I don't want to insult you." He couldn't take his gaze from her, as if fearing she'd disappear again.

"You didn't want to be around me earlier. Perhaps now I don't want your company."

He studied her face. "I think . . . I think that you do."

"Cocky now? *Le dément* reveals a brand-new personality." She didn't like that he was right, or that he *knew* he was right. Maybe she *was* as pathetic as he'd deemed her. "How did you get loose?"

"Pulled my shoulder out," he said, his tone indicating this wasn't even worth a mention.

She quirked a brow. Intense man. "*Naturellement.*"

"Come inside with me."

"You're ready to let the lapdog inside? And here I didn't even beg at the door. Why do you even care what happens with me?"

"I just . . . do. So return with me," he said. She could tell he wanted to snatch her arm and drag her in. "Dawn's coming."

She feigned tapping her chin. "Hmm, I never would have suspected if not for that big orange ball rising."

"If you won't come inside, then I have no choice but to stay with you here."

"What about *the sun*? Are you crazed— strike that. Are you a fool?"

"Tell me what happened tonight or come inside. One of the two."

"*Allez au diable.*"

"Then I'm staying with you." He sank beside her, flaunting that stubborn mien.

"Then I'll leave."

"And go where?" he asked. "Is this where you usually go when you're not with me?"

"No, I'm out here because you wouldn't stop shouting in my house!" she snapped, at the end of her patience. "I don't know why this happens. At the same time every month, I dance. I can't stop it, can't control it. And then once I've danced my heart out, I get to have it stabbed. Month after month."

"You said you were alone here."

"I am. I don't see Louis. I don't see the knife. I just can . . . I just feel it."

"I've heard of ghosts compelled to reenact certain aspects of their deaths."

"Well, now that I know I'm not alone in this, it's all better. You may go now. *Adieu.*"

If Néomi had previously appeared breezy and confident, now she looked like a shaken girl, off by herself to lick her wounds.

But Conrad had believed what he'd said earlier. She wanted him near—even if she was prickly with him. Of course she'd still be angry with him about earlier, but he also thought she was upset that he'd seen that dance. He figured women were like that—whenever they showed a bit of vulnerability, they came out with claws bared.

"Come with me, Néomi."

Her delicate hand rose to her forehead. She seemed drained, her image flickering, her eyes weary and not as luminous.

The changes in the house, the music, and all of those ghostly surroundings had to have been fueled by her, by her very essence.

"Why should I?"

Because he needed to keep her close. Because what he'd just witnessed had *done* something to him. He was altered. This was more than his determination that she was *his*. It was more than his resolve to do something about it and more than his new need to protect her.

He felt as if some foreign emotion had wedged itself inside his chest, and now it was swinging punches, demanding more room.

But he only said, "Why not?"

She was obviously so tired, but she still jutted her dainty chin up. "You feel sorry for me now. You don't have to babysit me. I assure you that I've gotten through this by myself before."

"I know you have." Each month for eighty years, she'd relived her death—alone. *Never again.* "You would come inside for no other reason than to save me from incineration. Because, *tantsija*, I can be as stubborn as you."

"What does that word mean?"

"It means *dancer*."

As tendrils of sunlight began to reach them, she pursed her lips. "Oh, very well." She floated to her feet, then accompanied him back to the house.

Though she grumbled, he was able to lead her into his room. She was likely too tired to resist. Inside, she drifted straight to the bed, then curled on her side, hovering just above the mattress.

Earlier, he'd noticed that she floated over chairs as though sitting. Now he knew she slept on beds as well.

In seconds, she was asleep. . . .

During the long day as he watched over her, her image grew stronger, which satisfied him more than anything in recent memory.

He experienced needs unknown before, inexplicable urges. . . . He wanted to lie behind her. Wanted to tuck her small body into him. Again and again, he ran his hands over the outline of her hair, imagining what the glossy curls would feel like.

He had the overwhelming urge to buy this place, fix it, and keep her safe within it—but only if he could prevent her from having to dance as she had last night. His hands clenched as he thought of her, cursed to feel that pain over and over.

Conrad had the knowledge necessary to do some spells—mostly crude protection or camouflaging spells—but could rarely access it on demand. Whenever he wanted a certain memory, it proved infuriatingly elusive. If he was able to utilize at will all the knowledge he'd acquired, could he figure out how to protect her?

What if the answer was there, already within him,

waiting to be retrieved? Nikolai had said Conrad could learn to do it.

He'd also said that there was only one thing that could compete with bloodlust—sex. And that there was only one thing that could compete with the overwhelming need to kill.

Now Conrad knew. The need to protect.

By dint of will, effort, and a rake he'd found in a ramshackle toolshed, Conrad had retrieved several of the newspapers on the drive that she'd been unable to reach. He intended to make a gift of them to his female.

Having no experience whatsoever with women and limited resources, this was the best he could come up with.

He'd just finished stacking up the papers in the room and settled in to wait for Néomi to wake when his brothers traced into the room.

Nikolai exhaled wearily to find him moving about freely. "How did you get loose?"

"Dislocated my shoulder."

Almost at the exact same time, all three raised their brows at the collection of papers. "You dislocated your shoulder to get to the newspapers on the road? You could have asked one of us if you wanted to read—"

"No. That's not it." *Why not tell them?* They already thought him mad. *What if one of them has encountered a ghost? What if they believed him?* "I got them for a female who lives here." He was sane enough to recognize how this sounded. "She likes to read them."

"The house is abandoned, Conrad." Nikolai pinched the bridge of his nose. "You know this."

He ran his palms over his pants. "I'm the only one who can see her. She's lying on this bed right now."

To a man, they got that anxious expression as though they were wondering whether madness was catching.

"If there is truly a ghost there, get her to move something," Murdoch said. "Can she make a door slam? Or rattle something in the attic?"

"Yes, she can move things with her mind."

Sebastian waved him on. "Then by all means . . ."

Conrad glanced from them to her, and back again. "She's . . . asleep." And he couldn't shake her to get her to wake.

"Of course she is," Sebastian muttered. He'd always been the most skeptical of the brothers. Conrad figured that even after three centuries, that hadn't changed.

"Damn it, I'm telling the truth."

"Yet you can't rouse her?"

Conrad considered explaining why she was so exhausted, but thought that would only make things worse.

Murdoch asked, "Why would we believe you're seeing a ghost rather than another hallucination? You're supposed to be bombarded with delusions."

"I was. Constantly. I'm not anymore. She's real." Right at her ear, he said, "Néomi, wake up!" No response. "Wake up!" he said louder, aware that he appeared to be yelling at the sheet.

Murdoch had a look on his face as if he couldn't decide whether to laugh or cry over Conrad's actions.

Finally, he said, "Kristoff has given word that there will be a battle tonight. So we likely won't be returning for two days."

Nikolai added, "We'll leave you free run of the property. The refrigerator is filled with weeks' worth of bagged blood, and I'll get my wife to stop—"

"I'll manage on my own," Conrad said quickly.

"Very well."

Surprised by the concession, Conrad said, "Free me completely."

Nikolai's gaze went from the newspapers to Conrad's eyes, and he exhaled. "We can't. You've come too far to relapse. Soon I'm going to ask you to make a decision. A critical one—but you have to be stable."

Conrad gave a bitter laugh. "Since when do you ask me to make a decision instead of making it for me?"

Nikolai's expression was grave. "Since I lost my brother for three centuries."

16

"Are you a betting man, Conrad?" Néomi was surprised her voice wasn't quavering.

He'd shaved, fully revealing the striking structure of his lean face. And she'd been given no warning. She'd breezed into the room, then stopped, speechless at the sight of him reclining on the bed.

Devastating male. And she wondered why she couldn't stay mad at him.

He frowned at her reaction. He obviously had no idea of his heart-pounding effect on women. "Depends."

Yesterday, once she'd awakened from her lengthy reverie, she'd found a stack of newspapers lying on the floor. He'd gruffly said, "I was able to get some of the ones that had piled up out of your reach." She thought that for a man like Conrad, this had been on a level with picking flowers for her.

Though the gesture had softened her, she'd still been hesitant when he'd wanted to stay close by. "Why should I choose to be around you?" she'd asked. "You're just going to hurt my feelings or start haranguing me for the key again." The key that she'd stolen from Murdoch and hidden away.

"My brothers were here earlier," Conrad had answered. "They said they aren't returning for two days. There will be a moratorium on the key. And I won't insult you."

Apparently, his brothers had allowed him to remain untied from the bed, with his manacles in front—even after he'd disclosed that there was a ghost living here.

The idea that he'd had to tell them that he *would* have gotten the spirit to prove herself, but she was *asleep*, was too amusing. The image of him yelling at seemingly nothing but a sheet was hilarious.

She'd decided to give him another chance. Which was why she held a deck of cards this evening. "I challenge you to twenty-one rounds of *vingt-et-un*. Whoever loses a round has to answer a question, truthfully and completely. Any question whatsoever."

He sat up. "Deal."

She hovered on the foot of the bed to face him. He had difficulty with the cards because his hands were still chained, but he wouldn't ask for help. And she had to use her most highly concentrated telekinesis, which would mean she'd have to sleep more. But still they muddled through.

After he won the first hand, his lips curved, not quite a smile, but she still had to shake herself. "I win."

Yes, you do. . . . In the game of attraction, lips like his should be ruled an unfair advantage.

What were the women of his time *thinking* to allow him to go unscathed? She wanted to fan herself with the cards she appeared to hold. "So ask your question," she absently said.

"Were you survived by any of your family?"

"*Non.* I never knew my father. *Maman* died when I'd just turned sixteen. I was an only child."

She dealt again. He had an ace showing, and she had seventeen. *Dealer holds.* "*Merde,*" she snapped when he flipped a ten of clubs.

He asked, "Why didn't you know your father?" When she hesitated, he repeated her words: "Any question whatsoever, truthfully and completely."

"I didn't know him because he was a scoundrel. He was rich, a scion of Nîmes, France, and my mother had been a young servant in his home. He was married, but he still seduced her. When she revealed to him she was expecting his child, he told her, 'Take the voyage to America, and I'll follow right after my divorce. We'll raise the baby there as a family.' But he never came. She waited for him—stranded here, pregnant, and without enough money to return."

"Maybe he died on the crossing. Who knows what could have happened to him?"

"*Non,* he sent *maman* a pittance that only served to let her know she'd been duped—a potential scandal decisively removed from *société's* eyes. To her dying day, she thought he would come for us, so she never remarried." Though there were certainly proposals in her line of work—some even legitimate.

Néomi had been unable to comprehend how Marguerite could turn away opportunities for a better life when they were offered to her, opportunities for a French émigrée dancer and her bastard to get out of the Vieux Carré.

In Néomi's mind, if a woman was silly enough to

wait for a man to save her, then she didn't get to be choosy about which man it would be.

Marguerite's life had taught Néomi well. She'd vowed never to be in that situation, dependent on a man.

She dealt once more. She had nineteen, while he had a jack of hearts showing. "Hit," he said. She did. "Hit again. And once more." He flipped his cards over. *Jack, two, three, six.*

Her lips thinned. This card game wasn't working out as she'd planned. She'd hoped to find out about his past and how he'd gone a lifetime without sex—not to get interrogated.

"Twenty-one the hard way. I win again. If your mother didn't remarry, how did the two of you live?"

"She worked."

"That's not a thorough answer."

"She was a burlesque dancer. I grew up in lodgings above the club."

He raised his brows. "This explains much about you, and your lack of modesty. But with your looks"—his gaze dropped to her breasts, then swiftly back up—"why didn't you follow in her footsteps?"

She gave him a bland smile. "Who says I didn't?"

He looked aghast. "But you were a ballet dancer!"

"Not always," she murmured.

"You can't leave it at that."

"Then win this hand." Twenty to her and seventeen to him. "I win." Finally. And if he was going to dig into her past, then . . . "Why aren't you more loyal to your family?"

He narrowed his eyes. "You're going to question my sense of loyalty?"

"*Oui*. Actually, I just did."

"I was in the Kapsliga for eighteen years. Then *they* turned on me. I fought side by side with my brothers for over a decade—*they* made me a monster."

"Why do you feel like you're a monster? I wish you didn't view vampires the way you do. You're growing on me"—*I'm infatuated with you*—"and I think your brothers are honorable men. The fact that you are all vampires is incidental."

"*Incidental*. My beliefs boiled down to one word." He fingered the edges of a card. "If you saw me in the midst of bloodlust, you'd think me a monster. Now deal. I'm keen to get to my questions."

She dealt. "Ha! I win. Why are your three brothers . . . different from you? Why did they never drink from the vein?"

"Sebastian prevented himself by becoming a hermit, staying away from any temptation. The oldest two joined an order, an army called the Forbearers. Their first law is never to take blood straight from the flesh. Though now I've heard they're allowed to drink from their immortal Brides."

"The Forbearers are King Kristoff's army, *n'est-ce pas?*" When he nodded, she said, "Why didn't you just join up with your brothers?"

"Kristoff's a bloody Russian!" he snapped, his broad shoulders tensing. "I fought those bastards for over a decade, in near daily battles, and then I was *killed* by Russian steel. I wake up, and I've got one's blood running in my veins, my brothers pledging *my* god-damned eternal fealty to him—a Russian *and* a vampire. There could be no combination I despised more."

"If these Forbearers fight tirelessly against evil vampires—"

"Kristoff has turned thousands of humans. The Lore balances itself, but not when he's creating vampires like that." Visibly making an attempt to calm himself, he said, "Deal."

"And the tide of twenty-one is turning," she said when she got *vingt-et-un*. "Tell me about your family."

He impatiently said, "My parents were a love match. My mother died giving birth to the last of four much younger sisters. My father was considerably older and never recovered from the loss."

"Three brothers and four sisters? You had seven siblings? I always wished for even one brother or sister."

"My sisters didn't live long—they died of the sickness. The oldest was only thirteen."

"I'm sorry, Conrad."

"I wasn't as close to them as I could have been. As I *should* have been. I'd already been fighting for the Kapsliga for years by the time the first one was born. They were closest to Sebastian."

"Why were you the son who was chosen for the Kapsliga?"

"Nikolai was the heir, Sebastian the scholar. Murdoch was the lover. As I had no pronounced interest, I became the killer."

"Why wouldn't you think of yourself as a *protector*?

You saved human life. You protected them from horrible fates."

"And then later I meted out horrible fates. Now deal."

"*Merde,*" she muttered again when she lost by one. "*Posez votre question.*"

"You actually took off your clothes in front of crowds of strange men?"

"Yes, I did. My mother had just died unexpectedly. My choices were to dance in the club at night and continue my ballet during the day, or go to the paper factory to work for the rest of my life." She'd had no marriage proposals in sight then. After all, she'd only been in her midteens.

He narrowed his eyes. "You said your mother died when you were sixteen."

"So?"

His lips parted, exposing those fangs that were somehow becoming very attractive to her. "But *sixteen?*"

"*Et alors.* I'm not going to apologize for it. Times were different then, and I actually enjoyed it for the most part. I kept that chapter of my life secret, not because I was ashamed, but because I knew people would have the same reaction as you—and do close your jaw, vampire."

"You weren't a virgin, were you?"

She blinked at him. "*Non, je suis Capricorne.*"

Ignoring her comment, he said, "And you weren't married?" When she shook her head, he gave her a look that said, *Ah-ha, one of those women.*

"Yes, Conrad, I am one of *those* women." She smiled as she dealt. "And I'm not ashamed about that part of my life either."

He hurried through the hand and won again. But when he hesitated with his question, she knew he was about to ask how many men she'd known—and Néomi didn't think he'd like the answer. . . .

17

"How many men had you been with?" he finally asked.

"Do you really want to know?"

Conrad nodded, though he wasn't entirely sure. He was still grinding his teeth over her stripping off her clothes for crowds of men in the twenties.

"Less than a score and more than a single," she answered.

"Truthfully and completely," he reminded her.

"Very well. I'd had four lovers b the time I was twenty-six."

"That many?" He scowled, bristling about the fact that four men had known her body and he hadn't.

"Alas, that few." Though I would have had a legion more if birth control had been more reliable." She was so open about this subject, even seeming proud of her experience.

At least she has some, he thought darkly. His own was nonexistent. And worse—Néomi knew it.

He'd been a young thirteen when he'd made the vow to the Kapsliga, long before he'd been able to understand exactly what it would mean to him.

Unfortunately, he had other men's memories of

sex. Not one among them was what he wanted to see, to experience—some made his skin crawl. He worked to block them out as soon as they arose. . . . "Is that why you broke it off with your fiancé? Because you didn't only want one lover?"

She shook her head. "I was tediously monogamous."

"Then why?"

"He hadn't done one thing specifically. But I always had a sense of disquiet about him. Regrettably, the only thing stronger than that was my need to have the very best. If there was another way to aim—except for the best, the most enviable—I didn't know of it. And Louis was the most eligible bachelor in the parish. He was extremely handsome, and the man had money—*oil* money."

A spike of some unfamiliar feeling hit his gut, settling there to burn. "So what happened with the *oil man?*"

"I knew I'd ignored my instincts about him for too long. And I'd realized that I didn't *have* to be married. Not to him, not to anyone. I was having too much fun on my own and doing just fine financially. So, after half a year of tempting him to marry me, I changed my mind. For Louis, that proved unforgivable."

"And how would a woman tempt a man to marry her?" Conrad asked, striving not to sound as intrigued as he was. He imagined her using her wiles on himself to get something, and the idea . . . *excited* him. He'd withhold whatever it was she wanted for as long as possible.

"I teased him. And then I didn't give him the milk for free."

Milk? "Ah. I see." At least she hadn't slept with the oil man.

"*Vingt-et-un.* I win," she said. "Now, tell me about the injury on your arm." When he hesitated, she added, "Any question whatsoever, truthfully and completely."

"Tarut, a Kapsliga demon, clawed me. It won't heal until he's dead." Conrad had been thinking that Tarut might be at that gathering. If Conrad could get free of these cuffs, he could go on the offensive and take the demon out.

"Why did he do that to you?" she asked.

"He thinks I should be dead—I disagree."

"How could he escape you? He must have been very strong."

"Tarut has a gang." Many demon species instinctively hunted in packs—Conrad would have to watch for them at the gathering as well. "Overall, demons are one of the strongest species in the Lore, and Tarut is older and powerful."

"How did you become an assassin?" she asked, the card game forgotten.

"I wanted the pay."

"Greed, Conrad?" she asked softly. "That doesn't seem like you."

"How would you know?" When she shrugged, he bit out, "I *needed* the pay. After the Kapsliga turned on me, I didn't know where to go or how to feed myself."

"Go on."

"They hunted me like a goddamned rabid wolf when I had no idea even how to survive as a vampire." Never had he been so weak, so bewildered. Half of his family had just died; the other half had become his enemies, and he was forever changed. "I was starving, and blood was everywhere I turned. Each night, I struggled not to drag a human down and feed."

"Then what happened?"

"Blood drawn from donors could be bought, but it was expensive. I stumbled upon a lucrative bounty for a shape-shifter, one that no one else would hunt."

"Why?"

"Because defeating a shapeshifter is a tricky thing. By the time you figure out how to contend with one form, they shift to another. I was exhausted from thirst, and the bastard roundly kicked my ass. Just when I was about to die, this new, overwhelming instinct took over." *His fangs had sunk into the shifter's neck and blood rushed before his eyes and slid down his throat. . . . Lost . . .*

"Conrad? Stay with me. Conrad!" When he finally faced her, she said, "You were talking about the instinct . . ."

"It was a vampire's instinct. It ruled me. I returned for the bounty with not only the shifter's head in a burlap bag but also his memories in my head. Suddenly I was in high demand."

She bit her bottom lip. "How many have you killed?"

"Countless. And then there were the targets I took out when I was human. I killed my first vampire when I was thirteen."

"So young? What was your life like as a human?"

"Most of it was horrifying, cold, and desperate. If the marauders didn't get you, the plague would. You didn't want to embrace a loved one who returned home because you didn't know if they'd brought death with them. We'd been rich—but there was no food or goods to buy."

"I'm sorry it was so hard for you and your family."

"That part's done with at least. What was yours like?"

"The opposite. For me, life was sensual, sultry, and passionate." Her eyes went dreamy. "I remember the throbbing heat of the French Quarter in summer. On every street, haunting music played. I frolicked in fountains and went *jazzmad*—which, incidentally, could be used as a successful legal defense in my time." She tilted her head at him, and her hair swayed over her pale shoulder. "I wonder what you would've thought about that time and place."

"It would have been alien to me. My culture worshipped the military and discipline."

"Mine worshipped jazz, hooch, and the relentless pursuit of pleasure. The warlord and the ballerina—as different as we can be."

"What did being a ballerina entail?"

"Performance after performance. Though I did like to play, when not on tour, I also trained six days a week without fail."

"I could tell. When I saw you dance."

"Ah, that's right. You witnessed it. The day before yesterday cracked up to be a bad day for Néomi, the lapdog."

He scowled but still asked, "Why are you so . . . patient with me? After the things I said?"

"Because I know you didn't mean them. And because I don't believe you're as bad as everyone thinks."

She had no idea. It would be best to end her flirting and playful looks of interest now. "Néomi, you have an idealized image of me in your mind. Let me make this plain for you. Less than two weeks ago, I killed a being, and I drank blood from his neck like a beast drinks from a gutter."

Wide-eyed, she said, "Well, that image certainly does dampen your attractiveness! But luckily you have a deep voice, which I like more than I should—so that neutralizes all that beast and gutter business."

He alternately liked and hated when she played as if she was attracted to him. "You make it sound so easy to dismiss."

"What's past is past, Conrad. Now you must learn from it and move on. If I'd had your mentality, I would always have been a burlesque dancer. I never would have aspired to being a ballerina, a profession that brought me great joy. Imagine all the things you're missing out on. Your Bride, a family, contentment. Unlike me, you can have a future—it's out there, just waiting for you to claim it. You have so much to look forward to, if you'd just stop looking back."

This was exactly what made her so dangerous to him—she *did* make him imagine all the things that could be. Such as having her as his Bride.

His dream . . . her doom. He shook his head hard. The curse couldn't touch her—even if it was real. She couldn't physically be harmed. But he still wanted to go on the offensive with Tarut. "Néomi, when my brothers come back, you have to get the key."

She gave him a mysterious shrug that said everything and nothing. "I'm tired, *mon grand*. I'm going to sleep."

He spoke French fluently. *Mon grand* meant *my big man*. A teasing term of affection.

"Where do you go?" When he'd searched the house for her, he'd seen that the master bedroom had a few spare pieces of furniture, but that wasn't where she went when she wasn't with him. She had to have a secret hiding place.

"Oh, here and there."

"Will you come back tomorrow?"

She sauntered over to him. "Honestly, vampire"— with a wave of her hand, she brushed his hair from his forehead—"if you stay charming like this, how will I ever be able to stay away?" With that, she disappeared.

But she was coming back. Because she *couldn't help herself*.

Suddenly Conrad found his lips curling.

18

And we'd been doing so well . . ." Néomi muttered, which only angered Conrad more.

Over the last three days Conrad's road to recovery hadn't been straight and even—more curving, filled with hairpin turns and many double-backs.

They were presently on a double-back.

"Néomi, make the vow that you'll get me the key!" He paced menacingly in front of the window seat she occupied. "My brothers will doubtless return tonight."

They were already a day overdue. "I've told you I don't want to talk about this." Giving him his freedom wasn't even an option for her. Murdoch had said that Conrad would relapse if released too soon, and she still feared he would attack his brothers if he went into a rage at the wrong time.

If her resolve wavered, she had only to remind herself that Conrad had spit blood at Nikolai's face less than two weeks ago. For centuries, his loyal brothers had searched for him—Néomi wasn't going to be the blunderheaded ghost who stupidly freed him just when he was improving.

Hiding the key from him was risky—she could predict the anger she was inviting, but she didn't want

Conrad to dwell on it, not when he was slowly but surely recovering. If he was aware that she had it, he would do nothing but browbeat her for it, obsessing over it.

She'd never lied to him, instead evading the subject, but she knew if he ever discovered she already had the means to his freedom hidden in a slipper in her studio he'd be murderous. . . .

He halted his pacing. "I know you see my brothers as heroes, but if I don't improve, they will kill me, Néomi."

She didn't believe that but knew she couldn't convince Conrad. "Do you think I would ever let you be harmed here?" Anyone who tried to kill her vampire would find himself tossed into the bayou *pour les alligators*.

"You don't understand what's at stake!" he snapped, raising his voice to just under yelling. "In case you didn't hear them, they're keen to 'put me out of my misery'!" A muscle in his jaw ticked—a portent that always signaled a rage was nearing.

Unfortunately, he still continued to have them. A male like him simply couldn't stand to be trapped. This situation was making him feel powerless on a continual basis, and he had difficulty moderating his aggression.

Sometimes he seemed like a powder keg about to go off. And yet she found an honesty, a purity about his fierceness. Louis had been all false faces and deception. Conrad's ferocity was raw and bare. You knew exactly what you were getting.

This didn't mean she would meekly accept it when he was hurtful. She'd once read an article about setting boundaries with the people in your life. If their behavior proved unacceptable to you, you didn't reward them with more attention. When Conrad grew unpleasant, she simply left—which had the lamentable outcome of angering him even more.

Eventually his temper would cool, and he'd find her at the folly or in the tangled garden. As he gazed at anything but her face, he'd hold out his hand and gruffly say something like "*Come*" or "*Do not stay away. . . .*"

"Damn it, Néomi! Why wouldn't you do this for me?"

When he punched her wall, she reached her limit. "I've asked you over and over not to damage my house, Conrad," she said in as calm a tone as she could manage. "My home might not look like much, but it's all I have. If you can't respect my wishes, then I don't want to be around you."

So he couldn't follow, she traced outside into the late-afternoon sun. Starting at the overgrown gardens. From there she floated along the buckling, overgrown path to the folly.

As she approached, she heard unseen creatures slipping beneath the water. They sensed her easily enough. Why couldn't others? Why did it have to be only Conrad *et les animaux* . . . ?

Anytime he tried to get control of his temper, he strode out here and paced. When she spied a worn path winding around the cypress knees along the bank, she felt another pang. *What am I going to do with him?*

He *was* trying so hard. And he had made progress. She'd seen him take a rag to his dirty boots, cleaning them as best as he could, like the soldier he'd once been. He showered every day, brushed his teeth, and shaved. Well, maybe he shaved every other day. But she liked the stubble. Every sunset, she battled her repugnance and brought him a mug of the blood left by the brothers, which Conrad drank only because it obviously cost her so much to serve it. Already his color was better, his muscles growing even bigger.

And as he improved, they talked more and more— two people who desperately needed to. Often they'd hit a rhythm, a bandying back and forth, as if their thoughts were interlocking pieces. She'd told him, "When we talk, I like how our words ebb and flow. There doesn't seem to be a need to remark on each comment, no need to clarify—it's as if we both understand that we understand each other. It's like dancing."

"Or sex?"

She'd smiled. "Only if it's great."

He'd given her a confident nod. "Then we would have great sex."

Lord, we would. . . .

They seemed to fit in every way. Yes, he was half-mad, but as a Prohibition-era ghost with a penchant for stealing condoms, moon pies, and bras, she wasn't exactly in touch with reality herself.

Conrad could see her; her presence seemed to be the only thing that calmed his mind. He was healing, and she was happier than she'd been in eighty years. Two broken souls together in this broken place had found a kind of contentment.

Maybe his being here wasn't the accident she'd thought it. She couldn't believe this was all random.

Maybe he was supposed to save her from this cursed afterlife?

And maybe she hadn't learned her lessons from Marguerite L'Are. If anyone was going to save Néomi, it'd be herself. . . .

At dusk, Conrad came to her.

Somehow looking both proud and contrite, he said, "I won't damage your house anymore."

"*Merci d'avance*."

He held out his hand. "I want you to come inside with me."

"No, Conrad, not tonight," she said, making him grind his teeth.

She knew her refusal frustrated him not only because he wanted to be near her. She believed he had a deep-seated need to *protect* her, as if she might actually need him to.

As if he felt that it was his right to.

Whenever he looked at her now, his eyes would darken in color and were becoming more and more possessive. . . .

"I might have damaged things, but I've repaired parts as well," he pointed out.

"*C'est vrai*." After finding some tools in the old shed by the drive, he'd fortified the manor, patching up or covering window openings and reattaching the front door he'd leveled.

Then, seeming to obey some undeniable instinct to keep her warm and safe, he'd set about rendering the master suite livable for her. He'd transferred the new mattress to the suite's bedstead, adding any available furniture to the area. In the attic, he'd unearthed an antique dresser and a chair that even she hadn't known were up there.

Once he'd miraculously cleared the chimney flue and was able to make a fire though he didn't seem to be cold and she certainly wasn't—he'd informed her that she would sleep with him in that room from now on.

His tone had reminded her that he'd been born an aristocrat and had become a warlord in the seventeenth century. Conrad Wroth was well used to having his will obeyed.

He'd seemed perplexed when she'd just laughed and deemed his domineering ways *très charmant*, and then he'd been angered when she'd reminded him that she already had a place to stay.

The fact that she had a hideaway she adjourned to every day annoyed him to no end . . .

"So you will come?"

When she made no move to, she could tell how badly he itched to force her inside. If she'd been corporeal, she had no doubt she'd be to force her inside. If she'd been corporeal, she had no doubt she'd be bouncing along over his shoulder as he hauled her away.

This mountain of a man was learning that his considerable might—which he'd clearly relied on for *everything*—was futile with her.

For once, her incorporeality was proving to be an advantage.

If he desired to be with her, then he either had to persuade her to come back or prevent her from leaving in the first place.

"I said not tonight." Willingly separating from him was just as miserable for Néomi. But she couldn't let him get accustomed to taking his anger out on her house—or her.

"Do as you will," he said in a seething tone, leaving her. But not before she spied that muscle tick in his jaw.

Late in the night, she'd just been dozing off in the studio when she heard his yell.

Before Néomi had even decided to, she'd traced to him. The second she arrived, he shot up in bed with another yell at the top of his lungs, so loud it rattled the windows.

When she hastened beside him, he swung his legs over to sit on the side of the bed.

"Conrad, it's all right. It was just a dream."

He held his head with his bound hands, elbows to his knees as he rocked. "My head . . . too full." He was squeezing it so hard, she feared he would crack his skull.

"Shh, shh, *mon coeur*." She gave a telekinetic stroke down his back. "It's over."

"I don't . . . I don't want to be like this anymore!" His tone was anguished.

"You're getting so much better," she murmured. "Soon you won't have these nightmares."

He narrowed his gaze at her, as if just noticing she was there. "You were . . . murdered—you remind me of the things I've done, of consequences," he choked out. "And you show me what I could have had . . . if I'd been . . . different." He grasped his head again and muttered, "You're what's wrong with my past. What has to be missing from my future."

She knew he would remember little to none of these words—but she would. "Conrad, your future's not settled. You can have good things in your life again."

"You're the perfect punishment for me."

"Oh." Stunned, she rose to leave.

He reached out to stay her. When he closed his big fist around air, he turned and struck the headboard with frustration. Eyes vacant, burning red, he rasped, "Did any man ever want his penance so much?"

She said nothing, just settled back beside him to stroke his hair from his forehead. She hated that he was in so much pain and wished she could draw it from him. He'd once been a hero, his life given over to something greater, but now he suffered.

Néomi had known that he was a broken man who needed saving. Over the last three days, she'd become convinced that he *deserved* saving.

Right at that moment, she realized it might just fall to her.

But how could she help him? She sighed, coaxing him to lie back once more. Néomi had been a dancer, raised in a demimonde concerned with little more than revelry and drinking. What did she know about bringing vampires back from the brink?

She'd simply have to use the tools she had at her disposal. And really, the medicinal values of Scotch and laughter were underrated.

19

"Who's your best friend, *mon grand?*" she cooed, levitating two bottles. "Who does Conrad love?"

He was kneeling at the fireplace, finishing his fire. Outside the night was blustery, but inside it would be comfortable. "What have you got?" He stood, brushing his hands off on his pants, then sat on one of the chairs in front of the hearth.

"A gift for you."

"A . . . *gift?*" Even he knew his tone sounded perplexed.

"*Oui,* also known as a *present.* Or as the French say, *un présent.*"

He accepted the bottles from her, dusting off the label of one. His jaw slackened. "This is Glen Garioch, nineteen twenty-five!" He hesitated even to read the other label. "My God," he breathed. "Macallan, 'twenty-four. Néomi, this is about a hundred thousand dollars' worth of whiskey. I can't drink this—you could sell it. Or have someone sell it for you."

"What would I do with money? I have plenty in my safe. Besides, I'd get much more pleasure out of seeing you drink it." She hovered just behind him, peering over his shoulder, which put her soft words right at his ear. "And then you must describe it to me, very slowly, in that deep, rumbly voice of yours. Is it smoky or earthy like peat? How does it unfold on your tongue? How long does it take for the heat to stroke through you inside?"

She could read the phone book and make it sound erotic. "You're sure?"

"Cheers!" She gave him an odd little smile as she said, "Á votre santé." To your health.

"Then I want to drink this and watch you dance."

She looked delighted with him; he'd never get enough of that look. "I want to dance and watch my vampire drink."

My vampire . . . Damn, he liked it when she called him that. He knew it was flirting at best, but he couldn't stem the flush of pleasure.

He opened the Macallan, letting it breathe. The scent of it hit him, and his lips curled. This would not be whiskey that he would *use*, as he had in the past. For one thing, he didn't need it to dull his rage as much as he had before. More importantly, a bottle like this *demanded* to be savored—

"I'll be back," she said, then vanished.

He tensed, anxious whenever she left, but she returned in minutes, bearing a windup gramophone over one hand and a crystal tumbler over the other. She handed him the glass, then positioned the gramophone on the floor. Once she'd wound it and set the record needle in place, scratchy music began to play, a slow jazz ballad.

Making her voice like an announcer's, she said, "And now! For the matinee! The supremely talented Miss Laress will perform for a lucky audience! Of one!"

She smiled coyly. "I've remembered an old dance I used to do when I was younger. I think you'll like it. . . ."

As his rare whiskey breathed, Conrad leaned back in the chair in front of the fire, watching the most beautiful female he'd ever seen dance solely for him.

Though Néomi wasn't blushing with color, she was still lovely to him—especially when she moved. *Hypnotic.* This dance was so effortless for her, she would turn to him in the middle of pirouettes or standing splits to smile or wink at him.

Néomi lived in the moment, laughed easily, flirted constantly. Her natural state was happiness, which both mystified and attracted him. Over his long life, that state had continually eluded him. But she had a theory why: "People think happiness will simply fall into their laps. You have to aspire to it. And sometimes you have to seize it when it's kicking and screaming."

Néomi had been murdered, possessed no body, and was still *seizing* all the pleasure she could. Conrad respected that.

Now she danced as if she knew by instinct precisely how to attract him alone. How to be irresistible to him. So why try to resist? Why struggle against his attraction?

Because even if she returned his feelings, he would only end up disappointing her.

He was improving here, but he wasn't *right* in the mind by any means, still suffering from occasional rages and grueling nightmares. How would he do once freed into the real world? Would he be able to keep from drinking his foes when he was addicted to harvesting their power?

For centuries his adversaries had been determined to discover anything he cared for. But then, that was an unspoken rule in the Lore. Immortals could be blasé about death after living so long—the best bargaining chip was revenge against family or loved ones. Yet for all those years he'd had no liabilities.

Conrad had acquired his first. Was running headlong to her.

He shook his head. No, his enemies couldn't hurt Néomi, could never abduct or wound her. Maybe that was part of the reason he'd found such an unusual feeling of ease with her—because he knew he couldn't harm her either. Even when he got free, he wouldn't be able to accidentally injure her if he lost control.

But how to get free? Not one of his brothers had returned since that day he tried to convince them of Néomi's existence—the day they'd left for Mount Oblak, the Forbearer Castle.

Conrad knew that meant one of two things had happened.

Kristoff had possibly discovered that they were keeping Conrad alive. The second law of the Forbearer order? *Kill the Fallen without measure.* Just by keeping Conrad alive, they'd been committing treason. Kristoff had likely imprisoned them at Mount Oblak, vowing to free them as soon as they gave up Conrad's location.

Which they would never do. For all their faults, they were as loyal as men came.

The other possibility? They'd fallen in battle. And Conrad didn't know how he felt about that. Over the last week, he'd become keenly aware that if not for his brothers, he would never have known Néomi.

Now that he was somewhat more rational, able to quell the worst of his rage, the thought of losing all three of them left him unaccountably troubled.

Revealing details of his past to her had forced his mind back to better times. He'd recalled how Nikolai had bailed him out of scrape after scrape. He'd thought back to the day the four brothers had made the fateful decision to take control of their country's defense: *No one else is getting the job done*. Conrad remembered being proud because not one of them had hesitated.

If his brothers lived, he would not be able to destroy them as planned. He didn't want to have anything to do with them, but he couldn't kill them. . . .

"Don't you want to try the whiskey?" she asked, pausing her dance.

"What? Yes." He'd planned to let it breathe a minute for every year of its age. But she looked so expectant. He supposed more than half an hour would be sufficient, and the taste would only grow increasingly complex with time. He poured a dram, swirling it in the tumbler, letting it coat the glass.

He took his first sip, just preventing his eyes from sliding closed in pleasure. "My God, that's what it should always be like." The taste was bracing yet smooth, the elements distinct but complementary.

"Is it better than what you usually drink?"

"Other whiskey or blood?" he asked.

"Either one."

"It shames other whiskey—and it's better than the blood I've been drinking."

Conrad instinctively knew that it wouldn't compare to hers.

"*Bien,*" she said, resuming her steps.

As his gaze followed her, he wondered what would it be like to pierce her pale skin with his fangs. If she were a flesh and blood woman, what would it be like to cup her breasts as he sucked her neck?

He had never touched a woman's breasts. He often tried to imagine what Néomi's would feel like from what he'd seen of them. *They'd be soft against his rough palms, giving to his grasp. . . .*

He'd always yearned for a woman of his own. He'd dreamed of not letting her leave the bed for days as he explored her, discovering how to pleasure her. He'd wanted to learn how to make his woman pine for him if he had to leave and cry his name as he entered her.

Cry his name in a sultry voice tinged with French.

Suddenly fantasies ran riot in his mind, of kneading her ass at the same time he suckled her nipples. Of petting her pale little body for hours until she came again and again for him—

"You look content, *mon trésor.*"

He coughed into his fist. "I have to say, I've been in worse jails." And having such a desirable cellmate didn't hurt either. Though the need to pursue Tarut grew more pressing with each hour, and a promising hunting ground awaited, he also found himself on edge from the idea of leaving her here for even a short time.

Suddenly, she twirled around and brushed a sizzling kiss on his cheek. His eyes narrowed suspiciously at her, but she merely laughed. "It's called—say it with me—*a-fec-shun.*"

He'd just assumed she flirted because that was her nature. Yet could she . . . could she truly be *interested* in him? Even be attracted to him—with his red eyes and scars? Maybe she wanted more, as he did.

But then there was no one else to attract her. He had no competitors here.

"Why would you show me affection?"

She answered, "Because I . . . feel it?"

"Why?"

With a laugh, she asked, "Why, why, why? Must you question everything good?"

"Yes, when it's illogical. You know nothing about me—"

"I know more about you than any other woman does, *n'est-ce pas*? You don't have to muster up the nerve to divulge your secrets to me, while secretly hoping I don't run away screaming. I know them all. I'm still here." Eyes bright, lips curling, she said, "And I know that you're my favorite man. *Dans le monde entier*."

"Because I'm the only one in the entire world who can see and hear you." She gave him that mysterious shrug. He knew she was likely playing, the flirtations meaningless. But damn it, her words still got to him. It was becoming easier to pretend the sentiment was real.

"You don't know what to do with affection, do you?"

"I . . . have no idea," he admitted. "I don't know my way around this. It makes me feel weak. You make me feel that way sometimes."

"How a man as powerful as you could feel weak, I'll never know. This disturbs me. What would you suggest I change so you don't feel that way?"

He scrubbed a hand over his face, struggling to convey what he was thinking. "You make me uneasy at times because you and everything you do are so unfamiliar to me."

"Like what?"

"Your laughter. It's as if you spend every second of the day merely awaiting a time to be able to laugh or tease."

"I sound *très terrible*. How do you stand being near me? It must be because of your saintlike patience and calm?" She topped off his glass.

20

Once she'd finished dancing, Néomi floated to the chair beside Conrad's.

The thoughtful vampire had pulled up two of them in front of the fire. He continued to treat her like a woman instead of a ghost. He opened doors for her, and though she could never take it, he often held out his hand for her.

Little things like this increased his already devastating attractiveness.

"Conrad, what was it like in the Kapsliga?"

"Regimented," he answered shortly, no doubt predicting where she was headed with this.

"Was it terribly difficult to abstain?" She'd been prying to uncover more about this part of his life. She was probably as tenacious at this as he was about the key. Or as he *had* been.

No longer did he ask her to retrieve it—because his brothers had *stopped coming*.

She suspected Conrad felt let down that they still hadn't returned. It must prey on him, wondering what had happened to them. Though he'd never admit it.

"Why are you so curious about this?" He swigged

his whiskey. Though she might've expected him to take from the bottle, he drank it neat from the glass, and slowly.

"Because I want to know more about you."

"Then why not ask me about the Great War, about our greatest victory or shrewdest defense—"

"Because I am also *a female?*"

"I can't argue that." He lifted his glass to her. "Ask what you will."

She made like she was sitting. "Did you abstain only because of your vow?"

"You heard my brother—Wroths keep their vows. That would've been enough. But there wasn't much temptation anyway. Healthy women near the front line were scarce. Especially any who weren't already obsessed with Murdoch." He contemplated the whiskey in his glass. "And the end was in sight. Service in the Kapsliga is from the age of thirteen to thirty seven. I only had a few more years left."

"I'll bet you were counting down the days."

"When there were lulls in the war, I did." His brows drew together. "But then I died."

"There was never a girl that struck your fancy? You never fell in love?"

"There wasn't any time even to contemplate emotions like that. I fought in battles all day and then warred with vampires each night. Survival was foremost on everyone's minds." He took a drink, his gaze turning distant for long moments. Was he reliving those horrors even now? Just when she was about to prompt him back to the conversation, he blinked and asked, "What about you? Did you love the oil man?"

"Not at all." And he hadn't loved her. That night when Louis had wielded his blade, Néomi had understood him better than she ever had. Louis had been frenzied not because he'd needed to be with her but because he'd wanted to punish her. No matter what sentiments he'd spouted over her body, he'd murdered her out of spite.

"The men you were with—did you love any of them?"

"I had great affection for them. But no abiding love for them."

"Why couldn't they win you?" He leaned forward, as if her answer was very significant to him.

"Oh, they didn't do anything wrong. I just never found my match."

"Did they . . . satisfy you?"

If they hadn't in the beginning, they had eventually. "I made sure of it. I wasn't shy about what I expected or needed from a man." He raised his brows. She could tell he was eager to question her about her words, but she wanted to refocus on him. "Conrad, how did you handle the physical need?" When his face flushed, she said, "Oh, I see."

"A lot," he admitted in a husky voice.

"Were you terribly curious about what it would feel like?"

He hesitated, then met her gaze. "Still am."

She exhaled a slow breath, for once thinking she might be in over her head with a man.

Néomi had thought she could easily handle Conrad, because men had never given her fits before. And she was experienced while he wasn't.

But Conrad Wroth wasn't an average man. He wasn't even a *man*, really. He was an immortal male who'd never had a female—when he'd clearly wanted to. She sensed a volatile passion inside him, just waiting for release.

How she wished she could be the woman who tapped into it! She'd never lamented the lack of a body as much as she did right now.

"Did you never touch a woman intimately? Never even . . . kissed a single time?"

His shoulders tensed. "That's enough questions. I've told you I don't want to discuss this subject with you."

He *hadn't*. "Why not talk about this?" *Mon Dieu, no woman has ever even given him her lips.* "Does the subject embarrass you?"

"Should it not?" He glanced away and grated, "Would any man want a beautiful woman to know this about himself?"

"If I didn't know better, I'd say comments like that are your way of flirting with me."

He scowled. "My way. As opposed to the regular way a man with more experience would go about it? I think you seek to keep me on edge about this. You like that I'm never able to settle in with you."

"Conrad, that's ridiculous."

"Is it?"

"*Mais oui.* I'll say this plain. If you were able and I were able, I would be seducing you, right at this very moment."

His fists clenched, and his lips parted, exposing white teeth and those sexy fangs. "You love to tease me, don't you?" He rose and strode to the window, glancing out into the tumultuous night. "You shouldn't say things you don't mean."

"I never do." This male was a sexually untutored, six-and-a-half-foot-tall, gorgeous immortal. And she was desperate to have him. There was nothing but truth to that.

"Then you're attracted to me because I'm all that's here."

"That's not so." She rose, crossing to him.

"Isn't it? Then am I similar to the men you used to bed?"

"Not in the least."

"Then *why* would you want to seduce me?"

She hadn't expected that question. "It's because I've never been with a man like you that I desire you."

His scowl deepened. "A red-eyed vampire?"

"A strong, virile male with large muscles I long to sink my fingers into."

He turned to set his glass on the windowsill, but she saw him swallow. Then he faced her, advancing, looming over her. As she'd done in the shower, she retreated until she reached the wall.

Raising his bound hands over her head, he again surrounded her with his body. "What if I wanted to do the seducing?"

He would. He was so deliciously domineering. "Why are you always caging me in?"

"Maybe I wouldn't, if you weren't always disappearing. You're as tangible as air, and it's so damned frustrating, *koeri.*"

"What does that mean?"

"It means *lure*."

She blinked up at him. "Your endearment for me is a synonym for *bait*?"

"You're luring me from madness." Lowering his voice, he said, "The only thing that could possibly tempt me from it."

She nibbled her bottom lip. "Would you follow me anywhere?"

"Into the sun." Conrad was all intensity. These weren't practiced sentiments—these were words he couldn't contain. "You said you'd teach me how to seduce my Bride. I want my first lesson."

She couldn't think. "Lesson?" He was too attractive for his own good. "Oh, yes. Well, if you had your female in a position like this, you could compliment her."

Staring down at her, he said, "So I could tell her that her eyes are striking? That I think about their color all the time?"

"She'd really, *really* like that. And then you could cup her face, and maybe brush her bottom lip with your thumb."

The muscles in his arms bulged, and she knew he was clenching his fists above her head, wanting to touch her. "And how would I know if she was interested in me?"

"She'd probably wrap her arms around your neck to hold you close," Néomi said, but she kept her arms to her sides, her own hands in fists. She yearned to twine her fingers in the too-long hair at his nape, ached to touch him in any way. But she couldn't and never would be able to.

I can never feel those muscles flex as he works my

body over the edge. Can never see that exact moment when any control he has deserts him and he's helpless to his own lust.

Néomi would never be able to enjoy him—she selfishly didn't want any other woman enjoying him either.

"And then what should I do?" His voice seemed whiskey-roughened and smoothed at the same time.

She felt as intoxicated as if she'd drunk it with him. "You'd meet her gaze, then lean in to brush your lips against hers."

"Brush my lips?" He was getting as caught up as she was, his natural reserve faltering. And she loved it. "What if I wanted to do something harder?"

Harder? Yes! She stopped herself. "But most females would want a measured seduction. You'd have to wait, to prolong it. But when your lady gasped, then you could take her mouth more forcefully."

"How?"

"Slowly slip your tongue inside, and tease it against mine—hers, rather." She shook her head. "Against hers."

He was rubbing his tongue over his fang, making her want to melt. "Tease?"

"Y-you can drive a woman wild from just a kiss if you do it right. Think, um, slow build."

He moved in even closer, until they were sparking electricity between them. "When would I get to touch her?"

As she stared up at his eyes, she saw them not as blood red, but as the red of flames. "If she moans, you could touch her neck. Maybe run the backs of your fingers from her ear down past her collarbone, then lower to the beginning swell of her breast. And if she likes that a lot, you might try following the same path with your lips."

"And then?" he rasped.

"What does your instinct tell you?"

"My instinct tells me"—his consuming gaze flickered over her ear, then dipped to her collarbone and lower to the swell of her breast—"to keep going down. To do whatever I have to in order to get my lips on your breasts. *Her* breasts."

Imagining that had Néomi subtly arching her back to press her chest up. "How would you kiss them?"

"I'd kiss all around her nipples, dragging my lips over her skin. Would she like that?"

"She'd probably be cradling the back of your head, moaning."

"Then I'd close my lips over one of your nipples—"

"You mean *her*, your Bride's."

He shook his head slowly. "When I think about kissing anyone, I imagine you. Only you. I can't pretend that this isn't so."

"That pleases me, Conrad. Because I don't want you kissing another woman," she murmured.

"Why?"

"I'd be jealous, wanting to scratch her eyes out for kissing my vampire." He frowned and opened his mouth, but she cut him off. "*Je suis sérieuse.* Now tell me what you'd do to me next."

After seeming to determine whether she was telling the truth, he said, "I'd take one of your nipples between my lips, sucking it in. . . ."

"Hard?" She gasped the word.

"Do you like that?" When she nodded, he didn't stifle his groan. "Then I would suckle it hard, licking you with my tongue at the same time."

Her eyelids threatened to slide shut. He was so sexy and manly. All intensity. How could she ever have been attracted to soft, docile businessmen with their *yes, darling* mentality? "I've fantasized about how your lips would feel on them."

A short, rough sound erupted from him. "I try to imagine what your breasts would feel like from what you'd shown me."

"Do you wish you could touch them, too?"

"God, yes," he quickly answered, then flushed.

"Do you think about them a lot?"

He briefly inclined his forehead near hers. "Some minutes less than others."

She gave a throaty chuckle, and he seemed surprised that he'd amused her.

"What would you be doing while I kissed them?" he asked.

"My hands would be rubbing all along your back."

Her eyes fluttered closed when he drew his hands down to reach for her. His palms were so big, fully covering the outline of her breasts.

She moaned softly when she felt tiny electrical shocks over every inch of them. "I'd sigh from the way your muscles worked beneath my hands. Then I'd clutch your hips to signal that I wanted more of you." He raised his brows at that, and she murmured, "I'd be getting desperate for you by this point."

"So you wouldn't stop me if I"—he swallowed and

his voice dropped an octave lower—"if I tried easing my hand up your dress?"

"Stop you? I'd place your hand on my panties."

He gave another groan. "I'd hook my finger under that black lace and pull them aside." He'd clearly been thinking about more than just what her breasts would feel like.

"Conrad, I'd be wet for you."

The deep rumble of his voice had turned to a husky rasp. "I'd be so fucking hard for you."

"Would you want to bite me?"

"*Yes,*" he hissed. "Would you let me?"

If he needed, she would give. "I'd deny you nothing."

"Then I'd take your neck and your breasts. I'd bite your white thighs right above your stockings."

Intense male. She stifled a whimper. "We're doing it again, exchanging comments, bandying."

"Like dancing."

She shook her head and whispered, "Like sex."

He stared down into her eyes, making her feel like she was drowning in fire. "Néomi, you make me want to be blooded. But only by *you.*"

21

This was Conrad's second sexual encounter, if he counted the time in the shower with her.

The female didn't have a body that he could feel, he couldn't get erect, and yet it was *powerful*. If they were this way now, he couldn't imagine what it would have been like if they'd met when they'd both been truly alive.

Of course, he'd known there was pleasure to be had. But he'd never suspected the rush, the savage thrill of discovering that a woman wanted him sexually. He'd never known the confidence that if he moved to take a female, she would be wet for him and clutching his hips for more.

She leaned up and brushed her cheek against his. He felt the same electricity but had no perception of her skin. He tried to imagine how soft her flesh would be. "I want to feel you, Néomi. I want to be inside you."

She closed her eyes and rubbed her lips near his. "My God, I wish I could be flesh and blood for you."

He groaned at the yearning in her tone. Their situation frustrated him to no end. He wanted her more than he had any other woman—he was convinced that she would have blooded him when she'd still been alive. And he truly believed she would receive him.

But I can't take her. . . .

With a bitter curse, Conrad dropped his arms through her, turning away. He prowled the room, pausing only to punch the wall with frustration—

He just stopped himself an inch from the crumbling plaster. He shot a glance at her, and she looked like he'd hung the moon. Damn, he *could* get used to looks like that.

Would she think him ridiculous if he asked her for more? They'd only known each other for a short amount of time. She was experienced and he . . . wasn't. To hell with it—he had to know. "Would you want to be with me? If you could? For more than sex."

She gave him a sad smile. "You have a destined Bride out there awaiting you."

"Néomi, you might be . . . mine."

At his words, her heart skipped, but she forced herself to ask, "Then why haven't you been blooded? Your heart hasn't started beating, and you still take no breaths. You don't . . . react to me in a physical way."

"I think my vampire instinct doesn't recognize you as my Bride because you're not technically alive," he said. "I need to know if you're merely playing at this, with me, because I'm here and you can."

"I am *not* playing with you. But Conrad, even if we had no physical limitations, I don't know that we could make this work between us. We're too different."

"How the hell are we too different?"

"All I've ever wanted is life. I covet it so much I

feel like I'll scream. But you . . . destroy it. And you're so *cavalier* about it."

"I kill. It's what I'm best at."

"If it was in self-defense or for a cause you believed in, then I could understand. But to extinguish life for money? I could never accept that."

"What if I . . . stopped? What if I told you that when I'm near you, I want to be a better man? Does that count for nothing?"

"It counts for everything!" She raised her hand to her forehead. "This is a moot point anyway. Unless you know of a way to resurrect ghosts . . . ?"

"No, I don't. But that doesn't mean there isn't a way. I'd search for centuries if I had to."

Centuries. Hundreds of years more of sliver moons and monthly torture.

"And understand this, Néomi—I'll do it whether you want more with me or not. So don't let that affect your answer."

"Conrad, do you really mean that?" Words bubbled up—*I need to be with you . . . I want us to try . . .*

He opened his mouth to answer, then stilled. "Someone's outside." Crossing to the window, he cracked open the drape. And scowled. "Excellent. My sisters-in-law are dropping by."

Néomi sidled up to him to peek out. Two petite women were hurrying out from a sports car into the stormy night. "Those are Valkyrie? They're stunning. Is that what Lore women look like?"

"Some. The redhead is Myst the Coveted. She is Nikolai's. Kaderin the Coldhearted is Sebastian's blonde."

Néomi had heard so much about those two that she felt as if she knew them—

"I'd planned to kill them, too." When Néomi glared up at him, he raised his chained hands. "Past tense. See? Already I'm improving."

Lips thinned, she studied his expression. He seemed earnest.

The Valkyrie began arguing in the muddy drive, drawing Néomi's attention back to them. Myst seemed intent on keeping Kaderin from the manor. When the clash turned physical, Néomi went wide-eyed. *I don't know them at all.* "They're *punching* each other," she said in disbelief. "I figured they were fierce since Kaderin is an assassin, but to hit each other?"

Conrad shrugged. "Nature of the beast, I'm afraid. They like to fight."

"I won't let you do this!" Myst struck out with a jab that connected with Kaderin's mouth.

Kaderin swiped her sleeve over her bleeding lip. "Just like that first Talisman's Hie—still sucker-punching me!"

"I'll do worse. If you turn Conrad over to Kristoff, deep down the brothers will never forgive us. If they wanted him given up, they would've done it themselves!"

With a shove, Kaderin said, "I don't know about you, but I want my husband back!"

Kristoff had imprisoned them? And wouldn't free them until he had Conrad? Néomi glanced at him. His expression was inscrutable as he said, "And that answers the question of what has happened to my brothers."

"I want mine as well!" Myst said, returning the shove. "But this isn't the way. For ages, Nikolai has searched for Conrad. All that worry, all that effort, for *nothing?*"

Apparently, Nikolai was still putting forth the effort—he hadn't turned Conrad over.

"Wait a second." Myst narrowed her gaze. "What in the hell are we doing? We're *Valkyrie*—we take what we want."

"What do you mean?" Kaderin asked.

"Kristoff won't let our men go? Then Kristoff needs to be taught a lesson. I say we capture the whole bloody castle."

There was a dangerous light to Kaderin's eyes. "*Fucking A.*"

"Just in our coven alone, Regin, Cara, and Annika would spoil for a chance to war with vampires, any vampires. They wouldn't care that they'd actually be helping a few. And I know the inside of Mount Oblak like the back of my hand."

Kaderin's lips curled into a threatening grin. "More fangs for my collection."

Then they were gone as swiftly as they'd arrived.

"Go get them, girls," Conrad muttered.

"Those small women couldn't really start a war?"

"They might be small, but either one of them could lift a train." His tone absent, he said, "Kristoff's sitting across the world—with no idea that hell has just been unleashed against him."

22

When one is insane, it's best to simplify things.

To get by in life, Conrad had organized his existence into a system of rewards and obstacles to rewards. He'd identified the reward he wanted: Néomi in the flesh, his to possess.

The obstacles: his captivity, her lack of a body, and Tarut's possible curse.

Essentially, Conrad had a list of things to do, a short list. *Get free, execute Tarut. Figure out how to resurrect Néomi.*

The last wasn't *im*possible. Conrad just had to find and coerce the right sorcerer to do it. He knew that there were only so many in the entire world and all other dimensions who *could* resurrect beings. And even fewer who *would*.

As for his captivity—the bottom line was that his brothers were not coming back, or at least, not soon. Not until after a war. If they got out alive.

Could the Valkyrie take Mount Oblak? Certainly possible. But it would take time to prepare.

Time he didn't have. His blood supply wasn't infinite, and the threat of Tarut weighed on him.

Tonight Conrad would get started on his list.

When he'd awakened this evening, Néomi had brought him a cup of blood, then set off on the paper quest. *Good.* He wanted her away. Collecting a bath towel, he started down the stairs.

One way or another, Conrad was going to remove the chains. He couldn't break them, so that left him with one other option.

He'd found a woodcutter's ax in the old toolshed. A cutting stump sat behind it.

If he was drinking heavily of blood, he could regenerate a hand in three to four days. He'd have to do them one at a time of course, so regenerating would take at least six days. Which meant he would miss the gathering, a promising hunting ground. Killing tended to get complicated without hands—

Suddenly, he heard . . . *a phone ringing?* Frowning, he hastened after the faint sound, coming upon a small sitting room downstairs, well off to the side of the house.

The ringing seemed to come from inside the wall. Tossing the towel over his shoulder, he raised his bound hands to slap his palms against the wall—it sounded hollow. His lips curled. *A moving panel.* He'd seen them in older houses before.

After determining the edges, he scanned it for a latch. Maybe it was in the wainscoting? He felt along the dingy white wood. *Got it.* When he pressed it, a faint click sounded.

He shoved the panel open and found newspapers were stacked behind it, but then she wouldn't have to enter through an opened door.

Inside, he narrowed his eyes. The room was a

studio—her dance studio, with attached barres and mirror-covered walls. *So this is here-and-there, her secret place.*

The space was overtly feminine, decorated with faded pinks and reds, silks and crumbling lace. But the mirrors were all broken, with strike patterns as if someone had taken a fist to them—or a shot of telekinesis.

Against a far wall was a small cot, padded with blankets that would never warm her. An unused pair of ballet slippers was tossed casually atop them. Beside a safe on the floor, he spied a sizable pile of pebbles and stockpiled cases of liquor.

On a table, he found masses of odds and ends displayed like treasures. Among the offerings were Sebastian's money clip, Nikolai's now quiet cell phone, and the hair comb from Murdoch's pocket. Néomi had probably treasured the comb because she found it *pretty.*

She's going to have a thousand of them.

He'd stumbled upon a little ghost's nest, filled with trinkets stolen from the living to connect her to them. Feeling dazed, he sank onto the cot. *This is everything she has. And Elancourt is the entire world to her.*

Yet you threatened to burn it down.

He tried to imagine being trapped alone here, if their situations were reversed. Yes, he was trapped as well, but he'd always known that sooner or later he'd get free.

No wonder she'd cleaved to him so strongly. She'd been desperate.

The back of his boot hit something. Bending down, he found a leather scrapbook. He brushed off a

layer of dust and cracked it open, the stiff leather pro-
testing.

The pages were neatly marked, the contents—
playbills and articles about her successes—meticulously
lined in wax.

He glanced up, half expecting her to appear and
start haranguing him for trespassing in her secret room,
but she was doubtless after that paper like a terrier
starving for a bone. So he read. . . .

One article was entitled *Bastardizing Ballet? Not
Just for the Cultural Elite Anymore*. Néomi had made
sure that children from the French Quarter and Story-
ville were guaranteed seating at her performances.

According to another article, Miss Néomi Laress
had violated parish decency laws with her coterie on
more than one occasion.

Local Ballerina Courted by Russian Prince, read
another headline. Conrad's fingers bit into the leather.
Always with the bloody Russians!

When the interviewer asked Néomi if she was
moving to Moscow anytime soon, she'd answered,
"Leave New Orleans? Never, especially not for a man,
prince or not. The city's in my blood." At least Néomi
had been prophetic. Even death couldn't make her
leave.

Why would she ever choose Conrad when she'd
refused a prince? Disappointment settled over him like
a weight on his chest. She'd said they were too different. In any other situation, he wondered if she would
have glanced twice at Conrad.

But then, everyone was a prince in Russia!

Just as he was setting the album away, he found an

article in the back that seemed to have been clumsily tacked on and was disintegrating in places without the wax treatment. Brows drawn, he read what he could:

Famous Ballerina Savaged by Spurned Oil Millionaire

Néomi Laress, a colorful and well-regarded citizen of New Orleans, died in her home Saturday night when Louis Robicheaux, a first son of the city, stabbed her in the chest. Immediately after, he turned the blade on himself, slitting his own throat.

. . . from a past shrouded in mystery, Laress rose in the ranks of professional dancers, gaining national recognition as a prima ballerina . . .

"It was so awful," one witness said on the condition of anonymity due to the illegal alcohol served at the party. "She was still breathing when he twisted the knife in her chest and told her to feel it for him! There was blood everywhere, all over her. I thought I would faint."

Conrad's shaking hands fisted on the sides of the album. He stared up at a mirror, and his eyes were redder than he'd ever seen them.

Not only had she been murdered, the monster had made sure she'd . . . *suffered.* Conrad had known she'd been stabbed to death, had imagined her pain a thousand times. He couldn't have imagined anyone would have taken hold of that blade and twisted it in Néomi's fragile chest—while telling her to feel it for him.

And I can't even slaughter the miserable fuck.

Stunned, he cupped one of her diminutive slippers in his hand, stroking his thumb over the silk. Her death had been horrific, her afterlife wretched—but he could make her existence better.

As soon as he got free.

Even if she didn't want him as he wanted her, she was good and deserved more, certainly more kindness than he'd given her.

His resolve renewed, he set the slipper away, then headed outside.

When he reached the cutting stump, he grasped the ax. This operation would be problematic with his chains, but he thought he could get enough leverage to swing for one clean strike.

Was this more madness? *No.* He would do this for her. *Then what are you waiting for?*

Raising the ax, he regarded his hand pitilessly.

Obstacle.

23

"aybe I can reach it," Néomi murmured as she gazed at the paper. "And maybe I can't."

In the end, she decided it wasn't worth the trouble. She was turning her back on a possible paper, and she didn't care. As she floated down the drive, a placid breeze blew and the stars were out in a cloudless night sky, and she couldn't stop smiling over last night.

She'd decided that she was going to give Conrad the key this eve, because she believed that he would make the vow never to harm his brothers.

And that look in his eyes . . . She thought he truly wanted a future with her, impossible though that might seem.

Just as she wanted more with her fascinating vampire.

Would he be angry about the key at first? Without a doubt. But after a rage, he'd soon calm. And if his brothers were trapped somewhere else, there really was no other option. . . .

As she closed in on the manor, she spied movement near the toolshed. She frowned to see Conrad. What was he doing out there?

She blinked for focus. Because it looked like he

was holding an ax at the cutting stump. *What the devil is he doing? Why would he—*

The horrific answer dawned on her; the ax dropped.

Everything began to spin.

The sound of the strike was still echoing as the blood spurted . . . he staggered silently. *Silent, doesn't want to alert me with a yell, doesn't want me to stumble upon him quietly removing his own hand in the dark.*

Mère de Dieu. Her energy flared and dimmed. He shoved a towel to the wound. The white cloth was red and dripping with blood in seconds.

Madness . . . A storm soon boiled overhead. *Too much.* Just as the rain began to fall, she finally had enough air to scream.

His head jerked up, and his big body lurched. He was gritting his teeth against the pain as they made their way to each other.

"Don't be upset, *koeri*," he bit out, his eyes rapt on her face. His expression was drawn in agony—but not over his own pain. "It will . . . regenerate."

She could barely hear him over the roaring in her ears. "But . . . but . . ."

"I did this for us."

"*Oh, God . . .*" The pain he must be suffering!

His face was wet from the growing storm, his black hair lashed over his cheeks. "Can you . . . do you think you can help with the other one?"

"Conrad, no!"

"You can do this, Néomi. It will save days . . . of healing time. Have to get these goddamned things . . . off me."

"Why?" She began weeping in earnest.

"This is the first step. I made a conscious decision. You're looking at me . . . like I've gone completely mad again." His voice faltering, he asked, "H-have I?"

"I . . . that's not why I'm so upset!" Rose petals swirled around her body. Her hair began whipping, yet not in time with the strengthening wind.

"Then why are you looking at me like this?" He narrowed his eyes, realizing her reaction was more than horror. "What is happening to you? To the sky?"

She gazed up at him, her eyes awash in tears. "Conrad, c-come inside so I can tend to you. I have to t-tell you something. *D'accord?*" Lightning struck close by.

"No. Tell me now." Even after what he'd just done, he got that stubborn look on his face.

"*S'il te plait*, let me just tend to you—"

"Now, Néomi!"

"I . . . I'll be back." She unsteadily traced to her studio. It took three tries before she could get hold of the key. When she returned, fear for him sat cold and heavy inside her. "I-I was giving it to you tonight," she whispered, offering the key.

His brows drew together as if he couldn't comprehend what it was. Then his eyes went wild. He threw back his head; his unholy roar of fury echoed in the night.

She gasped, energy funneling out of her.

"*What is this? Néomi, what the fuck is this?*"

She focused on his face, trying to keep the world from spinning. "J-just let me help you."

"Don't come near me!"

"Conrad, please, listen! I was going to give it—"

"Bullshit! *Cease your lies!*" he bellowed.

She squeezed her eyes shut, only opening them once she heard the rattle of chains. He flung the manacles to the ground in front of her.

And then she learned what rage truly was.

Can't comprehend . . . what I've just learned . . .

Fury threaded through his veins, drowning out the pain. She'd willfully kept him here. Lied about the key. Again and again.

Not her. I didn't want her ever to betray me.

He could hear himself beginning to speak, but didn't register the words, just had this rage he had to unleash before it seared him inside.

As the rain fell harder, the sparks glittering off her grew more intense. With each word, her face paled, her image flickering even more. Her lips parted as if she was horrified, as if she didn't recognize him at all.

He dimly heard her say, "Y-you're going to say something you regret, something you can never take back. . . ."

And then he must have.

"Oh," she murmured, looking like he'd struck her. Tears spilled from her eyes. Just before she disappeared, she whispered, "*Good-bye, vampire.*"

Somewhere out in the night, he heard her crying harder. An answering roar of pain was ripped from his chest.

24

Free of the chains, Conrad could finally trace. He ignored the throbbing from his injury and returned to his cabin deep in the Estonian marshes.

Inside, he peered around. *I'm glad she'll never see this.*

It looked exactly like a madman's home would— the product of a disordered mind. Esoteric writing was crudely printed on the walls; belongings lay broken, destroyed in countless rampages. Scattered on the floor were books with the pages stripped and crumpled.

Dark sheets haphazardly covered the windows. Demon skulls hung nailed over the door. His furniture consisted of a threadbare couch, a table with one chair, and a mattress on the floor. The only things organized were his weapons, and there were hundreds of them.

Atop the table were the notes he'd kept on his search for his brothers. With his remaining hand, he flipped through them. Just as this cabin didn't fit Conrad anymore, neither did these writings.

He'd tracked the three all over the world, from Mount Oblak in Russia all the way to Louisiana. But the writings no longer made sense to him whatsoever. Because he was different. All Conrad could discern from the pages was an all-consuming need for revenge.

Even that was extinguished.

He lay back on the mattress, but couldn't sleep for hours. Vivid red streaks had begun slashing up his arm as his hand began to regenerate; the pain was punishing.

He'd severed his hand for her. For them. He'd been proud to take the pain. To get a step closer to discovering a way for them to be together.

She betrayed you, willfully kept you a captured plaything. Why was it that everything he gave a damn about ended up stabbing him in the back?

She'd played him for a fool, keeping his mind from hunting. He'd walked around that mausoleum high on her, complacent. Charmed by her every move, he'd been blinded to what was really happening. . . .

Hours toiled by before he finally passed out.

Sometime in the night, he jerked awake with a yell, cradling his arm, his body slicked with sweat. He'd seen Néomi screaming in terror, trapped in darkness where he couldn't reach her.

She wasn't here with him as she always had been. "Shh, *mon coeur* . . ." she'd soothed. "Good-bye, vampire," she'd said last night.

His brows drew together. *Stop thinking about her!*

She'd calmed him, surrounded him with laughter. She'd challenged him to rethink his blind hatred. *You'll never see her again.* Once his trust was lost, he didn't give it again.

He was disgusted with himself. Even after her betrayal, he missed her presence more than he missed his hand.

* * *

The silence within her home seeped into Néomi like a damp chill, until she thought she'd lose her mind.

Just as she'd known it would.

For the last three days, she'd aimlessly roamed her halls, a lonely, despairing ghost, filled with regret. And always she wondered where Conrad had gone, where in the world he was at that moment. Was he safe? Healing? Was he drinking from a glass—or from victims?

Is he thinking of me?

She hadn't known it was possible to miss another this much.

He would never return, and she could do nothing but . . . await. Await the years to pass, hoping for the arrival of someone, anyone.

Néomi was helpless, powerless to alleviate her own misery. She was as pitiful as he'd accused that night.

With a sigh, she exited the house into the drizzling rain, bent on getting the paper. Having long since read the ones he'd collected, she pined for something to take her mind from this.

She had no other escape. She couldn't unburden herself to a good friend or change her scenery. She couldn't drink. There was no television show or good book to absorb her.

At the property line once more, her hopes sank. Tears began to fall for the paper that was well out of her reach.

I'm in the driveway, crying over a newspaper. This was the low point of her afterlife. She was as weak and pathetic as Conrad had deemed her with his crazed, yelling words.

Next thing she knew, she'd be moaning, "*Woo-wooo.*"

To hell with this. She would not mope like a . . . a damned ghost!

Her sadness boiled to anger. She refused to feel guilt for what she'd done. She'd been trying to protect him and his brothers. For ages they'd wanted to save Conrad. He was the one who'd gone and lopped off his hand without so much as a mention of his plans to her!

With her new anger came realization. Had she actually thought she needed a man to actualize her? To save her from this cursed afterlife? Would she wait forever for his return, as Marguerite L'Are had done for Néomi's contemptible father?

Conrad called me pitiful—and he was right!

How much she'd changed. In life, she'd always been bold, taking her destiny into her own hands. After that year of burlesque, Néomi had told everyone at the club, "I want to be a ballerina," and they'd laughed. "Maybe you could make the leap from burlesque to vaudeville," they'd said. "There are a few who've made that climb."

But burlesque dancer to ballerina was supposedly an impassable divide. Which was why Néomi had had to make it.

How do I get from point A to point B? she'd thought, hour after hour, day after day. She had figured it out, and though it had taken her years, she'd *done* it.

Néomi had danced her way from the Quarter to worldwide fame!

I want to be the old me! She had to do *something*. *Think . . . think.*

But in the last eighty years, she hadn't been able to come up with any way to alter her existence—

Wait . . . Néomi possessed two things she never had before. One was a tool—Nikolai's cell phone. The other was the knowledge that at least one person on earth had been able to hear her.

What if someone else could? Someone like Conrad, someone from the Lore? If there was one thing Néomi was learning about this Lore, it was that assumptions were readily turned on their ears.

There were witches, they'd said, some with extraordinary abilities—like that Mariketa. Maybe witches could hear ghosts?

And maybe pigs can fly.

She frowned at herself. Why was she scoffing at her daring idea?

Because she wasn't the old Néomi who relished challenges. She supposed that being disembodied did that to spirits. After all, she couldn't recall a tale featuring a ghost worthy of rooting for. How many stories recounted the quests of intrepid ghosts?

But what do I have to lose? She gave a laugh. *My precious time?*

What if this Mariketa was powerful enough to make Néomi . . . incarnate? Néomi had to find her number. *Yet how?*

She floated through the tangled gardens to the sad little folly, turning it over in her head. *How? How?*

Nikolai had used their services—it made sense that their number would still be in his phone! In a flash, she traced back to her studio and raised the phone in front of her face.

When the rain outside faded and the night cleared to match her change in mood, she reminded herself, *Don't get too excited.* Even if she could divine how to operate the phone, the telekinesis to work it would be complicated and tiring.

Surely I can figure it out! In nineteen twenty-seven, telephoning had been difficult—today, it wasn't. Besides, a cell phone wasn't a totally alien object to her. She'd seen the brothers using theirs, pressing buttons without even glancing at them. And she'd read the reviews in the paper for all the newest products, learning about their features.

She squinted at the screen. Yes, she knew enough to recognize a battery graphic.

This one's was an angry red.

Merde! No, no, don't lose power. Not yet! Manipulating small touches to dial wasn't easy, much less while being panicked. Brows drawn in concentration, she painstakingly "scrolled" until she reached the address book. Within it were business cards that looked like actual paper cards that had somehow been copied into the phone. Searching under W, she found:

The House of Witches
Est. 937
1st Class Curses, Hexes, Spells, and Potions
We Won't Be Undersold!
ph: (504) WIT-CHES
info@houseofwitches.com
Member LBBB

Swallowing, she selected the card and pressed the green "call" button.

Mon Dieu, we're ringing! The phone made an ominous beep. *Hold on, battery.*

Two rings. Was no one there? *Ringing, ringing.* It was long after five o'clock. Businesses probably closed even in the Lore.

The red battery picture had begun flashing. Just as she was about to hang up to save the power, a woman answered in a creepy tone, "Helloooo, Clarice."

Néomi's jaw dropped. *This worked? I made a call? Who's Clarice?*

In the background, it sounded as if a dozen females were singing, drunkenly howling the high notes of some song. First they'd mumble, "Duh, duh, dun, duh, duh . . ." then they'd yell, "Ever-last-in' love!"

"Hello? Hello? Is this a crank call?" the woman said, sounding normal now." 'Cause let me tell you, you dialed the *wrong* coven. I can convince your dialing finger to make its legal residence where the sun don't shine. Got me?"

Throwing caution to the wind, Néomi silently begged, *Please be able to hear me!* then said, "This isn't Clarice. Can I speak with Miss Mariketa? My name is—"

The witch held the phone away and called out, "Hey, does anybody here speak Voice from Beyond?"

Néomi's eyes went wide. *My God, I love the Lore!*

Back on the phone, the witch cried, "I'm kidding! I'm Mari. Hey, how do you spirits keep getting on the cell lines? It's because you're all electrically and everything, right?"

Néomi could barely move her lips. "I, um, *electrically?*" she repeated dumbly.

"I keep telling everyone our conversations are *not* private. Hold up, I've gotta do this." She held the phone away again. "Hey, Regin! Firstly, stop peeking at my frigging cards. Secondly, get your *own* cigars. And C, check this—I've got a ghost on the line, and she's coming over the phone wire to see us right now."

"Ahhhhhhhhhhh!" a woman screamed. Néomi heard running footsteps, then a slammed door.

Mariketa chuckled. "Reege isn't scared of basilisks or twenty-foot-long centipedes, but ghosts make her freak balls. We just made one of the most fearsome Valkyrie on earth run for her life. Classic."

The music grew louder as a manic-tempo song played—the only lyric was the word *tequila*.

Sweet pandemonium. Néomi wanted to be there so badly it hurt. The phone beeped again.

"So what's your name, spirit?"

"N-Néomi. Néomi Laress."

"Oh, man! I've heard of you! Dancer, right? From the old-timey days? You refused to get hitched and got shanked in the ticker. We studied you in my Local Feminists 205 class."

People actually study *me?*

In a chiding tone, she added, "Which, Néomi, I might have passed if you'd called two years ago. So what do you want with me?"

This is so bizarre! "I need, um, I would be very grateful to be corporeal, and thought you might be able to help me."

"Do you have any money?" Mariketa asked, her tone instantly turning shrewd. "I don't do gratis."

"I have a drawer full of antique jewelry." The phone was beeping more insistently!

"Meh. It's my one girls' night out for the week, and I'm kicking ass at five card st—"

"There are more than fifty diamonds! One alone is four carats. You can have all of them."

"We're getting warmer, spirit."

Beeeeeep. "In the safe there are stock certificates from before I . . . died. They were worth twenty or thirty thousand dollars eighty years ago. They'd have to be worth a fortune today, since the companies are still in business."

"Which companies?" This Mariketa was certainly no-nonsense when it came to money.

"Um, there's General Electric and International Business Machines. I think it's called just IBM today—"

"Okay, I have cartoon dollar signs in my bulging cartoon eyes. I'll be right over. Knock on the mirror closest to you while I'm on the phone."

Did Mariketa need the mirrors for her spells? Néomi's heart fell. "But they're all broken."

"Doesn't matter. Just need a sliver." Néomi dutifully knocked, and Mariketa said, "And I've . . . *got it.* All right, when a witch of superlative gorgeousableness climbs out of your mirror, don't ghost out on me."

Climbs out of my mirror? "Oh, I assure you—"

The phone was now emitting a long, unbroken tone!

"Please hurry, Miss Mariketa!"

"Hey, just call me Mari." In a feigned somber tone,

she sighed, "And I shall call you . . . *Spirit Friend.*"

Smiling stupidly, Néomi turned off the phone and tossed it to the bed. She was giddy—she was . . . *hopeful.*

She began to pace anticipating Mariketa's—*Mari's* arrival. With their singing, music, and cards, those females were like the *bons vivants* she'd adored. And one was coming to visit!

Life was suddenly new and different and full of promise.

It couldn't be this easy. But, *what if, what if, what if?*

25

Conrad sat hunched in a tree atop a hill, overlooking the chaos of the gathering. He scanned the crowd for Tarut, but so far had spied nothing. Even in this throng, the demon would be easy to spot. He was eight feet tall.

Though the risk in being here was great, Conrad was prepared. His hand was nearly regenerated. The drugs had all but worn off. And he was holding strong mentally.

Bullshit.

He was addicted to Néomi. *I'm addicted to a ghost.* Conrad couldn't feel her presence, couldn't smell her scent. And it was killing him.

Behind his sunglasses, his eyes darted. Only his own survival mattered, he told himself again and again. She didn't matter to him. *Damn it, she doesn't!*

Yet over the last three days, as his anger abated, he'd come to realize that she hadn't withheld his freedom for malicious, or even selfish, purposes. Her expression had been tormented when she'd handed the key to him. As long as he lived, he'd never forget how she'd looked in the rain, the glitter of electricity all around her lovely face.

With each hour, he remembered more of his enraged tirade. He'd accused her of keeping him in danger from his enemies. Yet she'd been watching over him like a sentinel whenever he'd slept. If anyone had attacked Conrad at Elancourt, he didn't doubt she'd have put them on the ceiling.

And he'd questioned whether she would've let him starve when the blood supply ran out, demanding to know if she gave a damn about that at all—when in fact, it was Néomi who'd coaxed him to start drinking the bagged blood anyway. Every sunset she'd brought him a cup filled to the rim, though she detested the sight of it. "I just can't see it without remembering," she'd said. "When I died, I was bathed in it, in Louis's. . . ."

Conrad had known that—he'd seen it spilling out over her floor the night of her dance. Exasperated, he'd said, "Then why do you keep bringing it?"

She'd blinked at him. "Because you need it."

Why *would* Néomi let a self-professed murderer loose? She'd been tortured by one.

Go back for her, his mind whispered. And do what with her? He'd never soothed the hurt feelings of a female. He wasn't smooth with words like Murdoch.

Why would she want to have anything to do with him after the things he'd said? He'd been so damned hard on her. He remembered telling her to rot in hell—she'd whispered that she already was.

He grasped his forehead. *What is* wrong *with me?*

She'd endured eighty years of that hell, only to have a vampire destroying her home, punching her walls. And even before those years, Néomi had *suffered*. The bastard who killed her had made sure of it.

Robicheaux hadn't plunged the knife and then looked on in horror at what he'd done. He'd taken hold of that blade and sadistically twisted it.

And Conrad couldn't even torture and slaughter the one who had done this to her.

His eyes widened. But he could desecrate the bastard's grave for her! *Now I'm thinking.* And of course Néomi would want to know about Conrad's gesture because it would please her. He would have to return, if just to tell her.

The idea heartened him, made being here a fraction more bearable.

When her mirror bulged out, somehow becoming pliable, Néomi gasped. A briefcase flew out of the glass, landing with a thud on her studio floor.

Then came hands, parting the mirror like a curtain.

From the opening, a comely redhead crawled out, her face alight with a smile. Following her was an eerily pretty black-haired woman with arresting golden eyes—and pointed ears. The glass closed seamlessly behind them.

"I'm Mari MacRieve," the redhead said. She hiked a thumb at her friend. "This is Nïx the Ever-Knowing. She's a Valkyrie."

Shaking off her astonishment, Néomi said, "It's such a pleasure to meet both of you." Turning to the black-haired woman, she said, "Nïx? I know some people who are searching for you."

"They always are, dearling," Nïx sighed, then fogged and buffed her nails, which looked more like small, elegant *claws*. She asked Mari, "How are you doing with all these mirrors?"

Mari let out a breath. "Hanging in there."

"She's a captromancer," Nïx explained. "She uses mirrors for her spells and for travel."

"But," Mari said, "I've got this foreign greedy power inside me that makes me get all entranced in mirrors if I'm not careful. So I can't live with 'em, can't live without them." Mari turned in circles. "Wow, what a place!"

Néomi noticed that she had a piece of paper taped on her back that read, *I Do Ghouls*.

"Oh, dear," Néomi said, pointing delicately. "Mari, you have a . . ."

Mari patted behind her until she snagged the page. "Damn Regin." After reading it, she crumbled the paper, then glared at Nïx. "When is Lucia getting back? I can't handle Reege by myself anymore."

Nïx shrugged. "Don't worry, I've got Regin taken care of. Folly, a rogue Valkyrie and Regin's archnemesis, arrives next Friday at a quarter after four."

Mari exhaled with relief. "Ah, your foresight is a beautiful thing. I wish mine was a fraction as strong as yours."

"No foresight needed. I bought Folly a ticket. I'm flying her in from New Zealand first-class. Regin will be furious at the betrayal—but sometimes you have to be cruel to be kind."

"You are wise," Mari said, then returned her attention to a bemused Néomi.

"How is it that you both can see ghosts?" Néomi asked.

Mari answered, "Because I'm a witch, and because she's damn old and powerful."

"Old as carbon," Nïx agreed. "And so powerful I'm working on my demigoddess badges."

Néomi didn't think Nïx looked a day older than Mari, but what did she know? "Can either of you tell me how I became a ghost?"

Mari shook her head. "No one really knows for certain, but I've heard it has to do with a soul being too strong, even after death, to pass on. Oh, and usually you have to have a sturdy spirit anchor."

"Spirit anchor?"

"Yeah, if you die in a place that you loved or that had meaning for you, it can anchor your spirit there."

Néomi had loved Elancourt—the property had been all she'd had that was permanent and lasting. She'd wanted to plant roots, to watch children play in the gardens and the folly. To grow old here with someone she loved.

Why did Conrad's face flash in her mind when she imagined that?

"So what do you do for fun around here?" Mari asked.

"Fun? Um, I read the newspaper. And . . . oh, sometimes cats move in! And there's this family of nutria that come in the winter to root around inside the house. Their antics are so funny, I could watch them for hours." She frowned. "Actually, I do watch them for hours."

Mari cast Nïx a speaking glance. "Bones, we got here just in time!"

"Clearly, Jim," Nïx replied in a bored tone.

Bones? Jim? "So you'd heard of me?" Néomi asked.

"Yeah, I'd thought about doing my class report on you."

Striving for a casual tone, Néomi said, "But you didn't?"

"An older witch had already written a paper on a suffragist from Baton Rouge. I wasn't above using it. But I remember you were a burlesque dancer turned ballerina."

"Burlesque? That got out? But people never understand," Néomi said, wondering what these women would think of her—Conrad had been appalled. What if they wouldn't take her seriously about what she was seeking? "I only did that for three months. Four possibly. A year at the most. I was never *entirely* naked," she added. "Not many times at all. Back then it was called a strip*tease*. Not a *strip*, you understand. There were usually fans or big feathers—"

"But that's one thing people loved about you," Mari said. "These days burlesque is way cool. After your secret got out, people called you the ballerina with burlesque soul. You *fit* New Orleans."

"Oh, then," Néomi said on a breath. At last, people were seeing it as they should. "I'm actually mollified."

"Great. So, let's get down to business."

"Would you like to have a seat?" Having her own guests here was so surreal!

With a nod, Mari kicked her briefcase past the coffee table to the cot, then sat. Nïx hopped atop the display table to the dust-free spot where the gramophone had been. She surveyed Néomi's collection of condoms, bras, and Mardi Gras paraphernalia, but said nothing.

"I'd offer you coffee—"

"I don't ingest food or drink," Nïx said evenly.

Mari added, "And coffee on top of margaritas is courting the wrath of Cuervo." She took out a pen and a pad of paper. "So, Néomi, first some background just for my own records. . . . Why contact me now? I mean, you've been a ghost for decades."

"Well, I didn't even know about the Lore until the vampires moved in a couple weeks ago. I'd had no idea there were witches or Valkyrie—"

"*Vampires* moved in?" Mari interrupted, flashing a look at Nïx. "Funny. I just saw a foreign vamp at a bayou bar recently. What a coincidence."

Nïx mouthed, *"Who? Whaa?"*

"Yes, they're from Estonia," Néomi said, and soon the entire story flowed. ". . . and then Conrad cut off his hand and called me a pathetic ghost, and I realized I was, and I couldn't stand it. So that's when I rang you up."

"You're not seeking to be embodied because of the vampire, are you?" Mari asked. "To show him what he's missing? Because this is really serious."

Even if Néomi never saw Conrad again, she had to take action of some kind. *Because I can't stand what I've become.* "I'm seeking this, because *it's time.*"

"Okay, I'm just going to lay all this out for you." Mari set down her pen. "I can help you with your incorporeality problem, but it's a temporary fix, and it comes with a high price. Not just the monetary type. It's basically a shell spell that creates a target practice body. The spell will make you look and feel precisely like the human you once were, but you'll, well, you'll get killed soon after."

"Why is that?"

"Some folks call what we're discussing a *hail Mary mortality* play. You could set about righting old wrongs, using knowledge of the afterlife to screw with the present. Fate doesn't like these bids and shuts them down *forcefully*," Mari explained. "It'd be like you were walking around with a glaring target on your back. You'd get capped by some unnatural cause—a runaway trolley car or a plane crash or you'd be electrocuted by your hair dryer. Something pretty horrific would happen. Your shell body would expire, then disappear, and then your spirit would *die*, die."

"How long would I have?"

"A couple of weeks? A night? Maybe a few months. There's no way to tell. But the most I've ever read of in the Web forum was a year."

Néomi swallowed. "What happens after *death*, death?"

"That's the kicker. Nobody knows—it's kinda between you and your God, gods, goddesses, et cetera."

"Well, now that we're in discussions," Néomi began, "I have to ask—is there any way to make me corporeal for a lifetime? Maybe I have enough money for a full resurrection?"

Mari and Nïx shared a look. "I don't touch those. But what you're asking for isn't a resurrection. Your spirit's here and available. No need to suck it back to this plane. What you need is an embodying, which is highly dangerous in itself. And there are about a dozen different conditions that would have to be met. But even if everything were ideal, I'm just not skilled enough to try it. Not yet."

"You've never attempted it?"

"On a human? Not outside a simulator." After a hesitation, she admitted, "I did recently attempt it on my ghost cat."

"And?"

"And, did you ever see *Pet Sematary?*"

Néomi shook her head.

"No? Well, my Tigger came back *wrong!*" she cried, biting her knuckle.

Nïx rose to sit beside Mari, patting her back. "There, there, favorite Wiccan-type person."

Mari dabbed at her eyes, muttering, "Got some, uh, dust in my eye."

To Néomi, the Valkyrie said, "Mari's got oodles of power, but this would be a skill level of"—she frowned—"what level?"

"A fiver," Mari answered, regaining her composure. "Out of five."

"Why not practice on me?" Néomi said, making her tone bright. "I'm game."

Nïx shook her head. "For Mari to do a five, she'd have to commune with the mirror to unleash her full power. It's likely she would get entranced in her own reflection, unable to break away from it. Possibly forever."

Mari nodded. "But I'm going to face my reflection in fifty years, when I'm stronger and more skilled.

We've already got it marked on the calendar. If you can wait that long, I'll put you at the top of the list, for a nominal, onetime fee—"

"No. *Merci*, but no." Fifty more years of loneliness and sliver moons? Her death relived another six hundred times?

Or possibly a year of life. There wasn't even a question of which she'd choose.

"I'm sorry, Néomi. If I tried to embody you now, I'd probably get enthralled and you'd come back worse than dead. I know you're thinking that there's nothing worse than dead—"

"No. I don't think that." Néomi had just spent a lifetime worse than dead. She understood the concept, and why it'd be wise to avoid it.

"There's one other option as well," Nïx said. "In the Lore, there are Phantoms, a ghostlike species of immortals who can incarnate at will, like shape-shifters between life and death. If you can exist long enough in this plane as a ghost, you'd gradually regrow a physical form, accumulating strength to become like them. You'd be able to leave your spirit anchor, and still retain all your telekinetic abilities."

"How long?" This sounded perfect! "How long do I have to exist to grow a body?"

Nïx snapped her fingers. "A mere four or five centuries. It'll be over before you know it."

"Oh." The breezy way Nïx said that made Néomi wonder how old the Valkyrie could possibly be. "That's kind of out for me, too. I relive my death every month. I couldn't stand the fifty years option, much less five hundred."

"Ah, the perpetual ghostly reenactment." Nïx nodded in commiseration. "Your spirit anchor would probably get burned or torn down before then anyway."

"Is there anyone else who can do the embodying?"

Nïx quirked a brow. "No one you'd want to tangle with. There are a handful of sorcerers who can do this, but they'll make outrageous demands—like your first-born or something equally unfun."

Mari said, "Listen, Néomi, you don't have any reason to trust our advice on this, but I can provide a list of referrals who would be happy—"

"No, I trust you. How soon could you do the target practice body?" Néomi asked.

Mari seemed surprised that she was still interested. "Uh, tonight. But really, this whole thing is probably not something you'd want to consider. I mean, how bad could it be here?"

Pinning Mari's gaze with her own, Néomi said, "I'm trapped in an interminable hell that I can't even kill myself to escape. I perceive *nothing*, not until the one night a month when I have a knife plunged into my heart then twisted in my chest."

"Okey-dokey, then, sounds like we'll be doing the spell!" Mari pulled out papers and forms from her briefcase. "So, about that payment."

Néomi waved her hand over her shoulder at the jewelry armoire behind her, and a felt-lined drawer full of jewels opened. Another four practiced waves had the safe open. "Do your worst."

With a discerning air, Mari picked out a few diamonds and certificates and placed them in an inner compartment in her bag. Nïx wouldn't even glance at the intense glittering, instead exploring the studio. She continually cast puzzled glances at Néomi.

"Well?" Mari asked, spreading out contracts on the coffee table. "Are you reading anything on Néomi here?"

"I get *nothing* on her," Nïx said.

"Is that good or bad?" Néomi asked.

Nïx narrowed her eyes. "It's *rare.*"

Mari offered a pen to Néomi. "Can I get you to sign here and here? Just an X will do." Néomi used telekinesis to craft a sloppy X. "Okay, and here. Nïx, would you witness?"

Nïx scrawled her signature, *Nïx the Ever-Knowing, Proto-Valkyrie & Soothsayer Without Equal.*

"Do I need to do anything to get ready?" Néomi asked.

"Why the urgency? I usually make clients wait forty-eight hours to mull their decision when the magick is irrevocable. "

"I really like the Lore and want to see more of it. And there's this gathering tonight—"

"Ah, the *Liv der Lanking*, the Life of Lanking. A raucous party. We call it the Liver Spanking. Nïx here planned it."

Nïx nodded sunnily. "It's B.Y.O.S. Bring Your Own Sacrifice."

"Now, why do my spider senses tell me that Conrad Wroth might be there?" Mari asked.

"What? Will he, indeed?" Néomi said in a breezy tone.

Nïx added, "Naturally, you'll want him to see you flirt with other males and regret his words."

Néomi was uncertain what she planned to do if she saw him there. Part of her was dying to know if she could blood him. Part of her wanted to see if he'd held steady after three nights away. And yes, another part of her wanted to show Conrad that she wasn't pathetic, languishing away in her haunted manor.

"You can go with us," Mari offered. "My hubby's there with his kinsmen. He *loathes* girls' night out—throws a mantrum every week. So I suppose I could go relieve his misery."

"I'd love to go with you!" And if Conrad was there, maybe she should tell *him* to go to hell. To return the look of disgust and pity he'd given her. "I want to get dressed up and meet new people. I want to feel!"

"The gathering's going to be extreme," Mari said. "And you'll only be a human—with nary a ghostly power. Are you sure you'll be able to handle it?"

"I thrive on excitement."

"Adrenaline junkie," Mari said. "Got it. So this'll be a Cinderella redux. I feel all fairy godmotheresque." She peered at Néomi. "You're sure you want to do this?"

Néomi said, "My ball awaits."

"While I get ready, take a gander at the Liver Spanking live." Mari pressed her fingertips to the glass, studiously avoiding any direct eye contact with the mirror until after a scene had appeared. Raucous beings were dancing around a bonfire at least five stories high.

Beautiful chaos. Néomi yearned to be amidst it, even as she wondered if she could indeed handle being thrown into that pandemonium, a mortal among immortals.

"Check out my hubby." Mari altered the scene and pointed to a very huge and handsome male—who was scowling fiercely at his surroundings and then into his drink. "Damn, that werewolf melts my butter," Mari sighed. "He's so miserable," she added delightedly.

Néomi frowned. "That's Bowen MacRieve—your husband?" When Mari nodded, Néomi said, "He was supposed to come after Conrad in two weeks if he wasn't better. Could you get your husband to not, well, hurt Conrad?"

"I'll talk to him. But I didn't think you would care, seeing as the vampire called you pathetic."

"I do care, don't I?" Néomi sighed. She supposed she always would.

Because she might possibly have fallen a little bit—really a *tiny* bit—in love with Conrad.

"Why don't you go with the intent to forget all about him?" Mari asked. "After all, it's possible he could find his Bride tonight—and she might not be you. There'll be plenty of males there to distract you. Get Nïx to show you Cade and Rydstrom—buddies of mine and some of the hawtest demon brothers you'll ever see." She took her tiny cell phone from one of her many pants pockets. "Gotta make a quick call."

When Mari walked to the other side of the room, Nïx pointed out two *horned* males who were uncommonly attractive. "There's Cade, all flawless golden good looks and moral ambivalence. A perfect foil to mighty King Rydstrom with his scars and proud honor."

"Look at those eyes," Néomi breathed. Though one brother was lighter haired and one darker, they both had blazing green eyes.

"Oh, yes. They have eyes, too, don't they? Everybody says that's what has females begging to do the hula hoop under them. Either that or their accents—a cross between Aussie and *Sith Ifrican*. But I think it's the horns."

Shell-colored and pleasingly turned, their horns started just above their ears, curving back along their heads. Their shape and direction reminded Néomi of the laurel wreath crowns men wore in antiquity, though Rydstrom's horns were as battle-scarred as the rest of him.

"Yes," Nïx continued, "those sleek . . . rock-hard . . . lickable horns."

Had Nïx just growled? "It sounds like you want one of them. Or, uh, both."

"Oh, no, no. I'm Mike Rowe's beloved."

"Is this Mike down there?"

"No, Mikey's playing hard to get at present." Her eyes going vacant, she murmured, *"But it will do you no good . . . you naughty little scamp."*

Just then Néomi overheard Mari say, "Hey, Elianna. . . . Ha-ha, no, I don't need bail! I was wondering about that shell spell for ghosts. Is it *corpus carnate* or *carnate corpus*?"

Merde! The witch was having to get instructions?

Mari paused, then said, "I am too up for this. . . . Uh-huh, uh-huh . . . and that's why I won't get entranced, now, isn't it?"

Néomi was about to express concerns when Nïx

said, "I put that vampire in your house. And I still don't know why." She leaned in, appearing genuinely puzzled. "Especially since you're going to die."

Néomi swallowed. "How do you know Conrad?"

"I know his brothers." Her voice took on a dreamy tone. "And I suppose I have an affinity for Conrad. I have squatters in my mind, too."

"So, I'm back!" Mari said. "Have you seen anything on Néomi? What course should she take?"

Seeming to come back to the present, Nïx told Néomi, "I see very little on you. I'm called *ever*-knowing, not *all*-knowing. But I know—for a fact—that the day anyone discovers what you're about to do will be your last."

"What do you mean?"

"No one besides the three of us can know the conditions surrounding your transformation. None can discover that you will begin a countdown as soon as you assume the shell body."

"Conrad's going to demand to know," Néomi said, then hurriedly added, "If he's there, and if I blood him, and if he apologizes for his past behavior, of course." *And if he doesn't still feel that crazed sense of betrayal.*

Nïx snorted. "I'm sure you can find ways to get around that, if you—oh, I don't know—want to *live longer*."

"Then we vow that none of us will ever talk about this," Mari said. "We'll never reveal that Néomi's time here is definite or how she was changed. Agreed?"

Néomi nodded firmly. "*D'accord.*"

"Agreed," Nïx said. "I do so love unholy alliances."

"Good then. That's settled." Mari pulled out a compact mirror from another pants pocket. "And I'm ready for action. Are you sure, Néomi?"

Decades or even centuries as I've been versus even a single day of life? Néomi nodded. "Let's do it."

Mari opened the compact in her palm. "Okay, then. Now for the profound existential question." When she began to rub her thumb over the mirror, her eyes became silver, like mirrors themselves, reflecting Néomi's astonished expression. "What do you want to wear?"

26

Hours after he'd arrived, Conrad squeezed his head, grappling for control of his thoughts. This frenzied overload of the gathering was wreaking havoc with him. If the Fallen reacted badly to quick movements and loud noises, then he'd just stumbled onto a special kind of hell.

Return to her . . .

He just wanted to find a way to tell her what he was thinking. To tell her that if he could take back his words, he would.

Right when Conrad was about to trace to Elancourt, he saw Tarut. All eight feet of him. The hulking demon was towering over an area crowded with other species of demons, accompanied by his gang of Kapsliga swordsmen. Each was shirtless with a wide leather band crossed over his chest. Conrad had once proudly worn the same.

His eyes narrowed when a haze of smoke suddenly appeared in the same area. A group of seven demons stepped from it, the Woede among them. Conrad had heard they'd somehow lost their ability to trace. Rök, the infamous fugitive, must be teleporting them. Just then Rök opened his mouth, sucking the smoke inside him again.

Tarut and the Woede—all three targets here for the taking, and more easily than normal. When Conrad engaged the Woede, they wouldn't hit their rage state completely, not without risking Conrad's life and the information he held. Rage demons in full demonic state were incredibly powerful, but near mindless.

And Tarut? Conrad no longer had to worry about being clawed by him.

Rydstrom and Cade didn't clasp forearms with Tarut in greeting. Instead, their hands remained near the hilts of their swords. Then Conrad saw Cadeon stiffen, his eyes narrowing on Tarut as if in realization. He dragged Rydstrom to the side, gesturing heatedly, while Rydstrom scowled in Tarut's direction.

So the demons knew they were hunting the same target—Tarut wanting to kill Conrad and the Woede wanting to keep him alive, at least for a time. . . .

Conrad tensed to attack, his fangs growing sharp.

That was exactly when he heard Néomi's laughter.

"Did you have to conjure that last bottle of wine?" Nïx said under her breath, but Néomi still heard her, even over the noise of the crowd and her own delighted laughter.

Fire. Creatures from myth. Revelry.

She was in heaven! For the first time in eighty years, Néomi was freed from Elancourt!

And, yes, she was a tad tipsy—had merlot always tasted so exquisite?

Now layers of sound meshed with layers of sensation: the constant rustle of leaves beneath her new leather boots. The scent of night-blooming jasmine and spent gardenias. A band tuning instruments in the background. The delicious closeness of her new dress.

When asked what she wanted to wear, Néomi had answered, "Anything but this godforsaken black satin party dress. Something with color! Something short and really sexy."

Mari had conjured a scarlet "body-conscious sheath" for Néomi. The shameless garment was long-sleeved but backless, and was shorter than anything she'd ever worn.

Hardly the couture of the pitiful!

Néomi's hurt over Conrad's words dwindled with each second—because she *wasn't* pitiful. Again she'd taken control of her destiny.

By God, it was heady. *I'm like the old Néomi. The one who would roll the dice and laugh in the face of fate.* She was going to get "capped," and she didn't give a damn!

"I had to do the bottles," Mari murmured in answer. "You saw her—she was freaking out."

At first the change had been overwhelming. Suddenly thrust into a world of perception, Néomi had stood in her studio, wide-eyed and struggling to adjust to the onslaught of feeling.

The weight of her body had abruptly pressed down on her feet, against a floor that was impossibly rigid. Her hair had pulled heavily along her back, and shivers had glanced over every inch of her skin.

It hadn't seemed to Néomi that she alone was changed, but that the entire world was altered, as if she'd been living in a dim bubble. Her new corporeal self had been shaking with sensation, dizzy with it. She'd patted her face in astonishment and whispered, "M-maybe this wasn't a good idea."

Mari had called what she was feeling *hypersensitivity* and said she had gone through the same not long ago. It would improve. . . .

"And we never would have gotten her to climb into the mirror otherwise," Mari added. "It was like trying to dunk a cat in acid."

Women with small boxes fastened on chokers walked by. "What are they wearing?" Néomi asked, a tad too loudly by the look on Mari's face. Each box had individual decorations or sayings painted on it.

"Voice modulators. The Sirenae are being polite," Mari explained. "If they sing, they could captivate all the unmated males here. Not very sporting."

One box read: "Yeah, you're welcome." Another read, "Boom! I got your boyfriend." Néomi laughed with delight. *Sirens! Of course!*

A group of elven-looking women strolled by, wearing nothing but gauzy skirts. Their chests were bare except for body paint styled in intricate leafy designs.

"Goody," Nïx muttered. "The dendrophiles."

"The dendro what?" Néomi said.

"Tree lovers—the tree nymphs."

Their obvious leader said, "Well, if it isn't Nucking Futs Nïx and the hex hack."

"Well, if isn't the *hookers*," Nïx replied blandly.

"Oh, I'm sorry, nymphets, this isn't the orgy—that's down the road."

"Nïxie, every party is an orgy waiting to happen."

Nïx opened her mouth, then closed it, dragging Néomi and Mari away. "Well, you can't argue with reason, can you?"

And nymphs!

Almost at once, Néomi's excitement was tinged by a tug of disappointment. Murdoch had said that nymphs would be in attendance. These startlingly lovely women reminded her that Conrad might have one like them for his Bride.

Luckily, there were gorgeous males too, and soon Néomi, Nïx, and Mari were surrounded by a number. They were all huge. A couple were even taller than Conrad.

Néomi felt dwarfed, but they seemed to be making every attempt not to startle her, especially since Nïx had introduced her as "Néomi, *the mortal.*" Néomi smiled in greeting, while furtively peering around them for a glimpse of the vampire.

"This is Uilleam and Munro," Nïx said, indicating a pair of Scottish twins who were roguishly handsome. "We just call them Hot and Hotter, or is it Hotter and Hot?" She shrugged. "They're Lykae. And here are the demons Cade and Rydstrom, also brothers—the ones I was telling you about."

"Nice to meet you, sweet," Cade said. But he seemed preoccupied, absently rasping the blond stubble over his jawline.

"It's a pleasure, Néomi." Rydstrom gave her a smile that didn't quite reach his remarkably green eyes.

The brothers' features were so alike, and yet their overall appearances were so dissimilar. Their bearings and even their accents differed. She could hear the colonial British in them, but Rydstrom's sounded more upper-class.

Rydstrom turned to Nïx. "I've been looking for you, Valkyrie."

"Oh, why? Did you find the one who seeks him in sleep?"

"As a matter of fact . . ." Rydstrom took her upper arm and *guided* her to the side.

"Help, help!" Nïx cried over her shoulder. "I'm being ravished by a demon!" When Néomi started after her—as if she could do something—Nïx mouthed, *"I'm really not."*

"Here's Bowen!" Mari said. He'd seemed to be following a scent. When he caught sight of Mari, he charged for her, gathering her in his arms.

After receiving a deep, seeking kiss that had Néomi fanning herself, Mari introduced him. He smiled at Néomi, then glowered at Cade, who returned the look. *Intéressant.*

The musicians she'd heard earlier began playing a melodic ballad with a heavy drumbeat that, of course, Néomi didn't recognize. But the song flooded over her. She could feel the percussion in her belly, and for the first time in eight decades she *needed* to dance.

"Go on and dance, Néomi," Mari said. "We'll wait right here. Just don't go too far."

Néomi nodded happily. At the fire, the music commanded her and she obeyed. With each second she grew more used to her body, recalling how she could coax it to move, to glide. . . .

Everything felt dreamlike. It seemed a night of magick.

Soon, she sensed she was being watched. As she spun, she spied glowing red eyes in the dark, following her every movement.

Conrad. Like a lion stalking a fawn.

This *must* be a hallucination.

She can't be real. Conrad couldn't process this. He'd wanted to go to her tonight. Over the last week, he'd ached to be able to touch her.

Now, like an offering, she was here for him. In flesh and blood, so alive. Somehow she was no longer a ghost, no more black-and-white. Her cheeks were flushed with pink, her lips as red as her short dress.

How could this change have happened?

She looked like a pagan dancing by the fire with her wild flowing hair. The way her body turned and swayed was decadent, wicked. "*Tantsija,*" Conrad murmured.

As ever, when she moved, he grew hypnotized. But now instead of merely soothing his mind, her dancing made his body feel taut, stretched like a wire. She'd been beautiful as a ghost. Like this, she was beyond compare.

He could actually take that kiss that he'd burned for, could touch her full breasts. . . . No, he couldn't— she surely hated him now.

Even across the distance, he could hear her heart pumping with excitement, which meant that she could bleed. Which meant that he could hurt her. Or kill her.

He'd fantasized about sucking at her neck. *Would I ever be able to stop once I'd started?*

The ease he'd felt with her because he couldn't harm her disappeared, replaced by dread.

And now his enemies could target her. Tarut had just escaped him moments ago. Conrad bit out a vile curse when his arm began to ache under his bandage. *Because my most fervent dream just materialized.* What he'd coveted most was dancing right before him.

You have to have a dream to lose it. . . .

Yet his own heart lay dead in his chest. No breaths began to expand his lungs. Though Conrad was seeing her in the flesh, his blooding still wasn't triggered. Disappointment welled inside him.

Turn your back and leave.

Just when he was about to trace, someone yelled, *"Fight!"*

27

Bedlam broke out in seconds.

The fight spread like a wildfire on parched grass. Beings began to change, eyes turning color, demeanors altering utterly, weapons appearing from seemingly nowhere.

The delicate nymphs had somehow concealed daggers beneath those gauzelike skirts and brandished them with battle cries. In the distance, she saw Cade and Rydstrom wielding *broadswords*. The Sirenae fiddled with something on their voice boxes that allowed them to dispatch concentrated shrieks, dropping their foes to the ground with bleeding ears.

Néomi caught sight of Mari and Bowen hastening to her. "Stay there!" Mari cried.

"*Oui*," she said faintly. She was too shocked to move.

But then Mari got hit by a stray elbow, sending her flying. Bowen went savage, beginning to turn to his werewolf form. Néomi gasped. *Terrifying*. She was glad she'd been forgotten by the Lykae—until the frenzied crowd engulfed her.

How had she thought she could handle this? An

accidental jab of an elbow wouldn't kill the immortal Mari, but Néomi might not survive it. Was this how she'd get *capped*? So soon?

She tried to duck and run but kept getting caught back up in the current of beings. Each surge pressed her ever closer to the fire. The band played on, seeming as oblivious as the *Titanic's*.

Then she saw him.

He was hard to miss as he charged for her, towering over others. He had dark sunglasses on, but she knew his eyes were fixed on her.

Without ever turning from her, he dropped any being in his direct path to her. She'd never seen anyone who could fight like him, so methodical but vicious—so *practiced*. His fangs were razor sharp, his neck and chest muscles straining.

If warriors fought back, he twisted necks and backhanded them, sending them flying. *Thank God his hand had regenerated—*

A fist struck him in the face with crushing force. His sunglasses went flying, but he didn't even pause in his pursuit.

Fierce immortal, with his jet black hair whipping over his cheek. She felt an untimely surge of pride that a male like him was coming for her.

He wants me. Those burning, blood-filled irises were locked on her. He was looking at her as if she was his, only his. He'd talked of having new vampire instincts, animal-like instincts. There was no mistaking what his eyes said . . .

Anyone who kept him from what was his would die.

*   *   *

Conrad couldn't risk tracing to her—she was a moving target in the fray. *Can't take my eyes from her for a split second. Sprinting faster, fighting harder—*

He suddenly stumbled, feeling as if a mine had just gone off under his feet. Righting himself, chin down, he charged for her once more.

Another explosion; he tripped forward, losing sight of her for a moment. *What the fuck is happening?*

His lips parted as he comprehended. Thunderous bomb blasts again and again.

Néomi . . . it's her.

A rhythm to the echoing boom—his . . . heartbeat. Conrad was hearing his heartbeat for the first time in three hundred years.

Mine! Even as he ran, Conrad felt a savage triumph. His lungs began to expand, waking. She was bringing him back to life. *Just ten feet away from her, one more obstacle—*

His body was tackled to the ground with the force of a freight train. Strong hands gripped him, hauling him to his feet. Two demons had him. Néomi was watching agape. *Safe for now.*

Weak . . . can't shake them off. Vulnerable for precious seconds while he transitioned. *Can't break free.*

"A red-eyed Fallen in New Orleans," Cadeon the Kingmaker said as he stalked in front of Conrad. "You're the one who drained the warlock dry?"

Conrad's chest heaved as he sucked in air. With each breath, his strength returned and then some.

Power such as he'd never imagined began erupting throughout his body. "Be more specific, Cadeon," he sneered. "There were several."

"We've been looking for you, vampire." The demon's eyes turned wholly black, and his horns enlarged and straightened with menace. But he wouldn't completely hit a rage state.

Conrad heard Néomi murmur, *"Mère de Dieu."* And Cadeon wasn't even close to a full turning. Usually when one beheld this demonic sight, one was about to die. Yet Conrad was finally catching his breath, and his heart was thundering with readiness. . . .

He flung his arms out, hurling away the ones holding him. Then he lunged at Cadeon. He fixed his hands around the demon's throat, clenching with all his newly blooded strength.

Power roared through Conrad's veins. Red covered his vision. The need to drink and kill was undeniable. There *was* no going back from bloodlust—his brothers were wrong. He'd done evil; he always would. He slammed Cadeon to the ground, stunning him.

Conrad could smell the demon's blood, could hear his heart. *More power, here for the taking.* Instinct ruled him. He gripped Cadeon's forehead, yanking his head back to bare his neck.

Cadeon's skin began to darken to a deep red. His upper and lower fangs grew. The demon was finally turning, but it was too late. . . .

"Conrad, don't."

He glanced up to meet Néomi's wide-eyed gaze. Conrad knew exactly what he looked like to her, with his fangs dripping, his eyes glowing and frenzied as he craved blood. "Now you know what I am." He lowered his mouth to finish this.

"Now I know what you *were*. Conrad, please take me home."

The need to protect. He hesitated at the demon's neck. *Stronger than the need to kill.*

If you saw me in bloodlust, you'd think me a monster.

Conrad hadn't been exaggerating. If Néomi didn't know him, she would be terrified. But she did know him, and recognized that he'd restrained himself for her.

Here was Conrad at his most frightening, and all she felt for him was pride and tenderness—

Suddenly Cade took advantage, bashing his head against Conrad's so hard his skull had to be singing.

Then the other two demons were back, attacking him at once. . . .

Without her telekinesis, she was powerless to stop them. Others in the crowd had ceased their own sparring to watch this clash. They were abuzz that the fallen vampire wasn't drinking and that the rage demon hadn't turned fully.

As Rydstrom and four more rough-looking males closed in on the fight, he asked her, "You know this vampire?" Suddenly, the others with him had a sinister air, their eyes all turning black.

When they advanced, Néomi swallowed. "I . . . only s-socially."

"You're his *Bride*, aren't you?"

Am I his Bride? Whispers sounded all around her; beings scrutinized her with new interest. *Why?*

She retreated a few steps, and when Rydstrom's crew continued after her, she turned to Conrad. He was still contending with all three of his attackers. "Conrad!" she cried.

He was in front of her in an instant, arm shoved back to yank her into him. His body was a heated mass of muscle, his broad shoulders rising and falling with breaths—

Breaths?

She laid her ear against his back. His heart was pounding. *I blooded him!*

"A new liability, Wroth?" Cade asked, wiping his forearm over his bleeding face. "Introduce us to your Bride, then."

"If you think to harm her," Conrad grated, "then you invite your own end." He grasped her upper arm, pulling her beside him.

Néomi swallowed when some of the females gave her sympathetic looks. *What do they know that I don't? What will he do to me?*

This was an immortal assassin who'd just been denied a kill. Denied because of her. She could see a feral, possessive light to his eyes, along with a deep rage, as if not slaying those demons had taken something from him.

No one wanted to challenge him—a vampire protecting his Bride. He cupped his hand on the back of her neck in a show of possession for everyone to see. *"Mine. And I protect what's mine."*

Then . . . they disappeared.

28

When Conrad traced them to their room at Elancourt, he didn't say a word, just stared down at her. Rage mingled with desire in his expression, both so intense she shivered alternately with fear and need.

He released her, stalking around her, his gaze raking over her body. She turned as well, until they were circling each other.

"How did you come to be like this?"

"I have *ways*, Conrad. Maybe I'm not as friendless and pitiful as you thought me."

He gave a bitter laugh. "Pity is the *last* thing I'm feeling for you, *koeri*."

"What are you planning to do with me?" she asked.

"You're soon to see." His low voice rolled over her—she could swear she could feel it rumbling.

They continued circling, almost as if in a dance. Her long-dormant senses had already been flaring to life, and with every second, she grew more deeply aroused. "Why were some of the females regarding me with sympathy?"

"They think they know what's about to happen

to you. You're the Bride of a fallen vampire denied a kill."

Things were going on in his mind that she couldn't understand. All she knew for certain was that he was more animalistic than any man she'd ever known. "What do they think will happen?" She believed Conrad would never *intentionally* hurt her. But he did alarm her. He was unspeakably strong, and her new body was so vulnerable.

"That I'll throw you to the ground and shove myself between your legs, taking your neck in a frenzy." He sounded as if the very idea excited him. Without warning, he seized her upper arms, dragging her to his body.

"Let me go, Conrad!" She could feel his erection growing, pressing against her belly. "What are you going to do?"

"I'm going to claim my Bride. You've been given to me—to me alone! It was *you* that I wanted." He fisted his hand in her hair, pulling her head to the side hard. Eyes riveted to her neck, he rubbed his tongue on his fang, then rasped, "*I can see your beautiful pulse.*"

Stifling a cry, she said, "You're hurting me, Conrad." *Try to sound calm.* She intuitively knew she had one chance at this—one chance with him. She didn't believe he'd ever forgive himself for harming her. "Do you intend to punish me over the key? Or are you losing control again?"

Still staring at her neck, he drew his brows together. "Hurt you?" When she attempted to pry his hand from her hair, he released it. "Never hurt you." Even as he was saying this, his other hand was gripping her arm. "I was wrong about the key. Have regret for my words."

And just like that, with two simple, unmistakable sentiments, her anger dwindled. "If you want more with me, then don't proceed like this, when you're enraged and fresh from a fight." She twisted her arm from his fist. "Don't hurt the body I was just given."

He breathed in deeply, so clearly struggling for command of himself. "If I can get . . . can get control now"—his head jerked to the side and back—"you'll forgive me for losing it over the key. Say it!"

"Yes, if you can do this for us." Néomi dared to reach up and stroke the backs of her fingers along his jawline. She experienced a jolt of surprise—this was the first time their skin had touched.

And this vampire, so brutal and violent to others, leaned his handsome face into her touch. She laid her other hand over his thundering heart. "Conrad, *je crois en toi*. I believe in you. Go to the folly."

When he hesitated, she said, "I promise I'll be right here when you return."

He gave her a sharp nod, before vanishing.

Back to the foggy bayou, stalking his familiar path. His mind was in turmoil.

Now his body was as well.

He inhaled, shuddering as cool air continued to flood into his lungs. It felt just as his brother had said it would. *Heavy . . . good.*

Three hundred years he'd gone without this, but now . . .

Conrad had been blooded. By the lush little

dancer he'd wanted above all other females. God, she'd smelled like fire and wine and *woman*. Too good to be true. Maybe this was all another dream, more madness.

He hadn't wanted to let her out of his sight, dreading she'd disappear, but if he hadn't left, he would've hurt her. The urge to rip away her clothes and plunge into her warm body had been nearly overwhelming.

She was so delicate—so *mortal*. He could break her bones with an absent touch.

And he would rather die than give her pain. He might be fallen and newly blooded. But this was *Néomi*, the woman he'd coveted for his Bride—and had been given in the flesh.

Though he burned to know how she'd come to be like this, all he could think about was the unbearable drag of his pants across his engorged cock.

With each heartbeat, his shaft grew thicker. This had to be truly happening. He grimaced from the pressure, unable to concentrate, to handle these shocking changes within himself.

It felt like three centuries of lust was building, as if his shaft would explode, it throbbed so hard. Just when he believed the pressure couldn't possibly build more . . .

. . . it did.

He should leave here for good. But could he give this night up? Néomi was actually in their room, waiting to be touched. To be taken.

She believes I can do this.

She'd said she wanted more with him. He could finally experience what this would be like. The only obstacle to his claiming her was the threat he posed to her. He had to make sure he didn't hurt her.

But then he had to pleasure her as well.

At least before, his anger and instinct had commanded him. Now he wondered how he could possibly satisfy her. He bit out a curse—he'd never even kissed a woman before.

She's waiting for me.

His eyes briefly widened. She'd told him exactly how to proceed with her, to make her want more, to make her desperate for him.

As Conrad stalked toward her, she studied his face. He seemed less frenzied. Or maybe he was only disguising it better, turning it inward.

Once he'd backed her to the wall, he raised his hand. *What will he do?* She swallowed with apprehension. . . .

Yet he only cupped her face. The gesture was gentle, tender. When he grated, "Put your arms around my neck," she realized what he planned. How hard he was trying for her!

And this is why I'm falling for you.

At this exact spot in the room, they'd practiced their kiss, both of them imagining it. It felt so natural when her arms looped around his neck. She'd longed to be able to twine her fingers in the hair at his nape. Now she did with delight.

"My Néomi," he rasped, rubbing his thumb over her bottom lip. "So soft." Her eyelids fluttered. "More than I'd ever imagined." His hand was shaking.

He's never touched a woman before me. All this was new to him. She needed to remember that.

"For three hundred years my sword hand has been steady. If I'm to be overcome, I'd want it to be by a little dancer."

His scent, his heat . . . God, he smelled so good. "Conrad, I want our kiss. Won't you brush your lips against mine?"

"What if I wanted to do something harder?"

"Think slow build," she forced herself to say—because he still was barely in control.

He stared down at her with eyes like fire, then leaned in to give her what she'd yearned for. When he slanted his lips over hers, a shock of heat rushed through her. She cried out, and he slipped his tongue in.

But he allowed her to lead. She lapped at his tongue, teasing and licking, making him groan. Soon he began deepening the kiss, stroking his tongue against hers.

She held onto his shoulders, reveling in the power she felt in his muscles, and whenever he did something she liked she gave a little squeeze.

He caught on handily. So much so, that he became the one who teased her now, flicking his tongue and stoking her desire. *Clever vampire.* His kiss was ardent, erotic . . . demanding.

When he glanced the backs of his fingers from her ear down past her collarbone, then lower to the beginning swell of her breast, she shivered. Simply experiencing contact was a delight to her starved senses, but Conrad's touch was mesmerizing. . . .

He broke away, leaving her breathless and dizzy. As his lips followed the same path as his fingers, she grew nearly frightened by how aroused she'd become, not with *longing*, but with pure lust for this male.

Her breasts grew heavy, her nipples stiffened. She could feel wetness between her legs.

"Want my mouth on you." He fisted her dress in both his hands, about to rip it apart.

"Conrad, let me." She shimmied, tugging it until it was wedged beneath her bare breasts.

A rough sound erupted from him as he gazed at her. Then he bent to her chest. Just as he'd said, he kissed all around her nipples, brushing his lips over her sensitive flesh.

She cradled his head, holding him to her. "Forget what I said . . . about a slow build."

He ran his face against her but still teased. When he finally dragged his tongue over one of her aching nipples, she cried out, "Oh, God!"

"You wanted me to suck on it hard?" he asked, cupping both of her breasts in his hands.

She whimpered in answer, and he returned his mouth, tugging her nipple between his lips to lick it at the same time. He gave a husky groan around the peak, then suckled her.

"Yes, yes . . ." *Friction, moisture, bliss.* Her fingers dug in his hair, pressing him closer as she arched wantonly.

When he switched to her other breast, squeezing as he sucked her, she couldn't stand it any longer. She clutched his hips. And he remembered. He eased his big hand under her dress, his skin deliciously abrasive against her tender thigh.

"Higher," she panted. "Touch me. . . ."

While he slowly raised his hand, she began frantically unbuttoning his shirt, shoving it from him. Placing her palms flat against him, she rubbed down his torso over rigid indentations and swells. His firm, smooth skin . . . the crisp hair in a trail just below his navel—*heavenly*.

His hand worked higher, hers drifting lower. He shot upright, standing fully when she clasped his erection outside his pants. The first woman to touch him there.

As she began fondling his shaft, his lids grew heavy, his jaw slackening. He bit out what sounded like an oath, then hooked his finger under the edge of her panties, pulling the silk aside.

At his first tentative foray of her sex, she quivered, and a harsh groan burst from his chest. "Ah, Néomi, you're so *wet*. . . ."

She moaned as he caressed her, spreading the moisture as if he was fascinated by her body's reaction. Stroking him, she murmured, "And you're so hard."

His hand stilled. Their gazes met. They both knew what came next.

"Can't even think about taking your neck . . . hanging on by a thread . . ."

"Then take me to bed."

Clasping her up into his arms, he carried her there and set her down.

She worked free his belt as he yanked off her boots, then his own. With a hissed-in breath, he eased his pants past his straining erection.

Oh, my. Her first sight of him aroused. His thick

shaft jutted, pulsing in tandem with each new beat of
his heart. The sleek skin of the crown was stretched
taut, visibly slick. Even as part of her felt as if she'd just
unwrapped a tantalizing present, another part of her
felt a flare of alarm over his size.

But she shook away her fear. *I'm the old Néomi once
more*, she reminded herself. She'd make sure they were
both ready when he entered her. Confident, she lay
back and opened her arms for him.

His brows drew together in an anguished expression as he followed her down. "*Christ, I hope this is real.*"

29

"This is real," she murmured between kisses. "I'm really here."

"How?"

"I wanted to be with you like this so badly. And now I can." She placed his hand on her breast.

With a groan, he palmed one, then the other, his breaths growing ragged.

Néomi was aroused for him but overwhelmed, attracted yet anxious. His erection prodded against her hip, the wide head so hot and slick, seeming to scald her skin.

"Conrad." She wriggled her chest when he grew a fraction too rough. "A little lighter."

He froze. When he eased his grip, and she stilled, he said, "I can be gentle with you."

Releasing her, he softly rasped her nipple with the back of his fingernail, then dragged the pad of his finger over it. She moaned sharply when he did it again. "Better?"

She found herself nodding against his shoulder. Somehow the assassin was gentling his callused hands on her—such a contrast to his ruthless fighting tonight.

Back and forth came the rasp of his nail and the maddening drag of his finger, over and over, until her nipples ached so badly they pained her.

"Tell me—say you like it."

"Uh-hmm, I like it."

In a husky voice, he said, "I can feel them throbbing, *koeri*."

She moaned again, arching her back. He responded by leaning down, his hot mouth suckling her, those firm, cruel lips pulling on one peak, then the other. As he inched his hand up her leg, he began slowly grinding against her hip.

Nuzzling her damp nipple, he said, "Spread your legs, Néomi. I want to touch you inside . . . learn you." Even as she ached for his touch, she grew nervous. Though she wasn't a virgin, he could still accidentally hurt her.

He tugged on her knee with a wildly quaking hand.

"Part your thighs for me." After hesitating, she . . . did. "Ah, that's it. Let me see you there." With a last lick over one of her stiff nipples, he relinquished her breasts to sit up above her. When he stared at her between her legs, he exhaled in a rush, and his shaft jerked in his excitement.

This aroused her even more. As she reached her arm around him to smooth her hand over the glorious muscles of his back, he ran his forefinger along her sex.

She needed to kiss him, to lick his body, to get her legs wider for him—

His big finger entered her.

She squirmed and moaned from the filling sensation, as he delved deeper, inch by inch. When he could go no farther, she cried out.

He stilled. "Have I hurt you?"

"No, oh, God! *N'arrête pas!*"

He began thrusting his finger inside her, grating, *"Tight. So tight."* She'd never felt or imagined any man so hard, yet he took his time learning her body. But in the back of her mind, she wondered if his claiming her as fiercely as the others had predicted might be better than this seething need, barely contained—and building.

Slow build, she'd told him. But where did it end?

"Conrad, please . . ."

"Will you come like this?"

"Yes, and *soon*."

With his lips parted around ragged breaths, he watched his finger slipping in and out of her glistening sheath.

"Conrad, yes, yes . . ." she whimpered, seeming mindless with lust. She leaned up to lick his chest.

He was stunned by how slick she was getting for him, how hungrily her flesh milked his finger. "It's *perfect*," he bit out, his tone sounding awed even to him.

He'd never known a woman could become this abandoned.

Not just a woman. *My woman.*

Unfamiliar urges racked him. He had the strongest *need* to pin her to the bed, so she couldn't get away from him. He had the need to tell her how much she was pleasing him. He bent to murmur at her ear, but his words turned to an agonized hiss when she rocked her hips on his finger.

"Higher . . . with your thumb," she panted.

Groaning at how swollen her little clitoris had gotten, he circled it with his thumb.

She moaned, "*Yes, Conrad . . .*"

With the finger inside her, he could tell when her sex tensed, readying to come. He wanted to make her come, needed to so badly. Just from his fingers.

The idea of giving her his cock to glove like that made him wild, but he wanted to feel what it would be like when she orgasmed.

She was shuddering, quivering, so close. Then, with her nipples tight and pointing, she stiffened, her eyelids sliding shut on a wordless cry. Her legs fell open wide. It was everything he could do not to spill against her hip as she clenched his finger, coming wetly around it, again and again. *Amazing. . . .*

Now he was dying for her to do that around his shaft. As soon as the tension left her body, he knelt between her legs.

Her expression was partly dazed, but still hungry, and her hips undulated as if she ached for him to fill her sheath. Seeing her open to him like this . . .

He laid his hips to hers. Leaning over her on straightened arms, he thrust to enter her, but she rocked down at the same time. He yelled out when the head slipped along her damp folds. She went wild, head thrashing on the pillow.

Sweating, gritting his teeth for control, he tried again, but she rolled her hips once more. He gripped her hips to mount her, but pinning her to the mattress only made her arch her back, rubbing her stiff nipples against his chest.

"Still, *koeri!* Or I'll spill against you!"

"I don't care," she moaned.

"Are you . . . are you about to again?"

"Yes, yes!" When his cock slid up over her mound, she fisted the sheets, arching even more sharply, rubbing up against his shaft. "*Conrad,*" she cried out, jerking beneath him. When her big breasts quivered . . .

To his shame, the throbbing pressure exploded against his will. "Ah, God, you're making me come!" With a yell to the ceiling, he ejaculated against her, pumping hard jets out onto her belly and breasts. He'd never known such ecstasy . . . grinding against her clitoris, he bucked uncontrollably as it continued on and on.

Once he'd finished at last, he buried his face in her hair. Staggered by the pleasure he'd just received, he breathed in her scent.

Then he realized what he'd done. He'd tried to claim his Bride, and instead had humiliated himself by losing his seed before he could even enter her. Tightening his jaw with frustration, he hammered his fist into the mattress.

Yet then . . . she was kissing him. Happily. "We have all night, *mon trésor adoré.* By the fifth or sixth time, I'll bet you can last as long as you please." She nipped his earlobe, then sucked him there before murmuring, "Get a towel, darling. . . ."

Reluctantly he rose and headed for the bathroom, feeling as if she might as well have sent him on a years-long hunt for the grail. That was how difficult it was for him to leave her. He still dreaded she'd disappear.

He couldn't imagine how she'd become embodied since the last time he'd seen her, and burned to know. The situation was enough to make anyone start doubting his sanity. Again.

He knew that just days ago she'd been . . . dead. Now, she was blooming with life.

Yet with all his memories, he'd certainly seen stranger things in the Lore, and he had time to discover her secret. For now all he wanted was another chance to get inside her—and another chance to make her climax again.

The tales he'd heard had always made pleasing a woman sound impossible, fantastical even. His shoulders back, he reminded himself that he might not have claimed her properly, but he had made her come more than once on his first try.

Recalling her abandon made blood surge to his groin. Though he'd spent his seed till his body felt emptied, his shaft was already hardening before he'd even gotten a wet towel.

Five or six times? At least, koeri.

But when he returned, she was already sound asleep. Her lips were parted delicately, her lashes thick on her pink cheeks. Her arm curled beside her head, the back of her hand against her ear.

Any disappointment at having to wait was dimmed by the thought of how exhausted she must be after a night like this. Recently embodied, attacked, and likely intoxicated. Her lips had been wine-reddened, her mouth sweet with it.

Leaning over her, towel in hand, he cleaned her skin with gentle strokes, marveling at how she was formed. She had a strong, lithe body. A dancer's body—that had responded to his touch as if it'd been trained to. Nothing had ever felt so right to him.

My Bride, he thought, his chest filled with pride. *No vampire has a more beautiful one*, he decided easily.

Once he'd wiped her off, he studied her at his leisure. On his hands and knees over her, he gazed down. He feared he'd soon grow obsessed with her breasts. How they quivered and how soft they were. How her nipples had budded as if demanding his mouth on them.

With a groan, he stroked himself, still surprised by the unfamiliar stiffness. But he vowed the next time he came it would be deep inside her body and to the sound of her cries. . . .

He'd always regretted not having sex at least once in his lifetime. Curiosity had plagued him—now it tormented. Taking her would be mind-blowing.

Yet he was still too new to sex to predict how he'd react. *Mind-blowing*. He didn't know if that would work out well for the insane vampire.

And how could he keep from hurting her little body when he did it? Tonight he'd felt her inside, had discovered how tight she was—there was no way he could fit into her without causing her pain.

He tried to push aside the doubts. Ignoring the ache in his shaft, he lay back and dragged her warm body to him. He exhaled with pleasure when she slid her smooth leg up over his knees and draped her arm over his chest—exactly as he'd imagined them sharing this bed.

He knew he would be unrelentingly aroused

through the night, but he would savor it, relishing her touches, the way she was already squeezing his chest in sleep. All night he would get to enjoy the scent of her hair. He could feel her heart beating against him, and he eventually lost himself in the soothing rhythm. . . .

Near dawn, he shot upright in bed. Leaning over her side, he planted his hand across her body, caging her in protectively, eyes darting.

No one was there—just the wind.

She murmured in French and turned to him trustingly. His Bride was now so fragile, so . . . *mortal.* No longer was she invulnerable to harm. He would be endangering her just by keeping her with him.

The Woede now knew he had a weakness. They would be relentless trying to capture her. In their minds, she equaled Rydstrom's crown. Conrad would gladly give them the damned information if he could pull it up, but they'd never believe he wasn't simply withholding it—not until they were threatening her.

Before, Tarut's curse had constantly shadowed him—now it had become a thousand times more imperative to destroy the demon.

Conrad had been given his dream. Was some force out there even now seeking to take it from him? If he even remotely believed in the power of the curse, then how fair was it to stay with her? Or was the damage already done? If he deserted her now, then he could be leaving her vulnerable to attack. . . .

In any case, Conrad wouldn't consider her safe until he was in possession of Tarut's head.

Forcing himself to set her away, he traced downstairs. He knew a crude protection conjuring that would guard her at least while she was here. By the front doors, he dipped his fingertips in the crumbling plaster, using it as chalk to inscribe the ancient lettering. Once he felt confident no trespassers could enter their home, he returned to the bed.

Conrad would remain here only until sunrise. After that, he'd begin providing all the things she apparently lacked: food, clothes, women's things . . .

As he pulled her back into his arms, he thought back over the hectic night. In the past, Néomi had looked at Conrad like he was a hero and had called him a protector, even though she knew many of his sordid secrets. She'd told him she believed in him.

Tonight he hadn't disappointed her.

He'd never forget the absolute conviction in her eyes when she'd said, "Now I understand what you *were*." She'd been so sure of him that she'd already appeared *proud*.

But she didn't know of his secret fantasies of taking *her* neck in a frenzy.

I'm the worst threat to her.

Even in the midst of the mind-numbing pleasure she'd given him tonight, he'd experienced fear for her, for the dangerous things she made him feel.

If you care for her, you'll let her go now, his long-dead conscience whispered. And yet he found his arms squeezing her closer to him. *Mine.*

30

When he returned from errands that morning, Conrad heard the shower going. He made out her soft sighs under the sound of the water.

Tossing away the bags of items he'd purchased for her, he postponed his plans to discuss how she'd been changed from ghost to mortal. In seconds, he had his clothes off, then silently traced into the tiled stall with her.

Her eyes were closed, and she was leisurely exploring her body. Licking drops of water from her lips, she cupped her breasts, as though relearning them.

Making himself as quiet as if he were hunting, he stared, riveted. Her raven hair was pulled over her shoulder, draping her pale breast, her hard nipple peeking through it.

He didn't think he breathed as her fingers skimmed down her flat belly and her legs parted for them. But he had to wonder if she would hear his heart slamming inside his chest.

When her dark nails glinted in the light as she began delicately stroking her sex, he bit back a groan and fisted his suddenly aching cock. She focused on her clitoris, briefly slipping her finger inside, as if to gather moisture for her rubbing.

He marveled at the expression of building ecstasy on her face. He wanted to see her look up at him like that when he entered her. *Abandon.* Never in all his years had he seen anything as awing as this female pleasuring herself.

But even as he realized that he could watch her and learn how she liked to be touched, he resented that she hadn't waited for him.

He'd satisfied her last night, so why hadn't she? Perhaps he needed to remind her why she should have.

When her moan turned nearly constant, he stopped her before she could come.

Just before she climaxed, she heard Conrad rasp, "Ah-ah."

Her eyes flashed open. He was in here with her, and she'd never heard him?

At once, her gaze was drawn downward to his jutting erection. The last time they'd been in the shower together, his manhood had been splendid. Erect, it was mouthwatering. She knew from last night that he'd grow so slick along that wide head. . . .

Yet when she reached to stroke his length, he seized her wrists behind her, yanking her body into his.

They were both breathing heavily as the hardened peaks of her breasts rubbed against him, and his stiff penis pressed against her belly.

"Why didn't you wait for me?" He had that intense, dangerous air about him.

"I woke . . . the sheets were rubbing over . . . my nipples." She shivered.

"If you have these needs, I want to satisfy them."

"I didn't know when you were returning," she said. "But you're here now." She leaned up on her tiptoes to kiss him. What started as her gentle foray soon blazed into a searing kiss. He crushed her lips beneath his as their tongues twined again and again.

When they broke apart, both out of breath, she murmured, "Conrad, I need you to make love to me."

At her words, his shaft pulsed against her.

"I think I'll die if you don't."

Instead, he released her wrists and cupped her ass in his hands, lifting her. Before she could say a word, he'd turned his back to the water and raised her to his mouth as if she weighed no more than a doll. Cradling her with splayed fingers, he eased her back so she could lean her head against the tile. She buried her fingers in his thick hair as she held on to him.

Running his face against her thighs, he abraded her with the stubble on his lean cheeks, and she loved it. Everything felt magnified. Each drop of water that splashed her skin heightened her pleasure.

But would he enjoy taking her with his mouth? He'd never done this before, had never tasted a woman.

When his tongue first dipped to her flesh, he gave a harsh groan against her. Pressing his mouth to her core, he thrust his tongue inside her, licking her deeply, thoroughly.

"Yes!" With a cry, she jerked her legs, tightening them on his shoulders. But he held her fast.

"I'll never get enough of this," he grated, settling

back in to suck and lick. As his fingers clutched her ass almost painfully, his strong tongue snaked over her throbbing clitoris again and again.

"There!" she cried, then moaned, "Conrad, right there."

Flicking . . . suckling . . . hard. When she came with a scream, undulating to his mouth, he set in with a frenzy. He never allowed her to take a breath before he was making her moan for another orgasm, forcing her body to strain for release once again.

Even more powerful than the first, this climax overwhelmed her. Her eyes flashed open in surprise as she melted against his greedy tongue, helplessly rubbing her flesh against it.

Once it was over at last, she had to push at his head, because he was still slowly laving her, lingering with low growls.

When he finally let her slide down his body, he held her steady. She felt how hard he was, yet he still made no move to take her. His expression was inscrutable, his shaft visibly pulsing with need.

"Don't you want to make love to me?" Naturally, she was all about living in the moment and was eager to fully experience this virile, compelling male.

But now there was something more.

She also wanted to join with him, because for the first time in her life she wanted to give herself to a man she . . . loved.

I'm in love with Conrad.

Though she'd never fully admitted it before now, her feelings weren't new. They'd been growing since the first night she'd seen him in all his wildness.

"Conrad, do you want to?"

He shook his head.

"Oh." Her face fell. "I see." Then she frowned. "No, I *don't* see."

"I fear hurting you," he said, his breaths still ragged from what they'd just done. The way she'd rocked to his mouth to give him more . . . He stifled a groan. "I felt how tight you are. I've thought about this all morning and do not see how I can spare you pain. I . . . can't give you pain."

She tilted her head at him. "You'd forgo your chance to be inside a woman because of consideration for me?"

He grated, "*Of course.*"

Her lips parted, and she laid her palm against the side of his face. "You're such a surprise, vampire. Such a wonderful surprise." Her hand trailed down his body. "Honestly, I've never been with a man as big as you"—she cupped the underside of his shaft, making him buck to her hand—"in all respects. But if you make sure I'm prepared, everything will be fine."

He ground his teeth. *I don't know how!* He could do as he'd done last night, but would that be enough to *prepare* her? He'd barely fit his finger inside her, even when she was wet.

She must have sensed his thoughts, because she licked a drop of water from his chest and said, "If you take me to bed, I'll show you exactly what I need—"

Conrad had her swooped up in his arms before she'd finished the sentence. Not bothering to dry off, he traced to the bed and laid her in it, following her down. Water dripped along their sides.

Her lips curled. "I guess you like that idea, then?"

He nodded. If she could show him how to do this . . . *God, to finally be inside her.*

As he leaned over her on his knees, she lightly grasped his forefinger, using it to slowly stroke her sex, from the opening up to her clitoris and back. Once she guided it inside her, he began thrusting with it.

Soon she murmured, *"J'ai besoin de deux."* She needed two of his fingers inside her.

He swallowed, but began working another finger in. Her knees fell wide open, her wetness growing. "Perfect, Conrad." With both of her small hands, she pressed his palm firmly against her until his fingers were seated deep. Eyes heavy-lidded, she whispered, "Spread them inside me."

He did, shuddering with pleasure when her back arched.

"Now in and out . . ."

He thrust his spread fingers. "This way?"

"Ah, yes! More . . ."

He gave her more.

"Conrad, now."

"Are you ready?"

"I don't . . . care. I need . . ."

As much as he wanted to replace his fingers with his cock, he had to be sure. He caressed and delved inside her, until she grazed her teeth against his shoulder in frustration. "Are you still worried?" she asked, panting.

"I still do not see that we can . . . fit."

"This is supposed to be enjoyable, darling. Let me show you how well we'll fit." She nudged his wrist, and he removed his fingers. Once she'd gotten him to turn to his back, she crawled over him, straddling his hips.

As her breasts rose and fell with her quick breaths, her fingers dug into the muscles of his chest, just as she'd said she would do days ago. She appeared fascinated, her tender palms running all over him.

He felt a savage thrill to see the way her gaze roamed over him. *My battle-scarred body is good for more than taking hits.* It aroused her.

When she curled her fingers around his shaft to guide it inside her, he hissed in a breath. *This is finally going to happen. . . .* The anticipation had him rolling his hips. He swallowed loudly, wondering if he'd last any longer than the time before.

He was already struggling to hold on, his cock throbbing with seed. "Want this so much . . ." When she began to mount him, his hands flew to her hips, gripping her. "Néomi, I—"

Her flesh was hot and slick as it met his. His eyes rolled back in his head.

31

The only thing sexier than a completely smitten male was a smitten male who'd never been with a woman. And Néomi was on fire for him.

Yet even as she ached, she savored Conrad's reactions. Once she began to work the broad head inside her, he gave a short, stunned groan. His lips parted as he stared at where they were joining.

This was all new for her as well. She'd fallen for him utterly.

She was truly making love. "Is this everything you'd hoped?"

"Ah, God, *you* . . ." He tried to speak again, failed, then gave a sharp nod. "Didn't know . . . to hope for . . . this much."

The look of wonder in his eyes as he watched her move on him made her feel sexier than she could ever remember feeling. His big body was so incredibly strong, and yet she was in control of it now, was about to take pleasure from it.

She relished the power, moaning as she settled farther along his length.

Chin to his chest, he shuddered. "Hot," he grunted. "Tight." She knew he was beginning to lose control, his hands quaking on her hips. His muscles were already straining, from his corded neck all the way to the sharp indentations leading from his waist to his groin.

"Take it deeper, Néomi." His accent was so thick.

Biting her bottom lip, she rose up and eased down farther. She was aching for more, too, but his size was challenging.

"Need more," he growled low in his throat, his knees falling open. "*More.*"

She rocked forward, then sank back harder, but his hips surged up at the same time—his shaft plunged deep in a searing thrust.

"Ah, God, Néomi!"

She winced, unable to bite back a cry.

"Your eyes are watering. You told me you wouldn't hurt! But I've hurt you."

"Just give me a second, Conrad," she whispered. The fit was so tight that she could perceive him throbbing inside her. "Can you do that?"

He grated out the word, "*Somehow.*"

After long moments, she tentatively rocked up and back, then again. Each time she could take his length more readily, her body accommodating his.

Soon pleasure subdued the pain, and his heated reactions fueled her own arousal. When she began to ride him in long, steady strokes, he yelled out her name. Once she pried free his death grip from her hips and placed his palms over her breasts, he gave a desperate groan as he squeezed them. Dragging her nails up his inner thighs had him shuddering, drawing his knees up for more.

By the time he was on the brink, she wasn't far behind.

Néomi let herself go completely. . . .

This was what he'd missed out on. This was what he'd ached for.

Inside his woman, he'd never known greater pleasure. He'd been waiting his entire life for this. . . .

She threw her head back, arching. Her long hair swept over his thighs. Clutching his legs behind her, she rode him faster. Her breasts quivered as his cock disappeared inside her again and again.

Seeming lost in her own pleasure, she writhed on him, raising her slim arms, stretching and twining her hands over her head. She held her elbows as she whipped her hips.

When she twisted her body at the end of the motion, he rasped, "My God, *how you move.*"

With each snap of her hips, the pressure to come built within him, but he vowed she would first. "Want you to—" His words died in his throat when she lowered both of her hands, letting them graze down her body to her sex. He shuddered out a breath as she began masturbating atop him.

"Néomi!" His control slipping, he drove up between her thighs hard, bouncing her on his shaft.

But she gasped in delight. "Do that again. . . ."

He released her breasts to cup her plump ass, working her up and down his length as he thrust at the same time. "You like that?"

"Yes!" she cried, rubbing her clitoris faster.

"*Come on me, Bride.*"

"Oh, yes!" Her eyelids fluttered, she licked her lips, then she moaned loudly.

In total abandon, she climaxed.

All around his cock, he felt the tugging clench of her sex. *Control slipping.* Her sheath seemed greedy for his seed. He could barely resist the demand.

Instinctive drives overwhelmed him. He wanted to obey them. *Mark her, claim her, bite her.* He needed his scent all over her, in her. He needed her blood on his tongue.

Before he could stop himself, he turned her to her back, shoving her legs wide.

Pinning her hands over her head, he began pumping his hips between her thighs. "I'm losing . . . control. *Néomi!*"

His eyes were wild. His massive body loomed over her, his muscles rippling with strain. He could do anything he wanted to.

Néomi had feared she would never experience Conrad like this—her powerful warrior, captive to his own fierce need. Now she could, if she believed in him, if she trusted him not to hurt her.

She surrendered herself . . .

As if he sensed her yielding to him, he rose to his knees to take her with more force. Gripping her shoulders to hold her in place, he plunged his shaft into her again and again. She'd never known anything like this—being taken without mercy, helpless to do anything more than accept the pleasure.

With each buck of his hips, he gave a short, rough groan, each growing louder until he was yelling.

Her head thrashed on the pillow. "Conrad . . ." she moaned, lost in another boundless orgasm.

"*I feel you coming on me . . .*" He clutched the back of her neck and rasped, "You're *mine*, Néomi." With his body tensing all around her, his eyes met hers as he began to ejaculate inside her. His expression turned to one of shock, then anguish. As soon as she felt his hot seed jetting so strongly within her, ecstasy lit his face.

He held her gaze . . . until his back bowed and his head shot back from the strength of his release. On and on, he filled her. She dimly heard his husky murmur: "*Nothing better . . . nothing.*"

With a final shove, he collapsed atop her, his breaths harsh against her neck, his heart pounding over hers. Still semihard in their wetness, he continued to thrust over her slowly, as if he didn't want to relinquish his new discovery.

He muttered, "My God, Néomi."

She grazed her fingertips up and down his sweat-slicked back, sighing with contentment. "I could die happy," she sighed, then frowned. *I will die happy.* No, she wouldn't consider it dying. She was *leaving*—simply moving on to a new existence. And after sharing this body with Conrad, allowing them both to know this pleasure, she was even more confident with her decision.

He never would have experienced this if he hadn't been blooded. . . .

"How could I have lived without that?" he grated. "I never knew." He'd demanded . . . everything from her. She'd seen it in his eyes as he came. He'd wanted her to yield to him, to desire him, to love him.

And she did love this vampire, with all her heart.

When he raised himself up, he gave her a sexy, cocky grin that made her breath hitch. "I was good, wasn't I?"

She reached up and stroked his face. "The best I've ever had or imagined." When he went still, she said, "It's the truth. Some men are just instinctively better lovers."

The grin returned. "Imagine when I practice on you five times a night."

"I can't wait." At her murmured words, his shaft jerked inside her, hardening and thickening so fast, she gasped.

"Time for practice, *koeri*."

32

"Where did you go this morning?" Néomi asked, once she'd finished savoring the most delectable croissant ever crafted in the history of mankind.

After the second time they'd made love, he'd been ready—and raring—for another round, but she'd groaned, *"Food. Your mortal needs food."*

He'd asked her what she would like if she could have anything in the world. "A hot, buttery croissant, with café au lait and fresh-squeezed orange juice." So naturally, Conrad had traced to France and brought exactly that back to her.

"I had errands to do," he answered. It was then that she noticed his hair was freshly cut, though it remained a tad too long, as she liked it. The ends were still wet from his quick shower. And he was wearing crisp new clothes—understated, dark, but unmistakably moneyed.

He was handsome as the devil, and with those fiery eyes, he looked more than a little devilish.

Forever the red would remind her of fire.

"Errands? Like what?"

"I've brought things for you." He handed over shopping bags that said Harrods on them. *Lots* of bags.

Apparently, he'd been to London as well. "You needed clothes. And there are . . . gifts." He coughed into his fist, his voice gruff. And she knew with certainty that he'd never bought anything for a woman before.

There was *everything*—shoes, dresses, sweaters, slacks. She found a toiletry kit with shampoos, perfumes, and lotions.

"A saleswoman said this would have anything you could need."

Néomi dug into more bags, savoring the different fabrics and the expensive designs. And not a black satin party gown among the offerings! "Vampire, you have excellent taste!" she said in delight.

He shrugged, but she could tell he was satisfied that he'd pleased her.

She found a felt box with a jeweled hair comb inside. "Conrad, it's so lovely!" Then she frowned at the facets of light in the stones. "These aren't real, are they?"

"Of course."

"Are you rich, then?"

"Exceedingly." His shoulders shot back, his posture straightening. "I don't look like I'd have money?"

"Oh, that's not it. It's just so dear. I adore these types of combs."

"I know. You stole one from Murdoch."

With a sheepish grin, she continued exploring. She pulled out a tiny pair of black thong panties—one among many colors and styles—and quirked a brow. "Let me guess. This is what they're wearing in London?"

"It cost me much to buy you those."

"Were they expensive?"

His face flushed. "They cost me because I could scarcely walk after imagining your body in them. Women's undergarments have a whole new appeal now that I've felt and kissed what goes into them."

She nibbled her bottom lip. "You were aroused in the store?" He glanced away and nodded. She'd have loved to have seen that. "Next time you can take me with you, and I'll model them for you."

Returning his gaze to her, he said, "Néomi, tell me how this transformation happened."

And just like that, it happened. The question she had been dreading. "The specifics are my secret, Conrad. I made a vow never to reveal them. I'm sorry, but that's how it must be."

"You won't confide in me?" he asked, his tone astonished.

"*Non,*" she said firmly. "If you insist, I still won't tell you, and then we'll quarrel."

"I'm to know nothing about how my Bride went from ghost to mortal?"

"I'm going to ask you to do this for me. I'm going to hope that you won't question why, and that you'll just accept when something good has happened for us."

"I can't simply ignore this."

Making her demeanor businesslike, she said, "Then I'm going to have to make it one of the conditions for us to be together."

"One of the conditions? You have more?"

"Yes, as a matter of fact. You have to promise me that there won't be any killing while I'm with you. Unless it's in self-defense."

He narrowed his eyes. "I can make that promise."

"And I have a last one." This morning when she'd awakened, she'd realized how close he'd come to taking her neck last night. If Conrad drank her blood, it wouldn't matter how guarded they all were about the secret. With her memories, he could discover everything—he would know her secret, and then that would be the end of her.

Néomi's new existence was going to last as long as possible, just as long as Conrad didn't discover how short it was destined to be.

"I know I told you in the past that I wouldn't deny you if you wanted to drink from me, but I've had a change of heart."

"Agreed," he hastily said. "It will *not* happen."

She frowned. This was the answer she'd hoped for, but his adamant tone confused her. "I'd thought you would want to. Do you fear getting my memories? Perhaps of other men?"

"A vampire never sees his Bride's memories of other males. The way my kind fixates—it'd be impossible to get past that. I won't drink you, because I could kill you."

"But don't your brothers drink from their wives?"

"Their wives are immortal—they can't die like that. I could drain your body dry in seconds."

"Then you won't ever slip up?"

"I *can't* slip up."

She studied his face. "So you agree to my terms for our liaison?"

"Did you always spell out stipulations for the use of your body?"

Her lips thinned. "Yes, I did. Since I intend to use yours as well, I'd be glad to hear your terms."

He stood and paced. "There will be times when I have to leave, but I'll do it when you sleep. I've put a protection on Elancourt against intruders, so you must vow to me that you'll stay inside the manor when I'm gone."

"Very well, but I won't be sleeping much." *I can sleep when I'm dead.* "And why do you have to leave if you're not working again?" When he hesitated, she said, "I've witnessed your recovery, Conrad. I can't watch you succumb again."

"I have to track the demon who marked my arm and destroy him before he kills me."

"Then it's in self-defense?" she asked. He gave a single nod. "Will you drink from him?"

"I will do everything I can to prevent that."

"And what about Cade and Rydstrom? They'd been searching for you."

"For Rydstrom to reclaim his lost throne, he needs information I . . . acquired. They will be ruthless to get it."

"Acquired? You mean from the memories of the warlock you'd 'drained.'" He shrugged. "Can't you just give it to them?"

"I would if I could. My mind's clearer, but I still can't pull up memories at will." He returned to sit on the edge of the bed beside her. "Why did you believe I wouldn't drink that demon last night?"

"Because you're just not as bad as everyone thinks," she said, repeating her words from days ago. "And because you're starting to look forward instead of back."

He exhaled. "You can't really expect me just to ignore how you came back from death? To not know?"

She shrugged, and his gaze dipped to her bare breasts. "Depends on how badly you want to spend time with me."

His voice harsh, he snapped, "You know how badly."

"Then you liked our morning?" He scowled as if her question was absurd. "Just think, you can have a nubile female here for the taking." Making her voice a purr, she said, "You can do anything to me anytime you like. You'll go from never having had sex to having it whenever the mood strikes you. If you'll just let this lie." This offer alone might take care of his curiosity—but if not, she was fully prepared to demonstrate more of what he'd be gaining.

She grinned. It wouldn't be a chore.

"Just tell me who you were with at the gathering."

"Again, I won't say." She rose to her knees. "Let's drop this, *mon grand*."

Distracted by her hardening nipples, he absently said, "I can't do that." He ran his hand over his mouth, finding it surprisingly erotic that he was completely dressed while she was naked in their bed. He shook himself. "Néomi, I *won't* do that."

As she eased over to him, she got a look in her eyes. He didn't recognize exactly what it said, but it made him instantly hard—and *excited*, his heart pumping wildly.

When she was kneeling up beside him, she nuzzled his ear with hot breaths. "There are so many *other* things we can talk about." Her fingers were busily unbuttoning his shirt as she murmured, "Like any secret fantasies you've harbored and want to experience." She brushed his shirt away. "Or we can skip the talk and simply *do* them. Would you like that?"

Just as he'd imagined once, she was using her wiles on him. He'd planned to withstand her for as long as possible. How . . . *intriguing*—

He sucked in a breath when she fondled his cock through his pants.

"I need these off, Conrad." At once, he yanked his boots off, then shoved his pants past his already straining shaft. Her eyes went heavy-lidded, as if she truly loved that part of him.

"You think I can't see what you're doing?" Once he was undressed, he sat beside her again. "You intend to manage me with sex. You think to direct me."

When she moved to kneel on the floor between his legs, he forgot how to breathe. "*Néomi?*" His voice broke on her name.

She placed her palms on his knees, spreading them, then leaned in. "Is it so bad being directed"—she began licking down his chest, her destination unmistakable—"if you like where you're headed?"

His eyes went wide. *She's going to . . . ? I'm to have this . . . ?*

Once she'd reached his navel, his hands flew to her hair, cupping the back of her head. Then came the first touch of her moist little tongue—

He yelled, "*You good*— ah!" While he stared dumbstruck, threading his fingers in her silky hair, she lovingly licked the swollen head and circled the crown.

With a groan, he opened his knees wider, hands shaking uncontrollably as she took him deeper. Her mouth was feverishly hot on his sensitive flesh. His shaft began to throb under her tongue, and he couldn't stop himself from thrusting it up between her lips.

Never slowing her ministrations, she moved his hands to her high breasts. As he hefted them and thumbed the peaks, she sucked him even more hungrily.

He wanted this never to end, but she began pumping the base of his cock with her soft palms at the same time, and the pressure to come intensified until it pained him. When she moaned around his length, he knew it was over for him.

Have to warn her. On the verge, seconds from losing his seed, he bit out, "*About to . . . come!*"

His jaw slackened when she didn't draw away, instead taking him more greedily. "Néomi!" He rocked his hips up, releasing into her waiting mouth. "*Wicked,*" he groaned in bliss as he shot against her tongue. . . .

Afterward he lifted her to her feet, clutching her against his chest. As Conrad held his female, he was staggered by the pleasure, wrought from him in a way he'd only ever imagined before.

Did he still need to know what had happened with her ghostly state? Of course. But when she placed his hand between her thighs to her feel her damp arousal, the need faded. They were together—that was all that mattered for now.

The rest was just details.

33

Within seconds of Néomi's tentative rap on the studio mirror, Mari appeared, diligently avoiding her own reflection on the other side. "Hold on, I've got to put you on screen. Okay, there you are!"

Néomi had known she couldn't go through the portal of the glass without Mari, but she'd figured she could knock at the door.

"It's about time you contacted me!" Mari held out her hand, breaching the surface of the mirror. "You want to come over?"

"Conrad will be back soon, and I wouldn't be able to hear him. Maybe you can come here?"

"Can't." Mari snapped her fingers to someone out of sight, and a teenage girl brought Mari an enormous cup that said Slurpee on the side. "We're hazing new witches at the coven house today. The innocent lambs are vying for my old room." She plopped into a cushy chair. "We'll have to teleconference via mirror."

Néomi dragged the cot closer to the glass and settled in. She was delighted to be able to talk to Mari, and not just for enjoyment. It would help take her mind off her worry over Conrad. Every time he left to hunt, she grew anxious.

"I see how you're going to be—use me for my spells, then I don't even get another nod for five whole days?"

"It's been so busy!" And the only times Conrad wasn't with her were when she slept. She'd happened to wake early this afternoon. "Are you all right from the gathering? I saw you get hit."

"Oh, yeah, just ducky. But you should see the other guy. He will *never* accidentally elbow another witch again. Even after his elbows grow back."

"That's good to know, I think. Was Nïx terribly disappointed that her gathering devolved into chaos?"

"I asked her the same thing, but she just laughed. I eventually got her to admit that she'd started it. Apparently you and the vampire weren't the only couple thrown together in the melee." She curled her legs under her. "So I take it you blooded the vamp?" When Néomi nodded happily, Mari tilted her head. "Wow, check you out—you look fantastic! A new haircut? And new duds."

She flushed from the praise. "Conrad's been taking me shopping. A lot." In the first few nights, she'd hit Paris with a frenzy, frothing at all the new styles to be had. And she'd had her hair trimmed in a boutique there, but only by a couple of inches, as each snip seemed to physically pain Conrad. "I offered to pay my own way, but he bristled. I tried to point out that I have scads of money, but he wouldn't listen."

"You have . . . *scads of money?*" Mari asked innocently.

Néomi stifled a grin, making her demeanor stern. "Yes. I looked up my certificates. Evidently thirty thousand dollars' worth of IBM and GE stock in the twenties equals approximately a hundred and fifty million today. Though a witch nabbed about twenty-five of it."

Eyes wide, Mari cried, "Who? What! Damn, those witches!"

Néomi couldn't stop a chuckle. She would've given Mari all of it.

"Speaking of witches—you missed girls' night out." Mari set down her Slurpee to cross her arms over her chest. "I don't know if Nïx explained this to you, but GNO is not optional. You will receive demerits for missed attendance. And by demerits, I mean you have to buy drinks for thirsty Wiccae."

"I'm still in the honeymoon phase. Don't I get a pass? Besides, I'm not supposed to go out in the city, not with Cade and Rydstrom in New Orleans."

Mari's expression turned serious. "They'd never hurt you, Néomi. They actually saved my life, back before I'd grown into my immortality."

"Would they hurt Conrad?"

"In a heartbeat," she admitted. "Most of Lorekind hate red-eyed vampires."

Néomi sighed. "Do you?"

"Ah, snap, put Mari in the hot seat! Well, I used to be very certain that I did. But everybody at the gathering was talking about how Conrad Wroth stopped himself from drinking Cade. Even Bowen is in a wait-and-see mode."

"Oh, that's a relief!"

"Still, I'd thought about checking on you anyway, dropping by with a type-A-positive pie or something."

"I'm glad you didn't—I don't want Conrad to learn

that we know each other. He'd do nothing but hound you for my secret." Even now, she listened attentively for his return.

He always went straight to the kitchen to get a mug of blood. She'd hear him open the refrigerator door and close it with the side of his boot. Then he would sit for a spell on the porch steps, drinking and seeming to decompress from the night's hunt. All they were missing was the *Honey, I'm home.* "Speaking of which—I don't suppose Nïx is ever wrong?"

"That would be *never.*"

"*Bien.* We'll keep the secret forever, and then I won't get capped." Néomi could speak Gang as well as the next former ghost from the Jazz Age.

"Néomi . . ." Mari was plainly troubled about her outlook.

"No, I know." She didn't want Mari to be. She was utterly grateful. "Every day I last is just a bonus. And really, I was born a mortal. That means any time I had on earth would *always* be uncertain."

Mari looked unconvinced.

"We just worked with what we had. I have absolutely no regrets."

"What'd you tell him when he asked how you came back?" Mari asked.

"I told him I had a secret, and that I wouldn't talk about it or we'd quarrel."

"And he just let it go? That's weird. Vampires are notoriously single-minded."

Néomi nibbled her bottom lip. "Well, I distract him. . . ."

"You distract—? Ah, I got it." She snapped her fingers again, and another teenager briefly appeared bearing a pastry box. "Beignet?" Mari opened the box and offered it through the glass.

Néomi *was* hungry. This would be her breakfast. Though Conrad escorted her to restaurants for most meals—he pushed food around on his plate and sipped "inferior" whiskey neat—she occasionally had to scrounge in the refrigerator. The shelves were divided in half, with his blood on one side and her juices, leftovers, and fruit on the other. "Café du Monde?"

"Where else?"

Néomi eagerly accepted, plucking one from the box. Still hot! She took a bite, sighing in delight as it melted in her mouth.

"Well, then . . . tell me, what's it like living with a vampire? Is it everything you'd hoped?"

"Better than. Besides shopping, he's been taking me to new places all over the world."

Tracing came in very handy when one had limited time and no passport. Though vampires could only trace to destinations they'd been to previously, Conrad had traveled all over the world in the last three centuries. "For our first foray, he made me close my eyes. When I opened them, we were on a moonlit beach on the Indian Ocean." The wave crests had been bright with luminescence, the breeze a balmy kiss.

It had struck Néomi then that she might just pack in a lifetime of experiences if she could last a year.

"I've never been. Bowen and I have got to travel more," Mari said. "So how's the vamp doing with the rages you told us about?"

"Anytime a male casts an appreciative glance my

way, I fear Conrad will attack him." He was still struggling to temper his aggression, still treading that path by the folly when he needed to cool off.

The men who regarded her had no idea they courted the wrath of a seventeenth-century warlord, ready to lash out over every long look. . . .

"Oh, you get used to that," Mari assured her. "Lore males can be really territorial with their females. But hey, aren't the females right back?"

Though Néomi wasn't of the Lore, she was extremely possessive of her vampire. With his towering, muscle-packed build and that jet black hair, Conrad's presence was beyond arresting. Add the sunglasses, and everyone mistook him for a celebrity. Women, young and old, stopped in their tracks to gape at him. "When one woman continued to leer at his backside, I wanted to pull her hair. Even though she was easily an octogenarian."

Mari snorted at that.

"Are all Lore males ridiculously overprotective as well?" Néomi asked.

"Don't even get me started."

Conrad could be so violent with others, but he'd proved to be protective of her to a fault. "At first I had trouble remembering that I can't float through doors anymore, and I kept butting my forehead—"

Mari thought that was hilarious, coughing on her Slurpee.

Néomi quirked a brow and continued, "But Conrad winces over each slight mark. And a splinter in my finger was rated as calamitous in his eyes."

Mari offered another beignet.

"*Merci.*" Néomi stretched to reach it. "Unfortunately, he's getting more and more suspicious whenever I say or do anything that shows no concern for the future."

"Like what?" Mari asked, brushing powdered sugar from her hands.

"He'd wanted to repair some things around the house, like parts of this studio so I could start practicing again like I used to. I told him there were just so many things I wanted to see now that I can leave the property." She did want to dance, but she had to make choices with her remaining time. "And then, just yesterday, he asked me why I wasn't worried about birth control. It got me thinking—should I be?"

Mari frowned. "I truly don't know. I'll ask around, post it to the discussion board."

What if Néomi could get pregnant? What if she could have their baby before she died? Would she trust the mad vampire assassin with her only child after she was gone? She thought of that fierce, protective light in his eyes whenever he looked at her.

Absolutely.

After a loud *slurp*, Mari said, "Tell me more . . . believe me, my minions are praying to Hekate that you'll keep me occupied all afternoon."

"Well, he's really *intense*. A few nights ago, he offered to desecrate the grave of the man who murdered me." Catching Néomi's gaze, he'd rumbled, "*Bid me to do this, koeri, and it's done.*"

"Aw, that's kind of sweet," Mari said.

"I thought so, too." Eventually. At the time, her lips had parted, and she'd murmured, "*Oh, how . . .*

thoughtful, Conrad." Again, she'd understood the offer was akin to an affectionate gesture from a male like him. "*But let's leave the, er, grave alone for now. I just want to enjoy you.* . . ."

Waggling her eyebrows, Mari asked, "So, is your vamp good in the sack?"

Néomi sighed, "Quite." Not only was Conrad insatiable, the male had *stamina.* He was discovering all the wonders of lovemaking, but she was rediscovering it with a virile male, forever in his prime. "I'd never been with anyone immortal before. There's certainly a difference."

By turns, he could be both gentle and fierce with sex. But he never hurt her, and she loved that she never knew what side of Conrad she'd get.

And the more self-assured in bed he became, the more domineering he grew. His growing confidence thrilled her, giving her delicious shivers because she knew it would only continue to get better and better.

Then she would remember she was *leaving.*

"I knew a witch who slept with a vamp once," Mari said in a lower tone. "I asked her what it was like, and she told me, 'You never forget for a second that you're with a vampire.'"

"*C'est vrai.* That is one hundred percent true. Conrad once told me of having new vampire instincts that overrode his human ones, and I can definitely see it."

Whenever he put his mouth on her, he held her down, until she felt like the caught lure he'd nicknamed her. If he kissed her mouth, he held her face and the back of her neck, as if he feared she'd get away. When he suckled her breasts, he'd greedily cup both of them from the sides, firmly gripping them. As he squeezed, she could almost hear him thinking, *Mine.*

Leaning forward in her chair, Mari asked, "Does he ever want to drink you? I've heard some chicks actually like it."

"I think he does want to, but he never has." Sometimes when they had sex, she sensed him skirting the edge of his control, especially now that he was growing so fatigued from hunting that demon. But she always pulled back from him, and he didn't press. "He's afraid of hurting me."

"He can't have your blood anyway. If he got your memories, then that'd be a surefire way to find out your secret. Think about it—you're never going to tell anyone. I'm not, and Nïx won't. How else could anyone find out unless Conrad drank you?"

"I know. Believe me, I know."

"So what are you going to do if he asks you to marry him or something? Isn't he from the seventeenth century? Guys from the past seem to get really weird about issues like marriage. And I should know, since I married one."

"I've thought and thought about it, and I've decided that I can't in any way promise my future when it's so uncertain." She didn't want Mari to think she was complaining, but pretending with Conrad was already difficult at times—Néomi didn't know how she could make it through even a short marriage ceremony. *Till death do us part . . . possibly next week.*

"Has he told you he loves you yet?"

"No, and I'm glad for it." Néomi knew he'd fallen for her as deeply as she had for him, but she dreaded that he would tell her he loved her. "Whenever I sense he's about to get serious, I keep the mood light."

"What would be so bad about him telling you that?"

"I wouldn't be able to stop myself from saying it back! And once he knows for certain how I feel about him, he'd never accept that I won't marry him."

"Yeah, that would be a strange conversation: 'I love you with all my heart!' 'Then you'll marry me!' 'Meh.'"

"*Exactement—*" She froze. "He's home! I must go!"

"Don't be a stranger, Néomi!" Mari made her tone ominous. "No. Really. Don't be. Or my crew and I will show you a bar tab you'll never forget."

Her worry for Conrad evaporating, Néomi laughed. As she dashed out of the studio and up the stairs to their room, she wondered what side of him she'd get tonight.

34

Vicious, eager to torture, and impatient to drink, he thought as he sank down onto the front steps with a weary exhalation, mug of blood in hand. So far, everyone he'd seized to question about Tarut had believed the notorious Conrad Wroth was the same as he'd always been.

Which was good—because he wasn't anything like he'd always been.

Staring into his mug, he reflected on his latest hunt. He'd chased down his final solid lead, and it hadn't generated any additional ones. *Another failed search.*

Conrad had nothing new to go on, and fatigue had begun setting in hard as he searched relentlessly for Tarut. When Conrad did sleep, his nightmares were grueling.

He dreamed of Néomi in ghostly black-and-white again, her cheeks and eyes shadowed. He saw her trapped somewhere in the dark, screaming in horror, choking on it.

The image was so agonizing to him, he wondered if it was some sort of dream demon's weapon that Tarut was wielding.

So Conrad had ceased sleeping for the most part, using the time to hunt longer in whatever part of the world was still night.

He'd gone to all of the demon's lairs, and to all of his comrades', mercilessly combing for leads. Conrad had been attacked twice so far, by human Kapsligas who didn't know better. He'd dealt them a lesson, but hadn't killed them—they weren't enough of a challenge to truthfully claim self-defense.

Yet no sign of Tarut.

Conrad had continually debated whether he was making things worse by staying with Néomi. Ultimately, he'd admitted what he'd always known: the damage had already been done. She'd been in danger since the night of the gathering. He'd been offered his dream—and he'd selfishly accepted it.

Even if Conrad was separated from her for a thousand years, she would still be what he treasured above all things—and what he feared losing most.

If only I could turn her into a vampire. Then she wouldn't be so utterly vulnerable. But he knew females never made it through the transition. Not one of his four sisters had risen. . . .

In a way, he'd always been relieved that they hadn't. They'd been sensitive girls—he couldn't imagine them waking from the dead with a cup of blood shoved in their faces. Now Conrad wondered if they would have grown from their childhood. Could they have adapted? He'd never know.

Once he'd finished the mug, he traced directly to the bathroom to shower and shave, allowing her to sleep longer. Under the hot water, he cursed under his breath. He'd forgotten to make plans for them tonight. *Where in the world to take her . . . ?*

Yet when he entered the room, he found her awake and smiling to see him. She made his heart speed up just to see her. "You're up and dressed? But not to go out?"

She was wearing a red negligee, with her creamy breasts spilling out. Her hair was long and free as she knew he liked it. Even his beaten body stirred behind his towel.

Every time he took her, he fell more deeply under her spell. After three hundred plus years of musing what sex would be like, he'd had high expectations. She continued to shatter them.

"I don't want to go out tonight," she said. "Maybe we could relax here?" She sat on the bed and patted the spot beside her. "I could rebandage your arm."

He eyed her suspiciously. "Are you intent on managing me for something?"

She plucked up the roll of gauze. "My intentions with your body are pure."

Once he sat beside her, she rose to her knees and wound the gauze around his arm.

"There's more to this hunt than merely striking first, isn't there?" When he nodded, she said, "Tell me."

"As soon as you tell me about your *secret*." Thoughts of what it could be plagued him.

"Are we to quarrel, Conrad? I'd rather spend the night massaging your back and making love, but if you insist . . ."

"You must know I'll only let this go for so long. I have unfinished business—but when I'm freed of that worry, I'll track down everything you keep from me."

Conrad had two theories. It was possible that she'd made a deal with a sorcerer—one of the very ones he'd had considered using to resurrect her. One like that could have embodied her, but they tended to extract devastating promises.

A witch could have done it as well, but Conrad didn't think this was the case. Though Néomi had said she had "lots of money," she probably hadn't factored in eight decades of inflation. Surely she didn't have the kind of money necessary to get even a meeting with a powerful witch. Conrad had heard of some turning their noses up at millions.

She sighed. "*Quel dommage.* What a pity, then. If you're after my secret, then we'll be quarreling often. So we might as well enjoy this night. Tell me, where did your hunt take you?"

"Moscow."

"Were you careful?"

"Always," he said, which wasn't remotely true. To get to a demon snitch, Conrad had ambushed a subterranean demon lair, fending off two gangs to drag his howling prey by the horns up to the surface.

Even though he had a reason to be more careful, with an actual person waiting at home for him, Conrad couldn't allow others to think he'd changed.

God, how he'd changed.

Tonight, Conrad had given the snitch his standard threat: "Talk. Or I'll drink you, harvest your memories anyway, and slaughter everyone I see in them." But the snitch had smelled of fear and cheap gin. Conrad had not only been *disinclined* to drink the demon; he'd found the idea repugnant.

The last thing Conrad had tasted before he'd left had been Néomi's sweet lips. *Drink the demon with the same mouth he kissed his Bride . . . ?*

The rumors of his past brutality were helping him now, but one of these days, someone would call his bluff. Would he be forced to return to his old ways to protect his Bride?

If he had to, Conrad would once again become the thing they feared.

"There. All done." She finished his bandage by brushing a kiss on it.

Strange, he'd had no reservations about entering that lair, and yet, as his gaze flickered over Néomi's smiling face, he realized that this one-hundred-pound, mortal ballerina scared the living hell out of him.

She hailed the end of life as he knew it. Was his life so great before her? Hell, no. But at least he'd understood it. Now it seemed he could understand nothing, was having to rethink everything.

A future, a family, a real home. Were these things now possible for a man like him?

"Do you worry about me when I'm gone?" he asked.

"Always. From the tidbits of information you've given me, I've gleaned that you're seeking to kill an eight-foot-tall demon who'll be surrounded by a group of swordsmen, ready to lay down their lives to protect him. Do I have that right?"

"You do."

She quirked a brow. "Oh, then what's to worry about?" She motioned for him to lie on his front. "How long will you hunt him?"

"Till I have his head," he said, stretching across the bed.

"How long will that take?"

"Considering our past pace—it could take weeks, months, even a year."

"That long?" she asked as she straddled him. "When you're out, do you ever come across information about your brothers?" Reaching forward, she began to knead his aching neck muscles.

He just stifled a groan. "No, nothing yet."

"Is there to be a war in the Lore?" she asked.

"There's always war in the Lore."

"But this concerns your family."

"I have other concerns right now."

"Because of your brothers, you're alive to be here with me right now." She pressed her thumbs firmly into his shoulders, unraveling the coils of tension there. "Is it so bad?"

"Yes, I hate this."

She chuckled.

His brothers had said life could be better, that all he'd needed was his Bride. And now, his life was in no way fixed, but sometimes he'd found himself feeling . . . hopeful. He wasn't assured of their happiness together—she was mortal and vulnerable and seemed determined to make no commitment to him; he was still half-mad and had numerous assassins competing for his head. But there was indeed *possibility*.

He owed them for that. "Would it please you if I said I'll concentrate on them when I finish with Tarut?"

"Yes, *mon grand*. It really would."

Conrad would do nothing else until he'd first secured Néomi's safety. Life and death were beginning to have new meaning for Conrad. Instead of being only a taker of life, he was becoming a protector. The ease with which he was assuming the role surprised him.

No wonder all his foes had searched to discover if Conrad had a Bride. She was his sole weakness. And one he'd never anticipated having. Conrad hadn't exploited this vulnerability enough in his enemies, because he hadn't comprehended the unimaginable power of it.

Fear for her overruled *everything*.

Because if she died, he couldn't simply walk into the sun to join her. He had no delusions that they'd deserve to go to the same type of afterlife.

Again he saw three obstacles between them. Tarut's curse, her secret, and . . . his own dark needs. Each time they were together, he struggled not to take her neck.

It wasn't as if he hungered for her blood to nourish him—he'd been gulping back mugs of bagged blood to keep from biting her, drinking so much that he'd begun to put on more muscle. His body was strengthening even as his resolve was flagging.

No, his vampire nature made him resent that last barrier between them. He should know his own Bride's taste. His instinct was screaming within him that if they shared the connection of his bite, then she would cleave to him.

But he was strong—he could drain her so quickly. Her mortal body would cede its blood until she died with his fangs still in her neck. He shuddered with dread.

"Did I hurt you?" she asked, climbing off him.

"What? No, not at all." He turned to his back. "I was lost in thought." If he could just secure any kind of bond with her. "Néomi, I want to speak with you about—"

"Massaging my front?" She reclined with her arms over her head and a seductive smile curling her lips. "Indeed, I *would* love that."

They'd stayed in bed the entire night.

Though Conrad had yet to sleep, he remained awake once she'd nodded off, musing that he'd spent so much time and energy hunting that he hadn't been able to focus on winning her over.

Holding her to his chest, he pondered what to do. He'd already bought her a ring, and awaited the right time to ask her to marry him.

Sometimes when she looked at him, he was confident her feelings for him ran deep, and that she would say yes. Other times, he got the opposite impression— that she was merely biding her time, planning to leave him soon. How to convince her to stay . . . ?

What if he'd already gotten her pregnant? That would bind them together as nothing else could. But then he'd become a father. He waited for the wave of aversion that idea should bring.

When none came, he explored the thought more, picturing Néomi carrying their babe and Conrad protecting them against the world. The idea *felt* right. She'd nurture, and he'd provide. Very right.

He'd never wanted children before.

Now he wanted *their* children.

What if he *hadn't* already gotten her pregnant? An anxious feeling immediately seized him.

He set her on the bed, then rose to kneel between her thighs. When he spread them wide, she woke with a gasp. As she watched him with heavy-lidded eyes, he gripped his shaft, feeding it into her, then sank deep into her heat.

She gripped his hips, guiding him to thrust as she needed. With each slow plunge, her fingers tightened into his skin.

Her hair was shining, spread across the pillow. Her blue eyes gazed up at him with trust—and something more. He cupped her chin. "So beautiful, Néomi."

"Conrad," she murmured. "I . . . I need you." She said the words the way she might tell him she loved him for the first time.

In answer, he rasped, "I need you, too." Realization struck him. His brows drew together, his breath shuddering out. Néomi had once asked him if he'd ever been in love, and he'd easily answered no. Now he knew why he hadn't.

Because he'd never met her.

It somehow seemed right that he'd never loved before her. That *she* simply *was* the emotion for him, the two equaling each other.

I'm in love with her. . . .

In the hours remaining till dawn, he took her again and again. But when the sun began to rise, he left her sleeping and dragged himself from their bed. She turned with a whisper, seeming to seek him. When she wrapped her slim arms around his pillow, nuzzling it, his heart took up too much room in his chest.

He longed to stay here with her. To feel her breaths on his skin as she slept warm and soft against him.

But Conrad knew what he wanted. Knew the obstacles between them. Though he was exhausted, he rose and dressed, mindlessly pulling on his boots for another hunt.

I'll have her. Or I'll die trying.

35

My time's running out, Néomi thought at the beginning of their third week together.

She didn't know how she knew this, but she sensed it strongly. *Running out soon.* She'd become convinced that she wouldn't last through even the first month with Conrad.

And she couldn't stop thinking that he would probably be there to *see* her meet her end. She'd known they would be in a relationship when it happened, but she hadn't truly comprehended that he would witness her death.

The death that promised to be violent.

The guilt was heavy. *Why didn't I think of this before?* Even knowing that, she couldn't force herself to part from Conrad to spare him. She was greedy for every possible moment with him, and she knew he was as well.

Last night, when she'd run the backs of her fingers over the scar on his torso, he'd said, "I used to hate that scar. But no longer." He'd met her gaze, and the words had seemed to spill from him. "Néomi, it brought me to you. If I'd known what was in store for me, I'd have helped the Russian plunge his sword."

After hearing that, she'd become convinced that what he felt for her was more than just what a vampire felt for his Bride. He was as in love with her as she was with him.

Yet even with that realization, she felt like their little world was falling apart in general. He was so wearied, but tried to hide it, just as she tried to hide her growing tension and dread.

As though he sensed her foreboding, he seemed determined to make every moment count. . . .

That night his gift of a dazzling scarlet gown along with the promise of a surprise destination were enough to distract Néomi's mind from her fears, at least for a short while.

When he'd traced her to Italy for dinner, she'd become genuinely excited.

Her vampire had reserved a private garden terrace at La Pergola, atop Monte Mario. "Conrad, the view is spectacular!" Below them lay Rome at night, lit like a dream. "*Mon Dieu*, is that St. Peter's dome? I've only ever seen it on a postcard. This is such an incredible surprise!"

"Oh, this?" When he gave a casual shrug, it drew her gaze to his dark dinner jacket, tailored to perfection over those broad shoulders. "This isn't it. This is just nourishing my mortal until it's time for the real surprise."

"Better than this? You must tell me!"

"Then it wouldn't be a *surprise*." He gave her a wry grin. "Also known as *une surprise*. . . ."

Once they were seated in plush chairs, the server brought by a trolley filled with chilled champagnes. As he poured, the man barely did a double take at Conrad's sunglasses, but Conrad still tensed. She wished his eyes didn't bother him so much.

When they were alone, he rubbed his hand over the back of his neck. "You must hate them. The blood red."

She shook her head. "I think they're the red of fire. And the color deepens and darkens when you look at me—which I love. Besides, with the sunglasses, you look like a movie star."

"Or a drug addict."

"I don't believe the two are mutually exclusive, *mon grand*," she said, coaxing a grin from him. As she sipped her champagne, she asked, "Wouldn't one have to reserve this spot months in advance?"

"One would."

She quirked a brow. "But you wouldn't?"

"You should know by now that regarding you, I stint on nothing."

The meal bore this statement out. Dish after dish began to arrive, costly wines accompanying each course. As she savored some of the most delectable food and drink she'd ever tasted, she tried to get him to reveal the surprise. He sipped his whiskey, lazily forked some food around, and grinned smugly at her attempts to get him to crack. . . .

"You're so pleased with yourself, vampire."

"It's too good of a surprise to reveal. How's your food?"

Some dishes were bold, some subtle; each caressed her palate. She smiled over her wineglass. "*C'est exquis comme tes lèvres.*" Delicious like your lips. He shot upright when she rubbed her stocking-clad foot up his leg.

In a huskier voice, he said, "You can use your considerable wiles"—his gaze dropped to the low neckline of the dress he'd given her—"all you like, but I'll never break."

For dessert, the server brought to the table a miniature chest of drawers, handcrafted of silver. Inside each tiny drawer was a different kind of petit four.

"That's it," she said, sampling all the delights, "I'm never leaving,"

"Don't worry—we'll come back."

She forced herself to smile through the pang she felt. "At least once a week for the petit fours alone."

After their dinner, Conrad said, "Ready for your surprise?"

"Yes, I'm about to die!" she said, immediately wishing she could take back those words, but she masked her disquiet.

He covered her eyes, as he liked to, then traced her yet again. She sensed different weather, fresh smells. And she heard a new language—French.

With his other hand warm on her bared back, he led her toward a spot that sounded more crowded than where they'd arrived. Then he uncovered her eyes.

Her lips parted on a gasp. She was standing in front of L'Opéra Garnier, the lavish home of the Paris Ballet. Shivers skipped up and down her arms. Tonight's performance? *Roméo et Juliette.*

It was one of her favorite Shakespeare plays, and one she'd always dreamed of seeing choreographed. To experience it here? In Paris? Her eyes watering, she said, "Conrad, this is the most wonderful thing anyone's ever done for me."

And the most desirable man she'd ever known was offering his big hand to take her there. "Come," he murmured. "Or we'll be late."

Dazed, she let him guide her up the steps inside the palace. With the sounds of the orchestra tuning in the background, she was overwhelmed by the splendor, gazing from the artistry gracing the ceilings down to the elaborate marble designs beneath her heels.

When they took their seats—in the best box—she purred, "Oh, vampire, you're gooood. It's almost as if . . . you stint on *nothing?*"

With a sexy grin, he removed his sunglasses and said, "I'm glad you approve."

From the instant the curtain rose, her heart pounded nonstop. During the performance, she was in heaven, struck by how much ballet had both evolved and remained the same. The medium of dance perfectly suited the tale, the music its sublime partner.

Yet Conrad sat with his arms crossed over his chest, a critical look on his face. "You shame them," he grated, which just made her love him more.

"Well, thank you for that, but I believe I'd be a bit short and busty compared to these modern dancers."

"I happen to have a thing for short and busty ballerinas."

She gave him a slow smile. "I'm glad you approve."

"Exceedingly so." A hank of thick black hair fell over one of his eyes. "Do you miss it?"

"I do. It was thrilling to perform for an audience. And I miss the camaraderie in the troupe." She even missed her muscles aching from the exertion of a taxing rehearsal. "But I'm happy that I get to share this with you." His hand found hers.

Once the curtain closed, she teared up at the tragic ending—though it was expected and accepted—because it had a new meaning for her now. Néomi, too, would be separated from the man she loved. She didn't want to be, lamenting that she was in this position.

But it was expected. She'd accepted it. And she didn't regret a moment—

He slipped a felt-covered box into her hand. "What is this?" she asked, though she knew.

With a swallow, she opened the case. Inside lay an exquisite platinum ring, with a vibrant blue sapphire center stone flanked by diamonds.

"Be my wife, Néomi."

When she could take her eyes from the ring, she gazed up at him. He'd asked her *here*. Awash in the beauty of this place, her heart was full with emotion from the dance—and from loving the man who'd given this night to her. Under any other circumstances, she would have been crying with joy.

"Conrad . . ." The need to confess everything burned within her. But she feared robbing herself of this time with him. *It's running out.* Their gazes held. *And I can't tell you.*

Giving the ring back would be one of the hardest things she'd ever done. Though it was tearing her apart, she handed him the box. "I'm so sorry," she whispered. "I can't."

He accepted it from her without a word. But a muscle ticked in his jaw.

* * *

When Néomi refused his ring, the world tilted askew.

Like a punch in the gut, Conrad realized that even after everything—the time they'd shared, their enjoyment of each other—she still would make no commitment to him.

And she hadn't even needed a second to consider what he was offering.

The fatigue he'd ignored returned redoubled. The frustration from his stymied search mounted. He was failing at every turn.

Conrad couldn't find what he needed and couldn't secure what he had.

The more Néomi pulled away, the more crazed he felt. He wanted her to the point of madness. Conrad was a man who knew exactly where that point lay.

He decided at that moment that he simply wouldn't *let* her go.

Conrad had feared that if he took this stand, he would remind her of Robicheaux. That bastard had demanded she stay with him as well.

Yet there was a difference between never letting her go when she actually wanted to stay and keeping her only because he couldn't live without her.

Conrad believed Néomi wanted to be kept by him. He'd oblige her.

36

He was seething.

Néomi felt as if she were sidling around an untamed animal—one wrong move could provoke it to attack.

Endeavoring not to reveal her dismay, she behaved as if nothing were amiss, readying for bed as usual. In the past, her feminine rituals had seemed to fascinate him, almost relaxing him. Maybe they would tonight.

She removed her jewelry, donned a nightgown and robe of crimson silk, and applied lotion to her hands and legs.

Taking a seat at her dresser, she raised her brush, glancing at him in the mirror. Usually he sat on the bed, rapt as she combed out her hair, as if awaiting his turn to run his fingers through it.

Now he was in his customary spot, but his expression was drawn. The weather outside seemed to mirror the turmoil she sensed inside him. The wind gusted all around the old manor, and the lightning was already dancing. Though the rain hadn't yet started, it would. Néomi knew fall was turning to winter in the bayou's unique way—with overnight deluges, as if to beat the lingering heat into submission and batter the clinging leaves from the trees.

"What do I have to do, Néomi?" He ran his hand over his wearied face. "Who do I have to kill to keep you? Tell me what to do, and it's done."

She turned to him. "Conrad, not again. I thought we settled this on the morning after the gathering."

"How could I forget about your *conditions?*" he asked, sneering the word. "Tell me your secret, damn you! Did you make some kind of deal with the devil? Why won't you marry me?"

He rose and crossed to her. With his broad shoulders back, every inch the officer, he said, "You might even now be carrying my babe. What if I refuse ever to let you go?"

"*Let* me go?" she asked softly. "I've been through that before."

"Don't you compare him to me!" Conrad pulled her up from her chair, then cupped the back of her neck. "There's a difference between keeping a woman who wants to be kept and one who doesn't."

"And you think I want to be kept?"

"You do. By me. You want me to make it so that we never part again."

She turned away, unable to deny it.

"So now *I'm* going to tell you how this will be with us." With a straightened arm, he swept the items from the dresser, setting her atop it. "You—are—mine. Nothing will change that."

He seemed on the very edge of control, and she felt her body already responding to his ferocity. "Body and soul—you're all mine." He was breathing heavily. And as soon as I kill the one I'm hunting, then you will wed me."

"What does Tarut have to do with us?"

"You know I bear the demon's mark." Conrad wedged his hips between her legs, forcing her gown to ride up. "You know that it won't heal until he's dead. But there's more to it. If I can't defeat him, then my most coveted dream and worst nightmare will come true. When you appeared that night at the gathering in flesh and blood—that was my dream."

"I-I was?"

He gave her a short nod. "My nightmare is that you die again."

"That's why you've hunted so relentlessly?" For *her*?

"And I'll continue to. But after that, Néomi, I vow to you, the second I rid my body of this mark . . . from that moment on you'll be more than my Bride—you'll be my wife."

Again a male was demanding that she marry him with a wild look in his eyes. But there were such differences this time.

Conrad would never hurt her. He would rather die.

And Néomi was just as crazed for him.

She knew her eyes were wild with wanting him, too. "Conrad . . ." She yearned so much to tell him everything. To tell him that she loved him, and that she was so selfish and greedy for him that she couldn't leave—even though she'd only end up hurting him. "It can't happen—"

Cutting off her words with his kiss, he groaned against her mouth and fisted his hands in her robe.

Once he'd stripped it from her, he snatched the small case from his jacket and plucked the ring out. He seized her left hand and pressed the ring down her finger. "This shows my claim on you," he grated. "Take it off right now if you truly don't want to marry me."

The metal was hot like a brand, the ring fitting her perfectly. She could no more take it off than she could quit breathing.

"I want you, Néomi. Forever." Just before he took her lips again, he rasped, "*Want me, too.*"

As his kiss deepened, he yanked up her gown to her waist. When he sensuously palmed her sex, she responded as if he'd lit a fuse, growing damp in a rush. Her hands were desperately seeking all over his body.

When she unzipped his pants and tugged free his rigid shaft, the broad head nudged against her entrance.

With his hand splayed over her chest, he pressed her back to the mirror. She drew her bent legs up, placing her heels on the edge of the dresser, as open for him as she could be. With a groan, he swooped his arms under her knees, then leaned forward.

Caging her in, surrounding her, he entered her body. Possessing her. "I feel you pulling away from me." With a long, hard stroke, he murmured, "*Don't . . .*"

He watched her expression, the emotion in her eyes. *This is a good-bye.* Even as he was inside her, she was telling him good-bye. *And I don't even know why.*

With everything he felt for her, he took her, driving between her thighs. His shaft throbbed within her tight sheath as he struggled not to come, wanting this to last forever.

The more she pulls away . . . He would never let her go. Never.

Take her . . . claim her completely. The last barrier between them. Conrad needed to bite her, to *mark* her, like an animal. He *was* the monster they all thought him.

No! He had to fight . . . had to overcome the instinct.

He felt his fangs sharpening. As his hips bucked, he found himself easing toward her pale neck, drawn to the hectic pulse he could see so clearly. *Possess her completely.* He licked her, preparing her.

Lost . . .

He pierced her tender skin; the sweetest flesh he'd ever tasted closed tight around his aching fangs. Was she moaning? He could feel the sound.

His eyes flashed open when he began sucking her, because God help her . . . he knew he'd do this again.

As her rich blood hit his tongue and slid down his throat like silk and wine, he groaned in ecstasy. Heat seared through his veins. Her heat. Her essence.

"Stop now." Her words were faint compared to the exquisite beating of her heart in his ears.

No. Want more. Sucking harder.

"You'll hurt me," she whispered.

Must have this.

"Conrad . . ."

With a will he hadn't known he possessed, he stopped taking. But he left his fangs in her flesh, growling against her damp skin as his seed erupted from his body in mind-numbing waves. *Connection. Marked. Mine. . . .*

When he drew back from her, he studied her face. Her cheeks were pinkened. He hadn't hurt her.

He'd bitten her. He'd taken her blood. And it had felt like it was supposed to happen. He'd heard her moaning. She'd taken pleasure from his bite. *I didn't hurt her—*

She burst into tears. With her bottom lip trembling, her eyes glittering, she whispered, "How could you, Conrad?" She raised her hand to slap him—the closest to fury he'd ever seen her.

37

W hat is *wrong* with me?" At the folly yet again. All the night creatures around him were silent, as if they sensed his threat. "Why can't I be right?" he roared to the night.

Néomi hadn't been physically hurt, but she'd been inconsolable. "You have no idea what you've done!" she'd cried. The hand poised to strike him had faltered. She'd closed it to a fist before lowering it, without giving him the hit he'd deserved.

As her gaze had flickered over his face, the expressions he'd grown used to seeing had been absent. There'd been none of her looks of pride in him, or glances brimming with desire.

She'd appeared betrayed.

For an hour he retraced his habitual path along the water's edge. He scarcely registered it when the skies opened up and poured. Earlier when he'd left the room, he thought he'd heard her beginning to cry harder. To cry over him.

It made his chest feel hollow, and his new heartbeats pained him. Hell, could death feel worse than he did now?

The only thing that heartened was that she hadn't

removed the ring. They'd both glanced at it and then met eyes. He'd felt sure she'd throw it in his face.

But she hadn't rejected his claim on her. Not yet.

A sound behind him. At first he thought she'd followed him out into the rain, and he twisted around, words rising from his tongue. *I'm in love with you. I will do better. I won't hurt you again—*

Eight swordsmen greeted him, weapons drawn, Tarut among them. There weren't many males that Conrad had to tilt his head to meet their eyes, but this was one of them.

Goddamn it, how could Conrad have been so careless? His senses had never failed him before. The demon could have walked up right behind him and sliced off his head, before Conrad would even have known.

"Will you trace, Wroth?" Tarut said, raising his voice over the rain. "Or fight?"

"Finally ready to die?"

One last battle, then. If Conrad was defeated, then maybe it would for the best. When Néomi left him, the memories would take over once more, and he'd be lost anyway.

Or if he won . . . She hadn't taken off his ring. If he won, he wouldn't let her leave him.

Let fate decide my future.

There were eight swordsmen against him, and he was weaponless. But Conrad would be fighting for her—because he'd vowed if he killed Tarut and rid himself of the mark, then she'd become his wife.

Things became simple. *Kill eight; keep her forever.*

Conrad's fangs sharpened. He ran his tongue along

one, the blood like a hit of adrenaline. Obstacles stood between him and what he wanted. He sneered at the demons. They had no idea what they'd stumbled into. *Eliminate the obstacles.*

He charged the closest one. In a flash, Conrad's hand shot out, ripping the demon's throat from its neck. Blood spurt. In his mind, these beings kept him from Néomi. A surge of fury coursed through him. They were a threat to her very life.

Conrad reached the next one, grabbing it by the horns, twisting the head until vertebrae cracked. His fingers bit into the demon's thick skin, ripping the beast apart with his hands.

They'd dared bring death to his and Néomi's home. . . .

Rage erupted in him—never had Conrad felt its equal. And soon . . . he succumbed to the frenzy, doing what he did best.

As Néomi peered into the mirror at the two pinpoints of blood on her neck, she shivered all over again.

The bite that had given her such pleasure also spelled her doom. She'd never felt more connected to a living person, and once it was over, never more betrayed.

Now she felt only regret. Her anger with Conrad had been akin to chastening a beast of prey for hunting. He was a vampire; he'd bitten her. She knew he hadn't made a conscious decision to do it. He'd appeared confounded, appalled with himself as he'd grated, *"I'm supposed to protect you from men like me."*

She gazed down at the breathtaking ring he'd bought for her, but she couldn't bring herself to remove it. He'd told her to take it off if she truly didn't want to marry him.

But she truly did.

He wanted to put a claim of some kind on her and her future. She felt the same need for him.

Yet she'd already sensed that she'd be leaving soon. She didn't know where she was going, just knew it would be without Conrad.

Oh, who was she fooling? Leaving? She wasn't going on a trip. She was about to *die*. And she was afraid.

She drew away from the mirror to wait for his return. He'd probably gone to the folly again. She wished he would come back—the wind had begun churning, pelting rain against the windows.

Suddenly a deafening roar resounded over the property. "Conrad!" Oh, God, would he try to harm himself? She'd been so hard on him!

When she heard him yell in pain, she was on her feet in an instant, cinching her robe as she hastened for the door. Dashing headlong into the blustery night, she squinted against the rain, tracking the sounds to a clearing near the folly.

She drew up short at the sight of three mangled bodies on the ground. Five other beings, all tall and brawny, circled Conrad. His lips were drawn back from his fangs, baring them in his rage. Was he motioning for his opponents to come closer?

In a flash of lightning, she made out the black symbols on their bared backs. *The Kapsliga.*

They took turns lunging forward with their swords raised. Every time they lashed out, the circle would tighten, giving Conrad less space to maneuver. Why didn't he trace away?

When one demon sank his sword into Conrad's arm, he bellowed with rage, his fist shooting out. With a brutal hit, Conrad sent him spinning unconscious to the ground, snatching the demon's weapon as he fell.

With his uninjured arm he swung the sword down, decapitating the foe. *Now he has a weapon.* She was transfixed by the harsh lines of his face, by the savagery in his expression. When the dam burst, his eyes flooding with red, she knew he was going to kill them all. She would only hinder him. Though it went against every instinct urging her to help him, she began to back away—

Conrad caught sight of her. At that exact moment, she heard breaths behind her; an arm slid around her neck.

Tarut had Néomi.

Conrad tensed to trace to her, but the demon tightened his hold.

"Not unless you want your fragile human dead."

Can't get to her, can't reach her. She was wide-eyed in the rain, terrified. *This is all my doing—all my fault!*

She looked so small compared to the immense demon. If Tarut flexed a muscle, he'd snap her neck. In one instant, she'd be dead. "Ease your goddamned grip, demon—you'll suffocate her."

"Bad luck of yours to get a mortal for a Bride. They die so readily."

The rawest panic Conrad had ever felt surged

within him. "Just hang on, Néomi." To Tarut, he said, "Let her go if you have any care for living."

"I don't think so, vampire." Two of Tarut's henchmen seized Conrad's arms, and he was forced to allow it. "You know what I seek. I'll never let her go, not until I get it."

Tarut wouldn't let her go until Conrad was dead. Through the deluge, he scanned the area, searching for options, for a kill. There were none.

He could see no way to remove this power from the demon.

Néomi was shaking her head, struggling to speak. "*Trace away . . .*" she gasped. *So vulnerable.*

"I'll vow to free her from the curse," Tarut said, "and release her tonight. All you have to give me is your head."

Rewards and obstacles. Reward: saving Néomi's life. Tarut would be bound by that oath to free her.

The obstacle? There was no obstacle. *All I've ever wanted is life,* she'd said. And because of Conrad's past, she was in jeopardy of losing it.

If he could sacrifice his life to save hers, he'd do it proudly.

"*Conrad . . . no!*" she cried, blinking through the rain. "*Wait . . . I'm d—*" The bastard tightened his grip, cutting off her air.

"Stop!" When she dug her little fingers into the demon's arm, desperate for breath, desperate for life, Conrad yelled, "Do it, demon—swing your blow. If you vow that neither you nor your men will ever harm her."

Tarut gave a solemn nod. "I vow it to the Lore."

* * *

Néomi was weeping, fighting . . . frantic for breath to tell him the truth.

In the tumultuous storm, Conrad stood with his shoulders back, so ready to meet death for her. Her struggles were making his expression anguished, making him *impatient* for the blow.

But it'd be for naught.

Néomi had only thought she'd known what intensity was in this man. Now she realized that his fiercest emotion was . . . *love.* It blazed from his eyes. And she knew he *wanted* her to see how he felt.

Yet then her sight began clouding as her dizziness increased. A fog seemed to slide around everyone, hindering her vision.

Still holding her, Tarut advanced on Conrad.

"*No,*" she choked out. As the demon leveled his sword at Conrad's neck, she seized a breath. "*I'm . . . dying anyway! Leave here!*"

Conrad's brows drew together in confusion; Tarut swung his sword.

38

An instant before it sliced through Conrad, Tarut's sword—and the meaty arm that wielded it—dropped to the ground.

The hit happened so fast, what was left of Tarut's arm flew past Conrad's face, spraying blood.

Cadeon had struck Tarut from behind, lunging from the smoke demon's tracing to strike just in time.

At once, Conrad grappled against the two who held him, frenzied to get to Néomi. The clash of steel rang out over the pouring rain and howling wind as Cadeon's men engaged the Kapsliga.

Conrad's mortal Bride was in the midst of an immortal battle—

When Tarut twisted around to face Cadeon, dagger in his other hand, Conrad bellowed, *"No! Tarut's holding her!"*

But Cadeon had already given a jabbing thrust.

Tarut had used Néomi to shield him.

Time slowed; Conrad couldn't see her, but he could scent her flowing blood. . . . He could see Cadeon's shocked reaction as he drew back his sword.

The demon had run it through her.

"No!" Conrad roared, struggling frantically. *"Néomi!"*

When Cadeon raised his sword again, Tarut finally dropped Néomi to block the strike. Too late.

Just after Conrad spied Tarut's head thudding to the ground, he caught sight of her . . . collapsing into the mud . . . limp, eyes open and dazed, pooling blood from her mouth and stomach.

With a roar, he snatched out one Kapsliga's throat with his clenching fingertips. He caught the other one by the roof of the mouth to wrench his head back and off his neck. The other Kapsligas fled at the sight.

Freed, Conrad lurched for her, sinking to his knees beside her. "Néomi!" He clasped her body up into his arms. "You stay with me!"

She could tell the old madness was on the verge of reclaiming him. He was adjusting her sodden robe in jerky motions—as if to keep her covered and warm in the rain.

Néomi didn't want to look down. Strangely, there was no pain—only numbness. But the demon's expression had told her everything. The wound was a mortal one.

Cadeon turned to approach them. As he made his way, she dimly heard the others. . . .

"Cade did *what?*" Rydstrom yelled. "What the fuck did you say, Rök?"

"He's gutted the vampire's Bride," Rök said. "The leech is worthless to us now—you can't torture them any worse than this."

"I didn't see her," Cadeon told Conrad. "I never saw her."

She felt pity for him—after all, he'd saved Conrad's life. If only he hadn't taken her own.

Even Néomi shivered at Conrad's expression. With his eyes blazing red with malice, he said, "*A thousand times over, demon. Anything you love will die.*" Then he traced her inside their room.

As he cradled her head, he mumbled his thoughts aloud. "*Hospital. Where? A human hospital . . .*" His eyes darted wildly. His face was beaten by the Kapsliga, his jaw swollen and lip busted. "*You stay with me,*" he pleaded down to her in a tormented voice. "*J-just hold on for me! Need to think . . .*"

She wanted so badly to stroke him to comfort him, but her arms hung useless. *I know this feeling. So cold.*

Dying. Just as Nïx had predicted. *On the day I told Conrad the secret, but not as they'd expected.* Fate could be so cruel.

"Need to find a hospital . . ."

She shook her head as much as she could. She wouldn't make it to the hospital—it was too late for her. But she had to explain, so he didn't think this was his fault. "Conrad . . . was dying anyway."

"Don't talk!" His voice was raw.

Sounds were dimming. Blood left her body so swiftly, like it had just been awaiting the chance. "I called a witch . . . she came through . . . the studio mirror." Sight going blurry. "Made me alive . . . but only for a short time. Knew this . . . couldn't tell you."

"Your death was the deal with the devil?" He was

quaking beside her. "And you got just two goddamned weeks?"

"*Worth it!*" She weakly coughed. "*Love you.*"

At that, blood tracked from his eyes like tears. . . . But then his body suddenly grew still. "What witch, *koeri?*"

"*Mariketa.*"

Clutching her to his chest, he traced them into the studio. "Just stay alive, Néomi!"

After easing her to the cot by the mirror, he found a blanket and pressed it to her wound. "My brave girl," he rasped, "you stay with me." Then he faced the glass. "Witch!" he roared. "Come to me!"

As he continued to yell for Mari, Néomi fought to remain conscious, wanting to tell him that Mari couldn't help, that he was getting his hopes up only to have them crushed. But with each attempt, she coughed up more blood.

"*Mariketa!*" He punched the mirror in a frenzy, battering his hand. "*Come to me!*"

When there was no response, he sank to his knees beside Néomi. "Ah, God, *come to us!*"

39

Forgodsakes, lay off!" Mari's voice sounded from the mirror minutes later. "We're coming!"

Néomi cracked open her lids when Conrad sank down beside her on the cot. He gently cradled her head in his lap.

"Why do you always get to go first?" Mari's voice demanded.

"Because I'm bigger than you are," came Bowen's reply.

When the Lykae emerged from the glass, with Mari following, their eyes went wide.

Mari started for Néomi, but Bowen's hand shot out for her arm, shoving her behind him. After he scanned the area and scented the air, he turned to Conrad. "Who did this to your female?"

"Demon," Conrad answered, his voice hoarse from yelling. "Named Cadeon."

"That bastard!" Bowen snapped, drawing Mari to his side. "You should've let me smash him in the jungle!"

"Cade? Oh, Hekate, you can't be serious!" Mari hurried to Néomi. "So that's who's been trying to call me. It had to have been an accident."

Néomi weakly nodded, then coughed up more blood.

Conrad squeezed her hand too forcefully, looking to be teetering on the brink.

Mari's gaze landed on Néomi's neck. "You bit her. Did you see her memories?"

"No, it was just hours ago—"

"Then how did you know to contact me through the mirror?"

"Néomi told me after . . . after she was . . . Damn it, what does it matter? Just fix this spell, witch."

"I'm so sorry." Mari shook her head sadly. "I can't fix it. I told Néomi this going in."

"Heal—this—body."

"It's just a shell. Even if I could heal her, she'd just get killed again and again."

"If all she needs is a real body—I'll return directly!"

That's my Conrad. So intense.

"The conditions for the assumption of another's body are lengthy," Mari said. "Chiefly among them— the body has to be donated by its owner. Not, er, commandeered."

"Restore her old one. I knew warlocks who could revivify flesh, creating a body from a strand of hair." He was clearly trying so hard, struggling to say the right words. "You could do that with Néomi," he said, his voice breaking on her name.

Mari answered, "That's how they make soulless zombies."

Conrad said, "We have a soul, waiting right here."

When Néomi felt herself becoming less substantial, he murmured, "Stay with me, Néomi. *Please, baby.*"

"Embodying a spirit isn't a science. It's an art, and it'd be outside my skill set as it is, much less if I have to revivify her dead body as well. Normally, a witch would heal the body in one step, then implant the spirit in another step. Now you want me to do both at the same time? Even though I've never done either before?"

"Yes—you must!" Inhaling deeply for control, he grated, "A dream demon marked me. I think that curse had something to do with her injury. This happened to Néomi just before the demon was killed tonight."

Mari's eyes narrowed. "You mean a *dream demon* hijacked my subject to give you a nightmare? My mystickal signature was all over her. And some tool just ignored that?"

Bowen put his hand on her shoulder. "He might no' have seen it, Mari."

"Anyone immersed in magick of this sort would have seen it. That really pisses me off. I'm supposed to be the most powerful witch, and my spell got owned in two weeks."

Think . . . think.

Control—never had Conrad needed it more; never had he been more in danger of losing it completely.

Wait . . . "Witch, if you don't do something about this, everyone will think they can overturn your spells at will. Who would pay you for spells that don't take?"

MacRieve growled, just as Mariketa said, "You

think I can't see what you're doing? Unfortunately, it's working."

"You canna think of this!" MacRieve snapped.

Mariketa cast the Lykae a troubled glance, then told Conrad, "Vampire, understand that I've never done this on a human. And another problem—I don't even *have* her body. I'd need to scry for the location of it, again while I'm doing everything else!"

"She's fading." Conrad raked his fingers through his hair. "Time's running out! What do we have to lose?"

MacRieve said, "She could come back *wrong*."

Conrad met his eyes. "I'll do what's necessary if she does."

"It's no' only that," the Lykae said. "Mari can enthrall herself in the mirror. Her eyes will incinerate anything that comes between her and her reflection, and she'll get stuck in an eternal trance. I feel for you, vampire, but I will no' allow her to put herself at risk."

"Sebastian saved your life—and he spared you from an unspeakable fate. You owe him a debt."

MacRieve's gaze flickered over Mariketa and changed color with some fierce emotion. Hardening his expression, he turned to Conrad. "No' a debt like this."

Mariketa turned to Néomi on the cot. "Would you want this, honey? A mortal life?"

When she nodded weakly, Mariketa stood and crossed to MacRieve. Gazing up at him, the witch said, "I think I can do this. I have to try. I mean, look at the vampire."

Néomi had just gone unconscious—Conrad knew

he appeared on the razor's edge when MacRieve scowled.

"We're running out of time," Conrad grated.

Mariketa pulled MacRieve farther to the side. "You said that if I married you, you would never get in the way of my career. This is spectacularly getting in my career's way. Do you know how good this would look on my résumé?"

"I also promised your parents and your coven that I would no' let you get lost in the mirror again. You're no' ready yet, lass! It's too soon after . . . that last time."

"Bowen, this has sat ill with me since I did the spell on Néomi. And I know you hate Cade, but he and his brother did save my life. He's been calling for my help with this. If I save Néomi, I'll be able to repay my debt to them." She took one of his hands in both of hers. "Just believe in me. I can do this. I *feel* like I can." When he clenched his jaw, evidently a sign of defeat, she smiled. "Will you get my Big-Spell gloves?"

Muttering in Gaelic, he scuffed back into the mirror.

While MacRieve was gone, the witch told Conrad, "The cost is going to be high, vampire. I'm gonna need ten mil for this one. I accept real estate, stones, or bullion. Or stock certificates from the twenties that are exponentially undervalued. And you have to vow to the Lore to pay it, since we don't have time for contracts."

"Agreed, ten million," he answered easily. "I vow to the Lore to pay it. But you must agree to keep this secret. If the demons know, they will only come after her again."

"I'm bound by the mercenary code to keep our dealings confidential," she said, but she was clearly troubled, conflicted about hiding this from her demon friend, a demon who'd apparently saved her life.

"Good, then. For the record, witch, I think you can do this, too."

Her expression briefly turned grim. "Just be ready to make hard choices, Conrad, in case I can't."

Still surly, MacRieve returned with a strange pair of fingerless gloves. The palms looked to be lined with some kind of bendable mirror.

As Mariketa donned them, she took a deep breath, seeming to shake off her disquiet. She told Conrad, "I like Néomi—I'd have tried this for half that amount."

"I love Néomi—I'd have paid anything you could dream up."

"Oh, snap! Live and learn, eh? Okay, one vampire's Bride brought back from the grave." She slapped her gloved hands and rubbed them together. "Let's put the fun back in funeral!"

ariketa faced the mirror, tilting her head. "This is the first time I've really looked at my reflection in months." To the Lykae, she said, "No wonder you love me. Could I be any cuter?"

"You will no' charm me from my apprehension, so doona bother," MacRieve said. "You're tae pull back if you feel anything amiss. Do you ken?"

She nodded. "Got it. Now, I need two mirrors standing on both sides of me, stat."

Conrad eased away from Néomi. "The broken mirrors on this wall are all there is."

"Grab them. Bring them to me."

He ripped a sizable shard from the wall in the studio. Blood from his fingers ran along the edges as he shoved the jagged tip through the wood floor until it stood upright. "Will this work?"

Gazing at his blood, she absently said, "It'll have to. Do the second one."

He repeated the process. As she continued staring at the blood, her eyes went wide as if with realization, before they narrowed on the streak.

"Should I clean that?"

She hesitated for long moments. "Leave it," she finally said with a swallow.

Conrad grated, "Witch, what is it?"

She averted her face, as if with guilt. "We're ready."

Once Mariketa was nearly enclosed by the mirrors, she made her hands into fists and closed her eyes. When her lids slid open, her eyes were . . . mirrors themselves, gleaming and reflecting everything she gazed upon. Her fingers uncurled and light glowed from one of her gloved palms.

Conrad hurried back to Néomi, but she was fading. The more Néomi's form dimmed, the brighter the light in the witch's palm grew.

Just as Mariketa's toes left the ground, a language even Conrad didn't recognize began to spill from her lips, but he could sense that her words were throbbing with power. With one hand, she made a fist around the light, as if physically grabbing onto Néomi's spirit. "She's going to disappear now," Mariketa told him, never glancing from the mirror.

When Néomi's hand vanished from his own, madness threatened. Her robe, nightgown and the ring he'd given her remained on the cot. He swallowed. *Keep it together.*

He took the ring, determined to see her wearing it once more.

"Found her grave." The witch pointed the forefinger of her other hand down and stirred. "I'm beginning the body." Again and again, she circled that finger, seeming to be meeting great resistance. The spell began taking a toll. She grew out of breath, nearly hyperventilating.

"You can do this, Mariketa." Conrad swallowed. "Bring my Néomi back to me. . . ."

The light in her hands intensified even more. The air grew heavier, ominous. As if agitated by the tension, creatures began skittering in the walls surrounding them.

MacRieve peered around him. "This does no' feel right. As if we're doing something we ought never do!"

"Shut up, MacRieve," Conrad snapped, though he'd felt the same atmosphere, threatening, like they were challenging a force far greater than they—and might be crushed for their audacity.

She began chanting once more. *The light was building, building*. . . . She shoved her hands out, seeming to fuel even more magick into the spell. The house began quaking.

"Have to . . . break through. Need to age . . ."

Age?

More unintelligible chanting, louder and louder, until she was practically screaming the words. The studio windows exploded. Papers flew in a tempest. "Bowen, I'm . . . losing it!"

"Mariketa!" With a roar, MacRieve lunged for her, trying to heave her away from the glass. But the Lykae couldn't budge the small female from the mirror's hold.

The silver glaze of her eyes darkened, as if ink flooded inside them. They began to turn wholly black. "This is bad!" she cried.

"No, Mari, doona do this!" He cupped his hand over her eyes, but the skin of his palm began to burn away in two distinct holes.

"Oh, Hekate, no!" she screamed.

The light in her hands exploded like a bomb, so intense it briefly blinded Conrad. "What was that?" he yelled. "What is happening?"

Mariketa gasped for breath. "Néomi . . . embodied."

He yanked his head around. "Where is she? Tell me!"

"There's a problem! It—" Her body stiffened, unmoving. She stared unblinking at the mirror.

"Ah, God, no' again, Mari!" MacRieve used his other hand to shield her eyes, until two smoking holes appeared in that hand as well. He snatched at her again, but even with his strength, he couldn't wrest her from that spot.

"What was the problem, witch? Where is Néomi?" Conrad was frenzied to see her. "Where is she embodied?" He charged for Mariketa. "Wake your witch up, MacRieve!"

The Lykae peered over his shoulder, baring his fangs. "Watch your step, vampire. I'm a breath from turnin'."

"How can I find Néomi? Break the goddamned mirror!"

"No' a chance—it could kill her."

"Put something bigger in front of her!" Conrad bit out, struggling to control himself.

"She burns anything away!"

"How long could she be like this?"

"Fucking forever, vampire!" MacRieve roared, his irises turning ice blue, the beast flickering over his form. If the Lykae turned because his mate was in dan-

ger, even Conrad couldn't defeat him. "As I'd bloody told you!"

Pacing, Conrad stabbed his fingers through his hair. "Christ, I don't know where Néomi is!"

He'd dreamed that she was kept from him no matter how hard he fought to reach her. Nightmares of her being . . . trapped in the dark? He clutched his forehead.

She was trapped somewhere right now. And that was why the witch hadn't returned Néomi to him here. But where in the hell would she be?

Wait. If the witch had been able to restore Néomi's body and put her spirit within it, but then got interrupted . . .

The answer hit him.

"Ah, God, I know where she is!" And he couldn't trace to her because he'd never been there before. "I need a car!" MacRieve and the witch had come through the mirror. Nikolai had driven his away weeks ago.

The Lykae ignored him, curling his finger under the witch's chin. "Mari, love, this is goin' tae hurt like hell." He took a deep breath. And then he stepped in front of her gaze.

The skin of his torso began to melt away as if burned by lasers, but he gritted his teeth, took the pain. "Lass," he bit out, "after this we will have words."

Where am I?

Néomi woke in a dank, close space, blinking repeatedly in the darkness. She had no pain in her body, none at all. Her wound felt totally healed. Mari had done it! But where was everyone? Why was Néomi alone?

A horrific suspicion tried to take hold of her mind, but she fought it. Her breaths grew ragged, sounding so loud in the confines.

When her dizziness passed, she rose and immediately knocked her head.

"*Nooo*," she moaned, beginning to shudder. "It isn't possible." Tears began pouring from her eyes. *Mère de Dieu . . . This can't be happening!*

She was in her coffin, which resided in the French Society's tomb in St. Louis Cemetery #1. At least thirty other coffins lay within.

Conrad will come for me. Somehow he'll find me. . . .

But hours seemed to grind by. Gasping rank air, she fought not to think about the bodies decomposing all around her.

None of her bones were in her coffin—it was as if she'd reincorporated them. She was embodied, which meant she was alive once more.

Néomi had grown a body just in time for it to die. . . .

Then the insects came.

She screamed. She screamed hysterically until the foul air grew scarce.

41

F*uck!*" Conrad yelled to the sky. He had no car, no idea how to get to her.

Conrad couldn't trace to her. He'd never been to a cemetery in New Orleans.

The Valkyrie compound was near Elancourt. He could sprint the distance and steal a car. *Don't know where to drive to.*

Conrad had rarely let himself even *contemplate* asking for aid—but now that he had to, only one person came to mind.

Nikolai. Deep down Conrad was still a Wroth, and he needed his brother's help—the brother who was locked up in Kristoff's jail. . . .

Conrad traced to Mount Oblak. Though it was daylight outside, the castle was dimmed.

"Nikolai?" he bellowed as he began wending down shadowy corridors. The sound echoed, summoning the castle guard.

Soon groups of soldiers advanced on him, swords at the ready—no doubt astonished that a crazed, red-eyed vampire was loose in the Forbearer capitol.

Conrad took their hits, seizing weapons with his bloodied hands to toss them away. Descending even deeper into the bowels of the castle, he twisted necks, breaking them but not killing the immortal soldiers.

"*Nikolai!*" he yelled again.

"*Conrad?*"

Conrad followed the sound to a sizable cell. Inside, behind thick bars, were his three brothers.

They stared in bewilderment. Conrad knew what he looked like. He had blood across his face and body, gaping wounds all over him, his face beaten by those demons.

"What in the hell are you doing here?" Nikolai demanded. "And whose blood is that?"

Conrad studied the cell bars. *Obstacles*. "I don't have time for questions."

Murdoch said, "You have to leave—they'll execute you if they capture you."

He gave a rough laugh. "Defy them to do either." He clamped the bars. *Have to get to her*. . . . Gritting his teeth, he began to strain against them.

"Those are as protected as your chains were," Sebastian said. "The wood, the metal, and the stone surrounding them are all reinforced. You can't possibly—"

Conrad bent them wide, actually breaking the metal.

"*My God,*" Nikolai murmured.

"Need your help to find my Bride!" He yanked the wreckage free. "I'm not mad . . . but I need you to trace me to every cemetery in New Orleans. Do you know where they are?"

Nikolai gaped. "Your . . . *Bride?*"

"His heart beats," Murdoch said.

"Do you know where they are, or not?" Conrad bellowed.

Nikolai nodded slowly. "I know all the cemeteries. Myst and I hunt ghouls there."

"Will you do this?"

"Conrad, just calm—"

"Fuck calm, Nikolai!" Suddenly Conrad sensed great power behind him.

"So this is Conrad Wroth," Kristoff said.

Without turning, Conrad sneered, "The bloody *Russian*. What do you want?"

"I'd known the Wroths were genetically incapable of fawning to a king, but *a modicum of respect . . .*"

Conrad faced the natural-born vampire, surrounded by his king's guard.

"You've taken out my entire castle guard. Something a Horde battalion couldn't do. They didn't tell me you were *this* strong," Kristoff said in a casual tone. His pale eyes were expressionless, but he was calculating. Conrad could sense it—and he believed he knew what Kristoff wanted.

"But then, you've been blooded."

"I don't have time for this!" Conrad snapped. "I'll kill you just to keep you from speaking."

His guards tensed, hands at their sword hilts. "Kill me? You wouldn't know your Bride if not for me, if not for your brothers. You'd have been dead three hundred years ago."

"I've put that together!"

To Nikolai, Kristoff said, "He took out the guards

without killing a single one—almost as if he was making a point. You were right. Conrad isn't lost. He's . . . quite a few things, but he's not irredeemable. And I can concede when I made a mistake. Though you should have come to me instead of willfully breaking our laws."

Nikolai shrugged. "I couldn't take the risk that you would say no. He's my brother," he said, as if that explained everything.

Kristoff turned back to Conrad. "Swear fealty to me, and all of you leave today as allies. Otherwise we fight."

There wasn't any *time* left to fight. "I'll vow . . . that I'll never engage you or your army."

Kristoff studied him, then said, "It will do for now." To the brothers, he added, "Take a week off. And do get your Brides to cease plotting my downfall."

When the king and his men disappeared, Nikolai said, "Conrad, you must tell me what's happened for me to help you. Who is your Bride?"

Conrad hastily said, "Néomi, this beautiful little dancer. Love her. So much it pains me. Have to find her."

"Why do you think you need to go to a cemetery to find her?"

"She was a ghost, the one I told you about. But no longer. She died again tonight and might have been resurrected—or embodied, fuck if I know the difference—but the witch, the werewolf, and I lost her body. One of the bodies. Or else I just can't find it. I'm going to go to every goddamned cemetery in the city and listen for her heartbeat."

Sebastian raised his brows and said, "The ghost

thing again," just as Murdoch muttered, "Con's thoroughly lost it."

Conrad snapped his teeth at them. "This happened!"

"I don't know what outcome I'm hoping for," Sebastian said. "Conrad's either irretrievably mad, or his Bride is a spirit from beyond whose corpse is lost. This seems like a lose-lose."

"He always did things differently," Murdoch said, daring to slap Conrad on the back. "I would like to stay, but I have an emergency that's weeks overdue. Good luck, Con." He traced away.

"Nikolai, do you have this one?" Sebastian asked. "I need to make sure the Valkyrie stand down."

Conrad turned to Nikolai, struggling to calm his tone. He wanted to punch his fist into the wall with frustration, to howl to the ceiling with anguish. His little Bride was in the dark . . . was she frightened? He stifled a shudder.

To get to Néomi, he had to convince them that he hadn't lost his mind. "Know this sounds crazy. But I am . . . I am asking you to believe me in this. Just . . . just take me to the cemeteries."

Sebastian said, "I don't think he's *ever* asked for anything."

Conrad grasped his forehead. "Nikolai, please, she's going to be"—his hoarse voice broke with emotion—"she'll be . . . afraid."

Nikolai finally said, "Go, Sebastian. Tell Myst I'll return after this."

When Sebastian traced away, Conrad said, "You believe me?"

"I . . . don't." Nikolai ran his hand over the back of his neck. "I don't know if I can accept everything you said."

"Then why?"

"For whatever reason, you need this badly, and you came to me for it." Nikolai cast him a stern look. "Because I'm still your goddamned brother."

42

St. Louis Cemetery #1,
New Orleans

In the third cemetery they traveled to, the tombs had seen better days. Many were storm-damaged, with crumbling stucco and rusted iron fences. Markings were eroded.

Spates of rain were sporadic; it was well after midnight. And still this haphazard maze of tombs was *busy*.

Drunken ghost tour patrons laughed raucously as they smoked cheap clove cigarettes and marked Xs on a tall pediment tomb.

Nikolai muttered, "That's not even Marie Laveau's crypt. Though Myst says that the priestess does get a kick out of it."

Conrad roared at the group. "Leave—us!"

After a moment of thunderstruck silence, tourists shoved each other down into the wet gravel as they fled.

Once the place was emptied, Nikolai said, "Conrad, you have to prepare for the possibility that you might not find what you're seeking. Or that you might locate her grave only to find what this woman . . . what she *once* was."

Her remains. Conrad shook his head hard. "I understand," he said, then he went still, holding his breath to listen for Néomi, willing his own heart to slow its furious pounding. He strained to hear over the cicadas and distant traffic—

He jerked his head to the left. *There.* The faintest rhythm. "I hear her!"

"How can you be sure it's her?" Nikolai asked.

"Know her heart." He homed in on the sound, tracking it to a vast, bleached white tomb, standing at least seven tiers high. Dread built like ice in Conrad's veins. Was she truly within this place? In one coffin among so many? How terrified she must be. *I'd dreamed her choking on her terror . . .*

No! Can't think about that now, need to keep my mind focused.

He pinpointed the sound to a third-level bay. The marble closure tablet was eroded beyond deciphering.

Swallowing hard, Conrad punched in the marble, crumbling it. Inside the vault was a small black coffin.

He slid it out from the space, easing it to the gravel path.

"Conrad!" Nikolai clamped his shoulder. "Just be prepared."

Conrad nodded, then gripped the lid, wrenching it free. . . .

"*Néomi!*" he rasped.

Her eyes were closed, her body still as if dead. Remnants of rotting lace and ribbon were scattered over her naked body. Dust marked her pale face and long hair. With a yell, Conrad snatched her out, clenching her to his chest.

"My God," Nikolai breathed. "You weren't . . . does your female live?"

"Néomi, say something to me!" Nothing. Conrad brushed the backs of his fingers over her face. No response. But why? He held her away from him. She looked perfectly formed. Her skin was warm and pinkened. Jostling her in his arms, he said, *"Please, baby, anything—"*

Her eyes fluttered open. *So blue.*

She coughed, gasping, ". . . knew you'd find me." Then she burst into tears.

With his gaze averted, Nikolai handed Conrad his jacket to wrap around her. Once he had her covered, Conrad cupped the back of her head, pressing her too tight to his chest, but he couldn't let up.

Trembling against him, she whispered, "I-I knew you'd come for me, Conrad."

"Always, *koeri*, always," he murmured, gently rocking her. "My brave, brave girl."

Then he met Nikolai's astonished gaze. "My vengeance is no more." His voice broke. "You have my gratitude, brother."

"I'm sorry I doubted you," Nikolai said sincerely. Then he asked, "But did you just call your female *bait*? That's an endearment for you, Conrad?" At Conrad's annoyed look, he held up his hands. "None of my business." To Néomi, he said, "Welcome to the family." Then he traced away.

Conrad took her from there as well, tracing her directly into their bathroom at Elancourt. Without releasing her for a second, he drew a bath, then lowered her into the steaming water.

As he washed the dust from her skin and hair, she sat with her eyes dazed, still steadily crying.

"Are you warming up?" She gave a nod. "Néomi, are you . . . hurt?"

"*N-non*, just shaken. Can't seem to stop crying."

"This is killing me, *koeri*. Tell me what to do to help you."

"I'm sorry. It's just . . . even when I knew you'd find me, being in the cof— being there was . . . difficult."

He tucked her hair behind her ear. "I know it must have been terrifying."

She frowned. "Was that Nikolai with you?" When Conrad nodded, she said, "How did he get free?"

"I . . . broke them out."

"Did you go alone?"

When he nodded, she gasped. "Were you injured? I haven't even checked you over."

"Not at all," he said, pleased that she'd become more animated at least.

"What were you thinking?"

"I needed Nikolai's help to find you. I would've done anything to get to you."

"He welcomed me to the family. Did you tell him we were getting married?" Her big blue eyes glistened with tears. "Because if the offer still stands . . ."

Conrad exhaled. "We can speak of this later. When you're feeling better."

"Wh-what do you mean?" Néomi asked, beginning to cry harder.

"Listen to me—shh, love." He sounded like she was tormenting him. "All of this is my fault. The demons will keep coming. If they find out you're alive, they'll never stop."

Relief flooded her, and her tears eased. If that was all he was worried about . . . "Then keep me safe. I'll never leave here without you. I learned my lesson. I'll stay inside the protection."

"I can't do this. Néomi, I . . . I *love you*. Far too much to see you hurt again."

He'd said he loved her. As soon as she realized she didn't have to dread hearing those words, it dawned on her that she'd truly been reborn.

We're going to be together. . . .

"And you could . . . you could do so much better than me," Conrad continued, having no idea that this was as good as decided. "You have your whole life in front of you—why should I think to be the one to intrude on it?"

"Do better? And precisely what's wrong with the man I love?"

"The man you love," he murmured, obviously enjoying hearing that. But then he seemed to force himself to explain, "I'll never walk in the sun with you or share a meal. The Kapsliga and other enemies will continue to dispatch killers. And I'm still not one hundred percent . . . right in the head."

She rose up out of the water to her knees and laid her hands on the sides of his face. "I like my pale skin and never share my food anyway. And we'll be ready for the Kapsliga. As for your mind, you'll keep getting better each day just as you had been."

"I took your neck. I could have killed you."

"But you *didn't* hurt me. Conrad, I loved it."

"Then why were you so angry?"

"Because Nïx told me that the day anyone learned how I came back was the day I would die. I couldn't tell you. I wanted to so much! When you took my blood, I thought you might be able to learn of it through my memories. I thought I'd been doomed to die even sooner."

He lowered his forehead to hers. "Néomi, I had no idea."

"Now, let me see your arm." When he frowned, she said, "You vowed that from the instant that mark healed, you'd make me your wife."

He drew back. "But that was before you . . . died. Again."

"It doesn't matter." She unbuttoned his shirt with trembling fingers. "Don't Wroths always keep their vows?"

When he shrugged from his shirt, she began tugging off the bandage. He swallowed, just before she revealed . . . smooth, healed skin.

He exhaled, defeated. "Néomi, I'll wed you at the earliest opportunity if you'll take a chance on me. I never want to be apart from you again."

"Even if I'm just a mortal?"

"I want you with me *forever*. I'll find a way to keep you with me—you have to know that." He pulled the ring from his pants pocket.

She cast him a watery smile to see it. "I do so love that ring." As he slid it on her finger again, she said,

"And I love the man attached to it. Do you know how difficult it was to return it to you at the ballet?"

"About as difficult as it was to accept it back?"

"I'm so sorry, *mon coeur*. I had no choice. How could I promise a future I knew I didn't have? But now I can say how proud I'd be to marry you."

"Néomi, even if there was nothing to divide us, I . . . I fear I'll only disappoint you. I'll do the wrong thing or hurt your feelings. This won't come overnight—just know that I'll try not to."

"That's all I ask for." She frowned. "Actually, that's not all. I want us to live here, Conrad. Would you ever want to? Can we buy Elancourt from your brother?"

"I'll buy you an estate wherever you wish. Are you sure you want to be here? You were murdered here—how could you not be constantly reminded of it?"

"I've been here for eighty years. I've gotten used to it. Besides, if I hadn't been killed, I wouldn't have you. You told me you would've helped the Russian plunge his sword to be with me—I would've run into Louis's blade for a chance with you."

His brows drew together, the intensity of his emotion seeming to boil over. He kissed her then, a scalding possession. When they broke away, gasping, he rasped, "We'll stay. But only if I get to bring the place back to life for you."

"Why not?" She sighed, stroking his hair from his forehead. "You did with its mistress."

A crash sounded from downstairs, followed by a bellow.

Néomi gasped. "Was that Bowen? They're still here?"

"Oh, Christ, the witch!" Conrad said. "She got entranced."

"Take me to her, Conrad!" He helped her dry off and don a robe, then traced her to the studio.

They found Bowen clutching Mari to his chest. He was covered with blood and gaping wounds all over his body, while Mari was pale and dazed.

"It worked, then?" Bowen asked Conrad, but his attention was focused on the witch in his arms.

"Yes, you have our thanks—"

"I'm takin' the lass home." To Mari, he said, "And then you're on indefinite leave."

Mari nodded weakly. "Never glancing at a mirror again. Never."

As Bowen stood, carrying Mari into the glass, she peeked back from his arms, her expression pensive. Just before they disappeared, Mari put her forefinger over her lips, a warning to Néomi.

What does that mean? Néomi's brows drew together.

And then they were gone, leaving unbroken glass behind. As Néomi peered at the mirror, her reflection flashed to her ghostly visage and back.

43

The weeks that followed her embodying would have been the happiest of Néomi's life.

If not for the fact that I came back wrong, she thought, stroking Conrad's hair from his forehead as he slept. . . .

Shortly after her return, they'd married without fanfare. Initially, she'd been weak from the events of that turbulent night, but as soon as she'd recovered enough, Conrad had gotten a Lore officiate to perform the simple ceremony at Elancourt.

She'd felt guilty marrying Conrad without revealing her misgivings to him. Especially when she'd learned that Bowen had barely managed to pry Mari from the glass. The spell had somehow gone awry.

Néomi could feel it. She was altered.

She continued her new habit of sleeping during the day, but now she only needed about four hours. She could leave or take food, though Conrad had learned her favorite dishes and tempted her with delicacies from all over the world.

She'd tried to call Mari, but was told that she and Bowen were on an island off the coast of Belize or somewhere fantastic like that.

Though Néomi yearned to confess her new secret to Conrad, she didn't want to worry him—this was the best he'd ever done. He was just so excited, making plans for them, eager to start their life together. He'd already begun restoring Elancourt, and he was *happy*, genuinely satisfied with what he imagined the future held for them.

Yet when Néomi had healed from a small cut in under an hour, she'd been so confounded that she'd tentatively broached the subject. "I worry, Conrad. Sometimes, I don't think I'm . . . human," she'd told him.

"Of course, you are," he'd said, gathering her into his arms and spinning her around until she was forced to smile. "What else could you be?"

The morning after her embodying, Néomi had woken to the sound of hammering. Conrad had taken his task of restoring Elancourt very seriously. But once she was well on the road to recovery, his labors were hindered by the fact that she found his sweat-slicked body irresistible.

Whenever she came upon him with his shirt off and his muscles all hot and lathered, she had to have him. "I'm back to normal," she'd informed him. "And normal for me is quite lusty." He'd declared himself "eagerly at your service."

One day she'd found him in the studio, but hadn't thought he'd heard her. She'd gazed at him with pride and a desire so strong it had left her shaken.

As he'd lovingly oiled the mahogany barre, he'd said, "I'll see you dance here." His voice had been husky, as if he was imagining it even then. "I'll watch you for hours, then I'll taste your damp skin."

They hadn't made it even close to getting to the bed. . . .

His care had made her long to dance again, to use this studio as she'd never been able to. Once she'd gotten stronger, she'd begun practicing again, her love for it undimmed by time.

Néomi could never take the stage again, but she'd decided to open a Lore ballet school. There was not a single one in existence, and she'd been heartbroken to learn that many Lore children—with their horns and wings and siren screams—couldn't attend human classes.

When she'd asked Conrad what he thought about the idea of a Néomi Wroth School of Dance, he'd said, "If it makes you happy, then enroll every Lore pup who's willing to wear pink." Scratching his head, he'd added, "Though I'll need to figure out how to expand the studio. . . ."

Conrad stirred then—but not from a nightmare. Once he'd turned to her, she smoothed the backs of her fingers over his cheek, and he resumed sleeping deeply. Nightmares were rare these days.

Though he'd been apprehensive about taking her blood again, that one bite had already transferred her memories to him. Néomi had feared hers would be the ones that would send him over the edge, breaching the dam. Yet they actually seemed to be *helping* him. "I dream of music and laughter and warmth," he'd told her. "It's . . . soothing to be in your memories. Awake, I'm with you. And asleep, I'm with you. I like this."

She knew he wasn't yet cured. It would take time. She just wished she had even more time with him. Given a new chance at mortality, she'd become greedy for immortality.

Life held so much *promise*. . . .

Except for the fact that she had no idea what she was.

Sometimes when she looked in the mirror, or if she caught her reflection in a window, she saw glimpses of her spectral self. The shadows around her eyes and under her cheekbones would appear in flashes.

Her night vision was as flawless as it had been when she'd been a ghost, and when she slept, she dreamed of floating and moving things with her mind.

This twilight, Néomi had awakened with a rose petal clutched in her fist. . . .

Nïx had visited Néomi on several occasions. Each time, the Valkyrie blatantly scrutinized Néomi with those golden eyes, seeming fascinated. Just yesterday Nïx had come to Elancourt and said nothing, only blankly staring at her.

"Nïx, what am I?" Néomi finally asked her.

"Complicated?"

"I came back wrong, didn't I?"

Nïx sighed. "I can't get a sense of you whatsoever."

Néomi had no sense of her own self. She didn't feel as she had when human—or as a ghost.

Awkward doesn't begin to describe this meeting.

"Have a seat. Please," Nikolai said, waving to one of the chairs in front of his office desk. Sebastian occupied the other.

Conrad had traced to Blachmount Castle, Nikolai's home, to meet with his brothers—at Néomi's insistence. It was day in New Orleans, and she'd wanted to nap for the afternoon, so he thought he'd get this over with.

His brothers had questions about the past—and Conrad wanted to formally purchase Elancourt from Nikolai.

With his neck knotted with tension, Conrad reluctantly sat. He was already on edge from leaving Néomi for the first time since her return, but being back here made his uneasiness ratchet to another level.

"I thought all three of you would be here," Conrad said. "Where's Murdoch?" He would leaven this tense atmosphere.

"Missing in action," Nikolai answered. "We presume it's concerning his 'secret' Bride. I think for the first time in his existence, he's having woman troubles."

"Might do him some good," Sebastian said, then asked Conrad, "Does it not feel surreal to be back here?"

He nodded. This castle was where Conrad and most of his family had died. His young sisters had wept here as they'd succumbed one by one. Blachmount was where Conrad had been born and raised—and raised from the dead.

For three hundred years, Conrad had hated Nikolai for his decision that fateful night. Now Conrad was beholden to him for Néomi. Without Nikolai's choices and Murdoch's determination, he would never have known his Bride. He would never watch her readying for bed, brushing her long hair.

Just yesterday, he'd thought, *My Bride by fate, my wife by choice. . . .*

"I felt the same way when I first returned," Sebastian said.

Nikolai made a scoffing sound. "No, you didn't— you were too busy decking me."

"The second time, then."

Uncomfortable silence ensued. Conrad peered around the paneled study. Nikolai tapped a pen against his desktop. Sebastian jogged his leg.

Eventually, Nikolai rose from his chair. "I have something of yours." He pulled a file from a cabinet, handing it to Conrad. Inside were the deed to Elancourt and the contracts of transferral.

"I signed the property over to you and your Bride the night you got her back."

Conrad's tension cranked up even more. "I can pay you for it."

"It's technically Néomi's anyway, right? Consider it a wedding gift."

Conrad hated feeling beholden. "Wait." He traced to Elancourt. There, he checked on Néomi, tugging her blanket higher with a kiss. Then he snagged a bottle of whiskey from the crate. She'd suggested bringing one, but Conrad had gruffly declined. Now he returned to Blachmount and gave it to Nikolai.

Nikolai brushed off the label. "My God, this is . . . this is . . ."

"As good as you're imagining," Conrad finished for him.

Sebastian wasted no time, rising for snifters from the sideboard. "Then stop staring at the bottle and let's drink it!"

They did. Two hours later, Conrad decided that

speaking to his brothers with roughly twenty thousand dollars' worth of whiskey in his belly wasn't so awkward.

When Nikolai and Sebastian wanted to know what had happened to Conrad in the past three centuries, he told them. When they asked about Néomi, he found himself proudly relating his wife's accomplishments. "You've never seen a woman dance as she does. And she'd bought that property by herself—an unmarried woman in her twenties." Even to himself, his tone sounded impressed.

"Chains, drugs, and brute force couldn't control Conrad," Nikolai began in an amused tone, "but a tiny ballerina is domesticating him with ease."

"What are you going to do about her mortality?" Sebastian asked.

"Search for a way to make her immortal." When they gave him uneasy expressions, Conrad said, "I know the odds, but that's a more likely scenario than me following wherever she would go after death." Conrad finished his drink, then contemplated the bottom of his glass. "Do you not think of our sisters when you're here?"

Nikolai and Sebastian shared a speaking glance.

At length, Nikolai said, "We're bringing them back. We have the means to retrieve them from the past. Not to change history, but just to return with them to this time."

Conrad narrowed his gaze. Was Nikolai jesting? "How?"

With utmost seriousness, Sebastian answered, "A mystic's key."

Conrad flinched at the word *key.*

Sebastian topped off their drinks. "A goddess named Riora gave me one turn of it for the sole purpose of reuniting my family. I know for a fact that it works."

If skeptical Sebastian said it worked, then it did. "And you'd thought of returning my past self as well?"

"Yes, the offer still stands," Nikolai said. "Think of it, we could clear your eyes of the blood completely. And take away all the memories that plague you."

"And what would happen to my present self?"

"You'd fade," Sebastian said.

"I knew you'd had an ace up your sleeve." No wonder his brothers had been so confident about Conrad's recovery. "But I'm not interested."

Nikolai steepled his fingers. "You wouldn't want to be human again?"

Sebastian added, "No more red eyes, no more blood drinking."

Conrad shook his head. "And no more strength to protect Néomi. I need it to keep her safe. If history wouldn't be changed, then I'd still have the same enemies after me—and now her." Conrad drained his glass, hating this reality of their lives. "Why didn't you just do it? Why go through all the trouble of capturing me?" Especially when he'd been spitting blood at them and trying to murder them.

"We wanted you to get stable enough to make the choice," Nikolai answered. "We would've been taking away your immortality. And you would have lost your own memories from the last three hundred years as well. It was a major decision." In a lower tone,

Nikolai said, "I didn't want to make the same mistake twice."

"There was no first mistake," Conrad said firmly. "You made a fated decision, and I'm in your debt."

"Good. Then you won't mind helping us raise the girls."

Christ, their sisters actually would live again. He'd get a second chance to know them better. Hell, Néomi could teach them to dance. He grinned, shocking his brothers. "When do we go back for them?"

"Once Murdoch returns, we plan."

Conrad opened his mouth to speak, then froze. *Something's wrong.* A chill slithered up his spine. "I'll return," he said, immediately tracing back to Elancourt.

Straight into fire.

Néomi had been dreaming of floating and walking through walls again. But now she wanted to wake because her breaths had begun to taste of . . . *soot?*

She couldn't seem to get enough air, coughing with each smoky inhalation. And in the haze of her mind, she perceived fire all around her, thought she smelled the flames and felt their heat.

A fire! Why can't I wake?

Feeling so dizzy . . . she needed clean air. . . .

At last, she was able to crack open her eyelids. She blinked them in disbelief.

The room was choked with thick smoke. Flames licked the walls and crawled across the bowing ceiling. The boards above her whined under the strain.

"Néomi!"

Conrad! He was here? Through the flames between them, their gazes met—just before a beam snapped and a portion of the ceiling collapsed in front of him.

With a yell, he lunged for her to trace her away, but returned to the same spot empty-handed, as if his arms had wrapped around only air. When he failed at it a second time, he dived into the fire, tearing away the blazing timbers to reach her.

Why did he look so stricken? She wasn't hurt—hadn't even a scratch. In fact, she felt nothing. *No perception. Dim.*

Then she glanced down. *No, no, no* . . . Her body from her waist down was buried under the burning wreckage from the ceiling. It should be crushing her. *Why am I still conscious?* Where was the pain?

Then she realized . . .

I died . . . again?

Néomi was in her incorporeal form once more, wearing her old black dress and jewerly—

A thunderous rending above her drew her gaze. With the ceiling gone, she could see that the roof was sagging in pockets. The enormous rafters began to snap, one by one. Jagged wood hurtled down like spears, hammering into the floor.

Still grappling to get to her, he dodged them.

"Conrad! No!"

One caught him, stabbing into his body, slamming him down. A split second later, the roof crashed over him, shrouding him. With a shriek, she found herself rising through the debris covering her, floating admist the fire to get to him.

She couldn't find him, couldn't see! Then . . . she spied blood pooling out from under a pile of debris, the liquid reflecting the flames, boiling and popping.

Tonight Cade found himself in a familiar spot—sitting on the edge of a downtown apartment's roof. His female's building neighbored this one, and her top loft and private rooftop pool were readily viewable from this higher vantage.

Cade hadn't intended to come here tonight. He'd just *needed* to.

He gazed over at her balcony. And there she was.

Holly Ashwin.

His Holly. She was a math geek who wore glasses, no makeup, and her blond hair in a conservative bun; she was sexier than any female he'd ever known.

But as ever, he scratched his head at her antics. She was cleaning an already spotless apartment. *Mystifying human.*

She'd expire if she saw his place. Just another example of how unalike she and Cade were.

Holly was scholarly—he was deadly. Every aspect of her life was strictly organized. His idea of a day's schedule was *wake, eat a few meals, do things, sleep.* And any of those were optional.

She didn't even drink. He took a swig just then.

Was she having company over tonight? *Her tosser boyfriend?* Just as his claws dug into his palms, Cade heard footsteps approaching.

Bloody Rydstrom. His brother had found him. *So much for keeping my visits secret.*

"What in the hell are you doing up here?" Cade demanded.

"I ask you the same," Rydstrom said, treating him to a look of unmitigated disappointment.

I've never seen that one before.

"You told me you wouldn't come here anymore."

"Fell off the wagon," Cade muttered.

"Humans are forbidden to us as mates for a reason. If you haven't gotten that through your thick skull before, then you certainly should now. The accident with the vampire's Bride is exactly why mortals and immortals should never mix."

Cade narrowed his eyes. "Are you sure Néomi's even dead?"

With a nod, Rydstrom said, "I checked with Nïx."

Why did mortals have to die so easily? The smallest sword thrust had ended the girl forever. She hadn't deserved to die like that.

"If she's dead, then that vampire is out searching for something of mine to destroy." Cade glanced around them. *A thousand times over,* Wroth had vowed. Cade would be signing Holly's death warrant to approach her right now.

"So you have even more reason to resist her," Rydstrom said. "You have to forget her."

"You think I haven't tried?" Cade ran his hand over a horn. "You think I don't know how bad this looks? I'm stalking a girl, a human who's millennia younger than I am."

"Then it's fortunate we're leaving this town for good. Nïx has given us one last means to destroy Omort—a job to complete. This is our final hope to reclaim my crown. She's adamant about that."

"What's the op?" Cade asked, though he didn't give a damn. He'd agree to anything to take his mind from what he'd done—and from what he was tempted to do with Holly. Even Nïx hadn't foreseen his crazed plans for her.

"We'll receive instructions within the week. Just be ready to move quickly."

Cade exhaled. "I'm always ready."

"Again, brother, this is it—our last chance. I have to know that your head is in the right place."

"I said I'll be ready," he snapped. "Whatever it is,

I'll get the job done." Cade rose and gazed at Holly.

For a last time.

With a lingering glance at his female, Cade dropped from the roof.

No sooner had Cade disappeared into the night than Nïx emerged from the stairwell to join Rydstrom. "And how did he react?"

Rydstrom glanced at her, evincing no surprise that she'd found them. "You don't know?"

"I'm ever-knowing, not—"

"Yes, yes, not all-knowing." Rydstrom sighed. "Cade's vowed to do his duty."

When Holly came back into their view, Nïx's golden eyes fixed on the girl and her pupils dilated. Tilting her head, she asked, "And if he finds out Néomi still lives?"

"Lying to him sits ill with me," Rydstrom said. "You're certain I can't tell him?"

Nïx faced him. "I've gone over and over the decision trees. Billions of outcomes all trace back to this decision fork—*tell him or don't*. It must be this way."

"So you've seen my future?"

"Some of it," she said. "And it's a doozy."

"Tell me," he said, waving her on.

"Rydstrom, you really must learn *to ask*. In any case, I've got somewhere I need to be. A mystery will be revealed to me tonight, and I can hardly wait."

"You can't leave me like this! And what if we need to get in touch with you?"

She grinned at him, but her eyes were growing vacant, her mind already somewhere else. "Greedy demon, there's only so much Nïx to go around."

45

If Néomi had died again, then that meant she had the power to save him.

She could move things with her mind once more. With a wave of her hand, she easily tore through the wreckage, following Conrad's trail of blood. Two waves of her hand had the roof section covering him hurled up and out into the yard. He lay unconscious, pinned by that jagged beam.

As delicately as she could, she began extracting it from his body. Even unconscious, he yelled in pain. She was hurting him, but she had no choice. Flames still advanced from all around them. The entire structure of the manor was quaking.

Inch by grisly inch . . .

At last! She freed him of it. Finally able to escape the blaze, she traced him outside under a great oak to shelter him from the raining embers.

She couldn't feel them.

Floating beside him, she assessed his wound, shocked at how swiftly he was still losing blood. "Conrad! Please wake up . . . tell me what to do to help you!"

He'd said he couldn't die from an injury like this,

but his paleness terrified her. He needed blood. Without thought, she put her wrist to his lips.

She gasped. *Oh, mère de Dieu* . . . She felt herself growing corporeal once more, gradually, from her arm out, like an accumulation of form. She perceived the dew on the grass and the bayou breeze.

How can this be?

Conrad's instinct took over, and before she could blink, his fangs had closed on her flesh like a brand. His sucking was as dizzyingly provocative as she'd remembered. When he groaned against her skin, she nearly swooned with pleasure.

Too soon, he released her with a last lick. In moments, he was able to open his eyes. With a husky murmur, he said, "For that . . . I'm willing to be staked nightly." When he opened his eyes, his gaze flickered over her body, over the familiar black dress they knew so well. "You were a spirit again. But I just tasted . . . flesh and blood. What happened?"

Néomi could feel the bite mark on her wrist was already beginning to mend. *I don't know what I am.* She whispered, "I just changed. I don't understand it." They stared at each other for long moments. Out of the corner of her vision, she saw flames stretching high into the night sky. Smoke funneled out of the windows and chimneys. Heat reached all the way to them. "I'd realized something was wrong with me, but—"

"Nothing's *wrong* with you!" he said vehemently, already able to sit up.

"Then what *am* I?"

"I don't give a damn. As long as you're with me."

"I give a damn! What if I get stuck in that spirit

form again?" She hated that weird ghostly half-world. She'd nearly forgotten how alone and echoing and faded it felt. "I wouldn't be able to hold you when you're injured or sleep against your warm chest. Or have sex with you. And I want to—a lot! And I'm so sick of this damned dress!"

"So that's what you are," a woman cried from the oak above them. "It all becomes clear!"

They both glanced up. Nïx sat perched on a limb, with her sword strapped over her back.

"Up there all along!" Conrad bellowed, immediately grimacing and clamping a hand over his side. "And you didn't think to help us?"

Nïx stood and alighted from the limb as though stepping from a curb, landing without so much as a sound.

"What became clear?" Néomi asked, her tone tinged with fear. "What am I?"

She saw Conrad swallow and knew he wasn't sure he even wanted to know.

"You're one of those powerful Lore phantoms I was telling you about. Though your aging process was accelerated by a few centuries. Good timing, too." She furtively pointed at the manor, saying in a stage whisper, "Just between me and you—your spirit anchor is on fire." An explosion sounded at that moment, and glass shattered out from all the remaining downstairs windows. "And, yes, I did plan for that blast to punctuate my words."

A fantôme?

"Phantom?" Conrad rubbed his forehead, smearing ash there. "Spirit anchor . . . ?"

Néomi explained, "Nïx told me weeks ago that I might become like a Lore phantom if I lived long enough as a ghost. Phantoms can incarnate at will, they can trace, and they can move things with their minds. And they don't have to remain in one place where their spirit is anchored. But it would take possibly five hundred years for me to gradually grow a body to incarnate with. Evidently, Mariketa sped up the five centuries."

Wide-eyed, Nïx said, "Yes, clever, clever Mariketa—a spell maker and a rule breaker! There's a reason Mari is my favorite Wiccan-type person."

Conrad said, "I still don't . . . What are you talking about?"

"Mari broke the House's rules, or rather, she *bent* them. Witches are not allowed to create immortals." She faced Néomi. "But in theory, you were an immortal already. So Mari gave you a body, which jumpstarted the phantom aging process. And somehow she managed to add a touch of Lore blood to activate the transition from human to Lore being. Maybe the vampire cut himself as he was frantically fetching mirror shards for the witch's spell? I dunno."

Conrad grated, "Is she part vampire?"

"No. Your blood was merely an agent, a facilitator. Even Mari can't make a female vampire."

"No wonder she was so nervous," Conrad said. "She knew what she was going to try to do going in."

"Yes. You owe Mari much. Though she didn't break the letter of their laws, she broke the spirit. She could be punished severely for this if others find out—even branded as a rogue for what she did. In short, Mariketa the Awaited will *not* be listing you as a reference, and you should send her a nice card for Beltane."

"Does this mean I can change back and forth anytime I want?"

"You're a shape-shifter between life and death," Nïx answered. "Concentrate on disembodying."

Néomi focused. When it worked, Conrad listed to the side before righting himself. "Sorry, *mon grand!*" She attempted making herself whole once more. Again, gradually, she grew corporeal.

"But, Néomi," Nïx began with the gravest severity, "whenever you disembody . . ." She paused as if deciding how best to deliver tragic news.

"Yes?" Néomi whispered. Conrad was holding his breath.

Nïx finally finished, "You will be . . . *wearing that dress.*"

Néomi and Conrad groaned.

"Just think of it as your alter-ego-wear. Cosplay of sorts, with your rose petals and goth-looking face. Speaking of alter egos—I think we should call you the *Incarnatrix.* Maybe give you a spotlight beacon."

"I'm *immortal?*" Néomi said in disbelief, as all this sunk in. "And a part of the Lore?" That realm Néomi had loved so much.

"Yes. No more getting capped, unless you get beheaded in your corporeal form. Naturally. In your spirit form, you can't be killed at all. Your species is very envied within the Lore. You're powerful, yet with few vulnerabilities. Well, gotta run. I have at least four more appointments this evening. My job as Proto-Valkyrie and Soothsayer Without Equal is as crucial and involved as you'd think."

Néomi said, "But I have so many questions. . . ."

Nïx sighed. "I'll give you a prediction because I'm benevolent. And because I didn't get you a wedding present." Dramatically waving her hand in an arc above her, Nïx breathed, "I can see it now." Then she met their eyes. "No. Really. I can see it now."

"Tell us!"

"Néomi—wife, mother, and owner of the only Lore ballet academy in this plane. Conrad, adoring husband and father, who still slips into the crazies now and again but works hard to get past it. He'll be throwing a mantrum every time you go to girls' night out, sweating with white knuckles until you return, but he'll get better with each year."

Néomi frowned. "We'll be parents? Can I . . . can we have children?"

Conrad squeezed her hand. "Néomi, it doesn't matter—"

"I'll check my sources to be sure." Nix peered up, brows drawn as if she was thinking back. When she was actually thinking forward. Then she winced. "Ooh," she murmured with distaste. Another grimace. "Oh, now, that's not nice!"

Conrad's lips parted. "What in the hell are you seeing?"

"You'll have children, all right," Nïx said, her tone grim. "And that first set of twins . . ." She shuddered.

"*First* set?" Conrad said with a cough, looking dumbfounded. "What did you see?"

"What *didn't* I see. I'll give you a for instance—any time you try to give them a bath, they either hide in the walls or sink their baby fangs into the door so you can't pull them away. And the pranks . . . don't get me started on the pranks. Auntie Nïx will be unavailable to sit for those two decades."

Néomi said, "They sound . . . delightful?"

Nïx's tone softened. "Happily, they grow up to be strong with clever minds and proud hearts." She eyed them both. "For now, I'll be expecting you *both* on the front line this Accession." She started away.

"Wait!" Conrad said. "Did someone . . . did one of my enemies set this fire?"

Nïx turned back with a grin. "Unless you'd pissed off some wiring-hungry nutrias, then I'm going with *no*." She disappeared into the night.

Stunned to silence, Néomi and Conrad sat together on the ground, staring at her home of more than eighty years, blazing in the night.

When tears began to course down her face, Conrad reached over to brush them away. "*Koeri*, I'm so sorry about the house."

Yes, she was crying, but not for the reason Conrad believed. *There's nothing wrong with me.* No wonder she hadn't felt like a human or a ghost—she was a bit of both. She was overwhelmed because she was so relieved.

I'm an immortal now.

She surveyed Conrad's face, noting that his color was already returning. He'd swiftly heal his injury and be back to normal soon.

We're going to be together. And have terrible, terrible little children.

When the first wall of Elancourt collapsed, she started laughing. Flames were consuming her home, and all she could think was . . . *let it burn*.

"Néomi?" Conrad cast her a concerned expression. "Why are you laughing?"

She felt freed, ready to embark on the rest of her new life. "Because I'm happy."

"This is going to be one of those times when your happiness baffles me, isn't it? You told me this was your dream home."

Dreams can change. She knelt before him. "All that matters is that we're together. And now that I'm immortal, if we play our cards right, it'll be forever."

His brows drew together, as if the truth of that hit him just at that moment. "But you loved this place."

"I did. It was everything to me. *Before*, when I had nothing else."

In a dry tone, he said, "This does resolve the problem of how to expand the studio."

"*Exactement.*" She smiled, cupping his face with her hands. "We'll take our time rebuilding, have fun with it. Apparently, we have all the time in the world." She leaned in to kiss the vampire she loved.

With a grin against her lips, he murmured, "At least until that first set of twins arrives."